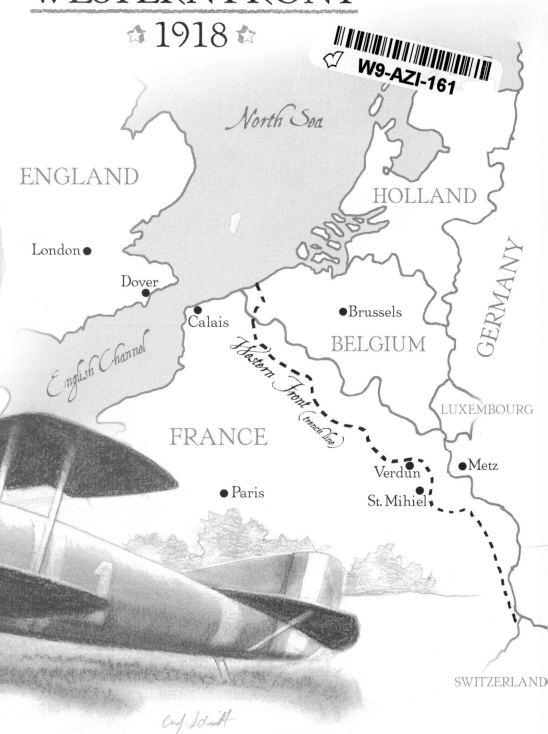

THE GREAT WAR
WESTERN FRONT
☆ 1918 ☆

W9-AZI-161

North Sea

ENGLAND

HOLLAND

London ●

GERMANY

Dover ●

● Brussels

● Calais

BELGIUM

English Channel

Western Front (trench line)

LUXEMBOURG

FRANCE

Verdun ● ● Metz

● Paris

St. Mihiel ●

SWITZERLAND

'TIL THE BOYS
COME
HOME

'TIL THE BOYS COME HOME

A WORLD WAR I NOVEL

JERRY BORROWMAN

Covenant Communications, Inc.

Cover illustration © Robert T. Barrett.

Cover design copyrighted 2005 by Covenant Communications, Inc.

Published by Covenant Communications, Inc.
American Fork, Utah

Printed in Canada
First Printing: March 2005

11 10 09 08 07 06 05   10 9 8 7 6 5 4 3

ISBN 1-59156-747-5

DEDICATION

This book is written in tribute to all the men and women who sacrifice their time working patiently with young people. Two are representative:

DAVID AGUIRRE volunteered for more than twenty years as an inner-city scoutmaster in a very tough neighborhood and then as an unpaid high school football coach. Dave worked hard at his profession nine months out of the year so he could volunteer three months without any earned income—and all because he loves to help young men. Even today, tears come to his eyes as he talks about the struggles and triumphs of the members of his teams and troops.

DAVID SORENSON was Young Men president while our three boys were growing up. A few years ago, David held a reunion for the boys he'd worked with, and dozens showed up from destinations near and far to express appreciation for a man who simply loved them for who they are.

One of my primary goals in writing this book is to illustrate just how profound a youth leader's influence can be in the lives of young people, as exemplified by these and so many others who work with the youth.

PREFACE

The primary reason I decided to write a story in this period was curiosity. Prior to starting my research, I had little knowledge of the First World War, having spent most of my adult life studying World War II. Yet it was clear that to fully understand World War II, one had to be aware of the First World War. To me, it was a jumble of images of pompous generals in odd hats and gaudy uniforms. The motorized vehicles they used seemed fragile by comparison to those used in the following war, making it difficult to take the First World War quite as seriously. In some ways, the images were almost comic. But eighteen million people had died—an appalling loss of life. So I decided to find out why the governments of Europe, as well as the soldiers who kept going back to the line, felt so strongly about the issues that they would make this kind of sacrifice. It turned out to be a fascinating study. As I learned more about the people and the times, the characters became real and the sacrifices personal. There's a poignancy in their hope that this awful conflict would prove so terrible that it would truly be the "war to end all wars." We know, from our vantage point, that their hope was vain.

Today, I almost feel as if I lived in that time, and I have enormous empathy for the families who lost loved ones, as well as for those who returned from the war disabled. Society was not nearly as forgiving and supportive of people with handicaps in those days, and even though the veterans were wounded in behalf of the country, they often returned to indifference or hostility.

This book is a tribute to those men, now mostly forgotten, for giving so much in the cause of freedom. In some small measure, I feel that I have come to know them, and I will always be grateful for their sacrifices.

ACKNOWLEDGMENTS

I'd like to thank my wife, Marcella, for her usual excellent job of editing the manuscript and for her help in keeping the story line consistent and logical. My books are always better because of her feedback and suggestions.

I'd also like to thank Tom Angle, a professional engineer, who reviewed the text for both technical and historical accuracy, as well as my daughter-in-law Hilary Borrowman for her thorough grammatical edit, and to Tina Foster, who gave me the confidence to write fiction in the first place.

Special appreciation is due to Chuck Jopson of Kuna, Idaho, for taking me up in a flight in his restored 1939 biplane. In learning the basics of how to manage the controls of this remarkable aircraft using the pedals, joystick, and throttle, I was far better prepared to describe the aerial scenes in the narrative.

A number of individuals read the manuscript at various stages in its development, encouraging me to continue the effort and providing their own insights into the story. Thanks to Sam Berrett, Ryan Morganegg, Analia Funke, Faith Cooper, Evan Rowley, Rob Perry, Kim Andersen, and an unexpected reader, Lane Jensen. Special thanks go to Cindy Schmidt for her illustrations.

Finally, thanks to the great staff at Covenant Communications, including Jessica Warner, who enhanced the book with her map and design, and my editor, Christian Sorensen, who worked so hard to prepare the story for publication.

Prologue

An American Aerodrome near St. Mihiel, France
July 1918

"Richards! You're flying with me. Let's go!"

"Yes, sir!" he replied crisply. The jolt of the alarm had already startled Trevor Richards and the other pilots, but his training asserted itself, and he was up and running for the door without even trying to process what was happening. After three days of rain, waiting and hoping for a break in the weather, there was apparently enough of a clearing to get up and out of the soup.

As they raced toward their Nieuports, a corporal intercepted Captain McMurphy with a hand-scribbled note that he'd taken down by phone from the control tower. As they struggled to get their gloves and headgear on, McMurphy provided a quick briefing: "Two Germans have been spotted harassing our trenches. Air Command wants us to drive them away. Cloud cover is low, but there should be enough openings to spot them. Shouldn't be too difficult." He actually grinned back at Trevor's broad smile. This was just the kind of mission they'd been looking for.

Their ground crews had the aircraft in position for take-off by the time that Trevor was ready to mount the first step on the lacquered wing to climb into the open cockpit. Calling out, "All clear," he flipped the switch to the off position so that Sergeant Getty could give the propeller a priming turn. Then, with the switch on, the sergeant gave a second spin of the propeller and jumped back quickly as the engine exhausted a black puff of smoke before roaring to life, the rhone-rotary engine spinning on its crankshaft at 1800 rpms. Waiting barely twenty seconds after Captain McMurphy started his acceleration, Trevor powered onto the soggy grass runway and followed his flight commander into the air. Even though he'd been flying for months now, the thrill of takeoff still excited him every time the wheels left the ground, even more so in the mist.

At five thousand feet, the sky cleared, and Trevor felt the warmth of the sun on his face for the first time in days. Free at last! Free from the ground and the petty concerns that go with everyday living. In the sky it was just the pilot, the air, and the occasional enemy. The excitement of aerial combat was almost addictive, and Trevor loved the challenge.

McMurphy executed some hand maneuvers to indicate that they should climb to maximum altitude to obscure their approach on the Germans. As Trevor watched his hand signals, he figured out the plan of attack. Not ideal—it would be better if they could fly past the Germans and come back from the east with the sun behind them—but it should work. Flying into the sun gave the Germans a natural advantage. But flying past them and then reversing course to come at them from behind would force them to fire in the direction of their own trenches, and the last thing they wanted to do was to kill some of their own men. This plan was the best they could hope for.

After approximately fifteen minutes of flight, they crossed the trenches. Five hundred miles of miserable mud trenches from Belgium to Switzerland. It was sickening to think that up to fifty thousand men could lose their lives in a single day. Straining to see anything that would signal an enemy aircraft, Trevor was frustrated to see nothing but blue sky above and intermittent cloud cover below.

McMurphy indicated a turn toward the south, so Trevor deftly executed a banking turn to the right, using the joystick and the rudder. The little French Nieuport responded instantly. After perhaps five minutes of travel in this new direction, with Trevor and McMurphy peering down anxiously, Trevor spotted a black spot that appeared for just a moment in the broken cloud cover below. He stuck his hand out of the cockpit and pointed down. McMurphy acknowledged then indicated that Trevor should go down first, so Trevor started into a high-speed dive on a trajectory that should bring him right on top of the other aircraft.

When he dipped into the clouds, he was temporarily blinded, so he relied on verbal counting to estimate the time before he reached the ground. At what had to be close to a thousand feet, he worried that he would have to pull up unless the visibility improved. Fortunately, the clouds cleared, and he broke under the ceiling to discover himself perhaps a hundred feet from a German Fokker that was busy firing at the ground. There was no time to fire off any rounds as the two aircraft ripped past each other in a blinding flash. It was obvious that Trevor's surprise was nothing compared to the German's, who went into an immediate retournement, looping up at maximum speed to escape. Trevor pulled up hard on the stick to follow the German and then pushed forward as the German turned toward the east at maximum speed. Off to his right, Trevor could see that McMurphy had followed him down and was having a similar experience with the second German aircraft.

The German pretended to ignore the threat by heading due east across his own lines. Trevor was able to bring him into his sights for just a moment and felt the satisfaction of firing off thirty or forty rounds. But at this speed and shooting against the narrow profile of the German from behind, the chance of a hit was minimal. Frustrated that the

German wouldn't fight, Trevor turned to see McMurphy holding the palm of his hand down, moving it in a motion that indicated he should slow down and back off from the pursuit. Trevor gave him a disgusted look, to which McMurphy pointed to his gas cap. "Of course," he said to himself out loud. "They're running low on fuel and probably ammunition. We got here too late." It was one of the most frustrating things about aerial combat in the Great War. Communications were slow enough that by the time the Army Air Corps could respond to a call for help, the battle was often over. Still, Trevor had engaged in enough fighting that he'd managed two kills at this point plus the satisfaction of having driven the Germans back on one more occasion.

He looked over at McMurphy to see what they should do next, to which his leader indicated they should fly east for a while. It was a good decision, because in another ten minutes they came under intense ground fire. At one thousand feet, there wasn't a lot of danger except, perhaps, from a stray bullet. But whenever the enemy threw up that much fire, it meant that they were nervous about something. The object of their concern came into view approximately sixty seconds later. There, on a muddy French road, was a fully exposed supply convoy. Trevor burst into a grin and turned to see McMurphy nodding in a motion that was as close to enthusiastic as it was possible for the captain to make. McMurphy made hand gestures to outline a plan of attack.

Trevor followed him down as they dove on the vehicles in the column. At just the right moment, McMurphy opened up with his machine gun, firing rapid bursts into the various lead vehicles. The first truck burst into flames, obviously with a hit to its gas tank. McMurphy damaged two or three others in the column before pulling up. Trevor followed him at high speed, about ten feet to the left to get hits on the vehicles that had scattered to the side of the road to get out of the way of the Allied attack. He was pleased to see that his run damaged at least a couple of vehicles, then he too pulled up to escape the hail of bullets being fired by what appeared to be every troop in the convoy.

Now they were to the east of the enemy. Trevor watched as McMurphy did a rudder-only turn to reverse direction. The skill of the turn was unbelievable. *The man is amazing! How does he do that?* Trevor executed a similar turn but without the same level of precision. This time they came in from behind the convoy. It was a good, clean approach, and Trevor was concentrating with everything he had to make sure he didn't shoot the captain while strafing the infantry troops that were firing at them. That's when he heard the uncomfortable twang of one of his wires snapping off to his right. That sound was followed by the thud of a couple of bullets slamming into his right wing.

He turned to see that in the heat of the battle, a German aircraft had joined their fracas and was now on his tail. McMurphy was still unaware of the danger, so Trevor pulled up in a horizontal vrille, which allowed him to come back down directly behind the German, having completed a full circle. Of course, the German knew he'd do this, but he was more interested in using the time Trevor was in the loop to close in on McMurphy, who was now forced to take evasive action of his own.

Trevor looked around the sky to see if the Bosche had friends, but the sky was clear except for this one intruder. At this point, McMurphy was doing a credible job of stirring things up with the German, so Trevor renewed the attack on the convoy. As he came in from the rear, he was delighted to see that about midway up the column were two trucks riding low on their tires. Fuel trucks—the best target a pilot could hope for. Blowing up a fuel truck was the best way to frustrate the enemy's offensive plans.

Still, it was a difficult shot because he'd have to pass over perhaps ten vehicles and two or three hundred men who would be shooting at him from the ground. He came in low and fast. As he reached the rear of the column, he heard the thud of bullets penetrating the fabric of the wings. When one bullet slammed up through the floor directly in front of him, he couldn't help but wince, but still he held his course.

When the first fuel truck came into his sights, he pulled back on the trigger and felt the concussion of his weapon firing. His line of tracers started kicking up the dirt behind the truck, then slammed into the back of it with small puffs of fabric thrown into the sky. The sky lit up in front of him as the truck exploded in a great fireball of crimson-orange light. It was a fascinating sight, the sky in front of him temporarily as bright as the sun at noon. Even though he was several hundred feet up, he braced for the turbulence that would quickly buffet him as his aircraft flew through the blast. His little Nieuport shuttered as it was slammed up fifty feet from the heat of the explosion. It took all of Trevor's skill to fight the natural roll the disturbance created.

A few moments later, he emerged on the western side of the black acrid cloud, both hands raised high in the air while his jubilant shout was absorbed by the deafening concussion of the blast. He kept the plane steady by holding the joystick in position between his knees. He pulled back on the stick as hard as he could to gain altitude. Turning back, he surveyed the mayhem behind him and was startled by a second explosion, at least equal in destructive force to the first. "I can't believe this," he shouted gleefully. "Two with one blow!" Then, to the German troops who were undoubtedly cursing him, "Take that, you Bosche—a little less fuel and ammunition to kill our doughboys with!"

In battle, there was never much time to celebrate however, so he quickly turned to see how McMurphy and the German were faring. He was pleased to see McMurphy coming up from behind with no German in view. With the objective obviously lost, the German had turned and headed for home—there was nothing to be gained by continuing a fight against two Allied aircraft. McMurphy indicated they should head for home.

Trevor's adrenaline began to wear off as they were crossing over the trenches on their way west. As a sign of respect for the ground troops, they dipped down a bit to signal they'd met with success.

Looking down at the American trenches, he sighed. Inevitably, as it did every time he crossed the Allied trenches, his mind turned to Dan O'Brian, his best friend from home. "Oh, Danny," he said quietly. "What are you doing down there in the muck of France getting shot at and having to shoot at others." It was so unfair—if anyone deserved to be home pursuing a career, it was Danny. *I hope you're still alive. I hope you're all right.* "Dear God, please help Danny. He needs you."

Part One

A SEASON
FOR OPTIMISTS

Chapter One

THE NEW KID IN TOWN

Pocatello, Idaho—Halliday Street Railroad Crossing
August 1911

"Oh my gosh, do you see that car?"

Danny O'Brian looked at Leonard Whitman with a bemused expression. "Yes, so they have a car. You'd expect the general manager to have a car, wouldn't you?"

"You're such an idiot, O'Brian. That's a 1910 Stearns. Sixty horsepower, a 550-cubic-inch engine, and a manual pump compression carburetor." He looked at Danny, who registered virtually no comprehension. "It has gas-powered headlamps, the most powerful in the industry." Still nothing. "Electric ignition," he said hopefully. Then, finally, "It costs $4,500!"

That got Danny's attention. That price tag was a fortune, and not even the general manager of the Oregon Short Line Railroad's Idaho Division was likely to make that much money. "How do you think they can afford it?"

"I don't know, but that is one beautiful car. Just look at the red enamel finish. I bet it's been polished a couple hundred times. That must be his wife and son." The two fifteen year olds stared at the sandy-haired boy climbing out of the front passenger seat of the Stearns. He was slender and short but looked fairly athletic. Maybe agile was a better word. If he wasn't their age, he was pretty close. "Do you think he's an only child?"

"How would I know? All my father has told me is that Mr. Jonathon Richards is a big shot from Salt Lake City who's never had to do a day's work in his life. You know how much my father likes management."

As the Richards family climbed onto the makeshift stage that had been created especially for this occasion, the crowd of mostly railroad workers quieted down so the mayor could start the program. "My fellow citizens, this is a proud day for Pocatello. After thirty-three years of crossing the tracks in the mud, we finally have a safe and easy way to get from one side of the tracks to the other. Because of a $250,000 grant from our largest employer, we're now ready to open the Halliday Street underpass, soon to be joined by the Center Street overpass just north of the Pacific Hotel. No one will have to dodge the trains any longer, and the road engineers can stop worrying about pedestrians." He looked up above his glasses and added, "Truly, it's a 'Great Gateway to the Gate City.'" The mayor silently congratulated himself on this marvelous turn of a phrase, particularly since it had prompted an appreciative chuckle from the audience. "Now I'd like to turn the podium over to one of our newest and most important residents, Mr. Jonathon Richards, general manager of the Idaho Division of the Oregon Short Line Railroad, who will dedicate the underpass and lead the assembled automobiles in the first procession to pass beneath these magnificent tracks that give our city a reason to grow and prosper."

Jonathon Richards stepped forward casually. If he found the crowd intimidating, he didn't show it. "My congratulations, Mayor Church, on the remarkable work the city did to get this important artery ready before the snow falls. After the floods we all experienced in January, which took out every bridge in southeastern Idaho, it's a miracle we could find enough engineers and laborers to get this done on time and within budget." Turning to the assembled dignitaries, he smiled and said, "Sorry, that's the manager in me coming out." Turning back to the crowd, he continued, "Since this is the first chance I've had to meet many of you, please let me thank you on behalf of my wife and son for the warm welcome we've felt since coming to Pocatello. We're about to settle into a new house, and we hope to make this our home for many years to come."

He paused briefly. "I see some of you straining a bit because of my accent. I'm afraid I'm British born, which makes it difficult for me to communicate the way sensible people should. My father brought me to Salt Lake City when I was twelve years old, and I've been trying to learn to speak properly ever since." The crowd liked him. His self-deprecating manner offset his obvious upper-class breeding. "With the new fifty-three-berth roundhouse to service the locomotives, icing platforms for the Pacific Fruit Express, the newest nine-hundred-ton coal chute in the western United States, and the new power plant and car shop, Pocatello now has the largest railroad facility between Omaha and the Pacific Coast. You have all worked incredibly hard to make this the linchpin in the system's plan to exploit the vast riches of the Pacific Northwest, as well as the mines and produce of Montana. Now, we look to this remarkable underpass as another example of how man's ingenuity and craftsmanship can solve any problem that presents itself. There are no engineers in the world as effective as those who work for the Oregon Short Line and our sister company, the Union Pacific, and we're pleased to provide you and your family a safe crossing. In spite of the more than seventy trains passing across the tracks each day, there will be no more dashing through the mud on a rainy day, Mrs. Church." The mayor's wife laughed and flushed at the attention he drew to her. "I can also tell all of you on behalf of the railroad that this is just the beginning of what we have planned for this dynamic city. I honestly can't express how proud I am to be the leader of the more than five thousand employees who work here in Pocatello and the rest of the Idaho Division."

"My father's going to have his hands full with this one," Danny said to Leonard. "Just look at him, standing over there glowering while everybody else is cheering."

"My father works for a union, and he's clapping."

"Your father's not a fanatic—mine is."

"Well, enough talking," Jonathon Richards continued, raising his hands to quiet the crowd. "We can talk about this underpass all day, or we can see if it works. Therefore, on behalf of the board of directors of the Oregon Short Line Railroad, I'm proud to dedicate the new Halliday Street underpass on this the twelfth day of August 1911." He raised the ceremonial scissors and cut the broad bow of the decorative ribbon that had been strung across the underpass entrance, while the crowd cheered. He and the other assembled community leaders then descended the steps and climbed into their cars to start the procession through the narrow, westbound lane of the underpass.

"I can't believe it," Leonard said breathlessly.

"What now?"

"The mayor is driving a Franklin! A seventy-horsepower Franklin like the ones that came through here on the great St. Louis-to-Seattle race a few years ago."

"You're beyond hope."

Leonard was used to this. Danny was one of his best friends, but they really had little in common. Danny loved music, art, and reading, while Leonard loved cars, trains, electric motors, telephones, and everything else mechanical or electrical.

"Look at that Richards kid sitting in the front seat. He's so smug. I bet he's never had to haul out a bucket of clinkers in his life."

"Probably not," Leonard replied. "But I'd sure like to get to know him so I could get a better look at that car."

"Well, I don't intend to get to know him. Just by the look of him, he's a snob, and I don't have the time to waste on him." Leonard shrugged his shoulders as the two boys started the descent into the pedestrian walkway on the north side of the underpass. It was pretty exciting to look down through the arched columns that separated the pedestrian passageway from the cars passing in the lane below them. Many of the drivers honked their horns to hear the multiple reverberations in the concrete tunnel.

"The underpass seems kind of narrow," Leonard said. Just then, they heard a scraping sound and saw Mrs. Morris's car careening off one of the center supports in the tunnel. Leonard laughed. "Well, I guess the underpass has truly been christened now. I'll bet there will be a lot more scrape marks on the concrete pretty soon."

After a twenty-minute walk in the morning sun, Danny and Leonard made it to the grounds of the high school on Main Street and Clark. As part of the day's celebrations, the railroad had scheduled a large picnic lunch with games and a host of track-and-field events. Leonard was entered in a relay, Danny in the 100-yard sprint. The events were set at 11:00 A.M. so everyone could run before eating lunch. At the appointed moment, Leonard took his place with his relay team. They were representing the west-side kids, competing against two teams from the east side of the tracks. When the gun sounded, the lead member of Leonard's team took off like a startled colt. He quickly took the lead but began to fade halfway around the track so that by the time the baton was passed to the team's second runner, they'd fallen to second place. Unfortunately, they lost even more ground in that circuit, but Jamie Winters made up some lost ground in the third leg. Leonard grabbed the baton and started out at a moderate pace, a maneuver that made the west-side crowd a little crazy. But he knew what he was doing, because instead of fading through the course, he simply continued to gain speed until he was neck and neck with the leader. With fifteen yards to go, they both poured on everything they had, but Leonard managed to pull ahead at the critical moment to break the tape. All the west-side kids, and even some of the parents, crowded in to congratulate him.

Next up was Danny in the 100-yard dash. Few runners even chose to compete because Danny was the acknowledged star of the event. Still, he saw four or five others line up, which made it fun to race. He moved into his favorite position, second from the inside, because it gave him the most room to maneuver. Then out of the corner of his eye, he saw someone with blond hair picking up a number. "The Richards kid," he said under his breath. "Well, this will be a good way to show him how things are around here." Danny used his spade to carve out a depression in the sand that he could push against with his foot when the race started. Then he crouched down into the starter's position. When the gun fired, he shot out at about the same speed as the blast from the muzzle of the starter pistol. His strategy was different from Leonard's—he liked to take the lead early and keep it. No sense encouraging any false hopes. It wasn't his practice to ever look to the side to see where the other runners were, since it could only slow him down. Plus, there'd never been any runners to look at. Which is why it was odd to see something at the extreme edge of his peripheral vision. Odd enough that it broke his concentration, and he turned his head ever so slightly to see what was there. What he saw infuriated him. The Richards kid was even with him, perhaps even ahead. *All right, guess I'll have to work for this one.* He lengthened his stride and increased the pace, pushing himself as hard as he could. *That ought to do it.*

But it didn't. A 100-yard race doesn't last very long and is completely unforgiving for those who need to make adjustments. Richards not only matched Danny's speed, but he beat it, coming in a good yard ahead of him. Most of the crowd applauded at the surprise victory, but Danny, gasping for breath, saw that his friends looked angry. He was grateful they didn't humiliate him by booing or yelling. He just wanted to get out of there, but before he could clear the track, the Richards kid came straight for him, hand outstretched.

"That was a great race—I thought you had me for sure."

"Yeah, good race," Danny mumbled lamely. He took Richards's hand with as little enthusiasm as possible, then dropped his gaze and tried to get away.

"My name is Trevor Richards. I'm new in town."

Brilliant—really brilliant. "New in town." "I'm Daniel O'Brian, but people call me Danny."

"Pleased to meet you, Danny." He acted like he wanted to say more, but Danny made up an excuse and turned his back on Richards, who was quickly surrounded by others from the crowd. Danny moved toward Leonard, who was hanging back toward the school.

Before he got to Leonard, he heard a voice behind him. "So the little hotshot finally got beat!" Danny grimaced at the sound of his brother's voice. "By a blond-headed English shrimp, no less." Danny stumbled as his older brother Kelly punched him on the back. He slugged him so hard that it would have knocked the wind out of most people, but Danny was nearly immune because it happened so often.

Danny wanted to shoot back some smart remark, but that would only give Kelly ammunition to further antagonize him, so he just shoved him back and said, "Leave me alone. You've got your own race to run, don't you?"

"I suppose someone's got to protect the family honor. Running and shooting used to be the only things you were good at, and now you've lost running. Don't worry, I'll make Father proud."

More than anything in the world, Danny wanted to turn and slug him right in the face, but Kelly weighed a good thirty pounds more than Danny and would have loved an excuse to beat him up. So he just kept walking while listening to Kelly and his lout of a friend, Victor, laugh at his expense.

"I can't believe he beat you," Leonard said tentatively. "What happened?"

"He just plain ran faster," Danny replied miserably. "I honestly gave it everything I had, but he just beat me. It's not fair—rich *and* fast."

"It looked like he tried to be nice to you after the race."

"Noblesse oblige."

"What?"

"Nothing—it means he could afford to be nice since he won the race. What does it matter to him that my father's likely to slap me or something for losing to a manager's son, particularly when Kelly gets done telling him all about it?" Danny groaned as he slumped down against the side of the building. It was all over so fast. He went from being the best at something everybody admired to just another one of the losers. It didn't count that most people loved to hear him sing, since that wasn't "manly" in his father's eyes. Whenever anybody complimented him on it, Kelly teased him, and his father shook his head in disgust. But not when he won races. His father liked it when he won races. Now that was gone. *Maybe not,* he thought savagely. *There will be other races, and I'll just have to work to beat him.* Danny hated the fact that a couple of hot tears were running down his face. He quickly wiped them away while turning his head from the crowd. Leonard must have seen, but he didn't say anything.

"Runners, take your positions." He looked up to see Kelly lining up for the mile race. With his muscular chest, powerful lungs, and long legs, there was no one who could beat him in an endurance race. That's why he was so powerful in football. *"Now that's a man's sport!"* he heard his father's voice say in his head. *"Football takes brute strength and endurance, but most of all, courage. Find somebody who's good at football, and they've got everything they need to make it in the real world."* It was almost like his father was a working man's Teddy Roosevelt, all bully and hale and out to prove how invincible he was. It was so strange that his father, a union rep for the Clark-Kimball Lodge of the Brotherhood of Locomotive Firemen, would relate to Roosevelt, who grew up as a sickly rich kid in New York. But the national union had made T. R. an honorary member, and that was good enough for Frank O'Brian. The biggest difference was that Roosevelt was an enthusiastic optimist while Frank O'Brian was a sulking, pessimistic union agitator who always had a gripe against somebody.

The sound of the starter pistol startled Danny, and he looked up to see the runners take off. He shook his head in unbelief. "Have I gone blind, or is that the Richards kid in the fourth lane?"

"You're not blind. It's him. Whoever heard of a short kid like that running a distance race?"

"He's actually got a pretty good pace going—not real fast, but not at the back of the pack either." Danny laughed. "He'll have to run twice as many strides as Kelly if he hopes to win. I wonder what he's trying to prove." Danny stood up and moved closer to the track so he could see what was going on. In spite of his size, the Richards kid ran with real heart and slowly but surely overtook the other runners one by one. When he moved into second place behind Kelly two-thirds of the way through the race, a lot of people in the crowd started cheering him on. Even from this distance, Danny could see that the noise was distracting Kelly and putting him off his stride. Kelly brought out two emotions in people: they either loved him because he could almost always outrun the opposing team tacklers (and he was large enough to shrug off the few that caught him), or they hated him because of his rotten personality. The split in the community was showing itself now. "This could actually turn out to be pretty interesting," Danny said with an odd tone in his voice. "I don't want Richards to win because he beat me, but it would be so amazing if he actually beat Kelly. I almost feel like rooting for him." Leonard laughed and seemed to secretly start cheering for Trevor Richards. As they approached the finish line, the frustration in Kelly's face was obvious. He tried everything he could think of to throw Richards off his course, including bumping him at one point, but Trevor quickly regained his footing and pulled ahead at the finish line. The crowd was ecstatic. August could be pretty boring, but not today. Two O'Brian kids beaten in the same day. It was unheard of.

Kelly didn't give Trevor even the slightest chance to congratulate him, spitting at his feet as he turned and walking from the field in disgust. He was muttering something about a pulled hamstring that slowed him down. He nearly knocked Leonard down as he and Victor stormed past. Leonard went up to Trevor and enthusiastically congratulated him, along with half the city of Pocatello. Danny stood looking on thoughtfully. His dark mood had passed, since Kelly would have to confess to his own defeat that night when their father got home from work.

An hour or so later, after an enormous lunch of fried chicken and watermelon, he and Leonard were walking down the alley behind Lander Street, talking about the strange events of the day, when they heard a disturbance between some of the garbage incinerators a little farther down. Instinctively, they drew close to the fence and inched their way toward the commotion to see what was going on.

"Think you're pretty great, do you, English boy?" Danny heard a familiar thud that told him Kelly had landed a blow. To his credit, Trevor Richards said nothing in reply but did his best to dodge Kelly's next blow. With Victor between him and an escape route, Trevor had no way out.

When Kelly knocked Trevor down and started kicking him, Danny looked at Leonard with a shrug and took off on a scream to tackle Kelly. Leonard took advantage of Victor's distraction to come up behind him and pull him down with his arms locked around his neck. It was stupid of both of them, because Victor and Kelly outweighed them and could easily beat them senseless. What they hadn't considered is that even Victor and Kelly together didn't equal three younger guys. It was just as Kelly was pounding Danny's face with his bare fist that Trevor Richards came flying at him from the side, knocking him to the ground and then pouncing on him with his own unique style of throwing a punch. It didn't come from the side, as Danny had been taught to fight. He punched straight into Kelly's face, almost immediately causing his nose to bleed as he cried out in pain. Danny actually had to pull Trevor off so that Kelly could cup his nose. At that point, the combined mass of Victor and Leonard crashed into the backs of Danny and Trevor, and a brief free-for-all left everybody bruised and gasping. When Kelly tried to join in again, Trevor somehow managed to trip him, which sent him flying face first into the dirt. That hurt his nose even worse, and he stood up bellowing like a bull moose.

"Had enough?" Trevor called out challengingly.

"I'll kill you, you little brat," Kelly screamed back, attempting to lunge at him.

"Stop it, Kelly. There's three of us and only two of you, and we'll kill each other if we keep this up. Just go home and leave this kid alone. You've done enough damage already."

"What are you talking about?" Kelly roared back.

Danny moved close to his ear and whispered, "He is the son of the general manager, for crying out loud. Do you really think it's going to help Father out for you to beat the manager's kid to death?"

Kelly looked stunned. It wasn't what he wanted to hear. "Father will be proud, and you know it."

"Probably, but enough's enough. Go home before you make it worse." Surprisingly, or perhaps because his nose was still bleeding, Kelly grumbled to Victor to come on, and the two of them lumbered down the alley, cursing as they went. Danny heard Kelly muttering that the jerk had probably broken his nose, which is why he hadn't fought back like normal.

"Thanks for the help," Trevor said, dusting off his pants.

"It doesn't mean anything," Danny replied. "My brother is a stupid oaf who had no business hurting you or anybody else. You'll know better than to cross him from now on."

"Well, it means something to me," Trevor said quietly. "I appreciate it."

"Come on, Leonard. Let's get out of here." Trevor stepped aside so Danny and Leonard could pass.

"You'd have beaten me today if you didn't lift your feet so high."

"What did you say?" Danny turned back to look at Trevor.

"You could have won the race if you changed your stride just a bit. I had a coach in Salt Lake who taught me how to do it. In a dash you have to lean forward so the bulk of your weight pulls your feet forward. It changes your center of gravity and gives you an edge. The truth is that you're faster than me. I'd be glad to show you sometime if you like."

Danny couldn't figure out what to do with this kid. No matter how hard he tried to get away from him, he kept coming up with stuff. "Come on, Leonard. Let's go."

"You go. I want to stay and talk for a minute." Leaning closer to Danny, he whispered, "About his car. I've got to know about his car."

"Fine, you stay and talk. I've got to go home and get cleaned up before my father gets back." He stomped off down the alley, shoulders slumped and head lowered.

* * *

Once he turned the corner and disappeared out of sight, Trevor turned to Leonard and asked, "What's wrong with him? Why does he hate me so much?"

"I don't think he hates you. It's his father . . ."

"What do you mean, his father? His father doesn't know me."

"You've got to understand that the two things his father hates most in the world are the English and management. He's a union rep and Irish. Your father is English and management. It's about that easy to understand."

Trevor nodded his head. "So that's it. His father hates my father, so he and his brother hate me, even though they've never met me."

"Danny is one of the best guys you'll ever meet. He'll be okay to you because he's a decent person. The trouble is that he has a hot-tempered father who loves everything about Kelly but has no use for Danny. It's pretty tough on him."

"What about his mother? Doesn't she have anything to do with it?"

"His mother is very quiet. She tiptoes around like a mouse so she doesn't set her husband off. She loves Danny and encourages him in his music, but she doesn't dare to stand up to her husband to protect Danny or she runs the risk of getting slapped herself."

Trevor shook his head. "Does his father really beat him?"

"Not with his fist or anything. He slaps him 'til it stings sometimes, and he probably uses a belt more often than most fathers. But he isn't a wife beater or anything. He's just angry about something most of the time. He has these great causes like, 'Workers of the World Unite!' Whenever Danny disagrees, they get in a fight. Personally, I get tired of listening to him and want to go home, but I feel like I should stay with Danny."

"What about his brother?"

"Kelly is mean. Really mean. He hits Danny hard, and since he's so much bigger, it usually does a number on him. Danny does his best to avoid him, but Kelly is always picking on him. I know you're not supposed to hate anybody, but Kelly makes it hard not to."

"I don't have a brother, and my parents never fight. My father is always cheerful and almost always proud of me. I can't imagine what it would be like to have a father who was mean or grumpy all the time." Trevor caught himself and turned to Leonard. "I hope your father is nice to you."

"My father is great. He's not like Danny's and probably not like yours either. He works in the locomotive roundhouse as a skilled mechanic, and he's very shy and quiet. He hardly says anything to any of us. But he loves us and spends lots of time helping me build things. I want to be a mechanic when I'm older too."

"I don't know what I want to be," Trevor said laconically. "Drive motorcycles or fly airplanes, I suppose."

"Airplanes?"

Trevor smiled broadly.

"Yes, airplanes. The first one to fly in Utah took off last year, and my father took my mom and me out to see it. It was the most incredible thing you've ever seen. The roar of the engine was unbelievable, and the propeller kicked up a breeze that about knocked the men holding the tail right off their feet." He laughed at the memory. "Once the engine was at full throttle, they released the tail, and it bounced down the field like an awkward little bird, and then just drifted up into the air like the most graceful swan you've ever seen. I wanted to be the pilot more than anything in the world." His voice trailed off, and he unconsciously raised his head as if to follow the image of the airplane into the sky.

"Speaking of incredible," Leonard said a bit sheepishly, "I couldn't help but notice that your family drove through the underpass in a Stearns. Is that your father's car?"

Trevor shook his head to clear the thoughts of flying. "It's ours, all right. Father loves automobiles and couldn't resist this one when it came to Salt Lake."

"But how can he afford it? I mean, that thing costs a fortune!"

"It helps that my grandfather owns a car dealership—he sells Buicks. He bought the Stearns for a promotion, mostly to show how great Buicks are in comparison, and gave it to Father after he'd driven it a couple hundred miles."

"Buicks. Wow. Your grandfather must be very rich."

Trevor nodded. "I suppose so. He's just Grandfather to me. He's every bit as cheerful as my father, so he's let me play around the cars ever since he bought the dealership."

Leonard shook his head in disbelief. "I mean, that's got to be heaven. A car dealership."

"Maybe we can go to Salt Lake sometime and you can meet my grandfather. I'm sure he'd like you, since you like cars so much."

"That's just too much to even dream about," Leonard said. He really couldn't say anything else.

"At the very least, we'll take you for a ride in the Stearns. Or my mother's Buick, if you like. Maybe you could come over Sunday afternoon. That's when Father is off work, and he always likes to go for a ride on Sunday afternoon."

"You have two cars? Nobody has two cars."

Trevor smiled. "Come over Sunday and we'll talk about it."

Chapter Two

SUNDAYS AT THE RICHARDSES' AND O'BRIANS'

The First Ward church occupied a prominent spot on the corner of Center Street and Garfield, just one block south of the high school grounds. The design was fairly common for the day, with steeply gabled roofs and small towers that resembled the Assembly Hall on Temple Square in Salt Lake City. Huge stained glass windows on each side of the chapel caught the sun and caused brilliant colors to dance across the chapel in the early morning and late afternoon. People had to climb approximately twenty steps to enter the chapel and another six to get up onto the podium at the front. The area where the leaders sat was created out of beautifully ornamented wood painted a brilliant, glossy white that gave it something of a fairy-tale feeling. The steep rise of the choir seats behind the pulpit, with the pipes of the small organ framing the view behind the speaker, inevitably caused one's gaze to rise heavenward. A small room was used for sacrament preparation on the right, while a circular staircase to the left led to the basement multipurpose room and classrooms.

Danny loved to get to church early and walk quietly up and down the pews, making sure they were clean. It was the teachers quorum's responsibility to get the building open and ready. In the summer, that meant opening the windows to get a breeze circulating through the building, while in the winter they had to light the ten or so coal stoves so that the building would be warm when priesthood meeting started. Priesthood meeting was from 8:30 A.M. to 10:00 A.M., followed by senior and junior Sunday School from 10:30 A.M. to noon, and then sacrament meeting at 7:00 P.M. Fast meeting was the second Thursday of each month at 6:00 P.M. for those who could make it. The teachers had to prepare the sacrament twice each week: first for Sunday School, and again in the evening for sacrament meeting. The little children attended Primary on Tuesday after school, and choir practice met later that evening. Relief Society gathered on Wednesday afternoon, the Mutual Improvement Association for the youth met on Thursday night, and there was usually some kind of ward dinner or activity on Friday or Saturday night.

It made for a full week, but Danny liked getting out of the house and hearing about lessons from the scriptures. Plus, as a member of the choir, he enjoyed the chance to sometimes sing a solo or descant. All in all, church activity was the biggest part of his life, which he was able to share with his mother. His father was a member but not very active, and Kelly had stopped going to church when he turned sixteen. He had started smoking, using the excuse that it gave him a boost for athletics. But it made him feel uncomfortable going to church. He said everybody was always "judging" him, even though a number of active members struggled with that part of the Word of Wisdom and no one made an issue of it. When their mother had protested, Frank had said a person ought to be able to decide for himself by that age. Not surprisingly, considering Frank's temper, she let it drop at that.

On Sundays, Leonard was usually second to arrive, with his father, who was the elders quorum president, followed by Elmer Peterson and Sam Carter. The four boys had grown up together and were presently the only members of the quorum. When Danny heard the door open downstairs, he looked up, expecting to see Leonard. He couldn't believe it when he saw a blond head come bobbing into view.

When Trevor saw Danny, he brightened up and said a cheerful, "Good morning. Are we the first ones here?"

Always quick to notice the obvious. "Yeah, but the other guys should get here pretty soon." He looked down and busied himself with refolding the sacrament cloths in preparation for Sunday School.

"Need some help?"

"No, thanks. We don't really need these 'til 10:30. There's not a lot to do in the summer."

Trevor shuffled around uneasily in the silence and seemed relieved to hear a commotion by the front door, signaling that other people had arrived. Soon Leonard appeared with his father, who introduced himself to Trevor. "Great races yesterday. It's kind of unusual to find somebody who's good at both sprints and endurance races."

"Thank you, sir. I just enjoy running. I like the way my lungs feel when I'm done."

Another group arrived, and Leonard introduced Trevor to Elmer and Sam. Sam was very tall and lean, brown haired with dark brown eyes and a sharply sculpted, good-looking face that made it look like he was very analytical and precise. Elmer was just a little taller than Trevor but much broader. He had the look of someone who enjoyed hard physical labor, so it wasn't surprising to learn that he worked in his father's construction business building houses. He had light brown hair, but his sideburns were an almost ruddy color that confirmed his Scandinavian heritage.

Even though Danny was the teachers quorum president, it was Leonard, the first counselor, who offered to show Trevor around the church before the meeting got started. Danny was embarrassed that he wasn't doing his job better, but he just didn't know what to do around Trevor. Their first encounter had kind of backed Danny into a corner that he didn't know how to get out of.

When Bishop Peterson called priesthood meeting to order, Trevor's face registered obvious surprise when he noticed that Danny had slipped behind the piano to play, and even more so when he accompanied the singing with virtually no hesitation. Bishop Peterson then stood to conduct the business of the meeting. "Would Brother Jonathon Richards please stand?" There was a muted gasp from the assembled brethren. Jonathon had slipped into the back of the meeting room unseen, so few knew he was there. When he stood, people almost gawked, since he was the first general manager in memory who was a Mormon. It was pretty unusual for the owners of the Union Pacific to let an LDS man reach such a high management position, even though the original track in southern Idaho had been laid by the Mormons who owned the Utah Northern Railway. When it had merged with the Oregon Short Line more than twenty years earlier, most of the new management had come from the East rather than from the Utah group.

"We've called Brother Richards to serve as an advisor to the teachers quorum and to help out with the Mutual Improvement Association activities when his schedule permits. All in favor, please raise your right hands."

Danny raised his hand in a bit of disbelief. Leonard leaned over excitedly. "This is pretty cool. I learned that Brother Richards's father owns a car dealership in Salt Lake, and he loves cars. This could be good."

"Yeah, real good." Danny swallowed hard. He was going to have to get to know the Richardses, whether he wanted to or not.

"Any opposed? Thank you, Brother Richards, for accepting this assignment."

When the opening exercises broke up, Danny made his way to the basement to conduct the class. With only four—make that five—members of the quorum, it wasn't really hard, but somehow it always made him nervous. As he was about to enter the classroom, the first counselor in the bishopric asked if he could have a few minutes to introduce Brother Richards. Following the introduction, he excused himself to do some other business, and the five boys were left alone with Brother Richards. The group had a reputation for being hard on instructors, but a new advisor was always a little intimidating—more so today because Jonathon Richards was so prominent.

"Well, then, let me introduce myself properly, and then I'll ask each of you to tell me about yourself. This getting together for priesthood meeting on Sunday is still rather new to me. Up until two years ago, the priesthood quorums met irregularly, perhaps just once a month or so, on a day and time of their choosing. These weekly meetings are a great change, but I'll have to adapt myself to preparing a lesson on such a regular basis." He smiled. "I come from a fairly prominent family in England, where my grandfather owns a lot of coal as well as the factory that gets it properly sized for use in railroads and home heating. When my father and mother joined the LDS Church, he disinherited us, since he believes that one should always remain a member of the Church of England. It's a matter of patriotism for my grandfather.

"Fortunately, my grandmother was independently wealthy, and she had previously made provision for my father so that he had enough money to move to the United States where he opened a car dealership in Salt Lake City. My older brother, Tom, works with my father in the business. I could have too, I suppose, but I prefer to keep Tom as a friend, and if we worked together every day we wouldn't stay friends for long. I can get pretty stubborn when I have an opinion, and Tom and I used to get into arguments. It's much easier to be in different lines of work. So instead of working at the car dealership, I started at the Utah Northern, only to have my job taken away from me when we merged. But I soon got it back, and here we are today. At any rate, I've been a member of the Church since age twelve, and I look forward to teaching you when we get together each Sunday. Any questions?"

There were none.

Brother Richards cleared his throat and was about to move on when Leonard tentatively raised his hand.

"You have a question? First, please tell me your name."

"I'm Leonard Whitman, sir," he mumbled. "I'm the first counselor."

"Very good, Leonard. One of my best friends has that name, and I've always admired the way it sounds." Leonard smiled.

"What I was wondering, sir, is that since you've lived in England and Salt Lake City, why would you ever want to come to Pocatello? It's so small here."

Brother Richards laughed. "It seems you feel inferior to people who live in larger cities." Seeing a puzzled look on Leonard's face, he continued. "What I mean is that you don't think you're as good as folks from larger and older cities. Well, let me tell you why I'm glad to be here. I have traveled extensively in the world, and I find that people are pretty much the same wherever you go. Some talk a bit differently, but we all are interested in having decent lives, raising a family, and figuring out why we're here. In a lot of regards, that's actually easier to do in a place like Pocatello where you can get to know everyone, rather than in a big city where you can go about with no one recognizing you. Think of it this way. If you did something really bad, would anybody else know about it?"

"Everybody would know about it," Sam said.

"Precisely. So you tend to be good because you don't want to embarrass yourself. If you're in London, with six million other people, there's no one who cares about what you're doing. In fact, there are lots of people who would like you to spend your money with them doing things that are bad. So it's actually harder to be good in a city."

"But don't people in cities know more than we do, since there's lots of libraries and things?" another boy piped in.

"Tell me your name, please."

"I'm Elmer Peterson, sir."

"The bishop's son?"

"Yes, sir."

"Well, Elmer, it's certainly true that people in Salt Lake City or New York know more about getting on a trolley than you do, since that's how they get around their city. They may even know more about the theatre or large symphony orchestras, since having more people makes it profitable for organizations like that to get organized. But they probably know much less than you do about hunting or fishing or hiking in the hills, since those things aren't available to them. So in the long run, we all know more about something than someone else. In many ways, you have the advantage because it takes less time to get around a town the size of Pocatello than it does New York or even Salt Lake City, so you have more time to learn things. Besides, I noticed the new Carnegie Library right across the street from the church, which means you can get the same books they have in the city."

"But a big-city library would have a lot more books than ours."

"True enough, but since no one could read all the books in the world anyway, the key is to get hold of the ones that you really want. And I bet your local librarian would order any book that you need." Then he added with a slight twinkle in his eye, "Plus, I have a bad habit of buying lots of books that get read only once and then wind up on a book-case somewhere in our house. You're all welcome to borrow them one at a time, as long as you promise to take good care of them."

The boys didn't know what to think of all this. They were used to being treated like children instead of talked to as adults.

"But now it's your turn to introduce yourselves to me. I need to know your names, age, your parents' names, and a little bit about your family, your best and worst subjects in school, and, finally, your favorite story from the scriptures." To make sure they remembered all that, he wrote the list on the black-slate chalkboard at the front of the room. "Now, I understand that you're in charge, President O'Brian, so why don't you go first?"

Danny stood nervously and cleared his throat. "My name is Daniel O'Brian, but everybody calls me Danny. I was born on May 2, 1896, so I'm fifteen years old.

"My parents are Frank and Julia O'Brian, and I have one older brother, named Kelly." Richards noticed the other students grimace at this piece of information. "My best subjects are music and literature and my worst is arithmetic. My favorite story from the scriptures is where Nephi is talking about how he'd like to be happy, but his sins and shortcomings make it hard, so he asks the Lord to help him."

"That's one of my favorites, too. Second Nephi, chapter four. Many people call it Nephi's Psalm because it's laid out much like David's psalms in the Old Testament. But I'm surprised that a fifteen year old would choose that as a favorite. I think it shows a lot of maturity on your part."

Danny blushed at the compliment and quickly dropped his eyes. It was particularly embarrassing to be praised in front of his friends. Still, it felt good to be recognized.

"Brother Peterson, I believe you're next."

"Yes, sir. As I said earlier, my name is Elmer Peterson, and my father is the bishop, Hans. My mother is Konstance, and I have three brothers and two sisters. My father builds houses for a living, and I work with him after school and in the summer. I like arithmetic a lot, but not reading. I'll probably be a carpenter like my father when I grow up. My favorite scripture story is where Ammon defends the Lamanite king's flocks from the bandits by cutting off their arms. He's real brave."

"Another Book of Mormon story. That's great—lots of action. Who's next?"

Trevor was seated between Elmer and Leonard and seemed reluctant to introduce himself to his own father. "My name is Trevor Richards, and I'm from Salt Lake City. You all know that this is my father, Jonathon"—everybody laughed to hear him call his father by his first name—"and my mother is Margaret. I don't have any brothers or sisters. I like shop and phys-ed best, and I do okay at arithmetic. I hate to write and to study English—diagramming sentences is kind of stupid." Groans from the others confirmed this assessment. "Because I'm short, my favorite scripture story is where David stands up to Goliath with nothing but a sling. It shows that a little guy can hold his own, even against a giant." Everybody, including Danny, laughed at that one.

"As you can see, Trevor has something of a comedic flair. What he didn't tell you is that he loves airplanes and pesters me endlessly to find some way for him to take a flight somewhere. Personally, I think flying is for the birds." The five boys groaned. "Yes, the pun was intended. Now, please save my dignity—Brother Leonard, is it?—and introduce yourself."

"Yes, sir. Leonard Whitman. My father is Matthew Whitman, and he works as a mechanic in the locomotive roundhouse. I have two younger brothers and two younger sisters. Reading and shop are pretty easy, but geography is kind of hard. I like the stories about Jesus in the New Testament, particularly when he healed the woman who touched his garment. I'd like to have faith like she had someday."

That one took Brother Richards by surprise and left him with nothing to say for a moment. Finally, he replied quietly, "It sounds to me, Leonard, like you may already have that kind of faith. Hopefully we'll add to it in the lessons we share in the next few years. Now, last, but not least."

"I'm Sam Carter. My father's a farmer, and I want to be a farmer when I grow up too. I like working with the animals and growing food for people. Arithmetic helps me learn how to run a farm. I don't like English and writing because I don't see that I'll ever use it. My favorite scripture story is Noah and the flood because he saved all the animals, and I don't think it would be a very good world without animals."

"Nor do I. Well, I can see that you're a very mature group of young men who must have paid attention to your Sunday School and Primary teachers. What I want to do each Sunday is to give you time to ask any questions you have about anything that affects your life, and then we'll see if we can find answers in the scriptures. If you don't have questions, we'll move straight into the lesson. How does that sound?" The boys murmured their assent.

"Unfortunately, my work requires that I often leave during the week, so I won't be able to join you as much as I'd like during Mutual Improvement on Thursday evenings. But I have an idea for something else that you might like. Each Sunday, Trevor and I try to make things easy on my wife by cooking a large breakfast right after Sunday School. We always end up making far more food than we can eat. So I'd like to propose that on the first Sunday of each month, the teachers quorum come to our house to join us for that meal. That way we can have an informal quorum meeting. Somehow it's always easier to talk when there's food involved. Since this is our first Sunday together, perhaps you could talk to your parents and ask them if it's all right if we meet today. Please apologize for the fact that I didn't give you much warning. Of course, if you can't come this month, you can start next month. Anyone have a problem with that?"

The four boys shook their heads in amazement at this invitation. Everybody knew that the Richardses lived in a large brick house just north of the Standrod Mansion on Garfield. It was the kind of house that only rich people could afford, and it was exciting to think of going there to see what it was like. Everybody agreed enthusiastically, although Jonathon Richards noticed that Danny had something of an anxious look on his face. He knew Frank O'Brian by reputation, although he hadn't had occasion to formally sit down with him yet. He could imagine that he was pretty stern. Hopefully it would work out.

A member of the bishopric rang a large hand bell to indicate that it was time to wrap things up, so Leonard gave a prayer and the group adjourned to go home to get ready to come back to Sunday School with their mothers and sisters.

When Danny got home, his heart was beating rapidly. As he walked through the door, he saw that his father was unshaven and sitting in his favorite reading chair with a copy of the union magazine in his hands. He didn't look up when Danny entered, so Danny moved over to the front of his chair and said quietly, "Excuse me, sir, but could I interrupt you for a moment?"

Without raising his eyes from the magazine, he said, "What do you want?"

"Our teachers quorum advisor has planned a meeting at his house after Sunday School where he's going to feed us lunch. I was wondering if it would be all right if I went."

Frank raised his eyes and replied, "It's not enough that the Church takes you—and your mother—out of the house both morning and night on Sundays. Now they want you in the afternoons too?"

"Only once per month, sir, on the first Sunday. It just turns out that this is the first time they want to try it."

"I thought I might go shooting this afternoon. But you wouldn't like to come along anyway, since it's Sunday. You might as well go, if it's all right with your mother."

"Thank you, sir." Danny turned and quickly exited to his bedroom. He was relieved to find that Kelly wasn't there—he was probably out with Victor somewhere. Danny was also relieved that his father hadn't asked where the meeting was to take place, although he had a sick feeling that it would come back to cause problems later. Still, he wanted to go to the Richards house. He liked Brother Richards and wanted to get to know him better. When it was time to go to Sunday School, he walked out the door with his mother. They both said good-bye to Frank, who simply mumbled something from behind his magazine.

* * *

It was a nervous group of four boys that showed up on the Richardses' porch at 12:30. The porch itself was six steps up from the sidewalk and was covered by an impressive portico supported by four brick columns. The roof of the porch provided a small balcony for the upstairs hallway. The house itself was a two-story Georgian framed in deep burgundy brick. An attached garage on the north side was an unusual feature, since most automobiles were stored in unused stables. On the south side, facing the Standrod Mansion (which the boys called "The Castle"), was a conservatory that had wonderful plateglass windows that reached almost floor to ceiling on the three exposed sides.

"I can't believe we're here," Elmer said a bit breathlessly after Leonard tapped the large brass knocker on the beautifully carved hardwood door.

Usually they would have changed clothes immediately after church, but they'd each come to the independent conclusion that a visit to "mansion corner" required Sunday best. Who knew how rich people dressed at home?

After a brief pause, Sam was so nervous that he was ready to leave, but the door swung open. The boys expected Trevor to answer, so they were all a bit speechless when his mother appeared instead. "Why, hello," she said pleasantly. "I'm glad to see that all of you were able to come. Jonathon and Trevor are in the kitchen, so why don't you come in and sit for a few moments?" Margaret Richards was a handsome woman with a slender build, auburn hair, and deep blue eyes. As the boys walked into the entryway, they were immediately intimidated by the new hardwood floor covered by a Persian rug. Danny was planning to walk around it until he saw Mrs. Richards walk across the corner as she moved toward the parlor on the right. There was a large cherrywood table in the center with a beautiful vase of fresh-cut flowers. The doorways on all sides were framed in a dark, carved wood, and a beautiful stairway with an amazingly shiny banister stood opposite the front door. Elmer almost tripped while looking up at the crystal-and-brass chandelier. "Why don't you wait in here?" she said, leading the way into the parlor. When Danny turned the corner, he couldn't help but let out a gasp. The conservatory on the opposite side of the parlor turned out to be a music room. In the center was a magnificent grand piano, the lid open and facing toward the parlor.

"Are you the boy who played for priesthood meeting today?"

Danny looked up, startled that he'd been noticed. "Why, yes, ma'am, I am."

"Trevor and Jonathon were talking about what a wonderful job you did. Would you like to play our piano?"

A look of terror came over Danny's face. "I don't think so. But thanks."

"Danny's best known for his singing," Sam chimed in. He seemed to immediately regret saying it when he caught the cold glare Danny directed his way.

"You sing? Could I hear you? I'd be pleased to accompany you."

"Really, I don't think so . . ."

"Come on, Danny, everybody knows you love to perform. Play and sing 'Danny Boy' like you did at the ward social." Leonard didn't care at all about the look on Danny's face.

"Please," Margaret insisted. "Trevor promised he'd learn to play the piano, but after a few lessons, it was more work to make him practice than it was worth. I'd like someone besides me to try it out. It may be a bit out of tune, since I haven't had time to have a tuner come over since the move."

Danny could see no way out of it. Besides, as he'd edged closer to the piano, he could see that it was a Steinway from New York. He'd heard about Steinways but had never actually seen one. The temptation to play such a beautiful instrument eventually won over his shyness, and he sat down on the padded bench. Adjusting himself to it, he marveled at seeing his reflection in the wood and gently rubbed his fingers up and down the perfect ivory keys. Looking up at Mrs. Richards, he said, "This is my mother's favorite song, for obvious reasons." Then he played the first chord . . . at least, he attempted to play the chord. The keys were very stiff compared to the usual upright piano that he played.

"A grand piano takes some getting used to. But once you learn its touch, I think you'll find it's far more subtle and responsive than other instruments."

He tried it again, with a little more strength, and the noise that welled up from the piano amazed him. The notes were so crisp, clean, and strong. After playing a few warm-up octaves, he started playing an introduction to "Danny Boy." The soft Irish melody was haunting in its effect. When he started singing, his voice blended so perfectly with the piano that it was difficult to separate the two. While his enunciation was clear and understandable, the words flowed together in a gentle and smooth way that made it sound effortless. While singing with a young man's voice, it was obvious that he would end up a tenor after his voice matured, and Margaret could only imagine how it would sound when mellowed by adulthood. She closed her eyes and listened as he sang the plaintive words of a song that expressed a mother's longing for a lost son. The thing that was most impressive in the performance, however, was the interpretation that Danny brought to the music, with his voice rising and falling to the changing moods of the verses. It was almost sorrowful when he struck the last chord and let it slowly fade into oblivion. Margaret was surprised when the other boys joined her in clapping enthusiastically for the performance.

"A remarkable performance—perhaps the best rendition I've ever heard." Jonathon Richards's confident voice broke the spell, and everyone turned in surprise to see him and Trevor standing in the doorway of the conservatory. "But unfortunately, the pancakes are ready in the dining room, and as far as I'm concerned, there's nothing quite so soggy as a cold pancake."

"Let's proceed to the dining room, then," Margaret said cheerfully. As Danny stood up, she leaned over and whispered, "I'd like to talk to you after lunch for just a moment, if you don't mind." Danny gulped and agreed.

The dining room was opposite the parlor on the north side of the house. A large Queen Anne table was filled with an overflowing cornucopia of breakfast foods and fresh fruit. After sitting down on the padded chairs, Jonathon asked if he might say the blessing on the food. Then he invited everyone to dig in. First the pancakes were passed, and Jonathon said, "I grew up with a tradition of having a variety of toppings for pancakes. As you can see, we have honey, maple syrup, fresh strawberries, raspberries, whipped cream, walnuts, raisins, and butter. We also have chokecherry jam and peach marmalade."

Leonard leaned over to Sam and whispered, "I never even thought to put such things on pancakes!" Sam nodded in disbelief—it was new for him too.

"There's plenty, so try one topping on one pancake, and another on the next. Of course we have bacon, ham, and scrambled eggs to offset the sweetness of the toppings. I'd serve the eggs over easy, but Trevor assured me you'd prefer scrambled." The boys could hardly believe it, but they started enthusiastically filling their plates. Not surprisingly, the only sound was of utensils clanking on china.

"Forgive me," Jonathon said, "but I expected there'd be a bit more conversation. Are you that starved that no one can talk?" The boys looked up anxiously. Finally, after no one else spoke up, Danny said, "Begging your pardon, sir, but we've been taught that only adults should talk at the dinner table."

"Ah, yes, I see. The 'children should be seen and not heard' philosophy."

"Yes, sir." The other boys nodded.

"I'm sure that your parents have taught you correctly. But tell me if my thinking is wrong. That policy makes sense if the dinner is primarily for adults, and children are simply invited to share the food. But in this case, you're the invited guests, which really makes it a meal for youth. In that light, it seems to me that it ought to be you who do the talking, while the adults remain mostly quiet. What do you think?"

The boys laughed, and Elmer said, "Forgive me, sir, but I've never heard anybody talk like that before. Is it because you're from England that you talk like this to boys?"

"Actually, no. They're even worse about such things in England. Sometimes no one spoke at the table, even my father and mother. It was dreadfully boring, and I always rather resented the fact that I couldn't talk. As you've probably observed by now, I'm a person who likes to talk, and I had a lot to say—still do!" The boys relaxed as Jonathon laughed at his own joke.

"The reason that I want you to feel free to talk around this dinner table is that I need to get to know you better so I can prepare better lessons for Sunday. I haven't been a boy for a long time now, and the only people I work with during the week are adults who talk only about business. So I need a refresher course in boys. Trevor had some rather noisy friends in Salt Lake City whom he had to leave behind, so this house seems unnaturally quiet. I'm hoping you'll fill it up with some noise once in a while. So does anyone have any questions about the Richardses or about our house or about any other topic?"

Elmer raised his hand. "I was wondering about all this furniture. Did you bring it with you from England?" That started a discussion of the furnishings of the house, which led to a discussion of the steam radiator that provided central heat and the fact that the electric wires were hidden inside the walls, rather than being in a conduit pipe running up the wall. When talk about the house had worked its way out, Leonard asked about the Stearns automobile.

"I love the Stearns," Jonathon Richards said. "It has a sixty-horsepower, four-cylinder engine in a 533-cubic-inch block."

Leonard gave Danny a knowing glance as if to say, *See, I told you so,* and then asked about the pressurized fuel tank.

"A car enthusiast, eh?" Jonathon then drilled down into some of the minutiae of the car's performance, including its 121-inch wheelbase, full leather seats, and modern array of instruments. Leonard held his own through the whole discussion. "It seems to me, Leonard, that you would love to meet my father. He owns a car dealership in Salt Lake City where he sells Buicks. They're a fine car company as well."

"Oh, I'll never make it to Salt Lake City. But it would be fun to visit someone who owns a car dealership."

"Why won't you make it to Salt Lake?"

"I don't know. We just never go there. Father's always pretty busy, and it would cost a lot of money."

Jonathon looked around the room and was surprised that no one seemed either surprised or upset by this sentiment. "Am I to understand that none of you has ever been to Salt Lake City?" All four boys shook their heads.

"Well, that's deplorable. To live five hours by train from the world headquarters of the Church and to never have been to Temple Square—we need to do something about this."

At this point, Trevor's face flushed because he knew that his father was about to come up with something outrageous. He always did, and it could be very embarrassing.

"I'll tell you what," Jonathon said in a conspiratorial voice. "The Church has asked that young men who are preparing for missions commit more than 120 scriptural passages to memory by the time they're ready to go. I say it's never too soon to start. So what I propose is that if every member in the group commits to memorizing thirty scriptures from the list by the end of next March, I'll take all of you to Salt Lake City. We can stay at my parents' home, and I'll show you the city while we're there. Any of your fathers who would like to come along are welcome. How does that sound?"

The boys were incredulous. "That sounds great," Leonard said in a hushed voice. Sam nodded in the affirmative. Elmer said, rather miserably, "I don't memorize very well, so I may not make it, and I don't want to ruin it for everybody else."

"Tough to memorize, eh? Well, I suppose that means we'll just have to help you out. I'm pretty sure we can get it done if you're willing to work at it."

Elmer smiled.

"And what about you, Danny? Would you like to go to Salt Lake?"

Danny didn't look up at him. Finally, he said quietly, "I'm not sure I'd like to go, sir, but that doesn't mean everyone else can't go." Jonathon was about to pressure him, but Margaret noticed the distressed look on Danny's face, so she jumped into the conversation.

"Jonathon, you're building everyone's hopes up before you've even had a chance to talk with the bishop and the boys' parents. You certainly can't take on a project like this without involving everyone else. It's no wonder Daniel can't answer you without having time to think about it."

Jonathon turned to his wife and, to the surprise of the boys, said meekly, "Of course, you're right, dear. Hopefully we can make it work, because it would be a grand adventure. In the meantime, it looks like most of the food is gone, so we'll have to clean up the table." He started to push back when he suddenly turned to Danny. "By the way, Dan, did Trevor tell you what an outstanding job you did in the race the other day? I don't think I've ever seen someone with such natural ability."

Danny looked up, a mixture of embarrassment and anger on his face. "But Trevor won the race."

"Yes, but I thought he was going to tell you about some changes you could make to improve your stride."

Jonathon looked at Trevor, who ducked his head, uncomfortable at having attention turned to him. Danny responded quietly, "He did tell me that, but to be honest, I thought he was just trying to make me feel better even though I lost the race."

"Oh, I see. You thought he was being condescending to you."

"Condescending?"

"Talking down to you. It probably made you angry, rather than feel better."

Danny looked up, surprised. "Yes, I guess it did make me a little angry."

Now Trevor was trying to disappear under the table, as everyone glanced back and forth between him and Danny. This was not the conversation he would have had his father bring up in front of the other boys.

Jonathon, however, was oblivious to his distress. "Well, I think you judged Trevor incorrectly. One of the things I admire most about Trevor is that it's not in his nature to be jealous or selfish. He had the good fortune of having some instruction by an excellent track coach who made some dramatic improvements in his performance, and I know from a conversation we had that he'd be happy to share those with you. Wouldn't you, Trevor?"

It was at this point that Trevor wished his father had never organized this lunch. He'd had a feeling something like this was going to happen, and now four sets of eyes were on him. "Yes, sir, but not if Danny doesn't want it."

The time had come for Danny to make a decision. He'd been hard on Trevor because he was jealous. Now he found that he had wonderful, kindhearted parents and that he was probably just trying to fit into a new place. Swallowing hard and facing Brother Richards—but really talking to Trevor—he said, "I was feeling pretty bad when Trevor offered, but I really would like to learn how to run better. I'd be glad to take some lessons." At that, Trevor looked up to see Danny smile a bit. Then Danny reached out his hand across the table. "I'm sorry for how I treated you. Can you forgive me?"

"Sure," Trevor said, brightening. "Maybe we could get together tomorrow after morning chores."

"It's settled then," Jonathon said. "Now, I believe I ought to get you all home before your parents worry. Who would like a ride in my Stearns?" Three sets of hands went up enthusiastically. Danny's was missing. This time Jonathon didn't push it. "Very good, then. Those who want a ride, let's adjourn to the garage. Danny, we'll see you tonight at sacrament meeting."

"Yes, sir. Thank you very much for the meal, Brother and Sister Richards. It was the best breakfast I've ever had."

As they stood up to leave, Margaret pulled Danny aside privately.

"Daniel, I don't know what your plans for the future are, but you should know that your musical ability is far beyond your years. I trained for the opera myself, and with training, I believe your voice is strong enough that you could sing professionally. Have you ever thought about taking voice lessons?"

Danny's eyes grew wide. He'd actually sung in the local theatre on the east side of the tracks, sometimes getting a leading part in the stage plays that the local acting company put on several times a year. More than once, people had suggested that he ought to sing professionally or perhaps try out for the Tabernacle Choir someday, but he'd never thought it a possibility.

"I don't think my parents could afford lessons. Plus, my father doesn't really like me singing in public. He says that it makes people vain."

Margaret bit her tongue. "I'm not sure he understands what a unique talent you have. As to affording it, one of my biggest fears in coming to Pocatello is that I wouldn't have anything meaningful to do with my time. I would love to teach you without charge just because I love music and I think I could help you." She watched as Danny dropped his head, obviously struggling with conflicting emotions. "You don't have to decide now, of course. But if you're interested, I'd be glad to speak with your parents. Plus, you can play our piano whenever you like. It would be nice to hear a young person's touch on the keyboard."

"Thank you, ma'am," Danny said quietly. "I don't know if I can, but it means a lot to have someone like you talk about my singing. Thank you." With that he quickly excused himself and slipped out the front door.

When Danny got home, he was surprised to find his father there. As soon as he walked in, he saw Kelly move into a corner, and he caught his mother's warning glance from the kitchen. He knew there was trouble when his father put down his magazine and looked up directly at him.

"So how was your teachers quorum meeting?"

"It was very good, sir."

"Have a nice lunch?"

"Yes, sir. We had pancakes with all kinds of toppings. It was really good." Danny had a sick feeling in his stomach.

"And how are Brother and Sister Sebastian? Are they doing well?"

Now Danny knew he was in trouble. He could lie, because he'd seen Brother Sebastian earlier that morning and knew that he was well. But, of course, he was no longer the advisor, and Danny had not been to his house.

"Actually, sir, I didn't go to the Sebastians'."

"No, you didn't go to the Sebastians'. Instead you went to Jonathon Richards's house. You went right up and into the house of the general manager of the railroad." He reached down and started taking his belt out of his trousers. "For some reason, you decided to lie to me so you could go over to a place where no O'Brian belongs. And you'd have gotten away with it if Kelly hadn't seen you coming out of his house not ten minutes ago."

"Begging your pardon, sir," Danny said desperately, "but I didn't lie to you." Out of the corner of his eye, he saw Kelly smiling. "Brother Richards was called as our teachers quorum advisor today, and he's the one who asked us to have a meeting at his house. So I really did go to my advisor's house." He looked at his mother miserably, but she just stepped farther back inside the kitchen.

"What did you just say?" Frank O'Brian had a perplexed look on his face. "Did I hear you tell me that Jonathon Richards is a Mormon?"

"Yes, sir. He's from Salt Lake."

"I know that he's from Salt Lake. But that doesn't mean he's a Mormon. What on earth is the company thinking?" Frank shook his head slowly from side to side. "A Mormon as a general manager. If that don't beat all." You could almost see the wheels turning in Frank's mind as he tried to digest what this would mean for his negotiations with Richards. At the very least, it meant that Richards would have to act civilized so as to keep up appearances of being a devout Mormon.

"So you didn't lie, but you still deceived me. You knew full well that I thought you were going to the Sebastians. Why didn't you tell me about Jonathon Richards earlier?"

Danny dropped his head. There was no sense trying to conceal the truth. "I was afraid you wouldn't let me go, sir, if you knew it was Brother Richards."

"Brother Richards. That just sticks in the throat, doesn't it? The only true brotherhood is among the workers of the world, yet you'd never call any of the men I work with 'brother.' But you'll call this management lackey your brother because he puts it to the workers six days a week, then shows up in church on Sunday acting all Christian and nice. Well, I can't spank you for telling a lie, but I can forbid you to go back to that man's house again. As long as you're an O'Brian, you don't belong there."

Danny started to say something but caught himself. In spite of his best efforts, tears welled up in his eyes. Seeing tears infuriated his father, who exclaimed, "Why are you crying? Fifteen years old and crying! You don't actually want to go there, do you?"

"It's just that I'm the teachers quorum president, and that's where they hold our meetings. I don't know how I can be the

president if I can't go to the Richardses' house." He unconsciously shuffled his feet while trying desperately to stop the
tears. He could hear Kelly laughing quietly back in the corner.
"I just want to be with my friends when they're there."

Frank started to say something but was startled to see his
wife step over to Danny. That was unusual. "Frank, he's only
a boy. I doubt that Mr. Richards spends his time talking
about railroad business when the boys are there. Plus, with
only five boys that age in the ward, it will be very embarrassing if he can't associate with his advisor and his son."
Frank stepped forward and was visibly irritated when both
Julia and Danny withdrew in fear.

Finally, he said quietly, "Dan, when I married your
mother, I promised her father that she could be active in the
Mormon Church and that she could raise any children we
had in the Church. I'm a man of my word. So if you think
you need to go to the Richardses' house to be active in the
Church, then so be it. You can even be friends with his brat
kid, if you want, even though he somehow tricked both you
and Kelly in the races you ran the other day. But I don't ever
want you to deceive me again. The only thing that's saving
you now is that you didn't lie about going to the Sebastians'.
If you have news that you think is going to make me mad,
you had better deliver it anyway, because I'll only be ten
times as mad if I find out about it later. Do you understand?"

Danny looked up. "Yes, sir, I do." Then the tears started
again. "I'm sorry, sir. I didn't mean to deceive you. I just
didn't know what to do."

Frank went over and put his hands on Danny's shoulders. "We're okay on this now. You don't have to talk about
it again. Now go wash your face and get out of your good
clothes. If I have problems with Jonathon Richards, they'll
be my problems, not yours." With that, Frank picked up his
gun and said, "I think I'll go out shooting after all. You want
to come, Kelly?"

"Yes, sir, I guess I do. Better than going to church."

Frank turned to his wife, who smiled at him. He decided it was all right that she'd stood up for Danny.

After they'd left, Danny turned to his mother. "Thanks for helping me out. The Richardses are really nice people, and we had a great time."

"I saw them in church today, and they do look like good people." She smiled. "Sister Richards seems very elegant and refined."

"She is, Mom. They have a baby grand piano that she let me play. And I even sang for her and the others. Afterward, she said that she'd been trained to sing opera, and she'd like to teach me how to sing. Do you think that would be okay?"

His mother gulped at that. "Your father said it was okay for you to be friends with the Richards boy, so I guess it's all right that you go to their house. One thing you can say for your father is that when he gives his word on something, he sticks by it, no matter what."

"But should I tell him about the lessons? I don't want him to think I'm deceiving him again."

Danny's mother stroked his hair and pulled his head to her. "Why don't you let me take care of that? I'll talk with him later tonight. If there's a problem, I'll let you know. Otherwise, just plan on it."

For the first time that day, Danny actually relaxed and smiled. It had turned into one of the best days of his life.

Chapter Three

BROTHERS

August 1911 was an unusually interesting month in
Pocatello. A popular railroad conductor named William
"Billy" Kidd was shot and killed during the arrest of two
robbers on board his train. Sheriff Sam Milton of Spencer,
Idaho, caught up with the two men on the train and was in
the act of arresting them on suspicion of robbing a saloon at
Monida. While he was attempting to handcuff the prisoners,
one of them, Hugh Whitney, lunged for his guns, which had
been placed on a nearby seat. When Kidd attempted to help
the sheriff, Whitney managed to shoot both of them. The
prisoners then pulled the bell cord to stop the train while
holding the other passengers at bay with the guns and jumped
from the train and ran into the nearby rocks, never to be seen
again. The injured deputy and conductor were brought to
Pocatello, where they were cared for by one of the Richardses'
neighbors, Dr. W. A. Wright. The deputy eventually recovered, but Conductor Kidd died of his wounds the next day.

One of the most exciting political actions in August was
the letting out of bids on a contract to build a city sewer
system. Most people in town used outhouses. A few of the
wealthy, like the Richardses, had their own cesspools and
indoor plumbing. Unfortunately, a lot of waste found its
way as raw sewage into the Portneuf River. The prospect of a
sewer system meant that the city was finally growing up.

Of course, both these events paled in comparison to the arrival on August 31 of the Ringling Brothers Circus—at least in the eyes of the First Ward teachers quorum members. Pocatello was the only stop scheduled for the circus in the state of Idaho, so excursion trains were placed into service to bring people from as far north as Ashton. The circus arrived on an eighty-four-car train, and a magnificent parade with exotic animals, strange performers in outlandish costumes, and vendors of every kind wound its way up Center Street. The circus itself was held in the open field on 12th Avenue, between Lander and Clark, and was a ringing success. The members of the teachers quorum all got to go with their families and were thrilled by the circus acts, which included trapeze artists, a lion tamer, and a troop of skilled horseback riders who rode around the ring while standing on the horses' backs performing amazing feats, such as juggling balls and doing flips. Everybody talked about it nonstop afterward, with the boys arguing about which act they liked best. In the end, Elmer settled the discussion when he said that as far as he was concerned the clowns were the best, which everybody agreed was true.

As for the teachers quorum, they took up semipermanent residence at the Richards house. Elmer came two or three times per week for help in memorizing his scriptures; Danny showed up as promised to learn how to improve his stride in running, then returned regularly for voice lessons and to play the Steinway. Leonard and Trevor explored every valve and bearing on Margaret Richards's Buick. They would have done the same on the Stearns except for the intervention of Jonathon Richards, who made it perfectly clear that only a certified mechanic was to touch that car. By the time the first Sunday in September rolled around, the boys were perfectly at ease entering the house.

At first glance, it appeared that Leonard and Trevor had the most in common, but in spite of their troubled beginning, it was actually Danny and Trevor who started spending the most time with each other. After practicing the stride best suited to Danny's sprints, he and Trevor started running two to three miles each day to practice technique. They were in good enough condition that they could talk while running. Trevor asked Danny dozens of questions about Pocatello and the various kids and teachers he'd meet when school started, while Danny was interested in what it was like to grow up in Salt Lake City, where Trevor had been so close to a true university and all the cultural events that a big city could support. While Danny had originally thought that Trevor would be conceited, just the opposite was true. Probably the thing that impressed Danny the most was Trevor's untroubled acceptance of the gospel and other people. He didn't even seem to hold a grudge against Kelly and Victor, in spite of the way they'd treated him.

While they walked to the Wirtz Candy Palace for a soda phosphate one afternoon, Danny remembered a question he'd wanted to ask Trevor. "I know how you beat me in the race on the twelfth, but how did you beat Kelly? He's clearly stronger and better suited for a distance run, and maybe the one good thing I can say about him is that he gives sports everything he has."

Trevor smiled. "Kelly could have won that race hands down. When I saw how fast he was pulling ahead of the rest of us, I figured it was over. But I must have unintentionally made some kind of noise, because I saw him turn and look straight at me. I could see it made him angry that I was that close, so he turned around and really started pounding. As I was bringing my left foot forward, I pitched some gravel with the toe, and it hit the back of his leg. That irritated him even more, and he turned to glare at me again. Every time he turned, he lost ground. So all I had to do was keep making him more angry. The closer I got, the easier it was, since I could start taunting him a little more." He laughed at the memory. "I thought for sure he was going to kill me when we got done, and I guess he tried until you and Leonard came along."

"You figured all that out while running a mile race?"

"What else do you have to think about while running that far?"

Danny laughed. "I'm glad you decided to be my friend, because I'd hate to have you as an enemy."

Trevor turned serious. "I don't ever want to have an enemy. Sometimes I worry that I'm too competitive. I really didn't have anything to prove by beating either of you. In fact, I knew it would probably make you and your friends angry, which isn't a good way to get started in a new town. But when I get into competition, I kind of go cold and try to find the weakness in what my competitors are doing. For you it was an inefficient stride. For Kelly it was his temper. I really wish I didn't do that."

They walked in silence for a while. "My father has a bad temper, and sometimes it scares me." That was the first time Danny had ever mentioned his father. Trevor didn't want to interrupt him, so he kept his peace. "I don't think it's because he's mean. It's just that he feels so strongly about things that he gets frustrated when people don't instantly see his point of view, and then he loses his temper."

"Has he ever hurt you when he's angry?"

Danny turned with something of a glare, as if the question alarmed him. "I shouldn't have said anything. Promise that you won't tell anybody what I said?"

Trevor felt a lump in his throat because he sensed the isolation that Danny felt, and he wanted to help him somehow. But now wasn't the time. He wished he hadn't asked that question. "I promise. It's your business."

The rest of the walk to the emporium was made in silence, with Danny retreating into his thoughts.

Arriving at Wirtz, Trevor said, with perhaps too much enthusiasm, "I think it's my turn to buy. You beat me pretty bad in our race this morning." Before Danny could interrupt, he added, "Besides, I did some work down at my father's office in the depot, and he just paid me."

Danny accepted the logic of that, and the two worked their way past the dazzling glass display case that was filled with hard candy of every color, including horehounds and fruit flavors. Sitting at the counter, they ordered strawberry phosphates. "Kind of amazing that they can have ice in the hottest month of the year, isn't it?"

Trevor sipped on the cool drink and replied, "My father says that it's the railroad that really makes ice practical, since large chunks are cut from the lakes near Park Lane in the winter and stored in the icehouse in sawdust through the summer. He says the ice here in Idaho is the best he's ever seen for purity. It's pretty amazing that even in the hottest weather, they never lose more than ten percent from melting." He finished the drink with one long slurping sound. "In Salt Lake we used to like to go down to the icehouse to watch them slide the big chunks along the trestle between the tracks so they could ice up the refrigerated cars of fruit and vegetables."

"We can do that here. The icehouse is out west of town on the main line. Want to go there tomorrow?"

"Sure." Trevor paid the bill, and they walked out past the warm cinnamon rolls that had just been put on a tray on top of the candy counters.

Danny was quiet on the way back down Garfield. Finally he broke the silence. "I'm sorry I clammed up when you asked me about my father. It's just something I've never talked about to anybody."

"I shouldn't have asked. It's none of my business."

"No, I want to talk about it. It's hard to keep inside." He turned his head and looked at Trevor earnestly, as if trying to figure out how much he could say. "My father isn't mean. He used to spank me quite a bit, but a lot of fathers do that.

Sometimes he'll cuff me when he thinks I'm out of line, but it really doesn't hurt much." Trevor tried to keep a steady gaze, even though he wanted to respond that not every father does that. "It's what he says that really hurts. I know guys are supposed to be tough, but he never says anything nice about me. You know how your father is always saying stuff like, 'One of the things I like about Trevor,' or 'Trevor probably knows a lot more about that than I do'?" Trevor nodded. "Well, my father never says anything like that. It's always, 'Why do you want to sing? It makes you look weak,' or 'Why do you want to go to college instead of getting an honest job?' and things like that. It's like nothing I ever do can please him."

They walked on in silence for a while. "The only time he ever says anything good about me is when I go shooting or hunting."

"You're good with a gun?"

Danny cast a quick glance to the side. "You know how good you are at driving your mother's car?"

"What do you mean?" Trevor asked with alarm.

"Do you honestly think everybody in the city doesn't know you go driving your mother's car at dusk? We've all seen you, even though you think you're sneaking off to Harrison Boulevard where no one is watching."

Trevor swallowed hard. "Okay, so I drive the car once in a while."

Danny turned and faced him squarely. "You don't just drive a car—you drive it almost as well as an adult. Leonard doesn't think I know anything about automobiles, but I know what sounds right. There's a certain time to shift in order to keep the engine operating at optimum performance, and you never miss. And I've seen you practicing turns and skids, and you've got awfully fast reflexes. I think driving must be the most natural thing in the world for you."

Trevor's face flushed at the compliment. "So maybe I'm a decent driver. What about it?"

"Well, that's how I am with a rifle. I don't know why, but I can draw a bead and hit what I'm aiming at nearly every time. When we go target shooting, I almost always hit within the bull's-eye. My father loves to brag to the other men about how good I am."

"That sounds pretty good."

"Except that he never says it *to* me—only *about* me. Plus, it irritates him that I don't like to go hunting." Danny started walking again, and Trevor matched his pace.

"Why don't you?"

"Because I hate to kill things. I know that we need to eat, so it's not that I think it's wrong. I just don't like doing it." He was quiet for some time, then said, "Maybe that's why I work so hard to be accurate. If I do have to shoot an animal, I make absolutely sure that I can kill it on the first shot so it doesn't have to suffer." He half-smiled and added, "In fact, it was on a hunting trip last year that I stood up to my father for the one and only time in my life. I was so angry I was trembling."

Trevor grinned. "Tell me about it."

"I have a rule that if someone in the hunting party shoots an animal and wounds it, they have about twenty seconds to reload and put it out of its misery. If not, I do it for them. One time, one of the guys got really mad at me for 'stealing' his shot. My father started in on me, saying I should butt out of his friend's business. I yelled back that if he ever wanted me to come hunting with him again, he darn well better know that I wasn't going to stand around and watch an innocent animal suffer, so he had to decide right then and there what it was going to be—me or the idiots who don't know what they're doing." Danny shook his head. "And all the time, this guy was standing right there."

"So what did your father do?"

"I thought he was going to kill me on the spot. But I was so furious, I didn't even care. He didn't talk for a couple of moments, and then he surprised me. He just said, in this really calm, steady voice, 'If you feel that strongly about it, then you should follow your conscience.' Then he turned to all his friends and said, 'Dan plans to shoot anything that you just wound if you don't take care of it yourself. So that's the way it is, and if anybody has a problem with it, you'll answer to me.'"

"Wow."

Danny stopped and turned to Trevor. "That's the problem. Most of the time he's sullen and cold to me, but every once in a while, he does something amazing like that, and it makes me think he cares about me. Then he'll turn around and do something that hurts my feelings again. It's pretty hard to deal with." He shrugged.

"Maybe your father really is proud of you but doesn't know how to show it. Whatever the reason, I'm sorry he's so hard on you."

Danny looked at Trevor earnestly. "Trevor, you've got to promise me you won't say anything to anybody about this. If my father ever thought I was talking about him like this, it would probably kill him—right after he killed me."

Trevor stood for a moment without answering, which increased Danny's anxiety.

"I've never told anybody this, but I actually had a twin brother," Trevor said quietly. Danny dropped his jaw. "He was born right after me, but there were some real problems, and they had to hurt my mother to try to save his life. He was born and lived for a few minutes, but then he died. It made it so my mother couldn't have any other kids, which is why I'm their only one."

"I'm sorry. I didn't know."

"Of course not. I don't want to have to go around telling people about it. But the point is that even though I haven't ever really known him, it's like I miss him. I've always wanted a brother in the worst way. I know that Kelly's mean to you, but I don't think all brothers are like that. Look how Leonard treats his kid brothers and sisters." Danny nodded. "The point is that something tells me you're about as close to a brother as I'll ever get. I mean, look at how well you get along with my mother. You love all the things she does, and I've never seen her as happy as since she's been teaching you voice and piano. And my father thinks you're one of the smartest kids he's ever known. He asks about you all the time."

Danny's face flushed. "He does?"

"All the time. And even though I haven't lived here very long, talking to you is so easy. It's almost like we knew each other in the premortal existence or something, and we're just picking up where we left off. So I don't know how you feel about it, but from my point of view, you're my brother— and unlike Kelly, I would never do anything to betray a brother. You don't ever need to ask me again not to tell something that you've shared with me."

Danny was stunned. His mind had trouble accepting what he'd just heard. Who would think that a kid like Trevor was lonesome for anything? Yet he was missing something in his life and thought that Danny was the one to fill the place. With that, he felt tears start to well up. Before he let them, he did something instinctive, yet socially unnatural for a boy that age. He reached out and hugged Trevor, hugged him really tight, as he whispered, "Brothers." Then he released him just as quickly and started away at a fast trot, a little embarrassed by what had transpired.

He heard Trevor yell, "Forever."

Danny smiled. *Forever!*

Chapter Four

MEETING PRESIDENT TAFT

High school started the first of September and was in session until the harvest was ready in October. At that point, everyone was excused for a two-week working vacation so the youth could help bring in the crops. Some went north to Blackfoot, which was rapidly becoming the potato capital of the world due to the unique characteristics of the volcanic soil prevalent in the area. Teams of horses would plow up rows of huge russet potatoes, while the students followed behind with wire baskets to pick up the potatoes. The baskets were then emptied into burlap sacks that were thrown onto large wagons to be taken to the potato cellars. Stored this way, potatoes stayed fresh for more than a year, ready to be shipped all across the country.

Just recently some farmers had started using huge steam tractors with wide metal wheels to do the digging. Although Trevor probably didn't need the money, he joined Sam, Danny, and Leonard on a crew. With his love of machinery, he watched the huge tractors with fascination, the roar of the fire and the smell of the burning wood filling the outside air as the tractors passed by.

Usually this time of year was discouraging to people, since they had to move inside earlier. Although most houses had electric lighting by now, it was usually a single bulb hanging from a wire in the center of the room. It was far brighter than the kerosene lamps most people had grown up with, but it was still hard on the eyes. The Richardses' house had been pre-wired for electricity, so the wires were hidden in the walls and there were multiple lights in every room. In the parlor they used a number of table lamps to cast a more even glow around the room. The most spectacular display was in the entryway and dining room, where crystal chandeliers had perhaps a half dozen lights each to shine through the brilliant crystal prisms.

Only a few houses had telephones, and they were all on party lines. One of the best forms of entertainment was to listen in on the conversations of one's neighbor. If someone tied up the line too long, the constant clicks of other subscribers picking up the receivers and putting them down usually became so annoying that the offending party would end the conversation.

After all the interesting things that had happened so far in 1911, it turned out that the biggest news of the year was that President William Howard Taft was going to visit the Gate City on October 4. That would make it nine years since the last presidential visit, when the wildly popular Theodore Roosevelt had ridden down Center Street in an elegant carriage imported from Salt Lake City.

While "Teddy" had been enormously popular in the western states, the same couldn't be said of Taft. With the election of 1912 looming, he evoked very different emotions from his predecessor, and everyone knew that he was in political trouble. Taft had presided over a series of social problems that left him looking weak and vacillating and that made him extremely vulnerable to the Democrats' popular new leader, Woodrow Wilson, governor of New Jersey. Taft's chances of reelection seemed slim.

Still, a presidential visit was a rarity for a small town like Pocatello, so the community rallied to make it as memorable an event as possible. The Center Street viaduct was nearing completion, and it was decided to make its dedication coincide with Taft's visit so that the first automobile across would carry the president of the United States. That would look good in the history books. Some people joked that it would also be the ultimate test of the strength of the viaduct, since President Taft was noted for his large girth and more than 300-pound heft.

As a community leader, Jonathon Richards was invited to be part of the welcoming committee that would accompany the president from his private railcar to the Bannock Hotel, where he'd give a speech and receive a key to the city. Taft would actually ride with a former governor of Idaho, while the mayor, Jonathon, and other dignitaries followed behind in their own automobiles. Jonathon invited his wife and Trevor to join him. When his assistant backed out of riding with them a few days before the event, he extended an invitation to Danny to join them in the car ride and at the ceremony at the hotel.

Danny approached his father cautiously that evening to ask him about it. "Excuse me, sir. Could I ask you a question?"

Frank looked up from the newspaper without a word.

"When President Taft comes to town next week, the Richardses are going to be in the parade and at the ceremony. They've asked if I'd like to ride along and have a chance to meet the president. I wondered how you'd feel about that."

Frank's face reddened, and he started to slowly clench and unclench his fists. His voice trembled as he said, "I can't believe I'm hearing this. Did you just ask me if you could ride in a parade with a manager of the Oregon Short Line to an event that will honor William Howard Taft? The same William Howard Taft who is in bed with every corporate interest in America? The same William Howard Taft who helped negotiate settlements of strikes as long as the employees agreed to bust the union? Is that the William Howard Taft that you're talking about?"

Danny gulped. He knew he had to respond, even though whatever he said would just get him into more trouble.

"I hadn't thought of it that way, sir. I just thought it would be an honor to meet the president of the United States. But I can see that it wouldn't look good for me to be with the Richardses."

"I can just see it now. I'm going to be there with Kelly and the men from the Brotherhood holding up signs for Eugene V. Debs, the only real friend the unions have in this country and the best presidential candidate ever put before the voters. Meanwhile, up there on the platform will stand my son, proudly shaking hands with that walrus of a president while Jonathon Richards beams proudly behind you. Everything I've worked for up in smoke so that you can have the 'honor' of meeting the president."

"I'll tell them no—" Danny was interrupted before he could continue.

"I knew that you've been spending too much time with that Richards kid and his father . . ."

Danny's stomach lurched at the thought of where the conversation was going. He desperately wanted to avoid being forbidden to go to the Richards house. Frank attempted to start a new sentence, but Danny intervened.

"Sir, I'd be proud to stand with you and Kelly at the demonstration in support of Mr. Debs. Who knows, maybe they'll take our picture showing the whole family in support of the Socialist party candidate. You know how the paper loves to show something like that."

That caught Frank's attention. He'd been holding a strategy session just the day before, trying to think how the union could turn the president's visit to their advantage. Maybe this was a way to get some coverage. It would certainly look good to the other union members. Plus, it would steal Jonathon Richards's thunder. Richards was always parading his wife and son around to show what a great family man he was. This would show that he wasn't the only one who had a family.

"You would really stand with me and Kelly?"

"Yes, sir. I'd really like to. I just didn't know how important this is to you. The truth is I don't know much about either President Taft or Mr. Debs. But I'd like to know more. Maybe you could teach me."

Frank O'Brian actually smiled—something not often seen. "You would, would you? All right, we'll go together. And I'll teach you what you need to know before we get there. We'll talk about it after supper." Aware that he'd given Danny a pass on the discussion about the Richardses, he picked up the paper without another word.

Danny turned and walked quietly to his room. His father had actually been nice to him. And he'd avoided the potential disaster of being cut off from the Richardses. That was a close call. He could see it was time for a crash course in politics.

When the day of President Taft's visit finally arrived, a crowd of thousands turned out to greet the president as he entered the lobby of the Bannock Hotel. The grand dining room had been decorated with dozens of red, white, and blue flags and bunting, provided by the new owner of the hotel, Mr. Kasiska. It was here that the president formally met the local politicians and leading citizens, including Jonathon Richards. The president was a genial man whose pleasant demeanor made him quite approachable. As he shook Jonathon's hand, he said, "I know you don't particularly like what we've done to the railroad trusts, Mr. Richards, but it's simply not in the best interests of the country to have a handful of citizens own our main infrastructure."

Jonathon smiled. "Actually, Mr. President, we're just an affiliated company of the Union Pacific Railroad, and the trust wasn't likely to do much for us anyway."

The president looked around and asked quietly, "By the way, before I speak to the main crowd up at the high school, can you tell me why they call this the Gate City?"

"Certainly, sir. It's because of our location. Our route from Lander, Wyoming, through southern Idaho provides the most natural route to the Northwest. It avoids the mountains of Utah and offers the easiest grade for trains going northwest to Portland and Seattle or due north to Yellowstone and Montana. All the switching is done here in Pocatello using the hump yard at the southern end of our property. We put more than seventy trains through each day, and that's going to increase. We're the Gate City to the Northwest."

"Ah, I see. That's very helpful." Then, in his normal voice, "Now tell me who these two people are."

"Yes, Mr. President. This is my wife, Margaret, who is one of your most ardent supporters. She wishes she were in a position to vote for you directly but will instead bring enormous pressure to bear on me to vote that way."

The president smiled. "Her wisdom provides excellent support for the suffragist cause, doesn't it?" He took Margaret's hand and gave it a light kiss.

"And this is my son, Trevor. I'm afraid he's far more interested in automobiles and airplanes than he is politics."

"I'd like to take an airplane flight myself," the president said coyly, "but I don't think they have one that could lift me!" He let out a great rolling laugh as he looked down at his portly stomach. Trevor didn't know whether he should laugh or not, so he just sort of smiled and accepted the president's handshake. "I hope you get the opportunity to become a pilot," the president said. "These are great times with great opportunities."

"Thank you, sir," Trevor said weakly. Then the president moved on to the other guests.

Breakfast was served after introductions. Fortunately, the hotel had been alerted in advance to the particular needs of seating the president. Specifically, all chairs with arms had been removed so the president could settle *onto* a chair rather than *into* a chair. It seems that one of the more embarrassing moments of his presidency had occurred when he settled comfortably into a bathtub, only to get stuck. White House staff had had to resort to smashing the porcelain tub so they could extract the president. On this occasion, the usual chair reserved for the head of the table had been replaced by a well-reinforced chair to make certain that it could hold President Taft without difficulty. All went well, and everyone enjoyed an abundant breakfast.

After meeting with the local politicians and leading citizens, the president's party made its way north to the grounds of the high school, where he gave a thirty-minute speech to an enthusiastic crowd assembled there. He'd invited the Richardses to join him on the reviewing stand, and they were with him in the pictures that the Salt Lake newspaper photographers took. The local paper, the *Pocatello Tribune*, was represented as well. When the paper came out the next morning, there was a prominent picture on the front page showing President Taft, the mayor, the Richardses, and, in the foreground below the reviewing stands, Frank O'Brian and his two boys holding up signs for Eugene V. Debs, "the Working Man's Candidate of the Socialist Party." Both families considered it a wonderful day.

* * *

As Christmas approached, the boys in the teachers quorum started working on their memorization in earnest. The Salt Lake trip was barely more than three months away,

and it had become their all-consuming passion to earn a trip
to Salt Lake City. Most were progressing nicely, except for
Elmer, who continued to struggle. Margaret adopted him for
the duration of the project and spent many hours reading
with him and helping him understand the context of the
scriptures so they were more than just words. Then she
drilled him until they stuck. Even at that, she worried that it
would be a close call.

While Christmas was considered an important holiday,
most homes in Pocatello limited their seasonal decorating to a
single Christmas tree and perhaps the hanging of stockings by
the fireplace. Not Margaret Richards. With the wonderful
plateglass conservatory to display her decorating talents, she
loaded up a magnificent Christmas tree with ornaments,
tinsel, and the new innovation of colored electric lights. As
cars or carriages made their way northwest on Garfield, her
tree shimmered in the crystalline night air. But that was just
the beginning. She had huge wreaths with large, red bows
hung above the garage and the covered portico. Inside,
garland looped from each corner of the entryway to the chandelier in the center. A magnificent Christmas flower arrangement filled the center table, with red holly berries, pine
boughs, and pine cones surrounding a live poinsettia. Fanciful
glass ornaments filled an imported crystal bowl on the dining
room table, and nuts and candy were placed strategically
throughout the first floor to tempt visitors at every turn.

In his role as general manager, Jonathon was expected to
host a number of holiday parties for community leaders,
officials of the railroad, and major shippers in the area, as
well as one for his staff and leadership. He and Margaret
hired a second cook to assist in the preparation of food and
were starting to interview prospects for a wait staff when
Margaret had an idea.

"Jonathon, when you take the boys to Salt Lake City, have
you thought about what they'll do for spending money?"

Jonathon looked up from the paper a bit perplexed. "No, I haven't thought about it. I suppose they'll spend some of their summer savings or get help from their parents."

"You're not with them as much as I am. Every one of those boys relies on his summer earnings to buy school supplies and clothing. Some even turn money over to their parents to help with food and other necessities. They certainly won't have anything left for your trip."

Jonathon smiled. "What's your proposal, Margaret?"

"I was thinking that we could hire the boys as our wait staff for our holiday parties. I'd have to train them, of course, but they're sensible enough to figure it out. Plus, it would force Trevor to do something to help out around here."

"You're going to trust five fifteen-year-old boys with your best china?"

She frowned. "I know it's a risk, but I think they can do it. Plus, I think it would be good for them to learn how to behave in a formal setting."

"I'll talk to them about it tomorrow at church. I think it's a great idea."

Then Margaret started talking, ostensibly to Jonathon, but mostly to herself. "Of course, we'll have to buy them all suits so they look good. We'll count that as part of their compensation. After that, they can use the suits when they go to Salt Lake."

So that's what this is all about. Jonathon smiled to himself. "We don't have a lot of time, so you'll need to get them fitted as soon as possible. You can use my account at Fargo's department store."

"Good," she said. "I'm glad we had this talk. You should pay more attention to such things."

* * *

There was only one serving bowl broken during the five events at which the boys served. Unfortunately, it was Elmer who dropped it on the tile floor in the kitchen, shattering it beyond repair. He was beside himself with grief. Margaret tried to console him by assuring him it was an unmatched piece that really didn't matter. Trevor was about to object when she shushed him. She knew that Elmer would never recover if he knew it was a bowl she'd inherited from her grandmother. Aside from that one incident, the boys did a superb job of serving, with plates served from the left, retrieved from the right. They were also a great hit with the guests, who commented on how sharp they all looked in their suits. One of the most significant moments was when Frank and Julia O'Brian arrived to the dinner Jonathon hosted for the various union representatives. Danny hadn't told his father about his "job," probably not suspecting that his parents were invited guests. Frank's face flushed when he saw his son serving in the house, but the obvious delight the other guests took in having the young men carrying out their duties so well quieted him down. Toward the end of the evening, the Christmas cheer must have rubbed off on him, because he quietly complimented Danny on how good he looked in his suit. It may have been the first time it registered with him that Danny was actually in charge of the group, and he was pleased at the way they responded to his leadership. For his part, Danny was immensely pleased to receive some encouragement from his father.

On Christmas Day, the boys were given strict instruction not to come over until well after their own Christmas dinner had been served so as not to interfere with their own family enjoyment of the day. The Richardses prepared their own meal for three so that their cook could be home with her family—a simple meal of roast turkey, mashed potatoes, and bottled string beans. Trevor was pleased with the clothing he received, as well as Mark Twain's *Tom Sawyer* and *Life on the*

Mississippi. Most fifteen year olds would have started with *Tom Sawyer*, but when Trevor saw the drawings of steamships, he was soon lost in the dream of becoming a riverboat pilot. He already knew what his big gift was, because it had to be delivered the day before, and he couldn't wait to show the other guys. Finally, the boys began to arrive.

"Merry Christmas," Sam said quietly.

"Thank you, Sam," Margaret said as she ushered him in the door. "Take your coat off and sit by the steam radiator. You look half frozen."

"Yes, ma'am. We gave the animals an extra feeding this afternoon before I came over, sort of to commemorate the animals who stood by Jesus while he was in the manger."

"What a nice sentiment. Your parents are certainly thoughtful people."

"Thank you, ma'am. By the way, my mother asked me to give you this." He pulled out a small plate of homemade divinity, which lived up to its celestial name. Margaret passed the dish around to the others and then spoke briefly with each of the other boys.

Leonard was the one who finally broke into the conversation. "Sister Richards, do you think it will ever be time to see what's in our packages?" He and the other boys had been anxious to see what they were getting since Leonard noticed the large gifts with their names a few days earlier.

She smiled and said, "I guess now is as good a time as any. Everybody get your package, and get ready to open them simultaneously, since you're all getting the same thing." The boys rushed the tree and then some sat down on the floor while others returned to their chairs. "On the count of three," she said, and then started the countdown. At zero, there was the sound of wrapping string being snapped, followed by shredding paper, then the disappointment of discovering that the boxes were filled with old newspapers.

The boys ripped the newspaper until finally a second, much smaller, package emerged.

"Not fair," Elmer shouted.

Jonathon laughed. "Okay, a new countdown." At zero, they tore open the smaller packages. Danny got his open first, and Margaret was pleased to hear him say an almost reverent "Oh, my." She watched as he gently turned the leather-bound copy of the Book of Mormon carefully in his hands while gently opening the gilt-edged pages.

Elmer said with a tone of fascination, "They've got our names on the front, in gold letters. I've never seen a book with someone's name on it."

"That's called engraving," Jonathon said pleasantly. "The book is yours forever. The cover is made out of leather, so try to keep the book dry. We hope that you'll all put it to very good use."

The boys thanked the Richardses profusely, particularly when Margaret asked Trevor to give them each a brand-new red pencil to mark special passages with.

"Okay," Trevor said. "I've got something else to show you. Come with me to the garage!" The boys set their books down carefully and raced with Trevor out the back door and into the rear entrance to the garage. There, next to the Stearns and the Buick, was a brand-new Indian motorcycle.

"Is that yours?" Elmer asked breathlessly.

Trevor smiled and nodded.

"That's a real beauty," Sam said. "One of my cousins has an Indian, and he says it has the best handling of any motorcycle on the road."

Leonard was simply beyond words. He crouched down on his haunches and rubbed his hands along the engine, feeling the smooth finish of the chrome.

"Mom and Father won't let me drive until the roads clear up. They say it's too dangerous in the snow. But once I learn how to ride, I'll be glad to take each of you for a ride." He cast a glance at Danny, who stood looking at it rather impassively. "What do you think, Danny?"

"I think it's great," he said. "I just hope you don't kill yourself on it. At least when you drive the Buick at breakneck speeds, you have four wheels under you." Everybody laughed.

"He doesn't always have four wheels," Elmer called out cheerfully. "I've seen him take some corners on two!" They really laughed at that.

"Be quiet, Elmer, my mom might be listening." He caught Leonard's eye and said, "Why don't you mount it and start the engine? It sounds amazing."

Leonard's eyes widened. "Really?"

"Of course. Behind every good rider is a better mechanic. I'll need a lot of help with this thing." Leonard didn't need any more encouragement. In a matter of moments, the dust was falling from the rafters as the powerful engine with a modest muffler filled the garage with noise. When the fumes started choking people, they returned to the house for hot cocoa and a mini-concert of Christmas hymns by Danny. The boys joined in the choruses, when appropriate. Then Margaret chased them away so they'd be home to spend the evening with their families.

Chapter Five

TEMPTATIONS AND TAUNTING

By March 1912, two things were clear. First, the boys were going to go to Salt Lake City, even if it killed Elmer. Second, Trevor Richards was born to ride. February and March were unusually dry, so Trevor took his motorcycle out most Saturdays. His reflexes were fast enough and steady enough that he quickly learned how to handle the bike and was constantly finding excuses to ride. He'd go to a large, open lot on North Harrison to practice his skills and soon learned to take even the tightest turns with very little skid. He quickly convinced himself that he was invincible and started driving accordingly—that is, until his father happened to drive by one day as he was tearing through a turn at breakneck speed. That's when some rules were imposed.

"I saw you driving your motorcycle earlier today," Jonathon said quietly. His voice betrayed none of the irritation he felt. Still, Trevor looked up in alarm.

"Where at?"

"Down by Harrison."

Trevor was instantly defensive. "I was just practicing. I don't ever drive that fast out on the streets."

"Good thing, because you'd be arrested if you did."

"Father, it's not dangerous. I know what I'm doing."

"You think you know what you're doing, but it's not as easy as all that. I know you believe you know everything about machines, but what you haven't learned is that they're unpredictable, and at the speeds you were traveling, even the slightest miscalculation could be deadly."

Trevor started to protest, but his father raised his hand.

"You're fifteen, and it's a privilege to drive, not a right. So you're going to have to follow a few simple rules. First, no passengers—at least, not until summer. Second, you have to stay on city streets and obey traffic rules. No trips out into the country until you have more experience and the weather is better. Third, no trips up City Creek Canyon or any of the other roads onto the benches on the west side of town." Jonathon held his gaze. "Those rules should be pretty easy to keep track of."

"But Father, City Creek?" The best riding trail for motorcycles was up City Creek Canyon on the dirt road that led up to the main water reservoir. The canyon road wound around in switchbacks that provided some wonderfully tight turns to test one's driving skills. The best turn of all was at the point where the road emerged out of the canyon in a sweeping turn around the rim of the foothills. Not only did it provide a spectacular view of the valley, but one had to drive extremely carefully or run the risk of falling down a hundred-foot bluff. It was one of Jonathon's favorite Sunday drives.

"You heard the rules. Your only alternative is to wait until summer when I can take you out practicing. So what's it to be?"

Trevor had no choice in the matter, which was evidenced by the huff he exhaled as he left the parlor. He understood that the rules were fair, but that had nothing to do with it. He hated the thought of having any restrictions on his riding.

Two Saturdays later, he took Danny for a ride around town. His father was working out of town in the morning, and this was the first rule to go. He knew the sheriff had been watching him, which encouraged him to watch his speed. Finally, he slipped across one of the bridges that took him to the west side of the Portneuf River, and before long he was on the street leading up City Creek. He stopped at the bottom.

"Why are we stopping?" Danny asked.

Trevor hesitated.

"Well?"

"My father said I can't go up City Creek. Says it's too dangerous this time of the year." Trevor rolled his eyes.

"Well, then, we better go back." Danny was pretty no-nonsense in these things. He knew better than to cross his own father, and he liked Brother Richards enough that he didn't want to get in trouble with him. He didn't know about the "no passengers" rule, or he'd have been furious with Trevor for breaking it.

"But if we went really slowly, we could at least see how it handles going up a hill. We don't have to go to the top, or anything."

"You know better than this, Trevor. I say we turn back right now."

"It's not fair. I've never had a crash or anything, and the bike is more than powerful enough to climb this hill. It wouldn't even get worked up."

Danny knew it would be pointless to argue. Once Trevor had his heart set on something, he never let go. He was a good kid, but pretty stubborn.

"If you're going, then let's get it over with. But you better be extra careful."

He was. He drove up the mountain road with little trouble, ascending out onto the bluff above the city, where they dismounted and sat down in the sagebrush, looking out over the city. After about ten minutes of talking and pointing out the different features of the rail yards, Danny said they ought to get back.

"Sure you don't want to go all the way to the reservoir?"

"I'm sure. You've pushed your luck already. Let's go."

They started along the winding road back down the canyon. Trevor was feeling a little more confident now, so he sped up. He also started taking the corners tighter to practice his control. As they reached the major turn where the road crossed the creek from the north side to the south side, then turned sharply back east down the canyon, Trevor sped up to get through the water without stalling. As he rounded the corner, he caught a movement out of the side of his eye and quickly swerved to miss a Model T Ford that was swinging wide in the opposite direction. To miss the automobile, Trevor had to gun it, and as he slid into the turn with the unexpected speed, he lost control and crashed into some trees. Danny was thrown from the bike, and Trevor's leg was crushed between a tree and the exhaust pipe, which burned his leg instantly. He cried out in pain as the driver of the truck came running through the trees. He was able to pull the bike away from Trevor, but not in time to avoid a serious burn. Plus, the front fork of the bike was twisted in an odd shape. When he got his wits about him, Trevor called to Danny, but heard nothing in reply. He lurched out into the trees, where he found Danny lying on his side, face away from the road.

"Dan, are you okay?" Trevor rolled him on his back, but Danny was motionless. "Oh, no," he cried, and called to Tom Runyan, the driver of the truck, "I need help!"

Just then, Danny opened his eyes and said, "I told you we shouldn't come up here."

Badly startled, Trevor nearly fell over backward. "Darn you, Dan. I'm already in enough trouble without you faking."

Danny sat up and rubbed his head, which was bleeding slightly. "I wasn't completely faking. I think I was knocked out for a couple of moments. Are you okay?"

They got up and checked themselves out. Trevor's leg looked like it had third-degree burns, with part of the skin black and jellylike. Danny was better off, and all he had to do was tear a piece of his shirt to hold against the head wound until the bleeding stopped. Tom gave them a ride back to the Richardses, where Trevor had to face his mom. After helping him bandage his wound, she told him to call his father, who was supposed to be back in town now.

"I'll talk to him when he gets home," Trevor said desperately. "No sense ruining his workday. He's got important stuff to do."

"Call him right now, Trevor."

"Yes, ma'am." Trevor slunk over to the phone and asked the operator for his father's private line. When his father didn't pick up by the third ring, he was about to hang up. Then he heard the receiver lift and his father say a crisp, "Jonathon Richards."

Trevor cleared his voice and told him who it was. Jonathon's tone relaxed on the other end and was pleasant— until he heard the reason for the call. Trevor's tone of voice changed quickly as Dan heard him say, "We're both okay. My leg got burned, and Danny got a little cut, but nothing bad." Then Trevor hung up. Dan looked at him expectantly. "He didn't yell or anything. He just said to wait here, because he'll be home in ten minutes."

It was actually thirty minutes, and Trevor and Dan sat in miserable silence. When Jonathon walked through the door, he went straight to the kitchen where the boys were sitting with Margaret.

"Are you okay, Danny?" he asked.

"Yes, sir." Jonathon felt his wound and decided it was all right.

"Let me look at your leg," Jonathon said to Trevor. He obediently lifted his leg so his father could unwrap the dressing enough to see the wound.

"You're lucky it didn't break your leg. As it is, we'll have to take you to the doctor to make sure infection doesn't set in."

"It doesn't hurt—much," Trevor said hopefully. He winced, though, when Jonathon touched the burned area.

"Danny, why don't you go into the music room? If you're feeling up to it, this might be a good time for you to practice." Danny's eyes grew wide. He'd never seen Jonathon Richards angry before. He got up promptly and left the room. Margaret brushed his shoulder gently as he left.

When Danny was gone, Jonathon turned to Trevor. "Why did you disobey me?" The look in his eyes frightened Trevor.

"I'm sorry, Father, but we were on that side of town, and I wanted to show Danny how the bike handles. We just went up a little ways."

"The two of you, in spite of your agreement about passengers. And on the way down you got in a wreck."

"It wasn't my fault. Tom Runyan took the corner too wide, and I had to swerve to miss him."

"So it was Tom Runyan's fault that you were in the canyon?"

Trevor started to protest, then figured out the jab and replied, "No, sir, it wasn't his fault I was in the canyon."

"Trevor, if you'd obeyed me in the first place, this wouldn't have happened. As it is, it may be that there was no way you could avoid this once you'd made the decision to ride up the canyon. But I believe that with more experience, you would have been better prepared. Plus, the creek wouldn't be running as high. That's why I made a rule. You knew about the rule, and you chose to disobey. Now your motorcycle is damaged, I assume, and you have a badly burned leg."

Trevor sat there in sullen silence.

"Just how bad is the motorcycle?"

"The front fork is bent. I don't know if there's other damage. We couldn't get it down the canyon."

"Well, I'll have to get a truck to go up and get it. Then we'll take it to the shop, where we'll store it until you earn enough money to get it fixed."

"But Father!"

"You can have a part-time job as a janitor at the depot, if you like. An after-school job has just opened up."

"But a janitor—"

"If you can find your own job, that's fine. But I'm not paying for a mistake that never should have happened."

"Yes, sir." Trevor refused to raise his head.

"Not only that, but you're restricted from driving for six months."

At that, Trevor looked up with real alarm. His face flushed, but he bit his tongue.

"Jonathon, I support you completely in disciplining Trevor, including restricting his driving privileges," Margaret interjected. "But I think six months may be too long."

Jonathon turned to look at Margaret. He was angry with Trevor and wanted to do even more than simply restrict his driving, but through the years, he had learned he should check his temper when his wife intervened.

"What do you think is fair, then?"

"First, you know that I don't like to drive in bad weather, so I'd like Trevor to continue to drive me to church. Second, if he does well in school and works hard at this job, I think you should let him drive at the end of June so he gets to enjoy at least part of the summer."

Jonathon looked at Trevor, who was so miserable now that not even the compromise held much promise for him.

"All right, then. Trevor, you may drive your mother whenever she needs you. But always two people in the car. If you abide by the rules, you may drive at the end of June. Are you willing to live by that?"

Trevor looked up and said a very sullen, "Yes, sir."

"Fine. Now, Danny will ride with me back to the station, where I'll arrange to pay for a truck to take us up the canyon. He can help me find the motorcycle. Meanwhile, you and your mother will go to the doctor. There's no sense making him drive over here." With that, Jonathon left the room without so much as a good-bye. Trevor was miserable but went with his mother out to the Buick for the trip to the doctor.

When Trevor saw his motorcycle later that night and sized up the damage, he felt even worse. "I'll be mopping floors for a year before I can pay for all this," he muttered to Danny, making sure he was in earshot of his father as well.

* * *

As the date for the Salt Lake outing neared, Jonathon went to each of the boys' homes to talk with their parents and to invite the boys' fathers to go on the trip. Sam's father was happy for Sam to go but had to decline himself because he'd be getting things ready for spring planting. Bishop Peterson agreed to go, along with Leonard's father. When Jonathon knocked on the O'Brians' door, Frank was surprised, to say the least, to see him there. He invited Jonathon in warily.

"I'm here on church business, Frank, not railroad. Mind if I sit down?"

Frank cleared a place for him at the kitchen table.

"Under the leadership of your son, the boys have been working to earn a trip to Salt Lake City on their spring break. They've had to memorize a series of scriptures, and I'm pleased to report that all but one has passed them off. Danny has been working with him, and we're confident that he'll make it."

Frank nodded.

"The reason I'm here is to request your permission to let Dan go on the trip with us and to invite you to come along as a chaperone, if you can."

"Danny told me about this trip when I asked about the suit he brought home. I personally don't think boys should be traipsing off to places like Salt Lake City, but I know he's worked hard for it. I also know it would be wrong for the boys' leader not to attend. So I'll give my permission. As for me, I have union business to attend to that weekend, so I won't be able to go."

"I'm sorry to hear that, but I understand. We'll be gone Thursday through Sunday night, the last weekend in April. We'll take the 11:25 A.M. Salt Lake City Special. At first I thought I'd take the boys on my business car, but the more I thought about it, I decided they ought to experience a typical passenger-train ride."

Frank nodded. "I think that's wise. Not everyone will grow up to get their own private railcar, so it's better not to make them think that's the way everybody travels."

Jonathon remained impassive.

Frank continued. "If it's the Special you're going on, I'll put in to see if I can fire on the run down to Ogden through Cache Junction. We can't let the boys ride in the cab, but maybe the engineer would be willing to let them take a quick tour of the locomotive before we set off."

"That's a great idea. Of course, it would be up to the union to decide, so if it's all right, I'll leave that in your hands."

"I think you can count on it," Frank said stiffly, then rose from his chair. Jonathon stood up and moved to the door, forcing a handshake on Frank as they reached the door.

"I want you to know, Frank, that you have raised a tremendous young man. He's a credit to both you and his mother, and I rely on him to get the work of the quorum done."

Frank mumbled something incoherent, and Jonathon started down the sidewalk.

"Why do you do it?"

"What?" Jonathon said, turning back to look at Frank.

"Why do you spend so much time with these boys? They're nothing in your world."

"They're everything in my world, Frank. Everything. The railroad is a job. The boys are the future." He turned and continued to his car. Frank watched as he drove away, shaking his head slowly from side to side.

Inside, Danny slipped out of his bedroom doorway into the living room. He was so excited he could hardly stand it. He wanted to run straight to Trevor's house and tell him that his father was going to let him go. He'd worried about that ever since learning about the trip back in August. *Thank you, Heavenly Father. Thank you for Brother Richards. Thank you for helping my father let me go.* He joined his father in the living room. "Thank you for granting your permission, sir."

Frank grunted. "You'll be needing some money on the trip—I don't want you living off the Richardses or any of the other boys. O'Brians pay their own way."

"I've saved money for it, sir."

"That's money you need to hang on to." Then he slipped Danny two silver dollars and a couple of quarters. "That ought to be enough for the trip. I don't want anybody thinking you're not equal to the other boys."

"Thank you, sir. Thank you!" Danny moved close to Frank to hug him, but his father stepped back. Danny asked if he could go out for a while, and Frank stepped aside silently. Danny raced down the street to find Trevor and tell him the news.

* * *

Temptation comes to even the best of people. Two weeks after his accident and just one week before the trip to Salt Lake, Trevor was home alone when an overpowering urge for a cherry-lime phosphate came over him. His father was on his way to Boise for a meeting, and his mother had just been picked up by another sister in the ward for a midweek Relief Society presidency meeting. It was cold outside, and he really didn't want to walk. Before he knew what was happening, he found himself in the garage, looking at his mother's Buick. *It's only four blocks going and four blocks returning. Nothing could go wrong.* The voice in his head recited all the reasons why it was unfair that he was restricted from driving. He climbed into the Buick, just to feel the seats, and, without thinking, reached down and made sure the parking brake was secure before impulsively turning the switch on the new electric starter to crank the engine. It started up beautifully. The garage door was down, so the room quickly started to fill with fumes. Trevor had a choice: turn the engine off or open the door. A quick wrestle with his conscience settled the debate. He stood to dismount, then reached over and turned off the engine. He turned out the light and went back in the house.

About five minutes later, his heart jumped in his throat as he heard the garage door open and the Stearns pulling in. *But Father's in Boise!* He waited nervously as Jonathon Richards came in through the kitchen door.

"Hi, Father. I thought you were in Boise."

"They cancelled the meeting because of a problem on the Ontario line. That division's general manager had to attend to it."

Trevor pretended to study his math.

"Trevor, did you drive the Buick tonight?"

"No, sir." He didn't look up.

"How did your mother get to church?"

"Sister Hall picked her up." He looked back down at his books.

"Trevor, then tell me why the garage is filled with gasoline fumes and why the muffler on the Buick is hot."

Trevor looked up. "Father, it's hot because I started the engine." His voice trembled. "I was tempted to take the car out because I want to drive so badly. But I turned it off after just a few seconds. I didn't disobey you, I promise."

Jonathon looked at his son. He'd never had this kind of trouble before. But it was obvious Trevor loved driving to the point that it was going to be a problem.

"I'm glad to hear that, Trevor. I should have been more specific. No starting engines in garages where you can asphyxiate yourself." He attempted to laugh, but Trevor was not in the mood. "Trevor, look at me." Trevor raised his eyes warily. "I know you think you're ready to be a full-time driver, but you're not. You're still immature, and I've got to help you learn to be more deliberate or you're going to hurt somebody."

"But I have fast reflexes. I can get out of scrapes that most people can't."

"Your reflexes didn't protect you in City Creek Canyon." When Trevor was about to object, he continued, "But that's not the point. The point is that even the best reflexes are no substitute for judgment. Now, here's how I'm going to help you. If you disobey me again by taking a car out when you're not authorized to, you won't go to Salt Lake with the rest of the group." Then, for added emphasis, "And I'll sell the Indian. Do you understand?"

The fire in Trevor's eye told him that he understood.

"I'm glad you didn't disobey me tonight. Three more months and you'll be driving again."

Trevor didn't respond. Instead, he asked to excuse himself in as cold a voice as he could muster and went up to his room. He was angry, as angry as he'd ever been in his life. But he resolved not to cross his father again. *I won't give him the satisfaction of selling the Indian.*

* * *

It was the kind of mistake you could only identify after it had happened. Danny could have worn his regular church clothes to sacrament meeting the Sunday before they were set to go to Utah, but he'd been asked to sing a descant with the choir so had dressed in his new suit. Sure enough, on the way to church, disaster struck in the form of an ambush by Kelly and Victor, who had been waiting weeks for an opportunity to mess up his trip. Their goal was simple—ruin his suit so he wouldn't have it to wear in Utah.

At first, Danny didn't know where Kelly was headed with his taunting. He thought it was just the usual stuff, so he simply shrugged when Kelly pushed him and said, "Think you're pretty big, going to Utah with the other children? Going down to see the rich relatives?"

"Cut it out, Kelly. Leave me alone."

"Too good for your own brother?" Kelly shoved him again, this time forcing him to bump Victor. Victor knew his cue and shoved him back hard into Kelly.

"Hey, knock it off, Daniel. Are you trying to start a fight?" Kelly shoved him to the ground.

Now Danny understood. He struggled to get up, but Victor was on top of him, doing his best to force his face into the ground. Danny had grown in the last six months, and Victor was having a hard time of it. That's when Kelly came from behind and sucker-punched him in the ribs. When Danny tucked up to protect himself, Victor started pulling on his jacket, ripping a button loose. Danny was in trouble and knew that no matter what he did to them, they'd win. *At least I can give them a fight.* He started punching back as hard as he could, but with little effect.

At this point, Kelly and Victor were involved enough in the attack that they didn't hear the Buick come up behind them. They did notice when Trevor tackled them full on, screaming that they'd better leave Danny alone. Their preferred way of fighting was two against one, but in this case, the odds were even, so they turned on Trevor and dragged him into the melee. All four were wrestling on the ground, punches flying and threats being traded. Just when the two bigger boys managed to roll on top of both Danny and Trevor to finish their work, the air was shattered by an ear-piercing whistle that would have deafened a small dog.

"What the . . ." Kelly said, rolling onto his seat and looking up. There, standing imperiously above him, was the formidable form of Margaret Richards.

"You boys stop this right now! All four of you!" Victor rolled off Trevor, and Kelly and Victor started scooting backward, crab-style.

"You ought to be ashamed of yourself," she said to Kelly. "Attacking your own brother—and when he's dressed for church."

"You can mind your own business, lady," Kelly said defiantly.

With that, Trevor leaped on Kelly with a fury that surprised everyone. "Don't you ever talk to my mom that way," he screamed while slugging Kelly in the face.

"Trevor!"

He rolled back and looked up at his mother.

"I'll handle this." Turning to Kelly, she said evenly, "You and your friend will get up and leave now, or I'll report you to the police."

"You rich people think you can control everybody. Well, the police aren't going to arrest anybody for hitting his own brother. Besides, he started it by bumping into Victor."

"It may be that they won't arrest you. But they will file a police report. And I wonder how that would affect a person's chance of getting a football scholarship."

"What did you say?" Kelly's eyes blazed.

"I said that I would report you and that the police report would be damaging to your college ambitions. Please don't make me do that."

Kelly was furious, but he knew he was bested. Trevor laughed to think his mom even knew about Kelly or his football. "You can keep the little creep," Kelly said while standing up. "He practically lives at your house anyway. He's become more English than Irish." As he picked up his hat, he gave Danny one last punch in the side. "Maybe you're not really an O'Brian, after all, but an adopted English boy!" Victor laughed, and the two of them stormed down the alley, acting as if they were angry.

"Daniel, let me help you up." Danny took Margaret's hand and stood, his face streaked, his suit filthy. He was doing his best not to cry, but it was clear that he was so furious he could hardly contain himself. "Your suit looks frightful," Margaret said calmly, "but it's not as bad as you think it is. We can clean it."

"But it's torn to shreds," he said, his voice trembling.

"Yes, and I know how to repair fabric. You leave this to me." Turning to Trevor, she said, "Your clothes can be dusted off. We need to return home and loan Daniel a pair of your trousers and a clean shirt. It's probably better if his father doesn't see this." Trevor raised an eyebrow, surprised by his mother's insight. "Let's hurry so Daniel isn't late for his solo."

"You're telling me to drive fast," Trevor said cheerfully, while feigning incredulity.

"Just this one time, Trevor. Just this one time."

* * *

Danny did a great job on his solo, and Trevor and Margaret dropped him off at his house on their way home. As Trevor drove quietly toward their house, he was lost in his own thoughts until his mother interrupted. "Why do you suppose Daniel's brother attacked him like that?"

"That's easy. He wanted to ruin his suit so he wouldn't have it to wear in Salt Lake City. Danny told me about it while he was changing clothes."

"Why doesn't Daniel tell his parents about Kelly's attacks? He's much smaller than Kelly and deserves protection."

"I asked him about that once. All Danny would say is that he did tell a couple of times, and his father did punish Kelly by spanking him. But then he spanked Danny for being a tattletale. So he stopped saying anything after that."

Margaret shook her head in dismay. "I feel sorry for Kelly. He must be an extremely unhappy person to be so cruel."

Trevor turned quickly and looked at her face to see if she was joking. She wasn't. "You feel sorry for him? How can you feel sorry for a bully?"

"Bullies are people too, Trevor. Often they do it because they're insecure and frightened."

"I don't think Kelly's insecure. His father loves everything he does. It's Danny who feels insecure."

"I think Frank O'Brian manipulates both of his sons. What he does to Kelly isn't an expression of love. It's insecurity on his part, so he encourages his son to act tough."

"Wow, you've named the two orneriest people I know, and you're feeling sorry for them. Maybe there's something wrong with me, but I just can't work up any sympathy."

They pulled into the driveway. After parking the car, Trevor escorted his mother in through the back door. She turned, looking at him earnestly. "Trevor, you should feel sympathy—or at least empathy. And you shouldn't judge. My experience tells me that most men father their own children the way they were fathered. So if Frank O'Brian has trouble being kind to his boys, it's very likely that he was treated harshly as a child himself. It's clear to me that he's not a happy person, so what good does it do for you to hold him in contempt? All it can do is make matters worse."

"I guess I just see what he does to Danny, and it makes me angry. He doesn't have to be mean. Even if he did have it tough as a child, he can change. That's what the gospel says, isn't it?"

Margaret nodded. "Yes, people can change. But it's harder than you might think. Until they invite the Spirit in, they spend their whole life fighting the 'natural man,' and too many lose the battle."

Trevor was quiet for a few moments. "If people treat their own kids like their father treated them as a child, then I should be a pretty good father someday."

Margaret smiled and pulled Trevor close to her, holding his head against her shoulder while she stroked his hair. In spite of his anger over his father's punishment, he could still say such a wonderful thing about Jonathon. "You'll be a magnificent father. Just look at what a wonderful son you are now. You'll only get better and better."

He snuggled a bit closer, then pulled away and said brightly, "I do drive too fast sometimes, so I'm not perfect." Then more quietly, "I don't think Father's ever going to forgive me."

"Oh, Trevor, you know he's doing this for your own good. You drive way too fast, and you need to stop it. I should have said you'll be a good father if you live long enough." They both laughed. Then Trevor turned serious again.

"I can't believe that Danny will treat his kids like his father treats him. He's nothing like his father."

Margaret sighed softly. "Danny will be different from his father. I'm sure he'll be very kind to his children. But there will be times when he'll find himself doing something unpleasant that's similar to the way his father did it, and it will probably distress him. It's almost inevitable, since the things we learn in childhood stay with us all through our life. Hopefully he'll recognize it when it happens and catch himself. Plus, there will be good things to emulate in his father as well." She smiled. "Besides, he's had the leadership of good men in the Church who are setting a different example. Your own father treats him like a second son."

"I shouldn't tell you this, Mom, and you've got to promise never to say anything because it's supposed to be secret, but Danny and I decided we're really meant to be brothers."

"It doesn't surprise me. He's been a blessing to all of us."

Just then, there was a knock on the front door, interrupting the conversation. It was Elmer coming to pass off the last two scriptures. Trevor invited him in and helped Elmer start reciting. He had to prompt him only once, which Margaret said was understandable. With a triumphant yelp, Trevor and Elmer raced over to the chart that kept track of each of the boys' progress. It was with great satisfaction that Elmer put two big Xs in the blocks at the bottom of his column. Margaret looked with satisfaction on the chart—an X in every block for every boy. It was going to be a wonderful week.

Chapter Six

SALT LAKE CITY
1912

By the time the final weekend in April rolled around, Trevor had made peace with his driving restrictions. He'd even started acting civil toward his father. It helped that his mom seemed to need him to drive her almost everywhere, so he was getting a lot of practice, which is what Jonathon had hoped for anyway.

Thursday was unusually cold, even for April. The five boys and Bishop Peterson and Brother Whitman stood alongside the massive locomotive, shivering in their coats. Frank O'Brian was giving them a brief tour to help them understand the mechanics of a steam-engine train. He pointed to the huge double-action piston, mounted at the front of the wheels, that filled with steam in each direction. The exhaust from the previous power stroke was forced out by the power stroke in the opposite direction, which provided continual power to the drivers. To keep the compound engine working efficiently, one of the yard maintenance men was busy oiling each of the great bearings that would rotate more than a million times on the two-hundred-mile journey to Salt Lake City.

"Excuse me, sir, but why are the wheels so much bigger on this train than on some of the yard engines?" Leonard asked.

Frank looked up at Leonard, pleased to have a question. To this point, the boys had been silent except for occasional whispered remarks to each other, so he had assumed they weren't very interested. "Good question. The weight of a passenger train is less than that of a freight train. Thus, a single stroke of the piston can propel the train a greater distance using the same amount of steam, but only if the driving wheel is large, such as this one. Plus, it offers a smoother ride to the passengers because there are fewer strokes for the distance covered."

Leonard nodded. Although he'd been to his father's shop many times, he'd never stood this close to a locomotive that was under a full head of steam, and he loved listening to the sound of the engine as it periodically exhaled the unused steam.

"How does the train avoid slipping when the rails are wet?" The boys looked at Elmer, and then back at Frank.

"It's the weight of the locomotive. There's so much pressure on the rail that it gains friction even in snow and ice. Plus, the coupled driving wheels increase traction, since all wheels are turning uniformly. Of course, sometimes, if the train is particularly long, you need helper engines to keep the weight of the locomotives great enough relative to the load. Occasionally, you even need an engine pushing from the rear of the train to reduce strain on the knuckles of the couplers that join the cars."

The next step in the tour was to mount the ladder up into the massive cab. For Leonard and Trevor, this was perfection, with dozens of gauges, levers, and valves. The gate was open to the firebox, and a hot, reddish glow roared under the multi-tube boilers. "This is Tom Newsome, our engineer. He's the one who gave you permission to come up to the cab. The engineer is responsible for controlling the speed and direction of the train under the supervision of the conductor." Frank stepped over near the firebox and glanced at a number of gauges. "My job as fireman is to control the pressure in the boilers to make certain it's adequate for the load." He pointed to a number of valves and continued, "To maintain ideal pressure, the fireman has to control the flow of water into the boilers. Not enough, and the pressure skyrockets until the available water is quickly used up. In the old days, that meant you ran the risk of an explosion. Modern engines have emergency release valves. On the other hand, if you've got a good head of steam and flood the boiler with too much water, you'll immediately drop the pressure and lose power. Make that mistake while climbing a grade, and you may not recover in time to make it to the top. So it's a job that takes constant attention and careful balance."

The boys were fascinated by Frank's instruction and stood largely gape-mouthed as he moved easily around the cab, showing them which valves he used to control the massive boilers. The sound of the blowers in the furnace that increased the heat of the flame added to the hissing sound of steam escaping from numerous joints in the line to produce an effect of sheer power.

"How exactly does a steam engine work?" This was the first time Trevor had asked a question. He'd always been wary of Frank, but his curiosity overcame his natural reluctance.

"Steam is admitted to the pistons by a control valve that is synchronized to the turning of the wheels. To pull this big of a load takes a lot of steam, of course. On our journey to Ogden, we'll burn almost two hundred fifty tons of coal." That brought an appreciative gasp. "Fortunately, we have automatic augers nowadays that will feed the coal forward so we can distribute it evenly along the length of the eight-foot grate. The furnace will actually start to glow red, it gets so hot. All around the furnace box are tanks filled with water, which the fire converts into superheated steam." When Frank opened the door to the grate, the boys shied back from the heat, then bent forward in turn to look in at the glowing fire. "It's burning orange now because we have no demand for steam. But once we get rolling, it will turn white-hot in there, particularly when we have a hill to climb." The boys just laughed as they felt a blast of heat from the open door.

"Time to sound the whistle," Tom Newsome said casually. "One of you boys care to pull the cord?" The engineer knew perfectly well that whoever was given the honor would instantly become the subject of both envy and esteem. The boys looked around, wanting to volunteer but reluctant to be the first to assert themselves. "How about you, Danny?" Frank said cautiously. "I don't think you've ever had the chance."

"Thank you, sir," Danny said, stepping forward, his face flushed. They gave him a short stool so he could reach the cord. Its pull was harder than he expected, and when the shriek of the steam-powered whistle sounded directly overhead, it startled him so much he let go. He wasn't the only one who was startled. All the boys and their fathers covered their ears and burst out laughing. It sounded a lot different than when you heard it from across town.

"Not bad, but not long enough. Give it another pull, and hold onto it this time." Tom held up his hand to indicate when he could let go. This time Danny pulled the cord with more confidence, and the piercing shriek of the whistle filled the air for at least five miles in every direction. When he let go, everybody burst into applause. Danny turned to the group and smiled. "Thank you, sir," he said to Tom, and then he glanced at his father, who was situated in such a way that the other boys couldn't see Danny's face. He mouthed the words, "Thank you," and his father smiled back. It was a moment unlike any that Danny had experienced. He'd never seen his father in his work environment, where all the other men treated him with both respect and regard. It was obvious that he was extremely competent at his job and that it was a difficult and important job. Danny was so proud he could hardly stand it.

"Well, we've got a train to run, so you boys better get back into the passenger cars." Frank and Tom took time to shake each of their hands and make sure they were safely off the cab. Then Tom Newsome turned to Frank and said, "A nice group of boys. Your son's a good-looking kid."

Frank flushed. "He's a real good boy. Not much interested in the things I like, though. Mostly takes after his mother. But he's a good boy." Then, almost to himself, "Real sensitive kid. It's tough to talk to him."

"By the way, we're picking up the general manager's railcar, so I'll need steam up about five minutes early."

Frank's eyes flashed. "I thought he said he wasn't going to take his car."

"I guess the big shots in Salt Lake want him to have it there so they can use it to entertain people this weekend. He seemed really embarrassed when he told me about it."

Frank smiled. "That's probably because of me. I told him the boys needed to see the train from a regular person's point of view, not from a private car. And he agreed with me. Now he's stuck in that big private car of his. I can see why he's embarrassed." They laughed. Frank shook his head. "But I guess it's okay if they get the whole experience. Richards wants this to be a trip they'll never forget."

"Tell me about this trip. Why's he doing something like this?"

"He's their teachers quorum advisor at church." Tom returned a blank stare, since he wasn't LDS. "It's the group that fifteen- through seventeen-year-old males belong to. Richards teaches them on Sunday."

"You're telling me the general manager teaches Sunday School to five boys?"

Frank laughed. "No, I'm not telling you that. Somebody else teaches them Sunday School. Richards teaches priesthood meeting, and he had a contest with the boys to win a trip to Salt Lake City. He's had them worked up over it for almost six months."

"Well, if that don't beat all." Tom lifted his hat and scratched his head. "Did you say he wants this to be a memorable trip?"

Frank looked at him quizzically. "Yeah, I said that."

"Memorable, eh? I think maybe we can push it a bit down by Clarkston—the track's pretty good there. If you'll give me the steam, I'll make sure they get a ride worth remembering." Frank roared at the thought. "Oh, I can give you the steam, all right. You just let me know when you want it."

* * *

Back in the passenger cars, the conductor told the boys they should sit in the last car. Trevor was getting a little worried because he hadn't seen his father yet. Jonathon would often show up to things at the last possible moment—his Stearns got a good workout every time he drove it—but it was just six minutes from the posted departure time, and Trevor knew that his father would never make a train late, even if it meant missing it. So he paced back and forth in the aisle. His friends were busy checking out the car, figuring out how the window blinds could be raised and lowered, watching the ceiling fans turning lazily above them to stir the air, and otherwise chatting cheerfully over the backs of their seats. Suddenly, Trevor was jolted by the movement of the train as it started backing. His quick reflexes kept him from being knocked into Elmer's lap, but he rather gracelessly sat down next to Danny.

"I don't know where my father is," Trevor said anxiously.

"I'm sure he'll make it. We must be backing onto a siding or something, because we were on the main south-bound track."

"By the way, your father was really neat with his tour of the engine. He has to know a lot to make that thing work."

Leonard leaned over from the seat in front and said, "My father says that word around the yard is that your father is the best fireman in the whole division. That's why they elected him the union rep. Nobody else knows as much as he does."

"It was really something, wasn't it?" Then Danny burst into a grin. "And I'm the one that got to 'blow the whistle.' Get it?" They laughed, and then Danny and Leonard started talking about what to expect in Salt Lake. But Trevor was too distracted. He kept turning around to see if his father had made it on board. *Probably on some stupid phone call.* Just then, there was a crunching sound, and the train came to an abrupt halt.

"We've hooked onto another car," Elmer shouted. The boys turned around and looked through the small window in the back door. Sure enough, the light that had previously shone through the glass had gone dark, and they could see the outline of another car. Just as soon as the brakeman hooked up the hoses, the train lurched forward and started to pick up speed. "We're on our way," Elmer said gleefully, not even trying to contain his excitement.

Now Trevor was agitated, at least until he heard his father's voice from behind him. "Worried that I wouldn't make it?" Everybody turned and smiled to see Jonathon Richards come striding into the car, wearing a sharp-looking suit. "Sorry," he said cheerfully. "Company business right up to the last moment. But we made it in the nick of time, and we're pulling out on schedule. That's important to a railroad man." He came and stood at the front of the little group, rocking back and forth to offset the motion of the train. "I'm afraid I do have some bad news, however." Everybody looked up in alarm. "I know that you all want to make the trip in the comfort of the passenger car, but it looks like we're going to be taking on a lot of passengers along the way, so I'm afraid we're going to have to move you off this car."

Everyone looked a bit perplexed. Starting toward the rear of the car, he said, "Gather up your belongings and follow me."

Suddenly it dawned on Trevor what was going on, and he burst into a grin. "He's hooked up to his private car! We get to ride in a private car all the way to Salt Lake City." It still didn't register with the boys what that meant, but they were relieved by Trevor's cheerfulness.

Entering the private car, they noticed a few things immediately, such as the highly polished ebony door casings and the doors that opened into two private sleeping compartments. There was even a private commode for each compartment. Next they passed into a formal dining room that featured a beautiful mahogany table with fresh lycut flowers as a centerpiece. Finally, they wound up in a large sitting room with sofas and wingback chairs. There were a couple of tables with games set out, but the best part of all was that the back door opened onto a covered patio.

"Go ahead and stand on the platform. It's fun to watch the city fade away as we make our way through the Portneuf Gap." The boys went out and stood with their hands on the rail, while the fathers who were chaperoning stood behind them.

"This is just like the president's train," Sam said. "Hey, look, everybody, I'm Sam Carter, candidate for president of the United States, and I want to tell all of you fellow citizens what an honor it is to stop here in, in—what's the name of this place, anyway?" Everybody laughed and bowed to Sam. Some of the boys moved inside and took up a seat next to one of the plateglass windows, while others sat at the tables. Everybody had been down through the Portneuf Gap on numerous occasions, since one of the favorite activities of the area was to go to Lava Hot Springs to swim in the natatorium. But they'd never seen it from this vantage point or in this kind of luxury.

"This is the best!" Elmer said confidently. "Some day I want a private railcar."

"If you really want that, there's no reason you can't have it," Jonathon said. "The world generally gives people exactly what they ask for, if they're willing to work hard to get it."

"Well, this is what I want."

"The only hard part is figuring out what you really should have instead of what you want." Elmer looked up with a puzzled look as his father sat down next to him. Jonathon continued, "I like having this car, but there's a lot of responsibility that comes with it. I have to be gone much of the time solving problems on location. That leaves Trevor and his mother home alone. What you find is that even the most comfortable private car can be awfully lonely when you're not with your family. Meanwhile, Elmer, you get to work with your father nearly every day in his construction business, and he gets to come home to his wife every night. So really, you have to wonder who has the better job."

Elmer turned and looked at his father in a new way. He'd always assumed the most expensive thing was the best thing. "I'm happy with what I do," Bishop Peterson said, "and I don't think I'd trade places with Brother Richards. Still, it's not often in life that people get an experience like this, so I'm going to relax and enjoy it. Care to play a game of chess, Elmer?"

"Yes, sir. But you know I always beat you."

"I know, but there's always hope, isn't there?"

Before they knew it, the train pulled into McCammon, where a switch was thrown, taking it off the main east-west line and onto the route of the original Utah Northern right-of-way. They headed down past Downata Hot Springs and through Red Rock Gap, where, Jonathon explained, the ancient Lake Bonneville had twice broken out of its banks, sending a torrent of water scouring its way down the Marsh Creek and through the Portneuf Gap. Eventually the water emptied into the Snake River, and then on to the Pacific Ocean.

Once clear of the gap and past Preston, Idaho, the train approached the Utah–Idaho border. They'd been traveling a respectable forty miles per hour, which was a delightful way to see the scenery. That's when Trevor noticed a change in the pace of the clicking sound coming through the floors from the metal wheels. Danny noticed that the pitch was increasing. Jonathon, who had spent many an hour on a railroad train, sensed the change in speed without really even thinking about it.

"Seems like we're picking up speed," Leonard's father said.

"A lot of it," Jonathon responded. Everyone instinctively moved to the windows. The scenery was definitely going by faster than it had been. Much faster. "We've got to be going at least sixty or seventy miles per hour. That's a little stout for this track." But it wasn't over—the train continued to accelerate.

Trevor burst out laughing and rushed out onto the platform to stick his head into the wind as it passed by. The others joined him as the train continued to increase its pace. By now the clicking sound was more like a continuous rattle, and the frame of the car actually became smoother as the miles passed under the train at a rate greater than one mile in every fifty seconds. Finally, they started into a long, gentle turn, which, at a speed of nearly eighty miles per hour, pushed everyone toward the left side of the train. Trevor was laughing and shouting, while Danny was braced up against a door casing. And Jonathon Richards was smiling from ear to ear. "This little display is all for you guys. Frank and Tom are pushing her right to the limit so you can see what a passenger train is capable of. Pretty thrilling, isn't it?"

Everybody showed their agreement by clapping. Then, as the curve sharpened, they felt the train start to decelerate. By the time it slowed to its normal pace, it felt like they were crawling, and Trevor moved inside to show his disgust.

Things brightened up a bit as they wound through the pass that brought them out of the Cache Valley on approach to Brigham City. Finally, some five hours after they had departed Pocatello, the train pulled into the yards at Ogden, Utah, the main switching point on the east-west Union Pacific Railroad main line, where UP trains were switched to Southern Pacific tracks and vice versa. As the train pulled into the station, Jonathon invited the group to get off and stretch their legs.

While walking toward the front of the train, Trevor caught sight of Frank O'Brian and Tom Newsome, who were being replaced by a different crew for the final stretch to Salt Lake City. He took off on a run and went up to the two, calling out, "That was the best! I can't believe it! How fast did we go?"

The two men closed on him quickly. "Quiet! We made the run at normal speeds and in the normal time." By now Danny had joined up.

"Oh, yeah," Trevor said in a whisper. "Mouth gets in the way of common sense." Looking around, he said quietly, "But how fast did we get going? It was so great to stick my head into the wind."

"I think it would be safe to say that we were not going eighty-five miles per hour," was all that Tom would say.

Frank agreed. "No, we never hit eighty-five. That's for sure."

Trevor shook his head appreciatively. "Amazing. Absolutely amazing. Thanks, Mr. O'Brian and Mr. Newsome. I'll never forget it. Not ever!"

They smiled. "You're welcome. It's kind of fun for us, too, once in a while." Tom Newsome moved off to the crew shack, and Trevor jogged back to the group.

When they were left alone, Danny turned to Frank. "Father, that was really wonderful. I never knew your job was so important. Everybody's talked about how they loved your tour. And Leonard's father says everybody respects you as the best fireman in the whole district. It's just great what you did for us."

Frank was clearly moved. He wanted to hug Danny, but there were so many people on the platform. "Glad you liked the trip." Then he turned to walk away. Danny stood motionless, not wanting to lose the moment. Frank turned back, walked up to his son, and punched him on the arm.

"You be good in Salt Lake. It's a big city, and the boys are looking to you for leadership."

"Yes, sir."

"Well, I better be going. Management wrote up one of our firemen for a stupid infraction, and he needs my help."

"Yes, sir." He watched his father head for the crew shack. He just couldn't leave it alone. "Thank you, sir! It was great!" Frank kept walking without turning around, but those walking toward him saw a quick grin cross his face.

* * *

When they finally arrived at the Union Pacific station in Salt Lake City, they found Jonathon Richards's father waiting for them in a brand-new Buick, along with two other cars with drivers. They quickly unloaded their luggage and climbed into the luxury automobiles to begin a trip through the city on the way to their temporary housing at the Richardses' home in the Avenues.

The first site that everyone strained to see was the Salt Lake Temple. All but Trevor had only seen it in pictures, and they quickly realized that photographs simply couldn't do it justice.

"The spires seem to reach right up toward heaven," Sam said in awe.

"And look at how the gold statue of the angel Moroni glistens in the afternoon sun," Leonard added.

"I wonder if he gets cold in the winter," Elmer said innocently, then laughed when the other boys stared at him with the perplexed expression they often had when considering one of his questions.

They wanted to stop, but Jonathon assured them they'd have plenty of time to tour the temple grounds on Saturday. The tallest building in Pocatello was four stories, so the recently completed Hotel Utah, directly across from Temple Square, seemed monstrous at nine stories. The Walker Building down the street was even taller. With the boys oohing and aahing as the cars traveled up South Temple past the magnificent Cathedral of the Madeline and the recently completed First Presbyterian Church, made out of native Utah sandstone. It was obvious that Salt Lake City was growing like crazy, as evidenced by the hundreds of motorcars making their way up and down the streets.

"I just can't believe this," Danny whispered to Trevor. "There are cars everywhere!" Just then a motorcycle roared past them between the lanes of traffic.

"So that's where you learned to drive," Leonard called out from the backseat.

Trevor laughed and said, "It's pretty neat, isn't it?" He didn't realize until that moment how much he missed Salt Lake, and he couldn't wait to introduce his old friends to the boys from Pocatello. He hoped they wouldn't be arrogant or anything, since a lot of city people thought everybody else were hicks.

Finally, the little convoy pulled up in front of a beautiful home on Second Avenue, and Eliot Richards invited everyone in. The boys were to sleep on mattresses thrown on the basement floor, while rooms were provided for the two fathers. Sandwiches had been set out, and the boys started eating eagerly once the prayer was said. Then, before sending them downstairs, Jonathon called a brief meeting.

"Here's the itinerary for the next three days," he said. "Tomorrow, after breakfast, we're going to go to the Utah

state capitol building for a quick tour. My father is a state
senator, so he's received permission to take you onto the
floor of the senate, and he'll explain how the government
works. They're not in session right now, so the only people
you'll see are some of the staff people. There's a chance that
we can meet the governor of Utah, but that will depend on
if he's able to step out of a meeting he has planned." The
boys nodded their heads excitedly. "Next up is to take the
Bamberger Railroad out to the Saltair Beach and Resort on
the Great Salt Lake. It's still a little brisk this time of year,
but it actually opened for the general conference weekend,
so you should be all right if you take a jacket. There are
amusement park rides and a huge arcade, and in the late
afternoon, we'll all go swimming in the Salt Lake. I've got
five dollars for anybody who can sink or swim to the
bottom."

"Elmer can do it, if anybody can," Sam said. "He's
nearly drowned on two previous outings." Elmer elbowed
Sam in the ribs as the other boys laughed.

"I think even the indomitable Elmer Peterson would
have trouble drowning in the Salt Lake with all its buoyancy.
Still, should he try, I'm relying on each of you to save him.
In fact, one of the rules we have to have is that you all pair
up with another boy so that you're never alone. That way if
somebody gets into trouble, or gets lost, he always has a
friend to help." The boys looked around to see who would
pair up. With five, it wasn't automatic.

"One of my old friends, George Smith, is going to join
us, so I'll go with him," Trevor said. He caught the glance
from Dan, who probably assumed he'd be paired with
Trevor. "Don't worry. We'll all go around together anyway.
You guys will like George a lot. Particularly you, Danny,
since he's a musician. He plays the violin and trumpet."

"The violin and trumpet," Elmer said incredulously.

"Yeah, he's a well-rounded guy."

"We'll eat at Saltair, then get home late. On Saturday, we're going to take a tour of the city in the morning and then go over to my father's car dealership. He has a track behind the car lot, and he's agreed to let each of you have a hand at driving one of his cars. The best driver gets to keep it."

Eliot glanced up sharply as the boys cheered.

"Just kidding about that one, of course. But there will be a prize for the best driver. That afternoon, we're going to have dinner at the Hotel Newhouse, so you'll need to change into your suits. It has one of the finest restaurants in the city, after all. We'll end the evening by driving up to an overlook behind the capitol building so you can watch the sun set over the Salt Lake Valley and then look at the lights of the city in the darkness. It's a spectacular view that I think is well worth seeing. Then, on Sunday, we'll go to stake conference at the Tabernacle on Temple Square, followed by a brief tour of the grounds. Then, after a nice dinner together, we'll change our clothes and catch the late train back to Pocatello. A busy couple of days, but it should be a lot of fun. Any questions?"

It was one of those times when there were a thousand questions, but none that really needed to be asked out loud. It was finally time to actually see the places they'd been dreaming about, rather than just speculating about it. Jonathon asked Trevor to take them on a walk through the neighborhood to use up some of their energy before bedtime. Just as they were turning to leave, he turned and said, "By the way, Danny, you need to talk to my father about something before you go to bed tonight, all right?"

"Yes, sir," Danny said, surprised to be singled out. "Should I talk to him now? I could catch up to the others."

"Good idea. Trevor, why don't you walk toward the baseball field first so Danny can catch up to you? He'll only be a couple of minutes."

Trevor looked puzzled but agreed and led Sam, Elmer, and Leonard out the etched-glass front door.

Danny walked over to Jonathon, who introduced him formally to his father.

"I understand that you like to sing," Eliot said.

"Yes, sir," Danny replied, his voice rising a bit at the end.

"One of my responsibilities on the stake high council is to help arrange music for the sessions of conference, and we have a priesthood choir scheduled to perform on Sunday afternoon. They're singing a special arrangement of 'Come, Come, Ye Saints' that calls for a tenor solo on the fourth verse. I was hoping that you might sing that for us."

Danny's eyes grew wide.

"Before you say yes or no, you should know that you will have to give up participating in the automobile driving on Saturday, since you'd have to practice with the choir. I know this is short notice, but our usual singer came down with a violent cough just yesterday. Jonathon had told me of your singing abilities when he talked about bringing the group down."

Danny still didn't say anything, so Jonathon interrupted. "You can think about it tonight if you want to, Danny, and if you're uncomfortable, they can just have the whole choir sing the verse."

"No, it's not that, sir. I'd love to sing with your choir. It's just that I can't quite believe this is happening. It's such a great honor—and all the Salt Lake boys probably have a lot more experience than me."

Eliot laughed pleasantly. "It is an honor. But from what my son tells me, it's one that you deserve. Always remember, Danny, God divided up all the souls of men so that they would be born where they're needed. A boy from Pocatello is every bit as important as the son of the king of England, because that's where God assigned you to be born."

"Yes, sir." Danny gulped.

"It's settled, then. After we get the boys going at our business, you and I will drive to the Tabernacle to practice. I can promise you that singing with the acoustics of that great building will be a thrill. I've never gotten over it, even after all the years I've lived here."

The shocked look on Dan's face told Eliot and Jonathon that he'd forgotten the conference would be held at the great Tabernacle. "Don't worry, son, it's really just a building—a great one, to be sure—but nothing you can't handle. You'll be fine."

"Thank you." Danny looked a little pale, but Jonathon's hug reassured him, and he turned and went downstairs in a daze.

"Seems like a fine young man," Eliot said amiably.

"A remarkable young man. Just this morning, before seeing me off to the train, Margaret told me that she believes he's something of a prodigy when it comes to music. He has no idea how good he is because he has no one to compare himself to. When he sings at church, the congregation just seems carried away, as much by the feeling he puts into a song as by the tenor of his voice. He's moving through her books at breakneck speed and soon will be beyond anything they can offer."

"Well, I'm glad to give him this chance, then. It's good to have you back here again, Jonathon. "

* * *

Friday was a long day. At the tour of the capitol building, they indeed met the governor, who treated them each very civilly and gave them each a small souvenir coin made out of native Utah copper to commemorate the day.

Saltair was a huge hit with the boys, particularly the arcade games, where Danny's marksmanship earned him a nice prize. Meanwhile, Trevor shouted gleefully on each of the ten rides he took on the roller coaster. For the four native Pocatello boys, it was the first time they'd ever seen a roller coaster, and riding it gave Elmer motion sickness. The most exciting part was the point in the ride where it went out over the water of the Great Salt Lake, giving every appearance that the cars in the train would fly off the rails and into the water. At the last possible moment, the track would assert itself, and the little train would jerk back in the direction of land before making a final descent to the passenger platform.

That evening, after taking a swim in the lake, they had dinner on the promenade and then watched as young couples took to the dance floor to swirl to a live orchestra. At around 9:00, Jonathon announced, to the disappointment of the group, that it was time to take the thirteen-mile ride back to Salt Lake City so they could catch some sleep before the next day's activities.

They were all tired, but not too tired to listen to George Smith tell them stories about some of Trevor's exploits before he moved from Salt Lake. By the end, they were in stitches, laughing so loud that Elmer's father had to issue a lights-out order, which quieted them but still didn't bring on sleep. George and Trevor talked to the others in low voices about how to act like natives as they walked about town the next day.

When they woke the next morning, they had a hurried breakfast and then made their way to the nearest line, where they caught a trolley into town. Before the morning was finished, they'd walked under the Eagle Gate, through the gardens of the Lion House and Beehive House, down Main Street with its hundreds of cars and thousands of people on the sidewalk, and into ZCMI, the world's first department store, before going out to the trolley barns at the end of the line. They had an amazing lunch in the basement of ZCMI and then went out to Richards's Buick dealership, where they got a complete tour of the facility. Leonard was beside himself with excitement as he saw the precision tool kits each of the mechanics had to work with. Eliot Richards personally conducted the tour, although he was interrupted a couple of times to chat with some of the finely dressed customers who came calling.

In the back of the dealership was a small race course, and, as promised, a number of used utility trucks and less expensive automobiles were put into service for the driving competitions. Everybody knew it would be funny because no one was really skilled at driving. Not knowing of his punishment, Trevor's grandfather asked him to do some exhibition driving to show the other boys how it was done. Trevor looked over at his father, who pursed his lips and shook his head. Trevor's heart sank, but he told his grandfather he couldn't drive. Eliot was about to protest when he caught his son's eye. Although he didn't understand what was going on, he quickly changed course and asked one of his mechanics to give a demonstration of the course. Trevor stood by the fence with his elbows on the fence, looking dejected as he watched the other boys head out onto the track.

As the boys prepared for their turn, Eliot motioned to Danny to join him for the drive into the center of town. Trevor asked if he could go along, but for once Danny failed him. "I'm already nervous enough, and the last thing I need is you sitting in the audience while I practice." Trevor went over and sat on one of the benches, refusing even to look at Jonathon. Most days Jonathon loved being a father. This was not one of those days.

After reaching Temple Square, Eliot parked his car in one of the angled parking spots that lined both sides of Main Street between the temple and the Hotel Utah. Walking through the east entrance, Danny almost fell over backward looking up at the temple.

"Magnificent, isn't it?"

"Yes, sir. I always pictured it as being beautiful, but I never imagined it would feel so spiritual just being near it."

"I grew up in England, where there are awe-inspiring cathedrals, but I never really felt very spiritual in them. That's why it was so shocking to me when these two young ragamuffins from America showed up at my door, inviting me to hear a message about the gospel. From the moment I laid my eyes on them, the Spirit of the Lord told me that the message they'd share with me was true. I found that hard to believe, since our ministers in the Church of England had all been to years of divinity school, but these two young missionaries soon proved that they had more than all the divinity schools in the world could offer." He reflected as he walked toward the Tabernacle. "I only wish my parents could have felt what I did. My mother was indifferent. My father was hostile. I was well established by then, so I didn't need their approval, but I still felt bad that they couldn't find the same inspiration that I did. At any rate, I still feel that same feeling of wonder whenever I come to the Salt Lake Temple. It helps me feel connected to heaven itself."

Entering the great Tabernacle, Danny nearly had a panic attack. The thought of singing to a crowd even half the size of what the Tabernacle could hold was overwhelming, particularly when he saw more than a hundred men assembling in the choir seats below the largest pipe organ he could ever possibly imagine. It had thirty-foot pipes fitted into an incredible breastwork of carved wood stained to look like mahogany. As they walked down the aisle, Eliot saw the look on his face and said, "So what's the largest group you've ever sung for?"

Danny didn't seem to hear.

"Pardon me for breaking into your thoughts, Danny, but I was wondering what the largest group is you've ever sung for."

"What? Oh, maybe two or three hundred," Danny said meekly.

"I don't know if Jonathon told you or not, but I am often asked to sing solos. I find that I'm most frightened singing in small groups, rather than in great big halls like this one."

Danny stopped short. "Why would you say that? This is . . . this is . . ." His voice trailed off.

"You see, Danny, when you're in a great hall like this, you can't really see anyone's face. There's color out there, and you know in the back of your mind that each color represents a person. But it's almost like they're not real. So I often just sing as if I were home alone practicing. But when you're in front of a small group, you can see each person's face, and that's much more frightening, as far as I'm concerned."

Danny started to get control of his breathing. "I guess I never thought of it like that."

"You probably haven't had to. But tomorrow afternoon this room will hold several thousand people. What you need to know is that every person who is sitting in the hall will be anxious for you to succeed. They're all here because they love being in the Lord's service, and they'll be sensitive to your fears. Most of them will have joined in the prayer that will be offered in behalf of everyone participating on the program during the invocation. And that includes you. Do you believe in prayer, Danny?"

"Yes, sir. I try to say my prayers every day, although I've never heard a voice or anything."

"Have you felt peace come into your heart when you've prayed?"

Danny thought about it. "Yes, sir, I have."

"Then you should feel at ease about tomorrow's performance because you will be well prayed for. I'm confident the Lord will bless you."

"Yes, sir." Danny gulped. *I'll need a blessing.*

Danny was glad that, as a guest, he got to sit on the front row. Only the boy sitting directly next to him said anything, and that was just a mumbled hello. The conductor was in a hurry, so he said they'd go through Danny's part quickly, undoubtedly assuming that he'd know what to do.

It may have been just his imagination, but Danny felt like the members of the choir resented him for being there—after all, it was their choir, and here he was, showing up at the last moment. He'd probably resent it too, if that happened at home. But then the music started. The organ was so deep and powerful that it seemed to lift him up and out of the chair. As he started singing the first verse with the rest of the members of the choir, he was overwhelmed by the sound of all those male voices singing together, and he was carried away by the sound of the music in the great hall.

When they reached the fourth verse, he didn't even think about the fact that he'd be alone; he just sang the part as he felt it. Perhaps no one knows exactly what the others in the choir expected, but when Danny's voice rang out so strong and solid, yet thoughtful, through the ponderous words, "And should we die before our journey's through, Happy day! All is well! We then are free from toil and sorrow, too; With the just we shall dwell!" there was an electric feeling in the air. When the group came in with Danny on the swelling words of the chorus, "But if our lives are spared again to see the Saints their rest obtain, Oh, how we'll make this chorus swell—All is well! All is well!" Danny was so overcome with emotion that he actually stopped singing for a moment, unable to get the words out. He felt the Spirit of the Lord flood his body and bear testimony that the great sacrifices of the early Saints had not been in vain.

When the song came to its conclusion, the conductor started over to shake Danny's hand and welcome him to the choir. Just then, there was a stirring in the choir, and Danny heard a low rumbling sound that included the words, "It's the prophet!" He and the conductor turned to see a tall, distinguished-looking man with a white, wispy beard approaching them.

"My dear young man, I hope you don't mind that I listened in on your rehearsal." Suddenly, Danny felt his hands enveloped in the warm grip of President Joseph F. Smith. "I was walking across the temple grounds when I heard your choir practicing. I've always loved a men's choir, so I slipped inside to listen. I confess I was startled to hear that verse sung by one so young, and it rather took me by surprise. As you perhaps know, I was in the original wagon company of pioneers and heard this hymn when it was new." Danny stood silently as the President of the Church seemed lost in reflection. "It was very difficult for my mother and me, and more than once I felt the loneliness of having my father martyred with the Prophet Joseph." He turned and looked beyond Danny to all the men in the choir. "As you good men sing this song in your conference tomorrow, you should know that it meant a great deal to us in those days when we felt that the world itself had rejected us. Hearing it again brings back many memories—good memories. Thank you for sharing your wonderful talent."

Then, turning again to Danny, he grasped his hand again and said a quiet, "Thank you."

Danny could hardly understand what was happening, but he had the presence of mind to say, "I've never felt my voice sound quite like that before, sir. It was wonderful."

"Ah, yes. Perhaps the Spirit knew that I needed a lift just now and used you to help me out. Promise me that you'll sing it again just that way tomorrow."

"I promise, sir. I promise I'll try."

Before turning to leave, President Smith again looked Danny squarely in the eyes. "You have been given a gift with your ability to interpret music. It's a talent that the Lord will expect you to put to good use in all the years of your life. You should always find a way to share it with others." He held Danny's gaze for a few unwavering moments, then turned to the conductor. "I've interrupted your practice long enough. Please accept my apology." He then spoke a final parting to the rest of the choir, thanking them for their service while providing his assurance that they would be blessed to do well in their performance the next day.

* * *

As Danny prepared to sing his solo, Jonathon was feeling lonely at the end of the bench, even though he was sitting next to Elmer and Bishop Peterson. Trevor had made a point of sitting on the opposite end of the group. But just as the song was about to start, Jonathon heard some rustling to his left and looked up to see Trevor scooting down in front of the other boys, squeezing his way next to him. As the song started, Trevor rested his head on Jonathon's shoulder. Jonathon's lower lip trembled just a bit as he reached across and pulled Trevor's head even closer, then he stroked his blond hair affectionately. Trevor turned his face up and whispered, "I love you, Father. I don't want to be mad at you anymore."

"I'm glad, Trevor. I'm so glad."

The song was even more powerful than during rehearsal, supported, perhaps, by the strength of the testimonies of the thousands who assembled to hear the conference. Danny felt a great confirmation of the Spirit as he sang out his solo. It was the greatest spiritual moment of his young life.

Later that afternoon, the boys were all crowing about the experience, proud that a boy from Pocatello had done so well. Danny accepted their congratulations quietly. It was only later that Trevor pulled him aside and said, "It's really too sacred to talk about, isn't it?"

"That's exactly how I feel. I almost want to cry every time I think about it."

"I know you didn't say anything to the other guys, but my grandfather told me about what President Smith said to you."

"He was so kind. When he took my hand, I felt like my heart was on fire."

"I had the chance to meet him once too, and I felt the same way."

"I know it's because he's the prophet, but there's something more than even that."

"It's because he's suffered so much in his own life," Trevor said. "My father told me that he's been persecuted from the day he was born. When the government seized all the Church's property and assets because of polygamy, they arrested him along with some of the apostles. He spent a lot of time in jail before the government granted amnesty. Through it all, the non-Mormons called him all kinds of terrible names. Yet he never has an unkind thing to say about anybody. He's strong, but in a gentle way. My father says that proves he's a saint, leading the Saints."

"Well, all I know is that I'll never forget this trip."

"Me neither. I know you don't want to take credit for it, but you did a great job today. I was proud to be your friend."

Danny smiled. He felt a strange contentment that often eluded him.

* * *

As the boys boarded the late train for Pocatello, they started to search for places to doze off. A whole weekend with very little sleep can be very exhausting. Before they faded completely, Jonathon gathered them around for an announcement. "I was speaking with my father on the way to the station, and he indicated that he has an opportunity that some of you may be interested in. He plans to sponsor a racing team this summer to promote the public's interest in automobiles—a lot of dealerships do it—and he could use some summer help." That piqued everyone's attention. "The offer is that any of you who would like to spend three months in Salt Lake City can work around the dealership and help out on the racing crew as it travels to local races to compete. My understanding is that there will be straight-track racing to see who has the fastest automobiles, as well as endurance races out into the country to see which cars do best in a cross-country environment. Housing will be provided at either my father's or my brother's house, depending on how many are interested. Pay will be minimal, but food and lodging will be part of your income. The main objective is to get experience in auto mechanics. Plus, there will be time for the professional driver to give driving lessons to those who are interested. Of course, you don't need to commit now. Talk with your parents and let me know if you're interested." He was gratified at the appreciative grins the boys gave each other.

As the boys settled down to sleep, Trevor came over and sat down by his father. "Thanks, Father, for setting this up with Grandpa. My bet is that you did it mostly for me." Jonathon simply smiled. "It'll be good for me to learn from a real driver, and I like the idea of spending the summer in Salt Lake." Jonathon acknowledged his thanks, and Trevor stretched out on the couch and rested his head on his father's lap. As he was drifting off to sleep, he looked up and added, "I'm sorry that I broke the rules." It was the first time he'd expressed genuine remorse for what he'd done.

"I only made the rules because I love you."

"I know." And with that Trevor drifted off to sleep.

Chapter Seven

TRAGEDY AT
BECKLER MEADOWS

Pocatello, Idaho
August 1914

War broke out in Europe in August 1914. Tensions had been simmering for years, particularly between France and Germany, and the assassination of Archduke Franz Ferdinand of Austria became the match that set the continent aflame.

In America, little notice was given to the outbreak of war in Europe. Americans had a long tradition of avoiding involvement in European affairs, recognizing that war was almost commonplace there, with national boundaries changing their lines every forty to fifty years. America had nothing to gain and everything to lose in the European wars, so people went on about their business.

In Pocatello, for example, the biggest news of the year was that the venerable Pocatello High School caught fire while classes were in session, and it was only through the quick actions of some of the teachers and students that everyone was evacuated safely and the north portion of the school saved from utter destruction. Classes were quickly transferred to nearby buildings, and the school district used the proceeds of an insurance policy to start reconstruction.

It was also the high school graduation year for the young men of the First Ward teachers quorum. For most, that meant the end of their formal education. Elmer was already working full time with his father who had been accepted as a major subcontractor on the construction of a spacious railroad depot just east of the new Hotel Yellowstone. Sam laid down his school books to work full time to save enough money to buy his own farm, and Leonard had been accepted by his father's union as an apprentice to work as a skilled mechanic.

While Trevor, Dan, and Leonard had spent the summers of 1912 and 1913 in Salt Lake City working for Eliot Richards, they decided to spend this last summer working at home, with Dan working with Elmer and Bishop Peterson and Trevor working as a messenger for the railroad. The training they had received in Salt Lake City working on the racing crew was invaluable. Trevor had applied himself and was showing signs of becoming an excellent race car driver. His reflexes were quick, and he instinctively adapted to each automobile, taking advantage of its peculiar strengths. Probably his single biggest asset was a love of all things mechanical.

Only Trevor and Dan (as he now preferred to be called) planned to go on to higher education. Trevor wanted to go to Idaho State Academy in Pocatello simply because he wanted to get school over with as soon as possible so he could take flying lessons and somehow start an aviation-related business. Although no one had found a really practical use for airplanes yet, he believed it was only a matter of time until they were something more than a spectacle for barnstormers and aerial circus stunts.

His father and grandfather wanted him to get the best education possible, however, and encouraged him to go east to a school like the Massachusetts Institute of Technology, but he balked at going so far from home. They finally settled on the premier university in the West—Stanford, in Palo Alto, California. Trevor wasn't particularly happy about leaving, but his parents made the well-reasoned argument that he could meet other enterprising young men at school who might later become business partners in a joint aviation venture. At least by going to Stanford, he could come home for holidays and summers using his father's railroad privileges.

Dan wanted to go east to one of the great music schools, perhaps in New York, but Frank was vehemently opposed, on practical as well as moral grounds. He couldn't afford it, and he didn't want his son joining ranks with the cultural elite. Jonathon's tentative offer of financial assistance was furiously rebuffed, and all the goodwill that had built up between Jonathon and Frank evaporated. Still, Dan held out against his father's express wishes that he join a union and start honorable work on the railroad. The final compromise was that he'd attend Idaho State Academy in Pocatello, where he could afford to earn his own tuition and live at home to minimize expense. He knew that this would hobble his ambitions to be accepted as a fully accredited musician with some of the nationally recognized groups, but he reasoned that it would give him time to grow up to the point where he could force his way out of Pocatello and out from under the dominance of his father.

Because of all these tensions, the August quorum meeting breakfast at the Richardses' was a subdued and somber event. With Trevor scheduled to leave for California in four weeks, the group knew that their happy association was about to come to an end. In spite of an occasional attempt to crack a joke or stir up conversation, the meal was eaten mostly in silence. It was Margaret who finally hit on an idea that lit things up.

"Do you all remember what a wonderful time you had on the trip to Salt Lake City the first year you were together?" Everyone mumbled their assent. "And since then you've found other activities." Heads nodded. "Well, why not one last, grand event to culminate your quorum experience?"

Jonathon looked up and said, "What do you have in mind? The boys all have jobs, you know."

"I know, but they could get a few days off, certainly. Maybe a trip to Boise or something." That fell flat. "I know," she said excitedly. "Jeanette Williams was telling us about a trip her family took into Yellowstone Park earlier this spring. They hiked to a remote location called Beckler Meadows where there are hot springs and interesting geological sites. Why don't you all go camping for two or three nights?"

There wasn't an immediate groundswell of support, but Leonard indicated that one of his father's friends had done the same trip and talked about what a great experience it was. Then Trevor added that if he could take his motorcycle or a car, he'd always wanted to go touring to places like Old Faithful and the Paint Pots. Before long, people were talking in earnest about how they could put a trip together on short notice, and soon plans were being drafted and assignments made, and the room became as cheerful as usual.

The final outline was that they'd all take off on the nineteenth of August and go to West Yellowstone on the train. Jonathon arranged to transport enough automobiles to get them to the trailhead for Beckler Meadows, which was barely inside the boundaries of Yellowstone Park. They'd do a fifty-mile hike in four days. When it was over, those who had to get back to work would take the train home, while those who had a few more days—Trevor, Dan, and Sam— would take a car to see Old Faithful and the other sites, returning a few days later. There wasn't much time, so everybody started getting ready.

Bishop Peterson was reluctant to take off work, but a fortuitous late shipment of lumber meant that he'd be idle anyway, so he agreed to go with the group. It was late enough in the season that Sam's father said he'd like to go, particularly since he hadn't accompanied the group on any of their previous trips. Even Leonard's father was able to take a few days of vacation, and it was a given that Jonathon would go. Frank wasn't happy that Dan was going to leave, but at eighteen, Dan was old enough to decide for himself, and even Frank wasn't up to another argument. He made it clear, though, that he wasn't going to go on any trip with "those hypocrites," a decision which pleased Dan to no end. He wished that he were in a position to move out, as Kelly had done the year before, but Kelly was going to school on a football scholarship. Unfortunately, there was no financial help for a music major. It was obvious from Kelly's grades that he didn't much care about school, but he did love playing football and was really quite accomplished at it.

The trip up to Yellowstone was beautiful as the train wound its way through the lodgepole pines of Island Park, arriving at West Yellowstone late that afternoon. They stayed in some rented cabins that evening and then set out for the trailhead at Beckler Meadows early the next morning. The first day was something of a forced march—they wanted to cover as much ground as possible early on so they'd have time to relax at the meadows. But they didn't make it as far as they hoped and ended up spending the first night camped about ten miles from the trailhead under the sheltering cove of a rock outcrop. The problem was that they'd had to ford the stream twice that day, and all the young men had gotten their feet wet—first Elmer who had tripped; then Sam, who had been shoved by Elmer for laughing; followed by Trevor, who'd rushed to Sam's defense; followed by Leonard, who'd lost his balance laughing; finished by Dan, who was attacked en masse by the group because he was whining about not wanting to get his feet wet. The fathers had been wise enough to get securely out of the way while the melee ensued. Wet feet and long hikes don't mix well, so the leaders had called a halt to the day's activities so the boys could dry out.

As the boys roasted their stockings by the fire, the conversation wandered amiably, with questions from the mundane to the profound. It was Elmer, the philosopher of the group, who asked why there was a new war once again in Europe. Jonathon kept quiet to see what the response would be, but generally no one had any really good answers.

"Perhaps because I'm from England, I've been following this more closely than most Americans. It's likely that some of the boys I knew in childhood will be involved." Everyone looked up expectantly. "The essence of the conflict is this: When Germany came into being as a state in 1870, it prevailed against France in the Franco-Prussian War, actually invading Paris. At the end of that war, the Germans returned to their own lines, except for keeping a fertile tract of land called Alsace-Lorraine on the French and German border. The French have hated them ever since and want that province back. Germany, meanwhile, has developed into one of the world's leading industrial powers, but Kaiser Wilhelm II doesn't feel it gets the respect it deserves. He's a small-minded man, vain and temperamental. He believes that Germany should really rule over a united Europe. In the past, when Queen Victoria of England was alive, she kept the peace. She was the mother, grandmother, or aunt of nearly all the crowned heads of Europe. The king of England is actually Kaiser Wilhelm's cousin. The problem is that Wilhelm is a lot of bluster and pomp and was almost insanely jealous of King George's father because of his distinguished standing in international affairs. To offset some of the prestige the British enjoy because of their navy, Wilhelm embarked on an ambitious program of expanding his navy, having built a dozen Dreadnought-class warships at incredible cost to the German people."

"So Wilhelm is the bad guy in all this?"

"The Germans don't think so, of course, but from my point of view, that's correct, Trevor. Of course, it's not just the kaiser. The German military is extremely aggressive and has a great deal of influence over the government's decisions."

"So why would anybody want to go to war? What good is it to kill people over a piece of ground?" The group was surprised, since Sam didn't usually talk much in settings like this. It was his father who replied.

"People don't usually fight just over ground. They fight over control. Our own Civil War cost hundreds of thousands of lives because the Southerners felt they were entitled to form their own country, while the Northerners thought they should stay part of the Union. My own father was killed fighting in that war."

Jonathon added, "In the case of the current war, it's as much a fight over ideas as boundaries. Germany subscribes to the theory that nature is improved by the struggle for the 'survival of the fittest' that Charles Darwin spoke of. The great German philosophers Nietzsche, Hegel, and Goethe believe that the strongest nations should prevail over weaker nations. From their point of view, war is a good thing, since the weak people are killed and only the strong survive. So while you see killing as a bad thing, Sam, some Germans see it as a glorious venture to prove the natural superiority of the German people."

"I think that's ridiculous," Sam fired back. "I work with animals every day, and if that were true, the lions would have eaten all the cows long ago. But the cows survive." He was obviously agitated. "War is evil, and I predict that this one will be awful. We have a lot worse weapons now than we've ever had before."

"You're probably correct, Sam," Jonathon said with a sigh. "But from what I read, both sides believe it will be over within six or seven weeks. They're both looking to knock out the other side with a massive initial assault."

"Well, they can't both be right. And if their first plan fails, then what?"

There was silence. The intensity of Sam's feeling was surprising, and nobody wanted to make him more agitated.

"It's really as simple as this," Jonathon finally replied. "Germany thinks it should stand preeminent in European affairs, France wants her property back, England wants to maintain a balance of power on the Continent, and Austria wants to regain some of her past glory. Italy simply hopes to share in some of the spoils of war. That's a lot to settle in one war, and, like you, Sam, I'm afraid the cost will be high."

Bishop Peterson ended the discussion by saying, "I do hope they're right about the war being short-lived. I hate the thought of people suffering and dying for national pride alone." Then he suggested they have a brief devotional before turning in for the night.

The mood brightened as they threw a few more logs onto the fire. Out there under the stars, it felt natural to speak of God and His creations, and the devotional soon turned into a testimony meeting.

* * *

The next day was enjoyable but long. The group covered the remaining fifteen miles to Beckler Meadows without any incidents. No one knew exactly what to expect, having focused all their energy on the task of just getting there; but when they did arrive, what they found was a large, open field surrounded by a thick stand of lodgepole pines, with three very different ponds in the center of the field. The first was a natural-temperature pond fed by the stream. The second was a small, bubbling hot pond that could easily boil eggs in a matter of moments. The third was a large, moss-filled pond the temperature of a warm bath. The two hot springs were filled with brightly colored rocks that seemed almost to glow in the deep blue water, caused by years of calcification of the minerals that were prevalent in Yellowstone.

The next day was to be filled with activities, such as target practice, swimming, and archery. It was tempting to go swimming in the larger spring, but they arrived so late that everyone was tired. After fixing a quick dinner, they hurriedly threw up tents. The adults carefully placed their tent with drainage in mind, taking the trouble to make trenches on the high side to divert water around the tent if it should rain. But with clear skies overhead, the boys skipped that effort and crawled into their bedrolls exhausted. At 3:00 A.M., they regretted their decision when a lightning storm lit up the sky, followed by a cloudburst that flooded rain through the floor of the canvas tent in minutes. Soon they were sloshing in their bedrolls, too miserable to get up and do anything about it, but freezing in the water. By sunrise, all five were shivering and desperate for warmth.

After lying there freezing for a while, Trevor said, "I'm going to go jump in that hot pool."

"Are you crazy? It's barely sunrise. You can't go swimming this early."

"I'm not going swimming. I'm going to save my life before I shiver myself to death." With that, Trevor crawled out of his bedroll and, in his underwear, raced across the marshy area between his tent and the pond. A loud splash followed by a contented cry encouraged the others. Soon, there were five boys floating and swimming and diving in the naturally hot water of the pond. The sulfur smell was a little tough to live with at first, but they soon became immune to it. The adults came out and groaned at them, but when they saw the condition of the boys' tent and sleeping blankets, they understood why. Jonathon patiently strung a rope between some nearby trees, and the fathers hung up all their boys' wet things to dry. Fortunately, with the sunrise, the storm clouds evaporated and the sun came out. After about an hour, Jonathon asked if the boys were hungry, but they weren't, claiming that they were still trying to get the cold out. After two hours, the leaders changed into their swimming suits and joined the boys in the pool. At around 10:30 A.M., Trevor declared himself boiled, crawled out of the pool, and found his way to a large, flat rock to dry off in the sun. Eventually they managed to get their clothes dry enough to get dressed and rebuild something of a campsite.

"You know, this is all because of lack of patience on your part," Jonathon said to Trevor under his breath.

"I know, I know. But things worked out."

"This time, because we were by a hot spring. But you're not going to find conditions quite so amicable in the future. The only way to assure your own survival is to be meticulous in your preparation. Never leave things to chance, like you did last night. You'll notice that the adults' tent stayed dry and toasty, while the five of you nearly froze."

It wasn't often that Jonathon Richards got grumpy, and it should have sobered Trevor to be spoken to so sternly. But somehow it amused him, and he burst out laughing. That really got to his father.

"I wasn't trying to be funny, Trevor."

"I know that, sir," he said, calming down. "But you've got to admit it's pretty hilarious that we had to pick our way barefoot through the marsh grass because of our own stupidity. I think this is a lesson that teaches itself."

Jonathon softened. "I hope so. Who knows what situations you'll find yourself in again?" Then, turning to the group, he added, "Remember, you should always carry a compass, and you should always keep your feet dry. With those two tasks taken care of, there's almost no situation you can't get yourself out of." Trevor loved it when his father slipped into his "English" style of speaking. He didn't realize that he was doing it, but it always came out when he was impatient or trying to make a point. The rest of the time his accent was almost unnoticeable.

After spending the rest of the day fishing, swimming, and relaxing, the group prepared to start down the trail to get a head start on their return to the base camp. They hiked for about two hours and set up camp at dusk. This time, the young men put their tent up properly, with drainage ditches that could have held most of the flow of the Snake River. Naturally, it didn't rain that night. Prior to turning in, they had another delightful evening around the campfire, eating and talking. The next morning they arose early and continued hiking.

At around 3:00 P.M., Leonard, Trevor, and Dan were out ahead of the rest of the group with just a few miles to go to reach the cars when Leonard saw a movement off to his left. Since they needed to wait for the others to catch up anyway, he said he wanted to see what it was. Dan and Trevor sat down on a rock to rest and started chatting.

A few moments later, Dan shushed Trevor and said, "Something's wrong, listen."

"I don't hear anything—"

Then they heard the whimpering sound of a small animal, followed by a roar and a crashing sound from the trees. Trevor jumped up and tore through the trees in the direction where Leonard had gone. He burst into a clearing to see Leonard standing between a bear cub and its mother. The huge bear was advancing on Leonard, who stood motionless with fear.

"Run," Dan shouted. Leonard turned and looked at him, and then took off running. But in running from the mother bear, he was heading directly toward the cub.

"This way," Trevor shouted, but Leonard didn't stop. In a moment, the mother bear had tackled him and knocked him to the ground. Leonard was flailing about desperately as the bear seemed to pick him up with her mouth and throw him around. There was no time to lose, so Trevor made the decision to run at full speed and tackle the bear from behind. He knew that if he got in front of her, she would attack him, so he planned his blow to land on the bear's back. With the full force of his weight crashing into the bear's body, he knocked her off balance enough to stop her work on Leonard. Trevor threw his arms around the bear's neck and made a mental vow to hang on, no matter what she did. The bear thrashed and turned, trying to flip Trevor off so she could attack him, but he wrapped his legs around her stomach and grabbed great handfuls of fur to give himself a grip. Raging and roaring, the bear stood up on her hind legs, while Trevor hung on desperately. Then she backed into a tree. Her weight crushed into Trevor's ribs and knocked the wind out of his lungs, forcing him to release his grasp. The bear lurched forward, and Trevor felt himself starting to fall to the ground. As he started sliding down the bear's back, there was a dull thud of a sound two or three inches in front of him, and he felt something splatter on his face. Without a sound, the giant animal dropped to the ground, lifeless. Trevor was in a tangle on top of the heap. Only then did it register that he'd heard the concussion of a rifle, and he turned to see Dan running directly for him, rifle in hand. He took a deep breath of air to reinflate his lungs and rolled off the carcass.

"You shot the bear!" he said incredulously.

"I didn't know what else to do. She would have killed both of you. Are you okay?"

Trevor wasn't okay. It was difficult to breathe, and his chest had an odd depression on the right side. "I think I broke a rib," he said breathlessly. "But I'll be okay. Go check on Leonard."

Leonard was a few yards away, twisting and turning in apparent agony. Dan could see that his left leg had been torn almost all the way off, and he was losing blood rapidly. Dan dropped to his knees and pulled off his belt. He wrapped it around Leonard's thigh and tightened it into a tourniquet.

In a few moments, the blood from the wound stopped seeping. Leonard was still writhing in agony, with wounds to his arms and face.

Dan looked up gratefully as he heard Jonathon Richards call out "What happened?" then, "Oh, no! Quick, we need help!" The others in the party came rushing onto the scene and moved in to help. Bishop Peterson had been trained as a medic years earlier, so he took over helping Leonard. They tore his pant leg off and attempted to bind his leg with a sheet that the bishop pulled from his pack. But it was obvious that the leg was far too injured to be saved. The best they could do was to get him to a doctor who could amputate it properly.

Meanwhile, Jonathon had sat down with Trevor and was holding his head in his lap. He could feel his son's broken rib, but in listening to his breathing, he didn't think it sounded as if his lung had been punctured. Trevor kept saying that he was okay, but he was awfully pale, and he kept trying to close his eyes. Jonathon talked patiently with him while they got Leonard stabilized. Sam and his father had immediately gone to work, cutting four poles that they used to build two stretchers. Leonard's father was comforting his son while the bishop worked to bind up his other wounds.

Finally, when they were ready to move the boys, Jonathon helped transfer Trevor to the stretcher. It was only then that he realized that Dan was missing. Jonathon wandered off a ways looking for him and soon found Dan sitting against a rock, sobbing. Jonathon came up and put his arm around him.

"You all right, Dan?"

"I didn't want to have to shoot, but I didn't know what else to do. The bear was going to kill them!"

"I'm glad you did shoot. You saved both their lives."

"Why did it have to be that way?" he sobbed. "The bear was only trying to protect her baby. Why didn't Leonard run the right way so she'd have left him alone?"

"People panic," Jonathon said evenly. "None of us knows how we'd have reacted if the bear had been after us."

Dan looked up and asked urgently, "Will they be all right? Are Trevor and Leonard going to live?"

"I think so. Trevor has a broken rib, but I don't think he has internal bleeding. Leonard's going to lose his leg, although he doesn't know that yet. But we've got the bleeding stopped. We need to go fast, but I want to make sure you're all right."

Dan looked at him miserably. "I'm all right. I just don't know why something like this happens. They're both such good guys . . ." He dropped his face again.

Jonathon felt his anguish. Dan's artistic temperament was revealing itself. The same emotional responsiveness that made him sensitive to music increased his distress at a time of trauma. "Look at me, Dan." Dan kept his face down. "Danny, I need you to look at me." Reluctantly, Dan raised his face. "Life doesn't follow a script, Dan. Sometimes bad things happen. That's part of why we have a mortal experience. When something goes wrong, all we can do is make the best decision possible in view of the circumstances and then go on. You made the best choice you could and, in so doing, saved their lives. I'm very grateful."

"I'm glad too," Dan said as he stood up, regaining his composure. "Who'd have ever thought that all the practicing my father made me do with the rifle would one day help me save somebody's life?"

"You just never know, do you?" Jonathon led the way back to the group.

When they got back to the site of the accident, Leonard and Trevor were trussed up on the stretchers, ready to go. But as the group started forward, they heard a plaintive cry above them.

"Oh, no," Dan said. "It's the cub." They stopped and looked up into the tree to see the cub huddling out of harm's way, crying out for its mother.

"Can we take him out with us?" Sam asked. "I could find a preserve or something to raise him on."

Sam's father put his arm on his son's shoulder. "There isn't time, Sam. We've got to get Leonard to the doctor immediately. And the cub will never make it on its own out here. He'll have to be put down so he doesn't suffer from starvation."

Sam pushed his father's arms off as he let out a strangled cry and moved as if he were going to stand between them and the bear. But then he dropped his head in sorrow as he realized the wisdom of what his father was saying.

"Maybe I could borrow your gun," Jonathon said to Dan. "I think even I could make that shot."

"No," Dan said, wiping away the tears. "I'll do it. I killed his mother, and so I should be the one to take care of him too. Besides, no offense, Brother Richards, but I want to make sure that it takes just one shot, and I know I can do that."

Jonathon looked at him tenderly. "All right, then. We'll move out just a bit, and then you catch up with us."

"Yes, sir."

Jonathon knew that Dan would need a moment or two alone to compose himself when it was over. About sixty seconds after they started down the trail, they heard a single rifle shot. A few minutes later, Dan caught up with them, tears streaming silently down his face. Sam wordlessly went up and put his arm around his shoulder, and the two of them hiked down the trail in silence.

In a matter of a few minutes, Leonard's life was changed forever. In some ways, everybody's life was different after that. While men were being killed on the battlefields of Belgium and France, a subdued group of nine made their way home to Pocatello, where Leonard would have to adjust to a new reality for his future. August had shattered its first dream.

Chapter Eight

STANFORD UNIVERSITY

Palo Alto, California, and Pocatello, Idaho
September 1914–May 1917

Trevor recovered without incident. His ribs had been broken, but some simple wrapping gave them time to heal, and it didn't seem to interfere with his range of motion very much. In time, Leonard was fitted with an artificial limb that allowed him to move around with a single crutch. But the railroad made it clear that there was no way he could maintain his apprenticeship. The risk was simply too high in the locomotive department, where parts weighed hundreds, even thousands, of pounds and quick reaction time was essential to maintaining safety. Jonathon got in touch with his father in Salt Lake City, and Eliot said he'd be pleased to have a detail mechanic to work on carburetors and other workbench-type products. So Leonard found himself moving to Salt Lake, where he took up an apprenticeship at Richards's Fine Automobiles. In time, he discovered that he actually enjoyed that type of work more than he would have liked the heavier mechanics he'd been learning at the railroad, and he was soon able to support himself.

Trevor went with his parents to Palo Alto, California, where he moved into university housing with three roommates. The San Francisco Bay Area had a delightful climate, and his father tried to make him feel good by complaining that he was really getting the best end of the deal, living amidst palm trees and the lush, verdant hills of the San Francisco peninsula. But Trevor was unmoved and told his father that they ought to change positions if he thought it was such a great place.

"You'd never settle down to manage a railroad," Jonathon replied. "It takes too much patience. You'd have trains going every which direction in no time."

"You're probably right," Trevor sighed. He moved in and determined to make the best of it.

Dan took up studies at the Idaho State Academy, where he found devoted teachers who did everything possible to help him advance his talents, even though his skill would have qualified him for a more established institution. Still, his principal teacher knew musical theory and had actually sung in the Chicago Opera, so Dan had plenty to learn from him. Margaret Richards had already put him through the basic textbooks, so his music instructor helped him craft an individual course of study in both piano and voice, with the promise that he could graduate in as few as two and a half years and then, hopefully, transfer to a full university to pursue a master's degree.

Trevor returned home to work for the railroad in the summer of 1915. Although no one formally set up the meetings, all the boys from the original quorum started showing up the second week of the month (since Jonathon still had the current crop of teachers meeting on the first Sunday) for an informal quorum meeting. They were all elders now and all still active in the Church. Leonard even attended twice, while home from Salt Lake visiting his family.

On their first Sunday together, Trevor told them about the great Pan-American Exposition that was built in San Francisco to honor America's role in constructing the Panama Canal, the largest single engineering project in the history of the world. Since the San Francisco earthquake nine years earlier had pretty much flattened the city, the goal of hosting the international exposition had given the local residents a target date to rebuild their city, and the results were amazing. Trevor explained, "Where nothing but flimsy earthquake traps once existed, tall buildings now reach to the sky, reinforced with concrete and steel. My engineering class studied how they've redesigned the buildings to do better in a future earthquake. The weird thing, though, is that the exposition itself is built out of plaster of paris and plywood. It's all fake! You go into a building that looks like a grand Italian palace, only to find that it's two-by-fours and chicken wire. Still, they have exhibitions on all the latest technology, including the most amazing nighttime display lighting you've ever seen. There's even a giant Underwood typewriter that's big enough for people to climb on, showing how important they think typewriters will be."

"I think they're important," said Jonathon, joining in the conversation. "For the first time, I can dictate to a secretary and have her issue orders that are legible. Nobody could ever read my handwriting." The boys all laughed.

Of course, the next inevitable question was how Trevor liked school and living in California, where it was warm in the winter. He replied by telling them about the air shows he'd been to and the fact that he'd actually started enjoying engineering since he could see it would help when he was ready to take up flying. He went on to say that he was ready to take lessons immediately but that his parents had made him promise not to until he got his degree. His father was about to say something when Trevor jumped in. "It's a fair requirement for them to place on me, because I know that if I got my pilot's license, that would be the last I ever stepped foot in a school again." Jonathon smiled appreciatively, and Trevor continued. "As to the weather, it's so perfect, it gets a little boring. The seasons are backward, with summer actually being quite cool and foggy as the heat of the land draws in mist from the ocean. Kind of weird, but nice."

When they asked Dan about ISA, he laughed and said that he was doing fine in his course work and could be certified as a teacher in another year. He hoped to move to a bigger city where he might be able to perform professionally on occasion, but he was getting reconciled to the fact that his future was teaching music, not performing it.

The next summer—1916—Trevor stayed in California to work with an engineering firm in San Francisco that was developing new designs for internal combustion engines. The next time he came home to Pocatello was in December 1916. By then, the Germans were threatening to launch unrestricted submarine warfare against all parties suspected of providing aid to the Allies because the British blockade was driving many Germans almost to the point of starvation. Germany's leaders felt they had no choice but to break the blockade. This, in turn, brought America to a fever pitch for war. Almost everybody was furious with the Germans and saying things like, "We need to go over there and teach them a lesson." Sam would always get into trouble because he'd reply with something like, "How many more lives need to be thrown into the meat-grinder before they learn the lesson? Do you really think American blood will satisfy the demons?" His anti-war rhetoric was not well received, since patriotism was running high. Even Trevor got into it with him, saying that Captain Moroni himself thought it was okay to take up arms to defend one's freedom. Dan listened silently to the arguments without really taking sides, but he felt like he probably leaned closer to Sam's point of view than Trevor's.

At the end of Christmas vacation, Trevor was up late talking to Dan when a thought struck him.

"Hey, Danny, why don't you come with me to California for a visit?"

"Why do you call me Danny? Nobody else does."

"I don't know. It just seems natural. I don't do it to make you angry. You've just always been Danny. Maybe it's that brother thing."

"I suppose it's okay, then, but only from you. Your mother calls me Daniel, your father calls me Dan, and you call me Danny. You are one mixed-up family."

Trevor smiled. "Easier to love because we're so odd?"

"I suppose so. Now what were you fantasizing about?"

"Oh, yeah. Why don't you come to California with me? You're done with school, and you don't have a teaching job yet. Why not come visit my friends and see Stanford? It's an amazing place. Plus, there are some very lovely ladies there, and I notice that you don't have anyone special here." He had a twinkle in his eye. "Leonard's married, Sam's getting married, and Elmer will probably never get married. Then there's you."

"Me? What about you? Do you have anybody special?"

"There is this one girl. She's probably the only other Mormon on the whole San Francisco peninsula. The nice thing is that she's really very beautiful, and I even think she likes me. But she thinks I'm reckless, and she's a practical person. I may be able to win her over someday, but right now we're just really good friends."

"I should meet her," Dan said. "She's probably just waiting for the right guy to come along, and . . . who knows?"

"Oh, right. Come to town and take my girl. That would be just like you. So what do you say? Can you come?"

Dan nodded thoughtfully. It was impractical, served no useful purpose, and sounded great. Plus, it would irritate his father. He'd moved into his own apartment a year earlier, so he hardly ever saw his father anymore, particularly since his mother had passed away six months ago from complications of the flu. At first he thought he should go over to see Frank on a regular basis, but they just sat in silence. When Kelly was there, he and Frank would talk about the union and things at work and ignore Dan. So there was nothing holding him in Pocatello, and he had enough money saved up from working with Bishop Peterson that he could probably afford the trip. He'd face up to long-term employment when he got back. One of the people at church had told him that there was going to be an opening at the high school for a music teacher, so he thought he might look into that, even though what he really wanted was to get an advanced degree and teach at the university level or maybe go to Los Angeles or some other place to sing.

"All right, I'll go."

"You will? That's terrific. I've got to leave in two days, so let's get cracking." They rushed downstairs to tell Trevor's parents, who both thought it was a great idea. Jonathon made a few calls to arrange their transportation.

Two days later, Dan found himself snuggled in a first-class seat on the Southern Pacific Railroad. From a scenery point of view, the most exciting part of the trip was the climb up the grade of the Sierra Nevada Mountains. The train had to pass through dozens of rock tunnels and over intricate lattice trestles that gave it a fairy-tale feeling. But most interesting were the snow tunnels at the very top, where the train would disappear for more than a mile into long, wooden tunnels that were designed to keep the tracks clear of snow. "It must be something to see the whole train disappear under the snow in the middle of winter," Dan said as they emerged from yet another tunnel. Trevor loved the mechanics involved in the railroad, especially now that he'd studied engineering. He readily agreed and entered into a lengthy discussion of the tremendous engineering work that went into building these tracks through seemingly impassable mountain traverses. Dan found himself fascinated, both by what Trevor had to teach him and by the fact that his friend had matured so much. Trevor had never taken school all that seriously, but it was obvious that he was really applying himself at Stanford. Dan smiled to himself to think that Trevor was actually settling down.

After reaching Oakland, they took a steamer ferry across the San Francisco Bay and registered at a hotel for the evening. After spending a day in San Francisco so Dan could experience a really big city, they found a train south to Palo Alto. Arriving late at the dormitory, Trevor awakened his roommates with his clunking around.

"Knock it off, Richards!"

"Quiet, Stu, you'll wake the others." Three pillows smacked him.

"So it's over," one of the other bodies said. "For three weeks we've been able to get some sleep at night because you were gone. Now it's back to Richards time."

"So I have trouble getting to sleep at night—at least you get the benefit of my company again."

"Who's this?" By now his roommates had given up on having a normal night's sleep, so someone turned on a lamp and six eyes looked out from two sets of bunk beds.

"This, my friends, is my brother Danny. But you have to call him Dan."

"I didn't think you had a brother."

"I do. We just weren't born to the same parents. You know about Danny—I've told you everything."

"Hi, Dan," one of them said, standing up and offering his hand. "I'm Stuart, this is Bill, and the quiet one over there is Jim." Stuart had an odd accent. It sounded English, but not quite. Stuart noticed the furrowed brow and said, "Australian, mate. Here on an exchange program. Except that I don't think I'll exchange my way back. The climate is good for my naturally masculine complexion." The others grimaced. "Plus, your brother there has about talked me into going into business with him building airplanes. Heaven help me if I know how to build airplanes, but I do seem to have a knack for business, so who knows? At the very least, we'll have fun wasting the investors' money."

Dan laughed. He could see why Trevor liked these guys.

"You can sleep on the couch over there," Stuart continued. "That is, unless you plan to move in permanently, in which case we'll have to find something more suitable." The room was hardly large enough for four, so the last proposition was ridiculous.

By now, Jim was awake. "Are you the one who's a musician?"

"I am."

"Do you play ragtime?"

"Ragtime, classics, musical theatre—you name it, and I'll figure out how to play it."

"And sing too," Trevor added. "That's what he's really famous for, singing."

By now Trevor was mostly unpacked and had changed into his pajamas. Dan had made a bed for himself and was also getting ready to fall asleep.

"I'll tell you what," said Stu. "There's a club in town where they have an open stage on Friday night. Maybe you can play and sing there."

Dan looked at Trevor blankly. "It's okay," Trevor said. "We may need to help some of them home, but the club is mostly for students, so it's a good environment. I think you'd like going there. You'll hear some really great music. Plus, I suspect you can show them something yourself."

"I guess if I ever want to get paid for my music, this is as good a place to start as any."

"Who said anything about getting paid?" Stuart replied indignantly. "We're all just poor starving college students who have to get by on our fathers' millions."

"Shut up, Stuart," Bob said. "The poor guy's only been here twenty minutes. Too much of you, and he's likely to die of boredom before he even sees the campus."

"Fine, then, would someone please turn out the lights so I can get my sleep? I have a very fragile ego. That's a Freudian term for those of you who haven't yet studied the good Vienna doctor, and it's been bruised tonight. So good night!"

* * *

The next day, Trevor took Dan on a tour of the campus and then drove him over to Half Moon Bay on the Pacific Coast.

"I've never seen the ocean. The sound of the waves crashing on the rocks is wonderful."

"It figures that you'd notice the sound. I see how big and flat it is. Think how great it would be to go flying out over it to see what the water looks like from the air."

"Have you ever been up in the air?"

Trevor looked like he'd been hit with a brick. "I told you I promised my parents I wouldn't learn to fly until I was done with school."

"I didn't say anything about flying lessons, and you know it. Have you ever been flying—as a passenger?"

"I have, actually," Trevor said nonchalantly, "at the Pan-American Expo."

"I figured." Danny laughed. "Well, what was it like? Everything you hoped for?"

Trevor glanced up and to the left, as if lost in thought. "It was a lot better than I imagined, and I have a pretty vivid imagination. You feel almost weightless up there, like you're suspended from the clouds. Everything on the ground becomes miniature, like when you're looking down on the city from the top of a tall mountain—do you remember how Pocatello looked from the hills above City Creek?" Dan nodded. "Except that in an airplane you can move around to get the precise angle you want. We circled the exposition and flew out over Sausalito, where I saw the fishing boats tying up. People waved and laughed on the ground. I hoped it would never end."

"So have you been up since?"

"No. I couldn't trust myself. I made a deal with Father, and I have to keep it. But I'm nearly done with school, and then I can do what I really want to do."

At this point they'd descended down to the surf. Dan loved how the cold water splashed up against his legs and watched as the tiny sand crabs burrowed into the sand, their presence evident only by the bubbles that gurgled up through the wet granules.

"Danny, I've got something on my mind that I'm afraid to bring up with my parents."

"Your parents? You can talk to them about anything."

"Not this," he said seriously. "I have strong feelings about the war in Europe. Two kinds of feelings, actually. First, everything that's happening in aviation is taking place over there right now. The United States has a grand total of twenty-six combat airplanes in the entire U.S. Army right now, while the British and French have thousands. We invented the airplane in America, and yet all the techno-logical development is taking place in Europe because of the war. We don't have a single factory that can turn out a competitor for the French Blériot or Spad or the English Sopwiths, to say nothing of the German Fokkers. If I'm really serious about working in aviation, I have to get over there before the war ends so I can learn how to fly in even the most adverse conditions."

"But America isn't in the war. Besides, the death rate for pilots is astronomical. Do you really want to run an almost certain risk of getting killed?"

"I wouldn't go over there to get killed. I'd go over there to fight for freedom. That's the second thing. What the Germans are doing is just wrong. They want to dominate all of Europe and turn everyone but the Germans into second-class citizens. The American Revolution was fought for freedom, and the leaders of the Church tell us that it was a good and noble thing. They say that the gospel couldn't have been restored if we didn't have freedom. Now it's threatened in Europe, and somebody needs to stand up."

"I don't know that I see it that way. It's like Sam says. The Europeans have been fighting for thousands of years. They started this mess, so they ought to finish it. Besides, how can you get in if President Wilson holds to his campaign promise to keep us out?"

"I think we'll be drawn in eventually. The Germans are desperate, and they're going to start sinking every ship in sight. When Americans get killed, how can we stand on the sidelines? Besides, I could always join the Lafayette Escadrille."

"What's that?"

Trevor shook his head in disbelief. "Where have you been? The newsreels at the movie theatres, the articles in the paper—everybody knows about the American air units fighting under French command. The Lafayette Squadron."

"Sorry, I don't like thinking about the war. Hearing about the trenches and how ten or twenty thousand men can be mowed down in a single charge just sickens me. Maybe I listen to Sam too much, but it really does seem like we're living in the days of the Book of Mormon when men's lust for blood is out of control. I mean, something like twenty million people have been wounded or killed. It's staggering!"

"I'm not saying it's right. But if we don't help, the Germans could very easily win. And once they've conquered France, then they'll consolidate their power and use their economic power to subvert England. And once they get England, they'll go into Russia, and one day we'll be facing a monster across the ocean. I really think this is a moral issue,

Dan, and it's wrong for us to stand by and watch the European democracies and Russia go down to defeat."

"When are you going to sign up?"

"At the end of the semester, probably May. I need you to be with me when I tell my mom and my father. I think they'll support me in it, but it's going to be hard on them. It would be better if we were both there."

Dan sighed. "Don't worry. I'll be there. But I don't think I'll ever volunteer. I haven't picked up my rifle since the day I shot that bear in Yellowstone Park."

"That was hard for you, I know. I've never brought it up because you did it for of me. I've felt sorry I put you in that position."

"Don't ever think that, Trevor. I'd do it again in a second. You and Leonard were in trouble, and I was glad I could save you. I just hated having to kill an innocent animal to do it."

"Can I ask you something about that day?"

"Sure."

"The bullet that killed the bear—it couldn't have been more than two inches from my head. I had to wipe blood off my face. Did you worry that you might hit me?"

Dan stopped walking and turned to face Trevor. "Do you remember how you once said that you go cold when you're in a competition?" Trevor nodded. "That's exactly what happens to me when I shoot. I knew precisely where that bullet would hit, and I didn't fire until I knew I could kill the bear cleanly without putting you in danger. That's why it took so long and the bear had time to back into the tree. I could have shot her earlier than that, but not without some risk." The pace of Dan's breathing had increased, but Trevor didn't say anything. "I'd never do anything that would hurt you, Trevor. Not anything."

"I know that," Trevor said as calmly as he could. "That wasn't what I meant at all. I always thought how scary it must have been for you to have taken a difficult shot like that, knowing that I may have had only seconds before the bear shook me off so it could turn to attack me. I worried about you. Anyway, I'm glad that you were there."

They started walking along the beach again. It was Dan who broke the silence. "To tell the truth, that's one of the reasons I've tried to keep the war out of my mind. I know that if I ever have to go to war, my marksmanship will almost guarantee me a spot in the infantry, where I'd have to kill people. I just don't want to do that. I know I would do it, because that's what is expected, and I even know it would be for a good cause. If you go to France, don't worry that I'll think you're bloodthirsty or anything. I'm glad that people are over there fighting for freedom. I just don't know what it would do to me if I was one of them."

There was nothing to say to that. Some battles were private.

Trevor and Danny began to race in the surf, the ocean breeze blowing furious and cold through their hair. They ran, as in the old days, until they could hardly take another step. The air at sea level was rich and moist, and it felt wonderful to be free from the cares of the day.

* * *

Friday night turned out to be one of those events that has the potential to change a life. Trevor and Danny met Stuart and the others at the Stanford Club. After a short performance by the regular musicians, the stage was declared open for anyone who wanted to show their stuff. Some of the students went up and sang, most doing a credible job, while others danced to songs played by the orchestra. Dan had about decided to pass when Stuart stood up and loudly proclaimed, "Ladies and gentlemen, if I could have your attention. We have the distinct privilege of having new

blood in the room. Would those of you who are sick and
tired of listening to my pal Bill stand before you each Friday
night please welcome Mr. Daniel O'Brian of Pocatello,
Idaho!" People cheered. Stuart was obviously a regular
whom everyone liked.

Dan's heart was pounding as he went onto the stage. He
was nervous enough that he didn't trust his voice to be
steady for the first number, so he decided to try to wind
them up with a medley of ragtime numbers on the piano,
beginning with "12th Street Rag," "Alexander's Ragtime
Band," and "MacNamara's Band." Although the songs were
a little old, his arrangement was unique, and his playing
absolutely sizzled. The crowd cheered at the end of the
number and called out for more.

Dan looked out and saw that a lovely young woman was
now standing by Trevor, who tipped a mock salute back to
Dan when he saw that he was looking. When the crowd
quieted, Dan stood and said, "I'm new here, but I like it a
lot already. I'd like to dedicate this next song to my best
friend, Trevor Richards, and to Sarah, who has joined him."
He then proceeded to do a piano introduction. The crowd
turned to look at Trevor and Sarah. Trevor bit his lip and
gave Dan a dirty look. But the moment Dan started singing,
the room went quiet and all eyes turned his way. His
delivery was perfect, and the timbre of his voice was rich and
easy. But it was the way he caressed the melody with his
unique interpretation that awed them.

When he finished, he received raucous applause, as well
as calls for more.

"What do you want to hear?" he asked.

"Tipperary!" someone called out.

Dan laughed. "So you want an Irish ballad/war song?"
He started the stirring march, march, march of "It's a Long
Way to Tipperary." In no time, he had everyone in the club
stamping their feet as if they were marching and singing

along with him at the top of their lungs. For the next forty-five minutes, he sang and played, while the crowd periodically joined in on the chorus. They sang their way through "Smiles," "Pretty Baby," and "Poor Butterfly." Then he sang solo. That brought them to their feet. If there were others who wanted to perform that night, they were out of luck, because the crowd loved Dan O'Brian. Finally, to end the performance, he sang a haunting rendition of "Deep River" by Harry T. Burleigh. The rich melody was moving and had a subduing effect.

"You're not going to end it that way," someone called from the crowd.

"You'll have to ask me back sometime," Dan responded cheerfully, then started down from the stage. The band musicians ordered a break, and people from the band and the crowd came up to congratulate him.

Trevor turned to Sarah and said, "I've never seen him so happy. He's usually pretty stiff, but tonight he just let loose. It's great."

When the band started playing again, Dan walked over to Trevor to formally meet Sarah Nichols. She was delightful—fun, witty, attractive. She obviously liked Trevor, and she mixed well with his friends. But it soon became obvious that the others wanted to start drinking, so Trevor said that the three of them ought to leave. "I'm afraid that Sarah and I inhibit them, which is probably a good thing. But I want to enjoy the evening our way, so maybe we can take a walk across the campus."

As they reached the door, however, an older man came up and asked Dan if he could talk to him for a moment. Dan was surprised, so he didn't react immediately. Trevor stepped in and said, "Let me introduce you two. Danny, this is Professor Bramson, head of the music department. Professor, this is Dan O'Brian, a friend of mine from southern Idaho."

"Pleased to meet you, Dan."

"Thank you, sir."

"I hope you don't mind my intruding on your evening, but I was surprised at your singing tonight."

"In a positive way, I hope."

The professor laughed. "Very positively, in fact. I know you only played popular tunes, but the way you form your words makes me think that you may have had some classical training. Am I correct in that assumption?"

"He has a bachelor's degree in music, sir. He started training six years ago with my mother and has since moved through the best teachers Idaho has to offer."

Dan's face flushed.

"Let me get right to the point, Dan. I have a theory about musicians who can perform both classical and popular music. Could you possibly arrange your schedule to visit with me and a number of other professors at the university tomorrow? I'd like to try an experiment, if you're game."

Dan hesitated but decided he had nothing to lose. "I guess that would be okay. Should I do something to prepare?"

"No, just show up at 10:00 A.M. I may ask you to play or sing a couple of numbers. Perhaps Richards here can help you find the way?"

Trevor assured the professor they'd be there.

The next morning Dan, Trevor, and Sarah arrived early and were ushered into a magnificent music room with dark, paneled wood and beautiful floor-to-ceiling windows looking out on the lush campus with its palm trees and sculpted gardens. Dan also saw a group of four professors seated at a table.

"Dan, allow me to introduce my colleagues." Professor Bramson then recited the names and credentials of his three colleagues. "I've invited you here today because there's some skepticism in the musical community that a musician can maintain classical skills while playing contemporary music.

Your performance last night makes me think that attitude is wrong. Would you mind telling us about yourself?"

This was more than Dan had bargained for, but he recited his history with music, somewhat apologetic that he'd never had formal training in a more recognized setting.

"Please don't worry about that," Bramson said. "All I'd like you to do is to play four numbers—two popular, two classical. Do you need any music?"

Dan's mind raced as he tried to decide what songs to play. He settled on Trevor's favorite popular songs and Margaret's favorite classical. He knew them all by heart. "No, thank you, sir, I can play from memory." The first song was contemporary piano, followed by classical piano. Then he did two numbers with voice, the final being an operatic piece that challenged his range.

The reception at the end was quite different than the night before. There was no applause, no cheers, virtually no response at all. The group thanked him and asked if he, Trevor, and Sarah would wait in the corridor.

Stepping outside, Dan said, "What's that all about?"

"I honestly have no idea. Bramson is well thought of by all the students, I know that. The others are pretty stuffy. They'd never go out to a student club."

After they had waited for perhaps fifteen minutes, Bramson invited them back in. The other professors were gone, probably through a side door that led to their offices. "Dan, I think you have an unusual talent, one that, if fully developed, could lead to some great opportunities both on and off the stage. Your performances last night and this morning support my theory that truly gifted musicians can respond to music of any genre. In fact, I believe that success in one area leads to a better understanding of the other. Can you tell me how you feel about that?"

"I agree completely, sir. Trevor's mother loved classical and opera, but she insisted I learn to play other types of music, probably because she knew that in Pocatello I'd have far greater opportunity to share with people if I could play a variety of music. I love it all—contemporary, classical, negro-spiritual, folk—I just love being part of it."

"Have you ever thought of going for an advanced degree, perhaps here at Stanford?"

That caught Dan so off guard that he burst out laughing when he should have shown more respect. It was just so preposterous that he didn't even consider whom he was talking to. "Me—at Stanford? I don't think so. We couldn't scrape together enough money to send me here if you garnished the wages of every working man in my family for the next ten years. Besides, my father wouldn't have anything to do with me attending a place like this. He's a labor man." Dan hadn't wanted to sound angry in his response, but he realized that his bitterness at going to ISA had never fully gone away.

"I understand perfectly. But I'm not easily dissuaded. When Leland Stanford and his wife created this university, it was their goal to create a West Coast equivalent to the Ivy League. The university was founded in honor of their only son, who died while they were traveling in Europe."

"I didn't know that, sir. I'm sorry." Dan was embarrassed now that he'd reacted as he did.

"The point is, Governor Stanford created more than an endowment for the university. He created a scholarship fund so that any student who has merit can attend the university without regard to his ability to pay. I believe you're the type of student that the governor had in mind. Since I have control over the music budget, if you would consider studying here, I believe we could work out a way to cover the costs."

Trevor slapped him on the back. "That's terrific, Dan. You can finally get the kind of direction you need. I may have to call you Dr. O'Brian someday."

Dan was having trouble breathing. It seemed impossible that he was having this conversation. Yet, there was Professor Bramson standing in front of him, and he knew that Trevor and Sarah were congratulating him, so it had to be real. Finally, he gained enough control to say, "I'd be very interested in your offer, Dr. Bramson. Very interested. I didn't think such an opportunity was possible."

"I have to go to class now, but why don't you come see me tomorrow at my office? We couldn't work you in until the spring term next year, but in the meantime we can work up a curriculum for you to study in advance of your matriculation. If you can be patient with us, I believe we can offer you a great future in music." He smiled and congratulated Dan and then excused himself, leaving Trevor, Sarah, and Dan alone.

"I can't believe this is happening," Dan said. "It's like a dream coming true. Stanford, with all its facilities and faculty. I just can't believe it!"

"Seems like we deserve some shaved ice," Sarah said pleasantly. "How would you two like to walk to my parents' house to celebrate your good fortune?"

"Thanks," Dan said. "For once I really feel like celebrating." He burst into a giant grin, and the three of them walked off hand in hand cheerfully singing their way across the campus.

Part Two

AMERICA IN
THE GREAT WAR

Chapter Nine

AN AMERICAN DECLARATION OF WAR

April 1917

Germany made two fateful decisions in the early months of 1917. The first was to begin unrestricted warfare on all shipping headed to Allied ports. In all previous wars, a hostile warship would stop its victim so that passengers and crew could disembark prior to the ship being taken or sunk. But in unrestricted warfare, the German submarines simply fired their torpedoes and then abandoned the scene, leaving the survivors to drown in the ocean. There was the risk to Germany that America would declare war over the policy, but at this point in 1917, it was becoming clear that full-scale submarine warfare had the potential to starve Britain out of the war, and Germany decided it was worth the risk of America coming in, since they calculated it would be at least a year or two before the Americans could make a meaningful contribution to the war effort. They hoped to end the war long before that.

The second fateful decision was made by the German ambassador to Mexico, Arthur Zimmerman. Relations were very chilly between the U.S. and Mexico. Germany sought to exploit that by offering to provide lucrative cash incentives for Mexico to join in an alliance with Germany against the United States, with the additional promise that Mexico could reoccupy its territories in Kansas, New Mexico, and

Arizona. Zimmerman sent this offer via a coded telegram. The British broke the code and released the contents to the United States. When it was released to the public, the furor was unbelievable. The thought that Germany was actively working against the U.S. outraged public opinion, and even long-time isolationists came out in favor of war.

On April 6, 1917, the United States Congress acted on President Woodrow Wilson's request that war be declared on Germany and her allies. An immediate surge of patriotism followed the declaration of war as hundreds of thousands showed up to enlist in the first week after Congress took action. Americans felt that Germany's actions were an insult to their national character and vowed that it was time to bring things to a resolution in Europe.

When Trevor Richards heard the news, he immediately went to the school administrators and announced his intention to enlist in the Army Air Corps. He wasn't the only one, naturally, so the school accelerated the date for final exams in behalf of any student who was leaving for the war. Trevor's early exit meant that he missed seeing his friend Stuart's graduation, but he wanted to get home to Pocatello as soon as possible to talk to his parents. Sarah was tearful at their parting but reluctantly agreed to Trevor's plea that they not make their relationship formal since there was too much uncertainty about the future. So they parted with nothing more than a promise to write and to see how they felt when the war was over.

Trevor made it home in late May and was met by Dan, who drove him directly to the Richardses' home. Jonathon and Margaret were solemn when he and Dan sat down with them. Trevor indicated that he would like to enlist with his parents' blessing, but even if they couldn't support him, he felt compelled to sign up for service. "The president says that democracy itself is on the line and that everybody must be prepared to sacrifice to save our allies from domination." He searched their faces for understanding. "Freedom is worth fighting for, and I just think this is something I have to do." Then he braced for their response.

Finally, Jonathon cleared his throat and said quietly, "We understand, Trevor. We've been expecting it, of course, because you're a loyal citizen and the country needs you. The world needs you." He was quiet for a moment and then smiled. "Plus, there are all those airplanes over there." Trevor relaxed a bit, which encouraged Jonathon to continue. "Trevor, all wars start out of selfishness and the desire for power, for property, and for vanity, usually on the part of the country's leaders. But innocent people suffer the awful consequences. While it's impossible to compare suffering, I believe that this war is the most gruesome in history. The kaiser—and his advisors—pours out destruction and pain with no regard for human life in a wholesale slaughter that approaches that of the last days of the Book of Mormon. Unfortunately, the realities of the battlefront are such that the Allies have responded in kind. They have to, because everything we cherish is threatened, and somehow this has to be brought to an end." He cleared his throat. "What I'm trying to say, Trevor, is that you will have to do things that in any other circumstance would be horrible. You're a man of conscience, and that might cause you to hold back. It can be fatal to hesitate. By making this your enterprise, you must do whatever is required of you without hesitation and . . ." He choked up. "And without guilt. I'm so sorry that leaders put young men in such a position, but they have, and now you must do your duty." Trevor didn't say anything because Jonathon looked so distressed. "Son, all of this could harden you. But not if you study your scriptures and say your prayers. The cause is just, and God will sustain you if you keep Him part of your life." Then, his voice tightening, he added, "And when you come home to us, you'll still be the same wonderful person that you are now. Changed, but still worthy. Promise me you'll stay in touch with the Spirit."

Trevor jumped up from his chair and ran to his father, throwing his arms around him. "I promise, Father. I promise." Then he sat by his mom and attempted to console her while she tried to hold back her tears for her only living son.

* * *

As it turned out, Trevor could have stayed in California for Stuart's graduation. In fact, he could have taken summer school. Even though the airplane had been invented in America, in April 1917, the U.S. military had just two hundred aircraft and virtually no infrastructure to support an air force. That was in contrast to the tens of thousands of aircraft in service by France, England, and Germany. The Germans and French now held a clear technical superiority in both the design and manufacture of airplanes, and America would never field its own aircraft in the war. Since it was assumed that the primary military use of airplanes would be as observers flying over the battlefield, the few military personnel who did work in air support were assigned to the Army Signal Corps, which was not a group accustomed to managing the kind of hostile encounters that the French and British air services were dealing with on the Western Front. Still, Congress recognized the need to increase support and voted the almost unimaginable sum of 640 million dollars to build a meaningful air service.

Trevor's departure to basic training was delayed until early September. In the meantime, he and Dan used those months to catch up with one another, going for a brisk run every morning at 6:30, as well as spending time together and with friends in the evening when Dan's work as a tutor at the academy came to an end.

* * *

The day Trevor left from the new Pocatello railroad depot was perhaps the hardest day of his family's life. They knew the statistics, even though no one talked about it directly. Aviators had the highest casualty rate of anyone who served in the military.

"Don't be reckless or foolhardy," Margaret said quietly.

"Everybody thinks I'm reckless," Trevor said defensively, "because I drive fast. But I'm not reckless. I'm always thinking and always engaged."

"I'm not criticizing," she said softly.

Trevor's lip trembled. "I know, Mom. I'll be careful. I promise." He hugged her tightly.

Jonathon gave his son a big bear hug and said, "You've grown into a fine man, Trevor. I'm proud that you're willing to stand up for your convictions. Read your scriptures and say your prayers. God loves you and will find a way to make what you're doing worthwhile. If it ever gets scary or lonesome, just remember that we're thinking about you and praying for you."

"Thanks, Father. I love you so much." He pulled away from his father's hug so he could look him in the face. "Nobody ever had a better father. No matter what happens, I've had a great life because of you. You'll be in my prayers too." They smiled and hugged again. Trevor couldn't remember if he'd ever seen his father cry, but the tears were flowing freely on this occasion.

Finally, he turned to Dan, Sam, and Elmer, who had come down to see him off. Leonard planned to see him for a few minutes during a train change in Salt Lake City.

"Did I hear that you enlisted?" he asked Elmer.

"Yep—last week."

"So where are they going to put you?"

"It's the strangest thing," Elmer said. "They had me take this math test. I thought it was easy. Then they asked me to take a harder test, which was different from anything I'd ever seen before. It had all sorts of strange mathematical patterns that you were supposed to group together. At any rate, I must have done pretty well, because they want me to go to Washington, D.C., to work in the Signal Service creating secret codes. Apparently I'll be trying to break German codes as well. It sounds interesting. But who'd have ever guessed?"

Trevor smiled broadly. "I always knew you were a diamond in the rough. You're going to do better in life than all the rest of us put together. I'll be relying on those codes you make, so make 'em good."

Elmer smiled. "I promise."

Then Trevor turned to Sam. "I know you have deep feelings against the war, Sam, and I respect you for it. I just don't see it the same way. But you've been a great friend, and I hope to see you when this is all over. It shouldn't take too long."

"I have even deeper feelings for you and the other guys, Trev—you're a lot more important than what I think about the war. I'll pray for you. If anybody can do well in an airplane, it's you. You're the best with cars and motorcycles that I've ever seen." They shook hands but recognized that wasn't enough, so ended with a hug.

Finally, Trevor turned to Dan. Moving close, he said, "I'll miss you most, boy. You're the best friend a guy ever had. You go to Stanford and make a name for yourself. I'll probably be hearing your songs on the gramophone someday, and I'll say, 'Hey, I know that guy!' and everybody will say, 'Yeah, right, Richards.' But it will be true, and I'll be your biggest fan."

"Darn it, Trevor, I wasn't going to cry." Dan wiped his face. "You've got to come back. I don't think I could stand it if you don't."

"I'll do my best. You can count on it."

The emotion was just too much. Saying good-bye was much harder than he expected. Yet, inside, Trevor was so excited he could hardly contain himself. He was finally going to get the chance to fly. This is what he had wanted since he was a little boy in Salt Lake City. So he straightened up, gave his mother one last kiss, and got on the train. He put the window down and waved as the train pulled out of the station. No one in the farewell group moved to leave the platform until the train was out of sight. Then they returned quietly to their homes.

* * *

Kelly O'Brian was one of the earliest Americans to enlist, entering service long before Trevor could get overseas. He left with a lot of bluster, but as he said good-bye to Dan, he said something interesting. "I was always pretty rough on you. I'm sorry if it ever got to you. You're not such a bad guy, really."

Dan smiled. "Thanks. I'll be praying for you."

"Well, if anybody deserves to have his prayers answered, it's you. You sure went to church enough."

Frank told Kelly he was proud. Really proud. Then Kelly was off.

Most Americans, like Trevor, didn't see service until nearly a year later, even though the British and French desperately wanted American replacements for their front-line troops just as soon as they could be sent into combat. After two and a half years and millions of casualties, they drafted every available young man as soon as he came of age. When America declared war in 1917, the Allies saw America as yet another source of human fodder for the "sausage mill," as it was called, and they hoped to have American troops standing next to theirs as soon as transportation could be arranged.

What France and England didn't count on was General John Pershing, the Allied Expeditionary Force (AEF) commander, who had very different ideas about how the Americans would be deployed. He insisted that the Americans fight in their own units under his command. So in spite of Allied pressure, he held back from releasing troops to the Allies except in the most desperate of circumstances.

For most Americans, Pershing's course was acceptable. But Kelly O'Brian wanted to get into action sooner and volunteered to serve with an Irish brigade under British command. After basic training in England, his unit was dispatched directly to the Western Front in October 1917. Kelly was sent up to the line just as an attack was being ordered. Not really knowing what to expect or what to do, he followed his sergeant up and over the ramparts of the trench and out into no-man's-land. He was cut down within the first sixty seconds after going over the top, the German machine gun tearing his torso into shreds. Frank received the telegram in mid-November. The individual who wrote the letter home said that he charged brilliantly, shouting at the top of his lungs as he went.

* * *

Dan came over to his father's house the moment he heard the news about Kelly. As he entered the house, Frank looked up dully.

"I'm so sorry, Father. I can't believe this happened to him—on his first day in battle."

"I guess it's why he was there. At least he died bravely, while charging the enemy."

"Yes, that would be like him."

There was a period of silence. Dan didn't know what more to say. His father broke the silence. "You never liked Kelly much, did you?"

Dan shook his head in disbelief. He was here to comfort his father and mourn the loss of his brother, and his father was saying something like this. "We weren't really close, but he was my brother."

"I always thought he embarrassed you. You and your friends were too good for Kelly. No matter what he accomplished in sports or at work, you made fun of him."

I will not lose my temper. I will not let him do this to me! "Maybe that's true, but Kelly wasn't very good to my friends. I can't tell you how many times he and Victor beat up on Trevor or me. It was kind of hard to be close to him when he was always hitting us." Frank didn't say anything. "But that's behind us now, Father. I'm just as sad as you are for Kelly. Nobody deserves to die like that."

Frank turned with fire in his eyes. "At least he died a hero's death. At least he was willing to serve his country instead of heading off to some rich boy's school while the sons and daughters of the working man are going to France to give their life for their country. At least he cared about something more than himself."

Dan felt a fury building up inside that he didn't know how to resist. "Just what are you saying? I deserve to go to Stanford. I've worked hard for it, and it's what I want to do. I know you don't care about my music, but I do."

"Yes," Frank said coldly, "your music is more important than anything or anybody in the world. More important than all those boys who are fighting in Italy and France and Russia and Persia and Turkey. Your music matters more than all of it."

Don't let him get to you. He's torn up about Kelly. Don't let him get to you. "Father, I don't want to have this argument. There's no reason for us to fight. I've registered for the draft just like everybody else my age. If they draft me, I'll go and serve. Until then, I'm going to do exactly what every other guy my age is doing, and that's to go on about my life. I'm sorry you don't like it, but it makes sense to me. I'd better be going now." He turned and started for the door.

"Go ahead and leave, you coward. You don't deserve even to be in the same house where your brother grew up. Just get out of my sight."

Dan turned in a fury and shouted, "Did you call me a coward? How dare you call me a coward! I've put up with you all my life, and believe me, that takes courage. Lots of it. A coward! I can't believe you'd say that to your own son."

"I have nothing more to say to you. It really doesn't matter what you do. Just leave."

Dan wanted to hit him, to pound him, to shake him until he owned up to all of the hurt and pain he'd caused through the years. His mother had died without having smiled in the last ten years of her life. Dan had never heard a kind word from his father since the day Frank had shown them the locomotive on their trip to Salt Lake City. But of everything he'd ever done or said, this was the worst. *A coward!* With that, Dan turned and slammed the door.

Acting on sheer impulse, he went straight for the army recruiting office. When the recruiter reviewed his application, he made a hand-penciled note that Dan would be a good candidate for one of the regimental orchestras that were being created to help maintain troop morale. Since he couldn't be sure his recommendation would be accepted, he chose not to tell Dan about it. He was about to dismiss him but hesitated when Dan said angrily, "Aren't you going to ask about my marksmanship? I'd think you'd want to know about that!"

The recruiter looked up, surprised. Most musicians wanted to stay away from the infantry like the plague. "You a good shooter, boy?"

"Put me out on the range, and I'll show you how good I am."

"Why don't we do that?" The recruiter stood up and escorted Dan into a shooting range and handed him a Springfield M1903, one of the most accurate weapons in the world. "Go ahead and see how you do shooting at that target down there. Take your time."

Dan raised the gun and fired off six rounds in rapid fire, then brought the weapon to his side. The instructor wheeled the target in and, at first, thought that Dan had hit the center bull's-eye once and missed the target completely on the other five shots. An odd pattern to say the least. But on closer examination, he made out six distinct strikes so close together that they were in a tight circular pattern, dead center. "That's . . . remarkable," he gasped. "You're going to be really valuable on the line. We have a special course of training for guys like you. They're called snipers, and every unit loves 'em because they're the ones for precision shooting."

"That's what I thought," Dan said furiously. "When do I report?"

"We won't need you for a couple of weeks. In the meantime, just sign this letter of intent to let the army know you're available. Of course, there will be additional paperwork to fill out, so why don't you come back the first part of next week? I'll talk with you more then."

* * *

Dan never returned home again. Since he'd already given up his apartment in anticipation of going to California, he asked the Richardses if he could live with them until it was time for him to go to basic training. They were happy to have him. Eventually, Jonathon prevailed on one of Frank's coworkers to go to Frank's home to collect Dan's remaining things. The fellow reported later that when he knocked on the door, he heard Frank call out, "Is that you, Dan?" But when he told him why he was there and that Dan had enlisted, Frank just pointed to his room and told him to take whatever he wanted.

When it was Dan's turn to leave, the group at the platform was smaller: Jonathon and Margaret, Bishop Peterson, and Sam.

"I hope you don't have to go, Sam," Dan said quietly. "You're kind of like the Anti-Nephi-Lehies, as far as I'm concerned. Maybe theirs is the best way after all."

"I don't know what the best way is. I know I can't go, even if it means I have to go to jail. But I think the fact that I own a farm will help me avoid a confrontation with the government. Hopefully I can fulfill my patriotic duty by raising lots of potatoes." Dan smiled. "It's not that I don't love America or appreciate freedom. It's just that I don't think that killing is the answer."

"I know. Don't worry, I know. I'm a lot more like you than you can imagine. I should never have lost my temper and enlisted. But what's done is done. It seems like there's an awful job to be done, and if Trevor and others are willing to go, I guess it's all right that I do my part. Right now, I just want to get over there and get it out of the way. Pray for me, will you, Sam?"

"Every day, buddy. Every day."

The Richardses were almost more distressed this time than when they sent Trevor off. It was not that they loved Dan more, but that it was the second time they had to do it. Now both boys were in harm's way, and it brought Margaret to despair. "Thanks for letting me teach you music," she said. "It was a hard time for me, moving to Pocatello away from my family and friends. I don't know what I'd have done if you hadn't come into my life."

Dan looked at her in surprise. "I had no idea. I just thought that you were an angel that Heavenly Father had sent directly to me so I could get out of my house into a world that I understood. You saved me."

She hugged him close. "Well, if that's true, then I don't want to lose you now. I know you signed up in frustration.

Promise me that you'll get over your anger so you can think and fight rationally. Promise me that you'll come home."

He looked at her and smiled. "I promise."

Jonathon reminded him that Leonard wanted to see him in Salt Lake City during his stopover there and that Jonathon's father was planning on him staying at his home.

Dan thanked him, then hugged him. "You'll never know how much it meant to have you as my quorum instructor. Now that I'm grown, I can see what a sacrifice it was. But it meant everything to us boys. We all love you. All of us. You're the world's best."

"Thanks, Dan. Be careful out there. I love you too. More than you'll ever realize." For the second time, Jonathon Richards started weeping.

That was just too much, and Dan started crying in turn. It was embarrassing, but he didn't care. He hugged them all again and then got on the train reluctantly. He'd been so happy for October to come so he could go off to Stanford. Now that dream was shattered, and he was off to kill men with whom he had no personal quarrel.

After the train pulled out of the station, Jonathon and Margaret made their way toward their automobile. As they rounded the northwest corner of the depot, they saw a man step quickly into the shadows. "Who is that?" Margaret asked nervously.

"It's Frank O'Brian. He must have watched Dan leave." Margaret squeezed Jonathon's hand and gave him a weak smile as they kept on walking.

Chapter Ten

FLIGHT TRAINING— ARMY AIR SERVICE

After basic training in the United States, Trevor and his combat group transferred by ship to Paris, arriving at Christmastime in 1917. In spite of the desperate fighting at the front less than a hundred miles away, the Parisians did their best to make life festive, particularly for the first crop of Americans. Everybody labored under a foreboding that the Germans were getting ready to make a massive assault to capture Paris before the Americans could arrive in strength, so the mood was somber. Still, the American flyers were invited into people's homes to share a modest holiday meal and then taken out to see the beautiful sights of the ancient city. Trevor was interested but frustrated. He still hadn't been up in an airplane, and the delay was killing him.

Then the momentous word came in written orders. *You are to proceed with all possible haste by motor coach to Tours, where you will begin flight training under the direction of French instructors assigned to the American Expeditionary Force.* Trevor's heart skipped a beat as he hurriedly packed his things, thanked the French family he'd been staying with for their hospitality, and headed to the assigned departure point, where he hooked up with Alan Gledhill, one of his friends from basic training.

"Do you think we'll get trained in time to see some action before the war ends?"

Trevor turned to respond to Alan. "I hope so. I was beginning to think my whole army career would be spent touring museums and restaurants." They laughed. "I hear the place they're sending us is the best in the country. Each of the instructors has air combat experience and really puts you through the paces. I even hear that Raoul Lufbery was taught by these guys."

"Really? Lufbery?"

Raoul Lufbery was a naturalized American citizen who had been serving in the French Escadrille, an American unit of the French military that had been fighting in the air war for more than two years. Lufbery had won many a daring battle, and his exploits had been in the popular press in America for years. He was universally respected by all the Allied fliers. "Wouldn't it be something if he stopped by the field? I'd love to meet a guy like that."

"Me too," Trevor said enthusiastically. "I've also heard that while the French used to take six months to train a pilot, they've learned how to reduce the training time down to about three months, so we could be in action by April. I hope so, because if not, I'm going to go absolutely crazy. I've just got to get up in the air and do something."

"I feel the same way." They piled into the backseat of what used to be a Paris taxi. Nearly all the motorized vehicles in France had been converted to wartime use. In the first days after war broke out, the Paris taxi drivers almost single-handedly moved enough troops to the front lines to turn back the German offensive. Without them, it's likely Paris would have fallen to the Germans in the first two months of the war, and there would have been a German mayor running the city. As it was, their driver spoke very little English, and neither Alan nor Trevor knew much French, so they started talking with each other.

"So where did you go to school?" Alan asked amiably.

"Stanford," Trevor replied.

"Ah, the West Coast Ivy League."

Trevor smiled. "At least that's what the governor wants us to be. Where did you go to school?"

"Me, I'm a Princeton boy, just like Woodrow Wilson. Everyone there agrees that Wilson was a breath of fresh air when he took over as president of Princeton prior to running for national office. I hope he's able to do as well at getting the country fully engaged in the war as he was at energizing the university. It's been nine months, and not a single American unit has gone into battle yet."

Yet there were casualties. Trevor thought of Kelly. He'd never liked Kelly because of the way he treated Danny. It was odd that he was one of the first American casualties, even though it would never be credited that way. Thinking about Kelly dying somehow made him nervous, so he tried to get back into a more relaxed conversation. "So I guess nearly all the pilot candidates are college graduates. That seems kind of strange to me. I mean, some of the best automobile drivers in the world come from the working class. Why keep them out?"

"You know what the British prime minister said in his speech last month—'knights of the air' and all that. It turns out that the only 'glorious' part of this war is the individual combat of the aerial jousters. It looks great on the recruiting posters and gives the public celebrities to root for. So naturally, England reserves that honor for the upper crust. I guess the same sort of bias has extended to America."

Trevor was thoughtful. "I suppose it also has something to do with the fact that pilots are expected to be officers, and since there aren't enough career military, they need to turn to the academies. Still, I have some friends who would do great if given a chance."

"They're probably the lucky ones," Alan said ruefully. "Not a lot of pilots live to come home, you know."

"So I've heard." Then, turning and smiling, he said, "But we'll be two who do—after becoming aces!"

Alan responded, "Richards and Gledhill, amazing aerial combatants, return to their heroes' welcome as the two leading aces of the Great War!" They laughed. And so the time passed pleasantly until they pulled up to the Tours aerodrome. Suddenly their confidence was shaken as they watched a trainee aircraft do an end-over-end flip on the runway. They turned and looked at each other with an expression of horror, then burst out laughing almost in unison when the pilot struggled out from under the wreckage and shook his head like he'd been dazed. "Well, maybe for now it's enough if the headlines read, 'Richards and Gledhill make it safely through pilot training.'"

* * *

After getting assigned to barracks, where Trevor and Alan were made roommates, they reported to the flight line for their first instruction. They were greeted by a stiff little man with a dark, greased mustache, who called them to attention.

"My name's Fouchard—Captain Fouchard, to all of you. My English is barely passable, so when you make mistakes, I'll yell at you in French. You may not understand the words, but believe me, you'll know what I mean!"

The fifteen young pilots laughed.

"You're all youngsters here . . . twenty, twenty-one or so. I'm an old man—age twenty-eight—so you must show me the respect of an elder."

The group smiled again.

Then, frowning, Fouchard went on, "If not because of age or rank, because I know what it's like up there, and you do not. Make no mistake, the Bosche is out to kill you, and he loves it when a new pilot comes out. The highest casualty rate is during the first two weeks in the air because everything happens so fast you won't know what's going on. That will make you, as you Americans like to say, a 'sitting duck.' So pay attention. If you have questions, ask them. If any of you choose not to pay attention, you'll be transferred to the infantry. Our reconnaissance tells us that the Germans are building up for a major offensive, and we need every aircraft in the air we can put up, which means we have no time to waste on those who are lazy, incompetent, or undisciplined. What I teach you can save your life. If you do not learn the lessons, we will lose a pilot and an aircraft." With disdain he added, "And we can ill afford to lose an aircraft." With that, he dismissed them to the classroom, where they began to study the mechanics of flight.

* * *

After a week in the classroom, where the students learned the principles of flight, they were taken to the field, where they were allowed to climb into the cockpit of the trainer aircraft. Trevor approached the wing cautiously but with so much suppressed excitement he could hardly contain himself. He looked for the small, black strip of rough surface where the pilot was supposed to mount so as to avoid putting a foot through the fabric of the wing. Climbing gingerly on the wing, he put his left foot in the assigned cutout, placed his left hand on the upper wing, and swung his right foot up and into the cockpit, where he placed it firmly on the seat. Then he lifted his left leg in and scooted his feet down into the well. Once firmly seated, he looked around at the various controls. In the previous days, he'd studied them over and over again so that he could act competently when first given the chance to manage the controls for himself.

As Trevor settled into the seat, he tried to take in everything about the new environment. He loved the smell of the varnished wood that rimmed the opening to the "office," as the experienced pilots called the cockpit. He rubbed his hand along the side of the fuselage to feel the shellac-smooth surface of the painted fabric. Looking forward, he tried to picture what it would look like to see through the small windshield and the rotating propeller. Then he placed his hands firmly on the joystick. He pushed forward and was surprised at the springy feel of the stick in his hand. As instructed, he turned and looked at the tail of the airplane and saw the elevator move up and down as he moved the stick forward and back. Then he pushed it slightly to the right and saw the right ailerons—the fins—on both the upper and lower wing rise in unison. Turning to the left, he saw that the ailerons on that side moved exactly opposite. Finally, after trying the sequence a couple of times, he gently touched the controls to the engine, careful not to change any settings, since he and the others had been threatened with their lives if they did.

Then the moment he'd been waiting for arrived. The command was given to turn the switch into the off position so that the mechanic could give a twist to the propeller and prime the engine. Once that was done, Trevor was given the clear signal, and he confidently called out, "Switch on!" The mechanic gave another swing on the propeller, and Trevor watched as a black puff of smoke issued out of the exhaust on the right side of the engine. He nursed the throttle until the engine caught hold and started to turn on its own. Most of the other students had trouble getting their engine to catch, but Trevor got it on the first try. He looked down to see Fouchard raise an appreciative eyebrow. As he raced the engine ever so slightly, he felt the incredible wash of wind thrown off by the propeller, and the blood pumped in his veins as it had the first time he took his motorcycle out. More than anything, he wanted to give it full power just so he could hear the confident rumble of the engine, but he knew better. There was only one mechanic holding the tail, and he could never hold the airplane in place by himself. So Trevor kept it at idle, taking in the smell of the rich fuel mixture needed for starting and takeoff. He could have stayed in there forever, as far as he was concerned, but Fouchard's hand signal told him it was time to shut it down. When the engines were silent, a gruff shout from their illustrious instructor brought Trevor and the other students in the first group up and out of their aircrafts in double time.

Some of the aerodromes taught pilots how to fly using two-seater aircraft with an instructor on board, but not Tours. They were to learn on the little Blériots, which had a single seat. Some of the students groused at that, since it meant their first flight would be solo with no one to help out in an emergency. But Trevor was glad because he wanted to figure the machine out on his own so he could train his body to respond without interference from an instructor. It's the way he'd learned to ride his motorcycle, and he thought it would work for airplanes.

When Trevor and Alan's group came out of the airplanes, Fouchard lined them all up and said simply, "Tomorrow morning, you take to the Penguins. Get a good night's sleep, because you'll need all your wits about you to control those flightless little birds." He smiled a sadistic smile and dismissed them.

"I don't see how it can be all that hard to run the Penguins up and down the field," Alan said anxiously. "I mean, all you have to do is keep the stick dead center and the pedals at neutral. What can be so hard about that?"

"Did you see those guys trying to control them last week?" Trevor replied. "It was the funniest thing I ever saw. They were going every which direction like a bunch of keystone cops. I kept expecting them to bump into each other. I thought their instructor was going to have a heart attack."

"But what's so hard about it? I just don't understand."

Trevor had already figured out that Alan was something of a worrier. Normally, Trevor would have thought that would disqualify a person for something like flying, but as he'd gotten to know Alan, he found out that Alan had raced high-performance automobiles on his summer breaks from college. Alan's father was a career army man who had a passion for the newest weapons of war, and he felt that motorized vehicles would assume an increasingly important role in the military. He had encouraged Alan to excel in all things mechanical, even though Alan's natural interests lay elsewhere. Apparently Alan had won a couple automobile races, more by being calculating in the way he'd positioned himself on the field than from quick reflexes and reactions. So Alan's musings about tomorrow were quite natural—he wanted to think everything through in advance. Trevor approached it a lot differently. For him, controlling a machine was an intuitive act. It was far more important to be familiar with the feel of the controls than to think about how to use them. He'd found that if he could learn the theory of how they worked, his body would quickly adapt to the actual operation. So he didn't let himself think too much about the Penguins.

Realizing how similar Dan was to Alan inspired Trevor to sit down and write a letter to Dan that night, regaling him with tales of Paris and the opera, where so many mysterious legends lingered. He'd seen an Italian opera that he didn't really understand, but he knew that his mother and Dan would love to hear about it, so he tried to write as much detail about the performance as he could remember. It was a long letter, but he felt good when it was done because it connected them once again and helped him keep both of his worlds active in his mind. Being in the military was so different from anything he'd experienced before that it seemed almost like Pocatello was part of another lifetime rather than simply another place. That night he fell asleep soundly, although he occasionally awoke enough to know that Alan was staring at the ceiling in the bunk next to him.

When morning arrived, the barracks attendant awakened them to a cup of hot cocoa or tea, then rushed them out the door to the flight line just as twilight started to yield to dawn. Fouchard was in particularly ill humor.

"This has got to be the worst day for the instructor," Trevor whispered to Alan. "This is where everybody in the whole aerodrome comes over to make fun, and it's got to be miserable for them to take the ribbing from the other instructors." Alan was somber, obviously nervous about his upcoming performance. "Don't worry," Trevor said lightly. "You're going to do fine. I know you flew that stupid, little clipped-wing midget two or three hundred times last night."

Alan looked at him a bit savagely. "At least I thought about it. You went straight to sleep and started snoring immediately. If I didn't sleep, it's because I had the sound of Rhone-rotary engine ripping away in the bed next to me!"

Trevor snorted at that, which drew the immediate attention of Captain Fouchard. "Ah, I see that Messieurs Richards and Gledhill are amused by our little exercise this morning." They both stood at quick attention, Trevor doing his best to suppress his smile while Alan tried not to collapse on the spot from the unexpected attention. "That's fine, gentlemen. I was going to give you some instruction, but it seems you think that unnecessary. Mr. Gledhill, why don't you go first, followed by Corporal Richards? At your convenience, of course."

The rest of the students looked at Alan with sympathy, because they all knew that he had the worst spot. Still, there was nothing to do but respond with a crisp, "Yes, sir!" Alan moved toward the little Blériot with as much confidence as he could muster, Trevor following alongside to be one of those who helped the mechanics hold the tail until the engine built up enough thrust to move out.

"Alan, you're going to be fine. Anybody who can handle a race car can handle this. Just remember everything you've studied and make your mother proud."

"I'm going to save the Germans a lot of trouble and kill you myself when I'm done."

"If that's the way you are, then I take it back. Go ahead and crash and die a horrible death in the fiery inferno. Of course, it would be a bit humiliating for your family to know that their son is the only person ever to die in an airplane that doesn't even have full wings."

"Would you keep quiet! I'm trying to concentrate." But by this point, it was a moot issue because they'd reached the airplane. On most days, the mechanics at the training school acted pretty bored by their job, but not this morning. The "flying" of the Penguins was the most entertaining day of the training cycle. So they helped Alan up and into his seat, reached in, and helped him with the restraining belts that came down over both shoulders and across his lap, then checked the setting on the engine. When Alan was settled in, they dismounted the aircraft and moved to their assigned positions on the tail and at the propeller. "Switch off," Alan cried out, and they gave a turn on the propeller. He looked to Fouchard, who gave him a nonchalant clear sign, then he called out, "Switch on." The great propeller turned, and the engine belched its black smoke, turned a few times, then sputtered to a stop. So they repeated the cycle a second time, and then a third time.

Alan was so humiliated he could hardly stand it. It was made worse when Fouchard came up on the side of the wing and shouted furiously, "The moment you feel it catch, you've got to give it some fuel! It's morning—your poor machine needs breakfast. Stop trying to starve it!" Of course, he'd been doing that very procedure, but next time he paid particular attention. He did nothing different, but the engine had finally started to warm up some and caught hold, and Alan nursed it to a smooth rumble. At that, Fouchard gave the clear sign again, and Alan revved the engine until the backwash was strong enough that it started tugging the little aircraft forward. He checked each of his controls to make sure they were in the neutral position, then increased the revolutions to the point where the men holding the airplane couldn't keep it restrained, and away he went.

For the spectators, Alan's first attempt was terrific. The little bird leaped out onto the field like a fox released before the hounds, and they could see Alan's head thrown violently to the right as the airplane twisted to the left. Before he could react, he'd done a complete circle and was now careening to the right. He should have shut the engine down but appeared to be resolved to regain control of the situation. That was a huge mistake. He managed to straighten out just long enough to pick up speed. As the airplane bounded down the runway it tried to lift off, but, of course, it couldn't, for lack of enough wing. As it bounced up into the air, Alan panicked and shut the engine down abruptly at precisely the same moment the aircraft again swerved to the left. The combination brought him nose down into the ground, shattering the propeller. Fouchard went running onto the field, shouting, "Sacré bleu," and other unknown words of French origin as the mechanics tipped the bird back upright and extracted its hapless victim from the seat. Alan staggered to the ground, oblivious even to Fouchard, his face a white pallor that showed just how frightened he'd been. He didn't even acknowledge Trevor as he staggered past on the arm of one of the mechanics. The other students were too nervous to make fun or even talk, although bystanders were certainly not restrained.

"Well, Corporal Richards, are you too frightened to give it a try?" Trevor straightened up and requested permission to mount one of the other aircraft. "You don't have to go as fast as your friend. Control is better than speed." Trevor acknowledged and mounted the aircraft. The mechanics buckled him in, and Trevor went through a quick pre-nonflight checklist. He tested each of the controls and finally gave the clear sign. Fouchard responded, and the mechanics gave the priming rotation of the propeller. Then he called out, "Switch on," and listened for the sound of the engine catching. At just the right moment, he gave it enough fuel for the engine to sputter to life and soon had it purring easily. Fouchard gave the clear sign, and Trevor increased the rpms until the wash of the propeller was adequate to pull the aircraft forward. He gave a thumbs-up signal to the mechanics, and they released the tail. The aircraft bounded forward just as it had with Alan. Without even thinking about it, Trevor noticed his left leg apply a bit of pressure to the rudder pedal, followed by a slight push on the right leg. As he gained speed, he could sense the aircraft as it tried to lurch to one side or the other, and he gently responded to both the control stick and the rudder pedals. At about fifty yards, he was maintaining a pretty fair semblance of a straight line, so he increased power. The plane started to jump a bit, but rather than panicking, he continued to make minute adjustments to the controls.

As he approached the end of the runway, he backed off on the power and began to execute a gentle arc to the left in an attempt to turn the aircraft around for the return trip. His ground speed was too high, though, and the aircraft started to slip to the right, and he could feel the left wheel sliding under him as the aircraft started to heel over. In a flash, he corrected with the ailerons while simultaneously reducing speed. The plane responded immediately, and he was able to maintain control through the turn. He opened the throttle wide and headed straight back for the hangar at full speed. As he approached the group, he powered down just in time for the aircraft to roll to a stop ten feet short of Fouchard. At the captain's signal, he cut the motor and started to unbuckle himself. A mechanic was at his side immediately to help him out.

"A very creditable job, monsieur," the mechanic said cheerfully. "A very fine performance for a new pilot."

Trevor tipped his hat to the mechanic and dismounted the plane, heading back to the group. The other students started clapping, until they received a fierce glance from Fouchard, who simply said to Trevor, "That is acceptable."

Trevor slipped back into line next to Lane Pritchett, who whispered, "I'll be happy if I can come in somewhere average between you and poor Gledhill."

Trevor saw that Fouchard was looking at him, so he waited until Fouchard turned before he whispered, "The secret is to not oversteer. The controls are really touchy, so use them sparingly."

"Thanks," Pritchett said, then turned to the next fellow in line and whispered the same advice.

After the next pilot started his attempt, which wasn't as awful as Alan's, Trevor slipped out of line and went over to the chair where Alan was sitting, still white. "It's okay, Alan. They tell me that some of the best pilots in the air had trouble their first time in a Penguin. You'll figure it out."

Alan looked up miserably and beckoned Trevor to sit next to him. "It's not the control thing that bothers me. I know I can figure that out. It's that I got motion sick with all the twisting and turning. My head is killing me right now, and I was afraid I'd throw up in front of the whole group."

"Ah," Trevor said simply. There wasn't a lot to say to that.

"I used to get carsick as a kid unless my parents let me ride in the front seat of the car. When I took up driving, it wasn't so bad because I could always see what was coming. But if I get sick in a Penguin, just think what it will be like in the air when you add up and down and banking motions to the equation."

Trevor decided to hit this one straight on. "Alan, it may be that you aren't suited for flight. But the only way you can know is to stay at it until you have a chance to go up in the air. I think it's just as likely that you're nauseated because you worried so much about this. Maybe we can get permission from Fouchard to practice after-hours until you know for sure."

Alan looked up and simply said, "Thanks. I'd appreciate it." Then he rested his elbows on his knees and cradled his head. "I really don't care about flying, but it's so important to my father. He's angling to get transferred out of infantry into the Air Service, and I just can't let him down. I don't know what I'd do if I washed out."

"First, I don't think you're going to wash out. Second, if you did, you'd transfer to the motor pool where you could wash out overeager pilots by making them carsick on the trip from Paris because of the way you drive. Either way, you'll do your part. So relax." Alan looked up and smiled. "Now let's go get in the line to watch the others before Fouchard writes us up for slacking." He helped Alan stand up, and they walked over to enjoy the fun of watching the funny little Penguins dance their way down the airfield.

* * *

Trevor passed out of Penguins after just one more trip and moved onto the next phase. Alan calmed down and learned to control the aircraft after five or six attempts. Even though he was behind Trevor and some of the others, the whole group had been slowed because there weren't enough of the funny, little three-cylinder monoplane Morane-Saulnier aircraft that provided the next step in their training. The goal in the monoplane was to bound down the field fast enough to use the elevator to take off and fly a few feet above the ground without really getting airborne. It was frustrating not being able to pull back on the stick and just take her up, but even Trevor realized that he wouldn't know what to do after he became airborne. So he used the jumps to practice taking off and setting the aircraft down. The trick was to keep the airspeed high enough that when you touched down, the aircraft didn't slam into the ground, but settled easily onto the turf. The students found out that it was harder than it sounded, so they spent upwards of a week improving their skills.

Trevor was excited when they finally graduated to the Caudron biplane with its powerful, nine-cylinder engine. After watching a number of instructors take off, rise up, circle out over the field, then bring it gently down, the students had their chance at it.

"We lose more airplanes in this exercise than I care to specify," Fouchard said with his usual air of disdain. "An airplane is really very easy to fly if you just trust yourself. Corporal Richards ought to do well, since it seems he takes everything for granted." Trevor couldn't tell if it was a compliment or criticism, so he held back the retort that would have come out naturally. "Once you find yourself airborne, remember to pull back on the stick to gain enough elevation to clear the trees at the end of the runway. You'll need to maintain full power until you're up. Then, once airborne, gently—I mean gently—pull your stick to the right so that you can start an easy banking turn out and around the airfield. Keep your power up so you don't lose altitude, and complete a wide circle that brings you into position to land. Straighten up and cut back on your power. Turn it off, if you like. Remember to keep your elevator up slightly so your nose doesn't come down. You'll be losing speed fast enough to bring the aircraft down, but you want your nose up in the air when you land so you don't go face-down in the dirt." He turned and looked at Alan, who had the common sense to blush even though Fouchard didn't mention him by name. "Now, I sense that disaster is impending, but to get things off on as best a footing as possible, why don't we send you up first, Corporal Richards."

This was what Trevor had been waiting to hear for twelve years—ever since he was ten years old in Utah watching the aerial exhibition out west of Salt Lake City. He'd dreamed about it, prayed for it, been frustrated at not getting it—and now his chance had arrived. For a brief moment, he thought of going up and giving Fouchard a kiss. He smiled at the thought—*It's a French tradition, after all.* But that would only take time, so he settled for a crisp salute and headed for the Caudron at top speed. Once strapped in, he completed his methodical pre-flight checklist to see that everything was in order. At last, he gave the signals and, when the prop was in position, shouted, "Switch on."

The engine roared to life with a thick cloud of smoke, and he quickly nursed it to its proper speed. The sound of the nine-cylinder engine was quite different from the little Blériot Penguin, and he thrilled as the prop wash flooded up and over his windshield. He turned to Fouchard, who gave the clear signal, and Trevor raced the engine to full acceleration. It ripped itself out of the hands of the mechanics holding the tail, and he was down the runway in a flash. As his ground speed picked up, he felt the thrill of riding his motorcycle on the back roads of Bannock County as the wind whipped his blond hair violently in the wash.

As he approached takeoff speed, his heart leaped, and in some remote corner of his mind, he had the feeling that this was what he'd been born for. At just the right spot in the field, he pulled back firmly on the stick, and the ungainly aircraft lifted gracefully and effortlessly into the air. He looked over the side and saw the ground falling away from him.

He checked the tree line in front of him and saw that he was easily gaining the altitude he needed to clear any obstacles, at which point he let out an unrestrained shout of exhilaration. He felt as if he and the airplane were soulmates and that he'd finally come home. With absolute confidence, he forced the stick gently to the side and noted the ailerons duly rise into the wind. The effect was immediate as the plane banked sharply to the right—perhaps a bit too sharply. So he backed off a bit and checked to make sure he was maintaining airspeed. He'd been given enough latitude to level the aircraft so he could learn to maintain level flight. Then he circled the entire airfield in a great swooping arc.

Finally he came into position for a landing, judged the best time to cut the motor, and was startled as he felt the airplane start to lose altitude rather quickly. It almost unnerved him—it was much easier to maintain control under full power, and without the acceleration of the propeller, the controls became more sluggish. He found himself twisting a bit in the wind, and he was using the rudder more than ever to try to maintain straight flight. As he descended to the open field, it felt as if he was going too fast.

He held his nerves steady, even though the aircraft seemed to twist at inopportune moments. Finally he felt the right wheel catch the ground. He was sagging a bit on the right side, and the impact caused the aircraft to bounce up. Instinctively he wanted to turn the aircraft, but he let it continue to drift down, compensating ever so slightly by depressing the left rudder pedal to bring the aircraft into a straight line again. This time the right wheel hit just a moment before the left wheel, and then the plane made firm contact with the ground. The impact jarred him, and he actually bit his tongue. But there was no time to think about that as he used the rough ground to eat up his forward speed, working constantly to keep the wheels straight.

The biggest danger now was doing a nosedive, and he avoided that by keeping the elevator up to provide drag to keep his center of gravity toward the rear of the aircraft. At one point, the tail wheel bounced up, and Trevor thought he was going to go face up, but at the last moment, it settled back down, and he rolled to a stop.

Unfortunately, his landing took up a lot more real estate than he had planned, and the group of mechanics who had been waiting to help turn him around for the trip back to the hangar had to scatter to avoid being run over as he came to a stop just a few feet short of a clump of trees. But he stopped in time, and his mechanics came up, clapping and cheering. His first flight had been a success, and Trevor was hooked forever. No matter what else happened, this war had given him the chance he'd always dreamed of, and he couldn't wait to go up in the air again.

Chapter Eleven

BASIC TRAINING— INFANTRY

Dan's first assignment was to basic training and gunnery school in New York state, just thirty miles out of Manhattan. On his first day, he soon found himself standing inside a barracks in nothing more than his underwear, at ramrod attention, while a mean-spirited sergeant shouted in his face. His head was cold, even though it was only October, because his hair was shorn. But his face felt hot because he wasn't the type to be yelled at without doing something about it. Still, he was guilty as charged—there was a wrinkle on his bed, as anyone who got his nose down into the folded corner could see. So he took his punishment like a man. The thirty push-ups weren't as bad as the indignity of standing there in front of the other men who had been given permission to get dressed. After the push-ups and an amazingly crisp, "Yes, sir" given in answer to the question as to whether he was natu-rally a slob, he'd been given permission to stand at ease and then to get dressed. The one thing he had going for him is that when the officers wanted him to yell back a response to a command, his well-trained lungs and vocal cords could fill the bill better than anyone else in the camp, which secretly pleased him to no end. He got to yell at them as a result of their own command. That seemed poetic justice.

Dan was fine with the physical training—he and Trevor had been running for years, and he enjoyed the challenge of competition. But he found it difficult when they started requiring the men to carry their packs on all assignments, since, at six feet tall and 140 pounds, he had a light frame and his pack weighed over sixty pounds. Plus, it seemed like nearly all the men in his unit were farm boys who were used to heavy physical work, while he'd been busy practicing music. But he made up in determination what he lacked in physical size.

In the end, Dan met all of the challenges of basic training and actually felt pretty good about the level of personal fitness he achieved. It was satisfying to feel his body respond to whatever challenge was thrown at it. He had the passing thought that he wished Kelly could see him now, but quickly regretted thinking that.

Still, he was glad when the six weeks came to an end. Standing in a perfect row and column, he marched among hundreds of other recruits who had completed this first phase of their training and was as thrilled as everyone else to hear the commanding officer accept the troops when presented by their individual staff sergeants. He'd received his papers a few days earlier, ordering him to transfer to a different part of the camp to start specialized weapons training. He knew he'd learn all the field weapons, including machine guns, but he had an inkling that he'd be singled out for the rifle.

The best news was that there still were an inadequate number of transport ships to move the troops overseas in any kind of volume, so the army had slowed down movement through the various schools. As a result, Dan was given a two-week leave of absence to rest up before starting weapons training. Most of the guys in his unit applied for a transportation voucher to go home, but Dan saw no reason to return to Pocatello, particularly since he would use up half his available leave on the train going and returning. So he decided to go into Manhattan to explore New York City.

He hadn't made any friends at that point, but as the others started to depart, he noticed a slender young man who stood back from the others. Eventually, it was down to just the two of them.

"So are you going home?" Dan extended his hand and introduced himself.

"I don't have any home to go to. I'm an orphan, and they were glad enough to lose me—one less mouth to feed."

Dan nodded his head in acknowledgment. "I don't have anywhere to go either, so I was thinking of going into Manhattan to see the sights and maybe take in some musical events or cabarets. I don't suppose you'd want to share a room."

The young man brightened and said, "I'd be glad to do that. I should have introduced myself—my name is Jody Wilkins from Cleveland, Ohio."

Dan shook his hand, and the two of them made plans to get transport to the nearest commuter rail station. Two hours later, Dan found himself emerging from the train station in midtown Manhattan. As he looked up and down the crowded streets, filled with more people than he'd ever seen in his life, he felt a wave of excitement overtake him as he picked up on the energy in the air. The elevated trains that rumbled overhead added to the noise of street vendors, automobiles, horses, and steam shovels, as well as the sound of a thousand other activities, to make the most dynamic aural environment he'd ever listened to. He took a deep breath and wasn't even offended by the rich assault on his olfactory nerves. He knew that he was in love with the place within the first sixty seconds.

Jody was really quiet but smiled when Dan shared his thoughts. "I've spent my whole life in the city—not as big as this one, of course—so this is nothing new to me. I find myself missing the trees and forests out at the camp. That was really the first time I've ever been to the forest."

"Well, my understanding is that France is filled with forests, and we'll be there soon enough, so I say we let loose and have a great time." Jody agreed, and they made their way to the subway station to travel downtown to a hotel they'd been referred to, in midtown near Madison Square Garden. The army had provided vouchers for up to ten days at one of the many hotels in the city, and they'd selected the Regis on the advice of one of their officers. Located on 25th Street between Broadway and Fifth Avenue, it put them in the heart of the city, within walking distance of the new subway lines that led north and south. After settling into their room, Dan studied their map and quickly oriented himself to the lay of the land.

As they started their walk, they couldn't help but gaze up in wonder at the Flatiron Building, the first skyscraper in New York City. They crossed the square to visit the famous Madison Square Garden sports arena with its grand arches and gates. Unfortunately, there were no events there that evening, so they just walked around the square, gawking at its size and grandeur. Dan wanted to see the East River before night fell, so they headed east on 26th Street until they crossed First Avenue, then continued on to the edge of the water. Across the great expanse they saw the lights of Brooklyn and, gazing down the river, the graceful cables of the Brooklyn Bridge. "I want to walk across that," Dan said excitedly. "Maybe we can do that tomorrow."

"Okay, but can we get something to eat now? I'm starved."

Dan laughed. "Sure. Sorry, but I guess I'm too excited to even think about food." So they started back in the direction of their hotel, stopping to eat at a street vendor along the way.

Over the course of the next ten days, they explored the city from north to south and east to west—or, at least, all of it they could. They walked on the elevated boardwalk of the Brooklyn Bridge while the motorcars and horses drove by on the steel deck below. They also found their way out to the Statue of Liberty, visited Central Park with all the magnificent new apartment buildings that were under construction on Fifth Avenue and Park West, and took time to go into the dozens of museums and art galleries that presented themselves seemingly at every turn. Because of their army uniforms, people seemed to go out of their way to be pleasant to them, belying the reputation New Yorkers sometimes had about being abrupt.

The best part of the trip for Dan was the variety of cultural events, including seeing Eddie Cantor in the Ziegfield Follies at the New Amsterdam Theatre, as well as hearing a symphonic orchestra in concert. But he loved the opera best—he'd heard and performed operatic pieces many times. To see the grand staging of an Italian opera was more than he could have ever imagined. After his first night at the opera, he went home and wrote a long letter to Margaret Richards telling her that he finally understood why she had been so excited to come to New York as a young lady.

Jody was tolerant of all this, but before they left the city, he asked for the chance to see at least one sports event, so they went to a couple of boxing matches at Madison Square Garden. It was amazing to see the crowds get caught up in the competition, chanting and jeering and even throwing things at the arena when a fighter faltered under the attack.

On their way back to camp, Dan was lost in his thoughts until Jody interrupted him. "So what did you like best about leave?"

Dan looked up, startled. "The opera. It was simply amazing to hear those performers fill an entire concert hall with their voices. I doubt I could ever sing as strongly as that." He'd previously told Jody a little bit about his singing.

"I've only known you two weeks, but I get the feeling that you're the kind of guy who can do about anything you set your mind to." It sounded like a compliment, and Dan decided to take it as such. It's possible that Jody was being a little critical, because he hadn't been nearly as excited to spend nearly every waking minute out on the streets doing something. Dan got the feeling that he would have been content to spend his time reading in the hotel or attending more events at the Garden.

"I hope it doesn't seem vain, but I really do want to do big things with my life. I know I didn't give myself the musical talent I have, so I think it's something that God must want me to do—at least, assuming I live through the war."

"I've never really thought much about God. Some of the orphanages are run by churches, like the Catholics, but the place I grew up was run by the city, and they didn't worry about church. Sunday was the day that we cleaned the place from top to bottom so we'd be ready to go to work on Monday."

"You didn't go to school?" Dan looked at him quizzically.

"When I was a little kid I went to school, but by the time I got to be twelve years old, the city sent me to work at a nearby factory, where I carried off clinkers from the blast furnace. Everybody had to work if they wanted a place to sleep."

"But how long did you work? I mean, when did you get to be a kid?"

Jody turned and looked at him, perhaps realizing for the first time how different they were. "I never got to be a kid, Dan. We worked at least twelve hours a day, five days a week, and half a day on Saturday. Saturday afternoon was spent washing our clothes, and then Sunday we cleaned the building. Sometimes we could play in a street baseball game or something on Saturday, but that's about it." He looked down dejectedly. "I never really had fun, but that's just what it took to stay alive."

Dan didn't say anything.

"They did let us do boxing pretty regularly. I think some of the schoolmasters and administrators liked to bet on it."

Dan was stunned. He'd always had to have a summer job, but he'd never had to work like Jody was talking about. For the first time, he felt some of the anger that his father must have felt about how the little guy gets taken advantage of. It also helped him understand why it had been so important that some of the child labor laws had been passed.

"Well, at least we had a great time together on this leave," Dan said as cheerfully as he could. Jody smiled and nodded. The one thing Jody didn't like was too much silence, so Dan started talking about everything they'd done to find out what Jody had liked. Before they knew it, they were back at camp, where a lot of the other guys had started returning from their leaves home.

* * *

Weapons training was a real eye-opener for Dan. He'd been target shooting often enough that handling a weapon was almost second nature to him. But he'd always had lots of time to break the weapon down when he got back home and to methodically clean every part. Here, however, everybody was judged by how quickly he could disassemble and reassemble his weapon, and it had to be in perfect working order at all times, cleaned, and lubricated until the barrel glistened. He loved the Springfield rifle, and, of the more than five hundred men there, he earned some of the highest scores on the target range. But he hated the machine gun. The thought of firing a weapon that could go through more than four hundred rounds per minute was disgusting to him. There was no precision required—just spray a pattern and hope that you hit your target. If you did, of course, you'd tear it to shreds in seconds. His instructors told stories of hundreds of men being mowed down when they went up and over the top of their trench to attack an enemy position because the artillery had failed to take out a machine-gun emplacement.

That's where Dan and the other top marksmen were to come in. While the average soldier seldom stuck his head above the level of the trench in daylight, it was the job of the sniper to stand in a reinforced turret where he could sight his weapon through a narrow slit in the parapet and fire on even the slightest movement across no-man's-land to take out a machine gunner, for example. They practiced endlessly, it seemed, spotting potential targets during all hours of the day and night and then drawing a single bead that would take them out on the first shot. The reality of the battlefront was that if they failed on their first attempt, they wouldn't get a second, because the gunner would duck down and eventually call in an artillery barrage on the estimated position of the sniper. If the machine gunner was killed on the first shot, however, then no one knew for sure where the bullet had come from. So the sniper could be either the salvation of a unit or the cause of its destruction.

Inevitably, before each day of training was over, somebody would ask a question that irritated the instructor because of its simplicity, and he'd order them all to run five laps around the field before turning in for mess. For his part, Dan was glad for the exercise. He'd always been extremely deliberate in his shooting, but here he was trained to react more quickly, and it took all his powers of concentration to keep up. The running gave him a chance to unwind.

When the scores came in, he was rated among the top in the class for accuracy but one of the lowest for his reaction time. His instructors cautioned him that he'd have to get over that if he wanted to stay alive. So he worked at it hour after hour, until his head hurt.

Finally, one of his instructors, after getting to know Dan a little, took him aside to talk to him.

"When you play classical music, do you have to do it with precision?"

"Absolutely. There's room for some interpretation, but it's very subtle. The music itself is so complex that you have to be precise."

"But you also play ragtime and popular tunes?"

"Yes," Dan said with something of a puzzled expression, wondering what the point was.

"I assume there's a lot of room to improvise?"

"There is. In fact, that's what makes it fun. One of the reasons they were interested in me at Stanford is that I could do both, which at least some of the teachers there think is impossible. So why the questions? I didn't know you were interested in music."

His instructor responded, "I'm not. I am interested in weapons. And I think, with just one small adjustment, you can be good enough to stand a chance of living through the war. Here's what I'm thinking. Being an effective sniper is like playing classical music—you have time to set up the shot carefully, and accuracy means everything, since you only have one chance. But in the normal flow of a battle, things happen fast, without time for set-piece actions. You have to simply react to the changing battle action without thought. Maybe that's like playing popular music, where you have to improvise and make adjustments on the spot. So you really need to be flexible enough to call on whichever skill set applies to the situation you're in at the time."

Dan nodded. "I hear what you're saying. I've always approached shooting in a very formal manner because . . ." he paused, "well, because." He didn't really want to explain his aversion to having to take more than one shot to kill something. "But it makes sense that I learn to loosen up when it's called for. I think I can do that."

"The point is that when you're up against a machine gun, precision doesn't mean a thing. They can throw so much lead that all you can do is take cover and hope for good luck or fire back fast enough and accurately enough that you take out the enemy before he can get you."

After that, Dan's speed and reaction improved noticeably.

* * *

When weapons training came to an end, Dan and the others awaited orders for their transfer. By now it was early spring of 1918, and the British were providing an increasing supply of troop transport vessels. Dan was notified to ship out for France in just ten days. It wasn't enough time to really do anything, so he decided to stay close to camp this time. Jody went with some other buddies into New York again, probably happy to have some guys who were less inhibited when it came to the saloons that he said he liked to frequent back in Cleveland. While in the city with Dan, Jody had never tried to coerce Dan into going into places like that, which caused Dan to respect him a lot.

But this time Dan stayed put. He figured it would just depress him to see the great music venues again, only to know that he was off to the mud and muck of the trenches. The one indulgence he gave himself was to send the Richardses a telegram to let them know how he was doing. A letter would have been just as good, but somehow he wanted to use up some of the money he'd saved so he didn't feel as tied to it. He wanted the Richardses to know that they were special, and he figured a telegram was the best way to do that. Who knew how long it would be before he could see them again? The war was certainly showing no signs of winding down. In fact, the officers told them that the Germans were making some remarkably fierce advances out of the trenches, even threatening Paris. The American doughboys were needed more than ever.

* * *

"Would you stop dancing around like that?" Dan looked at Jody fiercely, but inside he was almost as excited. Neither of them had been on a large ship before. Now they were standing at the railing of a converted ocean liner that was about to depart New York Harbor, and Jody was so full of nervous energy that he couldn't stand still.

The smell of the black smoke drifting down from the mammoth smokestacks filled Dan's nostrils with the familiar smell of the railroad yards in Pocatello. He could feel the great engines throbbing beneath the deck and watched in wonder as the massive ship swung slowly away from the pier and out into the channel of the East River. In a matter of moments, they were being pushed out of the harbor by the tiny tugboats nestled up against them on both sides. Once free of the docks, the tugs pulled away, and the ship's engines took over. Then they started to pick up a little speed.

Dan watched in wonder as the Statue of Liberty passed off to their starboard side. He recalled his visit to the statue during his leave. The tour guide who had led them up inside the statue to stand on the small platform at the base of the torch had told them the statue was a gift from France to celebrate the Americans' fight for independence and spoke about the role that France had played in helping them earn that freedom. He felt a surge of pride as they passed the Statue of Liberty, knowing that freedom of choice is as important as life itself and that sometimes men have to die in order for freedom to live.

His attitude had improved, and he was resolved to do his duty, no matter how unpleasant it might be. He knew that he thought too deeply about things, but in his thinking about death, he'd come to realize that it would be fine for the person who died, because they'd be back in the spirit world, where things would make more sense. He just worried about the people who would be left behind—specifically the Richardses, and even more specifically, Sister Richards. She had both Trevor and Dan to worry about, and he knew that it would be hard on her. He resolved right then to write them every week, no matter what else happened.

When they cleared the Verazzano Narrows that form the mouth of the entrance to New York Harbor, they joined a convoy with perhaps ten other ships—some troop ships, some supply—to travel across the ocean together. On their fifth day out, as they were approximately two-thirds of the way across the Atlantic to the Bay of Biscay, the convoy came under attack. The first ship in the convoy, a merchant vessel traveling with the transports, exploded without warning. The German submarine that hit the lead vessel had obviously been waiting patiently for the approach of the group. The torpedo must have struck the forward magazine, because there were two distinct concussions. The first was the torpedo going off, powerful in its own right; but the second was much larger and literally blew the front end off the ship.

Dan had been struggling with seasickness for most of the voyage and happened to be standing at the rail toward the bow of the ship when their neighbor was hit. He watched in horror as the front end of the ship went up in flames, and the whole ship nosed deeply into the water. The forward momentum seemed to carry it forward and thrust it down with almost no letup in speed. Before he could fully fathom what was happening, he watched the stern of the ship rise up in the air, and then the whole massive ship just slid forward with a mighty roar until it sank completely. Huge blasts of air erupted from the ocean as all the air inside the hull found its way out through the doors and windows that must have been blown off their hinges from the force of the pressure.

Although he hadn't looked at his watch, he was sure the whole spectacle occurred in less than three minutes. It was so distressing that he found he'd run all the way forward to the bow of the ship without realizing it, as if he could do something to save some of the men. He heard himself crying out to no one in particular, "There were more than a thousand men on that ship!" Vainly he gazed into the water to see if there were any survivors. The concussion alone would have crushed most of their lungs, and the quick plunge beneath the waves would have trapped the rest of them. It was almost too much to think about.

He was right. There was no time to think about it, because in the rush of events, he'd completely ignored the Klaxon horn sounding general quarters on his own ship. Now he became aware of the sailors running past him. One of them shouted, "Get to your assigned position, you ignorant sod." Dan turned and raced to the spot where he'd been instructed to stand in case of attack. He was glad that he was given a spot on the deck. He could face the prospect of getting blown up or even drowning, but he couldn't stand the thought of being trapped below deck if the ship started down and couldn't help but think of the men in the engine room, who spent every day knowing that if the ship were torpedoed, there was almost no way they could ever get out in time.

Their ship was next in line for attack, and Dan mentally braced for the blow that seemed inevitable. But then he saw the thick, black smoke of a destroyer pour over the side of their own deck, and he watched in amazement as one of the escort ships steamed past them at an incredible speed. Within a matter of minutes, he heard a concussion. The fellow standing next to him said, "They've released the depth charges. That ought to scare off that blighter of a submarine." Dan hoped so—oh, how he hoped so. By now their ship had turned to starboard, which gave him a better view of the destroyer in action. He knew that in a few moments, it would zigzag in another direction to make it more difficult for the German to sight in on them.

The sailors on the destroyer were rolling the huge drums to the edge of the ship and releasing them in a carefully timed sequence. A series of mushroom-shaped charges broke the surface of the water in an even pattern between their ship and the destroyer. This went on for probably twenty minutes, at which time the destroyer pulled away off their port side to continue the chase. The convoy, which had scattered with the first shot, now regrouped and started on the next leg of the voyage, with Dan's ship in front. Later that evening, the captain sounded the signal for "all hands on deck." He then conducted a very moving memorial ceremony for the men who had lost their lives earlier in the attack. His last words were to call on God for protection, that they might reach their port in safety. "Amen," said Dan and all the others around him, with unusual zeal.

That night, he had difficulty falling asleep. Each sound in the ship jolted him awake, and he lay there in something of a sweat, wondering if they'd be next.

Chapter Twelve

FIRST AIR COMBAT

It was obvious that Trevor was ready to graduate from flight training school, but Fouchard held him back with his group while giving him as much flying time as possible. Fouchard knew that with his natural skill and ability, Trevor would be immediately drawn to the thrill of battle, and he wanted to make certain that he had as much practice as possible to help him escape the inevitable problems he'd face in his first days at the front. No matter how skilled a pilot became, it was likely that his first encounter with hostile forces would leave him a bit bewildered and vulnerable because there was so much to watch out for. The only preparation was to refine his flying skills as much as possible so his mind would be free from thinking about operating the machine while he plotted an escape or an attack.

Of course, Trevor had no objection, since he was able to fly twice and sometimes three times a day. Like most pilots, the air was as natural to navigate for Trevor as the current in a river for a fish, and he soon learned to control his aircraft with little thought. If he wanted to go into a steep banking turn to the left, he simply had to think it, and the airplane was there. If he wanted to climb to practice a stall, the aircraft ascended until it could climb no more. He loved the feeling as the weight of the engine pulled the nose down into a dive and he felt the increasing g-force pulling him back against the seat. In time, he was taught how to do aerial spirals, keeping track of the number of loops as his plane circled toward the ground in a vertical dive. Fouchard told him that the loops allowed him to control the rate of descent while making himself a difficult target for any enemy that might be following.

Trevor loved it all and felt like he'd taken his motorcycle into the sky, where he could travel in all directions. His instructors recognized his ability, and one even actually compared him to some of the great aces of the war. Trevor enjoyed the competition in the class but recognized that no matter how skilled a pilot was, a stray bullet could cut him down as easily as the worst novice in the Air Service. So he put all thoughts of glory out of his mind and simply spent the days enjoying his time in the air.

Alan wasn't so lucky. He'd overcome his initial fear and had even gotten pretty good at managing the occasional airsickness that came over him. Yet he was hesitant in the air, waiting too long to initiate a maneuver and then reacting in a jerking fashion when his mistake became apparent. There was a real question about his qualification to fly, but in the end, his instructors cleared him for flight because the need for pilots was so great.

The next step in their training was to go to gunnery school at Cezeau, a quiet spot on the Bay of Biscay far from the front lines, where the pilots could practice firing harmlessly into targets on the ocean and the bluffs. They first started by shooting from a moving platform on the ground, then from a boat on the bay so they could learn to control their fire while in motion, and finally by shooting live ammunition from their aircraft. The instructors made it clear that a fighter aircraft was nothing more than a movable mount for a machine gun and that the pilot aimed the gun by aiming the aircraft. Trevor wasn't as adept at target shooting as he was at flying, but he got passing scores.

He was anxious to get to the front because the Germans had just launched their second massive Ludendorff offensive in April in yet another attempt to batter the British into submission. The need to put every available airplane into the air was urgent, and the British were pleading with General Pershing to release as many American pilots as possible. This time Pershing complied, and orders were cut to send Trevor and his class to a forward aerodrome to fight as part of the 95th Pursuit Squadron based at Villeneuve-les-Vertus in the Toul sector. Their instructors asked them each to go up one last time for practice, which they readily assented to do. Flying was now so second nature that they didn't even think about it.

Trevor ran out to his aircraft, one of the extremely agile and buoyant but highly temperamental Nieuport 28s that he would fly in actual combat. The Nieuport has a Rhone single-valve, nine-cylinder rotary engine that had the odd distinction of having the propeller mounted permanently to the engine block with the entire assembly rotating around a stationary shaft. This engine was air cooled, with the rotation of the engine block forcing air across the heat fins. It was a much lighter-weight engine than the standard water-cooled engine, which increased its maximum altitude, load-carrying capacity, and overall agility. The weight of the engine block and propeller turning at up to 1800 rpms also produced a gyroscope effect that took some getting used to. Plus, the engine was very noisy and had a tendency to shed oil back into the face of the pilot.

Trevor fired up the engine and had started the short roll for takeoff when the main bearing gave way. The entire engine assembly tore loose from its fitting, sending a shower of hot oil back into Trevor's face while the aircraft wrenched itself to the ground just as it was lifting for takeoff. The crash threw Trevor forward against his restraining belts, which undoubtedly saved his life, but his left arm was crushed in the wreckage of the airplane. Fortunately, the gasoline tank didn't explode, and the mechanics were able to extract him quickly. He had a severe burn to his left cheek which also bothered his eye, although the doctor didn't think it would do permanent damage.

His arm was a different matter. It had a compound fracture that required it to be immobilized for at least six weeks. Trevor was so furious and frustrated that he couldn't hold back the tears. If he'd been the type to swear, this would have been the time to do it. It was particularly tough when the rest of his class transferred out to their assault groups the next day. Alan stopped to say good-bye, and then Trevor was left alone. With the training grounds being so far from the front, there weren't a lot of casualties in the hospital, and he was left pretty much to himself.

After two weeks in the hospital, he pleaded to be sent to the 95th so he could join his crew, promising the doctors that he'd let his arm heal there. His face had cleared up to the point that the doctors felt it would be okay for him to go without bandages, although it was likely he'd have some pretty severe scarring. Trevor assured them he didn't care as long as he could get out of there. Since there was no real reason to keep him back, they agreed to the transfer.

When he finally arrived at the huge aerodrome in Toul, he was relieved to see some of the men from his training unit, including Alan. While he liked each of the men in the unit, he and Alan found they had a lot in common with another young American pilot named Josh Brown. All three were quite religious and refrained from taking advantage of the open bar at the officers' club as well as the other tawdry entertainment that sprang up around the military base.

Because his arm was still immobilized, Trevor couldn't go out on patrols. His flight commander assigned him to administrative tasks around the air base, such as keeping track of the pilots' logs, writing letters to the families of pilots killed in action, and so forth. It drove him crazy. At one point, he pleaded with his flight leader to let him go up in the second seat of an observation aircraft, but he was assured that it would put both him and the pilot at risk to fill a seat with an injured airman. Most of the other pilots in his barracks said they were jealous of his arm because it meant he could relax on the ground, far away from the danger. In fact, he learned that the most popular days were the bad weather days when no one could go up flying. On those days, the pilots slept in until late morning or early afternoon, a nice change from regular patrol days when they had to be up and on the flight line by as early as 0500. But Trevor wasn't satisfied and ached to get into action. His deep and abiding fear was that the war would end before he had a chance to see combat. Somehow he sensed that no matter what he did in civilian air, it would never be as exciting or meaningful as what he could do in the war.

In the fifth week of Trevor's recovery, two regular patrols were out and both alert pilots had been dispatched to take on a German Rumpler reconnaissance plane that had been spotted deep behind enemy lines. He was in the tower chatting with the dispatcher when the phone rang. He heard the sergeant's side of the conversation. "They're attacking east of Metz? I'm sorry, but both our alert pilots are out, and we have nobody here. Yes, I understand they're in trouble, but there's nothing I can do. If somebody lands, I'll send him up as fast as I can." Then he hung up the phone.

"Who's under attack?" Trevor asked anxiously.

The sergeant turned to him. "Ground troops report that some poor Frenchies in one of the new Broquet bombers are under attack on our side of the line, heading this way. Two Germans are attacking the Broquet, and it looks pretty bad for the French guys."

"I know where Metz is, I've been studying the maps until I've memorized every road, stream, and hill."

The sergeant looked at him suspiciously. "So what? You can't fly with that arm, and you know it."

"But, they're likely to be killed, and I could be there in under ten minutes."

"And a lot of good you'll do—you'll just get killed yourself."

Trevor looked at him desperately. "I won't get killed. It's my left arm, for heaven's sake. I can fly the aircraft with just my right arm and the pedals, and I have enough motion in the fingers of my left hand to control the engine." He stared at him earnestly, as if willing him to give permission.

"They'd have my hide," the sergeant said uncertainly.

"Then you just look the other way, and I'll go out on my own. I don't care if I do get written up. Somebody's got to help."

The sergeant opened and shut his mouth without saying anything, then finally said, "Okay, I'm looking the other way."

"Thanks," Trevor said breathlessly as he jumped up. With that, he raced down the stairs and started to the hangars at a dead run. The sergeant had already called ahead, so the mechanics were scrambling to get his aircraft in position for an immediate takeoff. When his mechanic came within range, he shouted, "You can't go up! You'll be a hazard to everyone in the air. You've never even been in combat before, and you shouldn't go out by yourself."

"I don't have time to talk. Just help me get strapped in. Now!"

His mechanic muttered something. Trevor knew that he was saying all this for show and that he really understood that Trevor had to at least try to help the bomber.

Trevor was soon ready to fire up the aircraft. In spite of the urgency, he still took time to go through his pre-flight checklist, test the controls, and check the windsock. "Switch off," he shouted. His mechanic gave it the priming turn.

"Switch on! Contact!" The little Nieuport sputtered to life, and Trevor switched on all twelve cylinders as the engine roared to full acceleration. He was off and up in the air, flying northeast toward Verdun at maximum speed.

He looked down to see the miles of trenches that showed he was just south of the front lines. The shock of seeing the trenches from the air for the first time subdued Trevor. The trenches snaked their way across the French countryside in weird patterns for hundreds of miles. Even with his thoughts occupied on trying to find the Broquet, he was able to appreciate the absolute devastation of no-man's-land, a dark, ugly scar of brown slicing its way through the otherwise lush and verdant countryside.

Still, there would be other days to explore this further. Right now, he was straining in every direction to see the bomber. He'd made a mental plot of where he thought it should be at this point, but he could see absolutely nothing in the air. After circling for a few minutes, he was completely frustrated. He even banked hard to the right, tipping the aircraft on its side, to give him an unrestricted view of the landscape below in case there was a burning bomber on the ground. But there was nothing.

Suddenly he saw two puffs of archy—anti-aircraft artillery—off to his left. The puffs of smoke were white, which meant they were Allied shells. At first he didn't pay attention; then a thought nagged him. Ground troops used archy to signal airplanes. The number and height of the puffs indicated the number of enemy aircraft, their altitude, and their general location. Without any hesitation, he banked to the left and headed straight for the place where he'd seen the puffs. The sky was still empty of everything except a few clouds. Then, out of the corner of his injured eye, he thought he saw a black speck down toward the ground. As he drew closer, it became clear that there was an aircraft down below him. Then he saw that there were three.

The leading aircraft was huge, the biggest airplane he'd ever seen in his life. The other two were obviously harassing it. Now was the time for action. He'd flown close enough to the front lines that he was now east of the scene. Even though it was late morning, the sun was still behind him, and he was at least one thousand meters above the Germans. He judged the moment as best he could and then shoved forward on the stick and started into a steep dive. He knew he'd pick up enough airspeed to overtake the Germans easily. They were dodging this way and that around the bomber, which meant the observer was being effective in holding them off with his rotating gun. He also observed that the pilot of the Broquet was executing some amazing maneuvers that seemed impossible for an airplane that size.

As the distance narrowed, he picked out one of the Germans and came flying in at a speed of at least 170 miles per hour. He tried to bring the German into his sights, but the German suddenly swerved to the left, still unaware of Trevor's presence. The move surprised him so much that he simply shot past the German on the right and had to pull up into a horizontal vrille to pull away from the ground. The little Nieuport responded beautifully, and up and over he went, coming back in behind the German a second time. This time he was prepared for any move, and at just the right moment, the German came into his sights. He pulled back on the trigger and was pleased to hear his gun respond. At a firing rate of 650 bullets per minute, he didn't have to hold the trigger very long. With every fifth bullet a tracer, he was able to follow his line of fire, and he immediately figured out that he was way off target.

He gripped the stick a little harder and brought the German back into his sights. This time when he pulled the trigger, the tracer line showed that at least some bullets had to have hit the German. Of course, that was just the first clue. The second was the startled response of the German attacker, who was now cast in the role of the attacked. He shot up like a small rocket and banked hard to the right to figure out where the Allied attack had come from. Trevor followed him into the turn, letting off a few more rounds before pivoting to the left. He'd seen the other German out of the corner of his eye and was anxious to separate him from the Broquet as well. He shot past the huge bomber so close that he saw the observer give him a thumbs-up as he crossed their path. The second German fighter came into view, above him but still in front. Trevor pulled up and fired up into the belly of the fighter. He saw his tracer trail cut across the belly, tearing at least a few holes in the fabric. The German fighter broke to the left side in a diving motion, now fully aware that there was another Allied aircraft on the scene.

From that point, things moved so fast Trevor could hardly keep track of the action. First he came under fire from one of the Germans while the other attempted to take on the bomber. Trevor responded with a reventment and got a few shots off at his pursuer while the bomber observer did his best to hold off his attacker. All the while, they were moving further behind Allied lines. Finally, both of the German fighters came straight for Trevor in an attempt to take him out so they could get a clear shot at the bomber without this nuisance, but he dove into a deep spiral that broke just a thousand feet above the ground. As he gained altitude, he managed to fire off a few rounds. Even though he was shooting pretty wildly, he saw that he must have hit a strut on one of the German planes, because the wing looked like it crumpled. At last both German planes reluctantly pulled away and turned for home. Meanwhile, the Broquet was almost out of sight, so Trevor banked to the west and started back—he hoped—to his aerodrome.

As he thought about it on the way back, he realized that he'd been crazy to come out with virtually no familiarity with the territory. The most amazing part was how fast everything had happened and how close the action was. He'd never imagined that he'd actually see the faces of his opponents as they tried to kill him and he tried to kill them. It was macabre, he decided. Still, he'd apparently succeeded in driving off the Germans, which wasn't too bad an accomplishment. It had been the most thrilling experience of his life.

When he finally glanced down at his watch, he was surprised to see that the whole thing had taken less than half an hour. Time had seemed suspended while he was in combat as his mind was fully occupied, coping with the changing battle scene. Now, as the excitement wore off, he felt tired, dead tired. He also became aware of deep, throbbing pain in his left arm. Even though he had mainly used his right hand and right arm in the combat, it was impossible for the left arm not to act in sympathy, if for no other reason than to maintain balance. Plus, with the sharp maneuvering, his arm must have been thrown against the restraints and side of the cockpit multiple times. At any rate, his arm hurt, his brain was overtaxed, and, worst of all, he was lost.

Each pilot was provided with a map of the battle area that was stretched between two rollers mounted in a compact, little device in the front of the cockpit. Trevor thought he had a pretty good idea of where he was, but he kept hoping to find a river or city to confirm his location. With the sun now directly overhead, it was difficult to even know in which direction he was flying. After ten or fifteen minutes of circling the area, looking for anything that resembled something on the map, he started to feel a bit of panic well up inside. For all he knew, he was behind German lines, slowly using up his fuel. He decided to go in the direction he was sure was west and to set down near any kind of installation he could find. He brought his plane to level flight and started marking the time. Occasionally he glanced down at his injured arm, holding the stick between his knees while rubbing the arm with his right hand. When doing this, he had to take short, quick glances up to make sure he was maintaining the horizon. With one of his glances, he was astonished to see two aircraft shoot past him, going the opposite direction. Cranking his head around, he saw them turn to follow.

At the moment he judged the aircraft were about to overtake him, he prepared to do a sweeping loop up into the sky, but he was surprised as one of the aircraft pulled even with him. Glancing over, he saw the insignia of another American aircraft. The pilot beckoned him to follow, and then executed a swift rolling turn to the left. Trevor inhaled slowly and followed him into the loop. They actually reversed course completely and started heading in the direction opposite where he'd been going. Trevor tried to catch him to indicate that he was running low on fuel and couldn't follow them into Germany when he saw the trenches appear below him. From the path he was now following, it became clear that he'd actually been on the German side of the line. Instead of heading back to his own aerodrome, he'd been flying directly into Germany! In another twenty minutes, he saw his aerodrome come into view, and the pilot he'd been following indicated with a hand movement that Trevor should land first. He was grateful for that, because his arm was now throbbing so badly it was almost the only thing he could think about. Completing a graceful loop that brought him into the wind, he settled the Nieuport gently onto the grass and rolled to a decent stop at the end of the runway. His chief mechanic, John Getty, came racing out to help him.

"You're alive," he shouted.

"Barely," Trevor said. "I didn't get hit or anything, but I almost made it to Berlin before those two pilots took pity on me and helped me find the way."

"Didn't get hit?" Getty said. "I think you better take a look at your airplane."

As Trevor stepped onto the ground, he looked at the fuselage and saw at least fifteen bullet holes. There were also holes through the left wing. "Oh, my gosh," he cried out. "I had no idea I'd been hit!"

"Look at this one," Getty said. "Another three inches and it would have gone straight through you." The bullet hole was just behind his seat, and as he walked around, he could see that the entrance and exit had passed within inches of the cockpit.

Trevor's legs turned to jelly and he collapsed to the ground with no warning. Getty burst out laughing. "Are you okay?"

"I don't think so. My arm hurts, my brain hurts, and my legs don't seem to want to work."

Getty reached down and helped him stand up. "Now, you just stand here for a minute. I don't want to have to carry you back to the hangar. You did all right for yourself, and you deserve to walk back under your own power."

Trevor wobbled unsteadily for a moment and then started walking on his own. "Thanks. Thanks a lot." Getty walked with him, just in case he buckled again, but he made certain that everyone who was rushing out to meet Trevor could see that he was walking on his own.

Josh and Alan had been out on patrol earlier that morning, but they were back now and were the first to run up to him.

"Are you okay?" Alan asked.

"Yeah, I'm okay," Trevor said quietly.

"You're the talk of the whole aerodrome," Josh said quickly.

Great, the other pilots have already told them how they found me flying the wrong way into Germany. That'll be good for my reputation. As he looked toward the hangar, he caught sight of his commanding officer, Captain George

McMurphy, who did not look happy. *Oh, yeah, and there's that business of flying against orders to deal with. Maybe a court martial to add to the list of things I should be worried about.*

"Are you listening to me?" Josh said urgently.

"What? No, I'm sorry. My mind's kind of rattled right now."

"We got a call from ground troops who reported that a crazy American airplane came to the defense of a French Broquet and actually succeeded in driving off two German attack planes. The dispatcher said that you took off to help them. Are you the guy the phone call was about?"

It took Trevor a moment or two to process this change in the conversation. "Yeah, I was the one. It was the most amazing experience of my life. Everything happened so fast."

"Well, that's what everybody's talking about. A green pilot with a broken arm taking on two German Fokkers. You have got to be one crazy fool!"

"You don't know the half of it. Just wait 'til you hear about my flight path home."

Josh was about to say something, but by this time they'd met up with McMurphy, so he wisely held his tongue.

"Richards!" McMurphy's eyes were blazing. "Just what part of the word *grounded* do you not understand? Is it possible that I wasn't clear in my communication with you?"

"No, sir," Trevor said quietly. "You were perfectly clear."

"So in spite of that, you decide to cut your own orders. Is that right?"

"There was no one here to help . . ." Trevor started to say, but then realized the futility of it. "Yes, sir, I went against orders."

About this time, the ground crew wheeled his Nieuport past the group, and McMurphy glanced at the bullet holes. "Not only that, but you got one of our aircraft shot to pieces."

Trevor didn't say anything. He just dropped his gaze to the ground.

McMurphy noticed him holding his left arm. Finally, he relented. "You did a fine thing, Richards. It was stupid, but fine. Did you wreck your arm?"

Trevor glanced up solemnly. "I don't know, sir. It hurts awfully bad." Perhaps it was the effect of all the excitement mixed with pain, but he felt hot tears dribble down his cheeks. He hated that, just hated it. But he couldn't stop.

"Brown, why don't you and Gledhill help this pilot to the barracks? First combat can be pretty rough—particularly for those who are stupid enough to try it all by themselves. I think he should lie down for a while."

"Yes, sir," Josh said crisply.

"Get your arm checked by the medic as soon as you're ready. Then report to me after you've had a chance to calm down."

"Thank you, sir."

"One more thing, Richards—if you ever disobey a standing order again, you'll be out of the air corps. Is that understood?"

"Yes, sir, I understand." Trevor was miserable.

McMurphy didn't want to embarrass him anymore, so he turned and walked away.

"Wow, you went up against orders?" Josh asked as they walked toward the barracks. "I figured they sent you up in spite of your arm."

"What was I supposed to do? We got this call, and there was nobody around. You know as well as I do that two German fighters would eventually wear out the Broquet. All the Germans have to do is use up the Broquet's ammunition, then leisurely shoot it from the sky."

"Well, I think you did the right thing," Alan said. "I just hope your arm's okay."

"Me too," Trevor said weakly. He really was feeling kind of faint right now and was glad that they were almost to the barracks.

Just then another aviator jogged up to their side. "Hey, lieutenant, are you all right?" Trevor looked up but didn't recognize the fellow who asked.

"I'm okay," he said tentatively. "I just kind of aggravated the problem in my arm."

"I heard about you going out to help the French bomber. That was a really great thing to do—and with a broken arm. Amazing!" Trevor still looked puzzled. A grin of recognition broke on the other pilot's face. "I'm sorry. I'm the guy who helped you find your way home."

"Oh," Trevor said with relief. "Well, then, I'm glad to meet you. I thought I was heading straight for home and couldn't figure out why you wanted me to turn around."

"You were heading straight for the kaiser, I'm afraid." They both laughed. "Well, I gotta go. Maybe you can come over to our side sometime and we'll have a hot drink or something. You were terrific for a first time out. Congratulations!"

"Thanks." Trevor started into the barracks. He looked at his buddies and said, "Seems like a nice guy. He probably saved my life today."

Josh and Alan looked at him in amazement. "Don't you know who that is?" Josh asked incredulously.

"No. Should I?"

"That was Jimmy Meisener, for crying out loud. You were rescued by Meisener, and he invited you for hot chocolate."

"Meisener?" Trevor shook his head to try to clear it. "One of the most decorated pilots in the French Escadrille, talking to me? I must be dreaming."

"You're not dreaming, but you probably should be. Come on, and let's get you into bed." Trevor didn't resist.

Chapter Thirteen

TRENCH WARFARE

Dan's ship finally pulled into port in the Bay of Biscay in mid-March 1918. After the submarine attack that destroyed the merchant ship, they experienced just two more alarms—probably false—that sent their escorts racing ahead of the convoy to lay down a shield of protective depth charges. While standing at the ship's railing one day, Dan remarked to Jody that he was glad he hadn't signed up for the navy. "I can't stand the thought of being below the waterline waiting for an explosion that may leave you deafened but alive while the ship heads straight for the bottom. Somehow, drowning seems the worst way to die. Better to do it in the open air." Jody thanked him for that sentiment later as they were forced to go below decks for lights out.

After landing in France, they were quickly assembled into their units and transported by railcar through Paris on their way to the front. Because of the recent German offensives, there was no time for them to stop and see the sights. Dan had to peer at the grand old city through slats in the frame of the car. Even with only quick glimpses, though, his heart thrilled when he saw some of the great landmarks, including the Eiffel Tower, still standing proudly above the city and within French control.

Their initial deployment was in an area known as the St. Mihiel salient, where the Germans had actually broken the stalemate to drive into Allied territory. They'd finally been stopped but had managed to hang onto some of the land they'd acquired. This required the construction of a whole new series of trenches so that when the Americans arrived to relieve the British on the left and the French on the right, they found the trenches relatively new and not yet fully fouled by human waste and rodents.

As Dan's unit approached the trenches at dusk, they were brought forward by motor trucks to a point within about one mile of the front. This was as far as the German infantry could effectively shoot their small arms with hope of hitting the advancing and retreating troops. Dan's unit's field commander, First Lieutenant Joe Stennis, formed them into a group to provide instruction. "It'll probably be a bit unnerving when you first hear enemy bullets whine past as we advance toward the trenches. While there's always a chance one can hit you, the odds are really against it. The Germans are firing from too far away. So go in standing up, moving quickly, with occasional changes of course to throw off an enemy gunner who may have decided to track your line of movement. About half a mile in, we'll enter one of the communications trenches. It's really narrow, so you may feel closed in at first. Don't worry. You'll get used to it soon enough, and if you're like most of us, you'll take comfort from the fact that the German bullets can't find you down there." He smiled at them, but they were too nervous to notice.

Stennis continued. "Stay close together because there will be a number of opportunities for you to take a wrong turn, and who knows where you'll wind up?" He decided to try humor once again, since a lot of men got killed their first day in combat because they became so paralyzed by fear that they lost their common sense when they first came under fire. "The trench system is pretty intimidating at first, since the trenches run for hundreds of miles from Belgium to

Switzerland. We only know of half a dozen or so men who got lost in the trenches and have never been heard from since. Rumor has it that one fellow made it to the Swiss border while looking for a latrine and decided to keep going south to fight with the Italians." He was disgusted when nobody laughed and decided this group was entirely too serious. These guys would have to lighten up if they hoped to stay alive. But such an attitude change wasn't going to happen today, so the lieutenant continued, "Once we get to the front, we'll post to our assigned location in the trench. The men you're relieving probably won't talk much, although they'll take time to bail the trench before leaving. That's part of trench courtesy. The single greatest cause of disability among our troops is trench foot, which is a condition of foot-rot brought on by living for days at a time with your feet immersed in standing water. In the winter, men have had their boots frozen to their feet, and the surgeons have had to cut the boot off to try to save their feet. That's why you should change your shoes frequently and always have a pair of dry socks to put on. The other thing you should always do before leaving the trench is share the work of shoring up the wood revetments that prevent the sides of the trench from caving in. If any of you were carpenters before the war, you'll find yourself very popular here, since the last thing anyone wants is to suffocate under a collapsed wall." He sensed their uncertainty and added, "Don't worry too much about it—we have enough experienced men mixed in with the group that they'll help you figure out the routine. It's not much, so you'll learn it quick enough. After that, your biggest enemy will be boredom. Any questions?"

The men were silent. Stennis was used to that, so he waited them out. Finally, one little guy raised his hand and said timidly, "Where do we sleep, sir?"

"Are you tired, soldier?"

"Yes, sir."

"Don't worry," he said sarcastically. "They'll have your feather tick laid out and waiting, and we'll send a note across no-man's-land telling the Germans not to fire their artillery tonight, since you need your rest." Finally, everybody laughed as the soldier's face went beet red.

Stennis saw another hand go up. "Yes?"

It was Dan. "Can you tell me what's the single greatest mistake soldiers make their first day on the line?"

No one had ever asked him that question before. "I suppose," he said after a moment or two, "that the biggest risk you'll face is to overreact to the danger. The guys who seem to make it the longest are the ones who somehow manage to stay the most relaxed. A lot of men die out there every day, and it may be that you'll be one of them before the war is over. But you only increase the chance of that happening if you fret about it. Somehow, when a person tenses up, it makes them less flexible in responding to real danger. So to answer your question, the best way to minimize risk is to simply proceed in a smart but relaxed fashion. What's your name, soldier?"

"O'Brian, sir. Second Lieutenant Daniel O'Brian."

"Where you from, O'Brian?"

"Idaho, sir."

"Never been there. I'm a Missouri man myself." Stennis observed the way that Dan held his weapon and concluded that he'd probably do all right on the line—which meant, of course, that aside from a random bullet, he had as good a chance as any to make it through his first week in the trenches. When there were no more questions, Stennis said curtly, "Then let's move out."

Dan had run dozens of miles on hundreds of occasions in the past ten years, so he was in good physical condition. But none of his conditioning or training could have prepared him for this journey. Loaded down with a seventy-pound pack, he moved out strongly enough, but as they entered the bombed-out areas, he was thunderstruck by the sheer scale of destruction. The only thing that even came close to describing the experience was the alien landscape he'd seen when the teachers quorum went on a summer camp to Craters of the Moon in central Idaho. At the time, he'd thought it otherworldly and exciting to see the great volcanic craters and cones thrown up in the middle of the desert floor. But here the craters were created by artillery shells, and the shattered remnants of trees and deserted, bombed-out farmhouses littered the landscape with debris. He was also sickened by the stench of rotting horses killed as they were forced forward with supplies, then abandoned where they fell. He stumbled over a skeleton at one point and found his heart up in his throat until he determined that it was not human. Then he heard the whizzing of a bullet pass not three feet from his head. In spite of all the training and the lieutenant's instruction, he hit the deck and lay there prone. The lieutenant heard the noise and turned around and laughed at him. As Dan picked himself up, he saw that he wasn't the only one who had gone down. A bit sheepishly, he began his forward movement again.

The Germans must have been lazy that night, because they fired only an occasional round, perhaps enough to let the newcomers know they had them in their sights. But no one was hit, and they finally reached the entrance to the communications trench, where they descended a gentle slope into the trench. They were taken in at dusk, since that put the sun squarely in the Germans' eyes. The risk was that the American soldiers created silhouettes as they came from the west, but after more than three years in the war, the Germans had learned to save their fire for when it would really count. Plus, it hurt their eyes to look into the sun, and few were willing to put up with the bother.

The air inside the trench was almost suffocating. Even though it was still cold outside, the musty smell was over-

powering and reminded Dan of the potato cellars near
Blackfoot. He stumbled forward along with the rest of the
troops, disgusted when his foot slipped off one of the planks
into the muck in the bottom of the trench. His boot was
covered in mud, and his foot started to get cold just a few
minutes later as the moisture seeped around the water-
proofing. After what seemed an hour of twisting and
turning, they came to a larger trench running perpendicular
to the one they were in, which meant they'd reached the
front. Stumbling to the left, Dan came upon a group of
soldiers who looked up without comment and started
collecting their personal effects. He was struck by how old
their faces looked compared to the youth of their bodies.
They were filthy, and as one brushed past Dan, he was overwhelmed by the odor. At this point he was standing next to
Lieutenant Stennis, who saw him wince. "These guys are
lucky. They get to go to billets for a week, where they'll all
get hot baths and good food. When you see them in a week,
they'll look like they're fresh out of high school." Dan didn't
reply, but he was dubious they could ever clean up well.

Their first night in the trench was spent shivering in the
cold, huddled up next to each other in one of the dugouts.
The Germans finally decided to give them a welcome and
pounded the ground around them mercilessly all through
the night. Neither Dan nor Jody got any kind of sleep.
Meanwhile, the men who had previous experience on the
line appeared to sleep soundly through the whole
maddening experience. The noise was both oppressive and
unnerving. Dan worried that it would damage his hearing,
so he pushed some of the cotton in his medical kit into his
ears, resolved that he'd do everything he could to protect his
hearing while in the war.

The next day dawned bright, clear, and cold. Lieutenant
Stennis was of the opinion that busy men were the most
effective, so he set them to work on the revetments, patiently

teaching them how to reinforce the sandbags that had started to sag or that were leaking and how to replace the wire that held them in place. While he moved around constantly, Dan noticed that the lieutenant never put his head above the surface, except for quick glances. Once their assigned area of the trench was shored up, the lieutenant spent the rest of the afternoon instructing them on how to protect themselves from various threats, such as a nighttime attack of Germans coming across no-man's-land to lob a grenade into the trench. He also showed them how to use the periscope they'd been provided to see up and over the trench. By the time night fell, Dan felt more assured that he could survive in this environment. It was unpleasant, but he could see that it was possible to get by if one was careful.

The next day gave them all a chance to see a man die in battle. One of the seasoned men crawled into the parapet to act as sentry. Dan happened to glance up just as the fellow leaned forward to look through the narrow observation slit. In the next instant the back of his head exploded as his body was thrown back and off the parapet. Lieutenant Stennis ran forward and lifted his body, but it was clear that he'd been killed instantly. The chance of a bullet finding that one spot was infinitesimal, but such was the chance of war. The lieutenant pulled the body to the back of the trench and assigned another one of the seasoned men to go up to observe. He then called for a crew to take the body back to the communications trench, where it could be sent back to the support and staging area for transport to a military cemetery.

A number of the newcomers retched when it all happened, and Dan had to suppress the response himself. But nobody said anything. *A man's just been killed,* Dan's brain screamed, but he kept his peace. There was to be a lot more of this before he was done.

On their third night in the trenches, Stennis asked for two volunteers to go with him out into no-man's-land. Men on both sides of the line used the cover of darkness to come up and out of the trench to repair their barbed-wire defenses, to recover the bodies of any men who had been killed during the day, and to generally keep their defensive perimeter secure. It was also the best time to reconnoiter the enemy's position. When no one stepped forward, he asked a second time. Finally, Dan and another soldier by the name of Gray volunteered. "We'll meet at 2300 for some quick instruction, then move out. Try to get some rest in the meantime." Stennis gave the rest of the group a disgusted glance and dismissed them. Fortunately, the German artillery was quiet, and Dan was able to get nearly three hours of sleep before being roused by Gray at 2230 for a quick bite of cold meat, a biscuit, and some hot tea. Dan chose not to drink the tea, settling for some hot water. Gray started to ask why but stopped short when Dan's glance made it clear he didn't want to talk about it.

Promptly at 2300, Stennis showed up and motioned for Dan and Gray to come forward. "Once we go over the top, it's essential that you maintain silence as much as possible. No talking whatsoever. If you see something, grab my leg and point. If I need to communicate, I'll whisper and let you know if you should whisper a response. Stay close enough that you can touch me. If we have even the smallest moonlight, you can follow my hand directions." He then showed them a number of simple hand gestures that would indicate how they were to proceed. "We'll be crawling out mostly to check on the Germans' wire and to see if it looks like they're planning any advances. I'm going to try to take us as close as possible to a machine gun emplacement that's been giving our guys trouble for the last few days. Whenever one of our men sticks his head up, these guys are all over him. I want to look for any vulnerability that could help us take them out. But under no circumstance do I want to start a fight tonight. Refrain from acting in self-defense unless return fire is essential—and I'm the only one who can judge that. There are only three of us, and we'd be easy targets. Understand?" They both replied in the affirmative.

"What if we're discovered and they start shooting at us?" Gray asked.

"Watch for my lead. If I think they're shooting in the dark, so to speak, we'll lie low until we can get out of there. If they start firing while we're returning, I may have you stand up and walk at a deliberate pace back to our trench."

"Stand up and walk?" Dan said incredulously.

"That's right, O'Brian. Most of the machine guns are sighted to fire near the ground to take out our men when they first come up out of the trench. As dark as it is tonight, they won't know exactly where we are and won't take time to retarget. By standing up, you run the risk of getting hit in the legs, but that's a lot better than having your vital organs shot up."

Dan could see that it was a lot more complicated than he had first believed.

"Right, then. Let's head out." Stennis quickly climbed, catlike, up one of the wooden ladders and over the top of the trench. Gray followed quickly. He was fairly short and of a slight build and moved with virtually no sound. As Dan put his foot on the lowest rung of the ladder, he felt his pulse quicken and had to gulp to slow his breathing. But he was up and over in no time and started crawling along the ground behind Gray and Stennis. He had his Springfield slung over his back with a full clip in the magazine, just in case. As they crawled along the ground, he found his clothing getting caught on their own barbed wire, which was annoying because he had to disentangle himself each time and then go even faster to catch up to the other two. For some reason, Stennis never got caught, and Gray acted like he'd been doing this sort of thing all his life. Dan felt clumsy and awkward and acutely noticed any sound he made, privately chastising himself each time he made a mistake.

As they neared the German lines, he heard some odd scratching sounds coming from in front of them. He couldn't figure out what it was until they started to encounter some of the German wire. Apparently, the Germans were out checking their barbed wire and making repairs where needed. He concentrated even more diligently on trying to move silently, wondering all the while how Stennis could possibly know where they were or keep track of how to get back. After perhaps ten minutes more of crawling in silence, Dan's heart was racing because it seemed as if they almost had to be right on top of the German trenches. His impression was confirmed when he suddenly bumped into Stennis, who was now lying perfectly still. Dan settled the weight of his body as quietly as possible into a position that he could comfortably sustain for as long as the lieutenant wanted to wait.

Finally, noiselessly, the lieutenant indicated they should start to withdraw. Dan backed out first, followed by Stennis, with Gray bringing up the rear. Dan made an attempt to move to the side so that Stennis could pass him but felt a tap on his leg indicating he should move forward. There was an urgency to the motion that made the hair on the back of Dan's neck stand up. Something was wrong, but he didn't know what. He tried to move faster but was hampered by the unevenness of the ground in this area. Suddenly the ground around him was illuminated in a bright, blue-white light that gave a ghostly appearance to the landscape.

Dan's mind raced through a jumble of thoughts as he tried to assess the new situation. *The British call it a Very Light, the Americans a Star Shell. But what color did they tell me a German shell is?* He desperately wanted to know if this shell was American or German. The sound of machine gun fire coming from behind him quickly provided an answer as he felt the ground around him churned up by the impact of bullets. He glanced back to see Stennis lying flat against the

ground, not moving. He moved his head ever so slightly to
see if he was alive and waiting or if he'd been hit.

The lieutenant blinked his eyes. Then three things
occurred almost simultaneously. First, he saw a shape rise up
slightly behind them, and somehow his mind determined
that it was Gray. Second, a brilliant orange flash blinded him
as an explosion ripped the air apart directly behind them.
The Germans had thrown a hand grenade from the machine
gun nest. He winced as a blast of searing air rolled over him.
Third, he saw Gray blown forward on top of the lieutenant,
who quickly rolled to the side.

What happened next was so fast that he didn't even
register it all. Gray tried to stand up, shrieking in agony, and
as he rose, Dan saw a figure back in the machine gun nest
raise up ever so slightly. In a reflexive action, he pulled his
weapon to his shoulder and fired, watching as the figure in
the nest fell backward. Gray was still attempting to get up,
even though the lieutenant was pulling him down, but it
was now obvious that his clothes were on fire, and he was
trying to run from the agony of being burned alive. Just as
the lieutenant managed to pull Gray toward the ground and
roll him over, Dan simultaneously heard the crackle of
machine gun fire and saw a second figure's head just above
the machine gun nest. Dan fired a second round and saw
this figure fall backward, at the same time registering the
sight of Gray lurching forward.

"We've got to get out of here!" Stennis hissed. "Help me
with Gray." Dan scooted back and brought Gray's arm up
over his shoulder as Stennis got under Gray's other shoulder,
and together they started crawling toward their line. By this
time, both sides of no-man's-land were firing, and Dan felt
the displaced air of bullets passing by. But they made
progress, finally reaching an Allied trench, where they
launched Gray forward and then slid into the trench face
first. It was deeper than Dan expected, with enough time for

him to roll so that he'd land on his bottom instead of his head. But instead of hitting dirt at the bottom, he found himself drenched in a pool of putrid water. It was freezing cold, and he couldn't help but let out a gasp as he thrashed through the water to dry ground. By this time some of the men in the trench had arrived to help, and they pulled Lieutenant Stennis and Gray into a relatively open area, where they laid Gray on his belly.

The moon had come out, so there was enough light to see each other in the shadows. When Dan looked at Gray, he could see that there was a bullet wound squarely between his shoulder blades. He must have been hit while they were carrying him.

"He's done for, then," Stennis said with an air of resignation. "What rotten luck."

Dan was trembling by now, in part from the cold dunking, but mostly from what they'd just experienced. "Lieutenant, how did you know we were in trouble?" he asked Stennis, trying to control the quiver in his voice.

"I'd expected the gunners in the machine gun pit to be asleep, but when we got within about ten feet, I heard movement that made it clear they were awake. I hoped they hadn't heard us. When I didn't hear anything for a while, I motioned for you to get going. I don't know what prompted Gray to rise up, but it was a terrible mistake. They must have been watching for any sign of movement. That's when everything broke loose."

Dan noticed that even though Stennis was attempting to talk in a calm, steady voice, his hands were trembling. That provided modest comfort to Dan, whose whole body was shaking. "Did I do something wrong back there? You told us not to fire at them, but I just did it on instinct when I saw the guy in the emplacement."

Stennis pulled him close and said quietly, "You did real good back there, O'Brian. You knocked out two of them, which is almost unheard of. I was furious when you shot until I saw that you were able to find your target in the dark. At first I thought it was just luck, but when you took out the second guy, I knew there was more than luck going for us. You undoubtedly saved both our lives." Then he smiled. "The Germans will have to think twice about using that machine gun emplacement again. My guess is that it will move down the line somewhere." The lieutenant settled back against the side of the trench. "I don't know why he had to rear up like that," he repeated quietly, then sat in silence for perhaps five minutes. Finally, with an air of resignation, he said, "We better make it back to our unit." It took a real effort to stand up, and Dan appeared to stumble. By this time Stennis had thanked the men who had helped them out of the sump, and together he and Dan carried Gray back to their area in the trench.

As soon as they reached their post, Stennis instructed Dan to get out of his clothes and use his blanket to dry off. "It's better to be cold and dry than to be wet." By now it was probably 0200, and Dan suddenly felt as if his limbs were made of lead. He did as he was instructed and got out of his wet clothing, then pulled his blanket around him, moving onto some dry straw in a corner of the dugout he and Jody had carved out of the side of the trench. A makeshift roof kept them dry.

"Are you okay?" he heard Jody ask quietly.

Dan didn't know how to answer. Of course, he was okay if you defined that as being alive and uninjured. But he'd killed two men and watched a comrade die. "I'm okay," he said. "It turned kind of ugly out there." Jody started to ask why, but Dan shushed him. "If it's okay, I'd like to talk about it tomorrow."

"Sure, I understand." Jody was quiet a moment. "Of course, I don't really understand, but I can wait. I hope you can get some sleep."

"So do I." He paused. "So do I."

* * *

Dan didn't really think he could sleep, but he must have, because he felt the sun on his face as he came out of a bizarre dream. He didn't know how long he'd been asleep, but he was alone in the dugout. As he sat up and stretched, he saw that his clothes had been hung over a little makeshift drying line, and when he felt them, they were dry enough to put on. He smelled terrible, but there was nothing he could do about it. At this point, no one had taken notice that he was stirring, so he sat with his back against the wall of his dugout.

He knew he shouldn't think about what had happened last night, particularly his part in all of it, but no matter how hard he tried to tell himself not to think about it, his mind continued to replay every event in sequence. It was almost like watching a motion picture in his mind, with the image of no-man's-land very much like the black-and-white movies he'd seen back home, since, in the nighttime, everything except the explosion of the hand grenade had been in ghostly shades of gray. When he got to the part where he'd shot the Germans, he felt a sense of panic well up inside. It almost overwhelmed him, and he had to suppress the urge to stand up and try to run away.

Then, something inside his mind told him to open his backpack. At first he resisted, but when the thought persisted, he leaned over and dragged the heavy pack to his side. He opened it and started rummaging without knowing what he was looking for. His hand felt the soft leather cover of a book. It was the Book of Mormon that Brother Richards had given him that first Christmas in 1911. He let out a little sob as he pulled it out and ran his hand over the cover. All the pleasant memories of Christmas at the Richardses' came flooding into his mind.

As he opened the book and fanned it, he found the letter that Jonathon Richards had handed to him as he was boarding the train in Pocatello. He'd read it only once, in the early days of his training, but it hadn't really meant much at that point. But today he needed to hear Jonathon's voice in his mind, so he started reading at the top of the letter. After getting through the part about how much the Richardses loved him, he came to a quotation that Brother Richards had taken the trouble to copy in full. It was from a talk Joseph F. Smith had given in general conference in April 1917. Congress had actually declared war while the conference was in session, and President Smith had deviated from his prepared remarks to talk about the war and what it meant for those who would serve. He reminded the Saints that "even in the face of conflict, the spirit of the gospel must be maintained." He went on to say that even in war, members should keep "the spirit of humanity, of love, and of peace-making," and then the prophet instructed prospective soldiers that they should always remember that they were "ministers of life and not of death; and when they go forth, they may go forth in the spirit of defending the liberties of mankind rather than for the purpose of destroying the enemy."

Dan put the letter down and closed his eyes. Had he fired to kill the enemy or to preserve liberty? He decided that the answer was neither. He fired to save Gray and Stennis. That wasn't exactly what President Smith had said, but as he thought about it carefully, he also realized that he hadn't shot out of hatred or bloodlust. He had done what was required of him. *Heavenly Father, I hope that what I did was all right. Please tell me it's all right.* He didn't feel anything for a few moments, and so he repeated the prayer over and over in his mind.

Finally, he heard Jonathon Richards's voice come into his mind, and he found himself transported to the Richards house on the day Trevor had announced he was enlisting. With remarkable clarity, he remembered what Brother

Richards had said to Trevor. He'd said that war could harden
a person, but not if they said their prayers and read the
scriptures. Then he'd promised Trevor that if he would stay
close to the Spirit, he'd come home the same wonderful
person he was then. Changed, but still worthy.

As he thumbed through the pages and reread the letter,
he determined that no matter what else happened, he would
never kill out of malice. He'd do what he had to in order to
protect himself and others and to help the Allies win the
war. It really was about freedom, and that was worth
fighting for. But not at the expense of his humanity. It was
then that he felt an incredible warmth flood through his
body, and the heavy feeling that had been oppressing him
seemed to evaporate. He had an incredible sense of being
enfolded in the Spirit, and he wept silently as he was
comforted.

Chapter Fourteen

ATTACK ON AN ENEMY AERODROME

The doctor scowled when he unwrapped Trevor's arm, and he failed to show any kindness in the way he examined the bone. Trevor winced in pain but successfully suppressed any kind of verbal response.

"You're a fool to do this to an arm that wasn't yet healed."

"Yes, sir."

"I should send you back to a hospital—not because of your arm but for a mental evaluation." Trevor remained silent. "All of you pilots are fools." The doctor looked up. "But I guess that's what's needed in this insanity." He took a warm wash rag and started vigorously scrubbing the skin, which had grown clammy and smelly under the bandages. Trevor winced even more at this treatment but still held his peace. The last thing he wanted to do was to anger a doctor and be put on the injured list again. Finally the doctor looked up from his task and locked onto Trevor's gaze. "The bone is fairly well knitted, but it's still fragile. Given the level of bruising, I'm amazed that you didn't break it again. I'm going to clear you for combat because it's obvious you'd go against my orders anyway. But," and there was a long pause to make sure Trevor was paying attention, "while you may be able to deceive your flight commander into thinking everything's all right, you and I both know that this arm is never going to be what it should be. Not for a long time, at least. Before you leave, I'm going to put a bag on that table over there. It'll just be sitting there full of bandages that a person could use to wrap his arm when it's stressed and painful. Of course, I couldn't give you those bandages, because that would indicate that you're not really fit for service. So I'm telling you that you shouldn't take the bag. If you're smart, you'll let me write you up on the injured list so you stand a better chance of living to the end of the war." He looked up expectantly, as if he hoped Trevor would take him up on his offer.

"Thank you, but no, sir. I wouldn't want you to write those orders."

"Well, then, I hope you don't have to use that arm too much in combat, because it could give way at any time." Trevor felt a slight surge of panic in his stomach, but he quickly suppressed it. "Now let's take a look at your face." The doctor was much gentler this time. Trevor had always been considered quite good-looking with his blond hair, blue eyes, and high cheekbones. Now he'd stopped looking at himself in the mirror because of the ugly, red scar tissue that had formed on his left cheek. It hurt intensely at first, became bearable when the scab had formed, and turned downright annoying when the new skin under the scab started to itch. He'd picked away at it until there was a layer of fresh, pink skin under his left eye. It was perpetually tender, but it didn't seem to offend people as much.

"You'd have done a lot better to let the scab come off naturally. Does your eye bother you a lot?"

"No, sir." The doctor looked at him searchingly, as if expecting more. "Sometimes it waters a bit when I get tired. But it's not too sensitive to light or anything."

"I'm sure." The doctor bent down to a group of papers, which he signed quickly. Because he'd been ordered to get a full physical, Trevor was sitting there with nothing on but his Skivvies. "You might as well get dressed. I'll clear you for action." Trevor let out a sigh of relief. "But," the doctor said, turning as he stood to leave, "I think you'd be smart to come back to me if anything gets worse—either your eye or your arm. There are millions of people fighting the war, and it's not likely that if you come off the line to heal up a bit, your absence will change the ultimate outcome."

"Thank you, sir. I won't be stupid about it."

"Well, that would be the first time for a pilot, but we'll see." The doctor stepped through the canvas door as Trevor quickly pulled on his trousers and shirt. Just as he was collecting his things to leave, a hand appeared through the opening of the door to place a bag on the table. Trevor glanced around, even though there was no one else looking, quickly picked up the bag, and departed.

* * *

Being cleared medically meant that Trevor could now take his place in the regular rotation. After catching up with his unit at the front, he'd initially been assigned to room with a stranger; but his bunkmate was killed in action a few days later, and Captain McMurphy moved Josh Brown into his room, probably so he could watch Trevor. No one really believed his arm was okay, but they all went along with him on it.

While McMurphy couldn't keep him off the line forever, he was pleased that the weather kept everyone down for the next couple of days. Trevor was anxious to get into the air again, but everyone else was relieved to get a break. Finally, the skies cleared, and McMurphy took Trevor and Alan up with him for a couple of raids into German territory. He preferred to escort newcomers onto the front because it was so difficult for them to spot enemy aircraft. At the end of each trip, he'd debrief them and ask how many airplanes they had seen. On the first trip, Trevor reported seeing four total, while Alan admitted to seeing none. "The actual count was three German Fokkers nearly two thousand feet below us, a Rumpler flying above us at twenty thousand feet, and a flight of three Nieuports that passed east to west directly under us—that's a total of seven." Trevor wanted to think that he was making it up just to intimidate them, but he knew better. A pilot had to train his eyes to see the smallest speck in the sky. It was easier when an aircraft was coming at you from an angle, but when they came from directly ahead at the twelve-noon position, it was really tough to see them through the windshield and propeller.

On their third trip out, McMurphy decided it was time to cross behind the German line, since that's where most of the action was. The Germans had only half as many airplanes as the French, British, and Americans, so they had to be cautious in how they deployed them. Their answer was to wait behind their own lines, where the Allied flyers had to use their fuel to find them. That gave an automatic advantage to the Germans. Plus, it meant that the Americans had to fly through German archy to get there, endure small-arms fire from the ground if they did any strafing, and lose any aircraft that went down with the pilot alive.

On this particular occasion, they flew due north to the ancient city of Metz, meeting virtually no resistance on the way aside from some mild archy as they crossed the trench lines. Circling high above the city, Trevor found it hard to believe how beautiful the city was from the air. Situated on a series of thousand-foot bluffs, the city was surrounded on three sides by the Moselle River, which is why it had been a virtual fortress for the past thousand years. As they circled down to take a closer look, he could imagine the battles that had raged across the centuries with the defenders sitting confidently in their perch, firing down on their attackers. It must have been so easy then, with just one approach to defend. But as they circled to less than three thousand feet above the city, he saw citizens scurrying for safety. The old river couldn't protect them from an air attack, and now the city was vulnerable to bombs. If he had had any on board, he could have dropped them at will, perhaps destroying a thousand-year-old cathedral or fouling the city's water supply. It was pretty disturbing to think about, and he was glad that he wasn't on a bomber crew. At least his battles were fought against military combatants, not innocent civilians.

As he made a gentle loop to gain a little altitude, he felt the concussions of some of the artillery positioned there to protect the city. It was pretty useless, actually. The chance of an aircraft getting hit by archy was fairly remote if it had any room to maneuver at all, since the aircraft could change altitude, direction, and speed almost at will. The few hits they did score were simple luck. What archy was good for, however, was breaking the pilot's concentration and forcing him to take evasive maneuvers that could break up his attack pattern. As he saw Captain McMurphy signal a retreat, he realized that the German archy had actually succeeded today by forcing them to withdraw.

With a fuel supply of about two and half hours left, they needed to make their way back to friendly lines anyway. As they were crossing over no-man's-land, McMurphy pointed down. Trevor dropped his gaze and saw a green-colored fog obscuring the American side of the line. He saw McMurphy mouth the words, "Mustard gas," and realized that the Germans had fired gas canisters into the Allied lines to cause confusion. That was always a prelude to an attack across no-man's-land. As McMurphy descended toward the ground, Trevor saw a group of German infantry coming out of their trenches. He knew instantly that McMurphy was going to go in for a strafing run, so he lined up to his right side and about two hundred feet behind. Alan should have lined up in a similar pattern behind Trevor so that the Germans couldn't run to get out of the firing line after the first aircraft passed. When he turned to look, however, he couldn't see Alan anywhere.

As they reached one hundred feet above the deck, McMurphy leveled off, and Trevor saw the line of tracers as he strafed the soldiers on the ground. Most of them dropped to the ground as an evasive maneuver, but he could see that a lot of them were hit as well. Saying a little prayer in his mind, he pulled the trigger and recoiled a bit as his own gun blazed to life. He'd practiced this very maneuver in the Bay of Biscay, where the students could see their bullets hitting the water. Now he watched as the stream of bullets churned up the ground, as well as any German soldiers who happened to be in the way. As he pulled out of the run, he realized that he'd been holding his breath and the muscles in his legs were tense, as though he had been getting ready to start a fifty-yard dash. Slowly he relaxed his clenched jaw and forced himself to relax the rest of his body.

McMurphy wasn't done, however. They hadn't used any ammunition earlier in the flight, so they started this battle with full belts. Swooping up above the battle line, McMurphy made an amazing vrille and came straight down on the line in a screaming dive. Trevor was right behind him, and together they made a second strafing run through the German advance. This time soldiers scattered in every direction. On their third pass, they found that most of the Germans had retreated back to the safety of their trenches, with men huddled up against the walls, where it was unlikely a stray bullet could find them. McMurphy made an indication for one more pass, but this time there was virtually no one to be found, so he signaled for a return to their aerodrome.

Luckily, it wasn't too far away, because just as Trevor was about to use his blip switch on the final approach to the runway, the motor cut out. He looked down to make sure he hadn't unintentionally hit the switch, but his finger was well above it. He checked the position of each of his engine switches and found that all were in the correct position. Regardless, he drifted to the ground with no power.

When John Getty came up to assist him, Trevor reported the loss of power. Getty just smiled and said, "Did you ever think to check your fuel level?"

"What?"

"Your fuel tank—it's empty."

"Ah," Trevor said, shaking his head. "Guess we got a little carried away on the trip home."

"At least you're in better shape than McMurphy."

Trevor turned to follow Getty's gaze. There, at the end of the runway, was his flight commander, the nose of his aircraft straight down in the dirt. He had run out of fuel a couple of moments earlier than Trevor, and his trailing wheel had caught the top of some branches, which brought the aircraft down face-first. McMurphy was being helped out of the plane, apparently unhurt.

Trevor jogged over to see him. "Are you okay, sir?"

McMurphy looked up and growled, "I'm the one to ask that question, not you. So stand easy, Mr. Richards."

Trevor smiled and saluted.

"You did good work back there, Richards. A lot of pilots freeze up the first time they have to do a strafing run."

Trevor's smile faded. "I didn't like doing it, sir, but it was our job."

"Yes, it was. You saw that we broke up their attack, I hope. That's why we're in this war—to protect our men and destroy theirs."

"Yes, sir," Trevor said stiffly.

McMurphy looked around. "At any rate, it's not every day that we know the results of our work so clearly. Who knows how many Allied lives were saved?" Then McMurphy interrupted himself. "By the way, where's Gledhill? I didn't see him after we started the attack."

Trevor was glad to change the subject. "I don't know, sir. I looked for him when we started down, but he was gone. I hope nothing's wrong."

They walked back to the hangar, headgear in hand, hoping that maybe Alan had gone down inside friendly lines. They were quite surprised when they saw his aircraft tucked neatly in its place, his mechanics giving it a once-over prior to regular maintenance. "What's this all about?" McMurphy said under his breath. "Where's Gledhill?" he called out sharply to his mechanics. They responded that they thought he'd gone back to his barracks. "Well, what's he doing back here? Did he have mechanical problems?" His mechanic reported that there were no problems with the aircraft but that Alan had reported that his guns had jammed when he tested them prior to the run. McMurphy pursed his lips, then asked very quietly, "And when you tested the guns, were they jammed?"

Alan's mechanic answered quietly, "No, sir. Lieutenant Gledhill reports that he was able to clear the jam just prior to landing."

"I see. Well, get this ship ready. It will be going up first thing in the morning."

"Yes, sir," was the muted reply.

McMurphy stood pondering in silence for a few moments. Trevor's arm was killing him, and he wanted to get back to his room to take off the bandages that he'd wrapped it with. He'd found that if he didn't wrap it, the blood would pool on long flights or when he made aggressive maneuvers, which left it in a lot of pain. Wrapping it helped because it kept it stiff and restricted, but then it ached by the end of a mission from being constricted. Either way, it usually hurt. Still, the last thing Trevor wanted to do was confess to McMurphy that his arm was hurting. Finally, McMurphy turned and noticed him standing there. "Richards? What are you doing here?" The look on Trevor's face helped him realize that he hadn't dismissed him. "Sorry, Richards, I guess I was doing a lot of thinking. Why don't you go relax for a while? Get an early start on your sleep tonight. I'm going to request that we go out at first light tomorrow, and I want you along."

"Thank you, sir. I will." He turned to leave. No one was really supposed to compliment a higher-ranking officer, since it was his duty to train and lead. Still, Trevor thought he should say something. He doubted he could have gotten through that exercise without McMurphy's leadership. Just as he was about to exit the hangar, he turned and said, "Captain McMurphy."

McMurphy looked up.

"I just wanted to say that I'm glad you were there to lead us today. It's a real honor to fly with you."

McMurphy's face softened a bit. "Thanks, Richards. Now, go get some rest."

Back in the barracks, Trevor went straight to his room. At first, he thought he'd go talk to Alan to see what had happened, but then he decided it wasn't his problem. Plus, he desperately wanted to unwrap his arm. Slipping his shirt off, he gently started unwrapping each bandage in turn. As the blood started to flow more easily, his arm began tingling, and a dull ache asserted itself. Still, it felt great to have the pressure off, and he lay back on his bed to relax. When Josh Brown came in four hours later, he tried to wake Trevor so he could get out of his clothes, but he couldn't rouse him. He settled for untying Trevor's shoes and slipping them off, then covered him with a blanket and let him sleep.

* * *

At 0430 the next morning, Trevor was roused from sleep by the barracks attendant, an older volunteer by the name of Smith.

"Pardon me, Mr. Richards, but you're on the active list for this morning. You need to be to the line in thirty minutes."

Trevor mumbled something incoherent.

"Thirty minutes is all, sir."

Trevor rolled over and, without opening his eyes, said, "Good, that gives me fifteen minutes to sleep."

"Yes, sir." Fifteen minutes later, Smith was back, this time unrelenting. "Mr. Richards, you're down to twelve minutes." That got Trevor's attention, and he sat bolt upright in his bed. Twelve minutes was the very minimum.

"Okay, gotta go." He jumped out of bed and started looking for his pants.

"You're wearing them, sir," Smith said patiently.

Trevor looked down and said, "Oh, yeah. That's good, it gives me a head start." He pulled on his boots without lacing them and raced for the door, grabbing the cup of hot chocolate out of Smith's hands as he ran. He bolted across the field as fast as he could run, skidding into the hangar precisely as the second hand swept 0500.

"Good to see you, Lieutenant Richards," McMurphy said mildly. "I trust you slept well?"

"Apparently, sir, since I can't remember anything after I left you yesterday afternoon." Against his will, McMurphy smiled.

Alan was already there, looking nervous. By the look on his face, Trevor guessed that he'd interrupted a conversation.

"Richards," McMurphy said flatly, "I'm about to have an unofficial conversation with Mr. Gledhill that officially will never have happened. I could excuse you, but frankly, I think it will be easier for Gledhill if you're here. Are you okay with that?"

"Yes, sir." Trevor had a sick feeling in his stomach.

McMurphy then proceeded to talk quietly to Alan, asking him for his version of events the day before. He repeated the story much as his mechanic had reported it.

"Gledhill, I have reason to think that things may not have happened exactly the way you described them." Alan started to protest, but McMurphy indicated for him to remain silent. "I'm not going to make you change anything in your report, but I am going to give you a chance to request a transfer out with no questions asked."

"I don't want a transfer, sir," Alan said defiantly.

McMurphy's voice got a colder edge to it. "Understand me, Mr. Gledhill. When I send a team into combat, I need to have confidence that all the pilots are up to their best work. I've had reports that your cockpit has had to be cleaned of vomit on some of your trips back, which might indicate a propensity to airsickness. I've also found it strange that in all the combat missions you've flown so far, you've never had occasion to fire a single bullet."

"But—"

McMurphy shushed him again. "So what I'm saying is, Gledhill, if you want out right now, I'll arrange it. You can give the government great service behind the lines. With your knowledge of flying, you could help us in supply and administration." He looked at him sternly. "You've got about ten seconds to decide. But if you say you want to stay in combat, then just know that we're going to go up today, tomorrow, and the next day. I'm going to take you to some of the hottest spots in the sector, where you're going to be guaranteed a chance to fire your weapon. Today, for example, you, Richards, and I are going to fly into the St. Mihiel salient. There's an aerodrome that's been vexing us, and I intend to cause some havoc there. I'm going to try to hit some Rumpler observation airplanes before they take off. If you come back without a shot fired, I'll relieve you from your duties, which is a lot worse than a voluntary request. So think carefully, but give me your answer."

Trevor didn't want to make eye contact with Alan in case it would add to his embarrassment. But he looked up and saw an agonized look on Alan's face.

"My father . . ." Then a hard look came over his face. "Sir, I respectfully request to stay on duty with you and Lieutenant Richards."

Trevor sagged.

"All right, then. Go to your aircraft, gentlemen. We're off to St. Mihiel."

Trevor walked with a heavy heart to his airplane. Even though the mechanics had been out of earshot, the look on John Getty's face showed him that they understood what had happened. When Getty raised an eyebrow, as if to ask, "Why is he going?" Trevor could only shrug his shoulders. After he was strapped into the cockpit, the signal was given, and he fired up the Rhone engine. Glancing to his left, he saw that Alan was already taxiing out onto the field. Trevor thought about the many hours of conversation they'd had together. Alan was a literature major, his father old-line military. Straight As and acceptance to Princeton apparently weren't enough to please his father. No matter how hard he tried, Alan confessed, he never felt it was enough. When the war had broken out, Alan's father had seen it as a great patriotic endeavor, a chance to export American democracy around the globe. It had gone without saying that Alan would serve and, with his college degree, that he'd be an officer. The only place acceptable to his father was in the Air Service. Never mind that Alan had no desire to fly. So here he was, doing something he was ill suited to do, just because it was easier to face death than an ignominious return home. Instinctively, Trevor thought of Danny, who, even now, was somewhere getting ready to go into the trenches when he should have been at Stanford. *Why does war do this to people?*

With no good answer to that question, he turned his attention to the task at hand. They ascended quickly and headed slightly northeast so they'd be east of the aerodrome when the time came to attack. McMurphy had briefed them on his plan of engagement. He wanted to ascend to nineteen thousand feet, gaining as much altitude as they could squeeze out of their Nieuports, so observers on the ground would be unaware of their presence as they crossed enemy lines. His goal was to be as far out of sight as possible when the sun broke through, and then they'd go into a steep dive at precisely the moment when the sun would be in the eyes of the German maintenance crews and archy gunners. When they reached ten thousand feet, they were to kill the engines so their attack would be silent. At one thousand feet above the deck, they could restart the engines so they'd have power to pull out of the dive. He wanted to fire as many rounds of ammo as possible into whatever aircraft were on the ground. At this point in the war, Germany's industrial capacity had fallen below that of the Allies, so every airplane they could destroy on the ground was one less airplane the enemy could send up. "If I had my way, we'd disable every aircraft and leave every pilot alive," McMurphy said somberly. Trevor agreed with the sentiment.

Even though it was summer, the air was remarkably thin at nineteen thousand feet, and as the little group reached their individual ceilings, the air was probably below thirty degrees Fahrenheit in real terms, much colder than that with the wind chill. They were all dressed warmly, but it was still hard for Trevor not to shiver in the cold.

Although he knew it made Alan nervous, he couldn't help but turn to look at him occasionally. Trevor secretly hoped he'd change his mind and head back to the aerodrome for reassignment, but he was always there.

Eventually McMurphy indicated that they were in position, and they started down, careful not to accelerate too rapidly and risk tearing the upper wing loose. At ten thousand feet, McMurphy leveled out and started a large, lazy circle. Trevor cut his engine with the blip switch and followed suit. He turned to see that Alan was in the pattern behind him.

As they circled, Trevor had to adjust his eyes a couple times and wipe some tears away. Coming out of the cold at nineteen thousand feet to the relative warmth at ten thousand feet was strange. Even stranger was the way his head seemed to clear as it received more oxygen. Finally, McMurphy started into a dive directly to the west. Trevor started in after him, followed by Alan. There was absolutely no sign that any of the Germans had heard or seen them. There was no archy, no ground fire, and no one hurrying on the runway. For its part, the runway crew could not have been more accommodating. There were two Rumplers sitting in front of their hangars and six Fokkers that had undoubtedly been assigned to support them. It was like a treasure trove, and the three American pilots set out like pirates to plunder it. At one thousand feet, Trevor released the blip switch and waited anxiously for the engine to catch. The little Rhone proved its worth and fired up on command. With a great belch of black smoke, it roared to life as Trevor leveled out of the dive to follow McMurphy across the deck of the aerodrome. When the distinctive sound of the Rhones fired up, the Germans on the ground started to scatter. There was no mistaking the sound of a rotary engine, and the grounds crew knew immediately that they were about to be fired on. McMurphy chose to attack the large Rumpler on the left, so Trevor zeroed in on the one on the right. He hoped that Alan would fire at the Fokkers, because if they managed to get airborne, it could be as bad as six to one against them.

As he flew level above the deck, he heard the pinging sound of bullets from the ground firing through the canvas wings. He watched as McMurphy's tracers found their way in a long arc across the backbone of the first Rumpler.

Trevor pulled his trigger and concentrated on bringing his line of fire across the path of the second Rumpler and was pleased when he saw it start to rip the aircraft apart. Apparently, he hit the gas tank, because as he roared over the stricken aircraft, there was a huge explosion below him that sent his aircraft jumping up through the heat. He pulled back on the stick and went into a high-powered revensement loop so he could pull up above the airfield and come in for a second run.

Reaching the top of his loop, he looked straight down on the airfield as Alan passed beneath him. If there were any tracers being fired, he didn't see them, and Alan passed harmlessly above the Fokkers. Coming out of the loop, Trevor saw that at least two of the Fokkers were taxiing down the runway. They had to be dealt with momentarily, but for now he followed McMurphy in for a second strafing run that decimated three of the remaining Fokkers. He looked for Alan to follow but couldn't find him in the sky.

At the start of his second revensement, he found that he had company. One of the Fokkers was headed straight for him, guns blazing. Trevor banked to the right, which was an extremely dangerous move while in such a steep climb. The aircraft started a steep slide as the airflow over the wings was temporarily lost. He let the aircraft fall a bit before reasserting control. By now the Fokker had shot past him and was maneuvering for a return encounter. As he pulled level for a head-on approach to his enemy, Trevor saw Alan pass just feet underneath him, apparently flying on a perpendicular heading. Then Trevor looked and saw that a second Fokker was headed straight for him from his right side. Essentially, Trevor was positioned perfectly in the crosshairs of a crossfire. It was going to take some maneuvering to get out of this one. As he tried to think whether he should mount or dive, he turned to see Alan's progress in firing on the Fokker to his right. He could see the tracers from the Fokker firing into Alan, but he saw no return fire.

"Break off, you fool!" he shouted into the air, but Alan held his course. As the two aircraft came closer to each other, he could see that the German was going to kill Alan at any second. But in spite of the hail of bullets, Alan held to his course. The German must have figured out what Alan had in mind at exactly the same moment as Trevor, because the German suddenly shot up at maximum acceleration. Alan anticipated his move and shot up as well. The crash of the two aircraft at a combined airspeed of over three hundred miles per hour sent debris flying for nearly a mile in both directions.

Trevor was so transfixed that he almost forgot the Fokker approaching from head on. He looked up to see that they were perhaps a thousand yards apart. With defiance in his voice, he shouted to the wind, "I'm not going to do the same thing, you Bosche," and he pulled his trigger, starting a lazy arc that worked its way toward the Fokker. Bullets were slamming into his own airplane, so it came down to whoever hit the other one first. When Trevor thought he had to break off or collide, he saw the Fokker erupt in flames and start to lose altitude. He climbed straight over the top of the German with just enough room to look down and see the expression on the other pilot's face. There was no way the German could avoid crashing, but Trevor was left to wonder if he'd make it out alive.

Doing a quick banking turn to the left using full rudder, Trevor quickly reversed course and watched as the German crashed to the ground. There was no hope that the pilot made it out, because a second fireball shot up into the air. Trevor felt his aircraft wobble under him, and he turned to see if he was under fire from yet another aircraft. All he could see was open space. Then he looked down to see that his right hand was trembling on the control stick. He forced himself to bring his left arm down, and he quickly brought the plane into control with both hands on the stick.

At this point he was flying west, away from the aerodrome, but he couldn't see Captain McMurphy. In spite of the archy that the Germans were now throwing up, Trevor reversed course and headed back. He was still pretty low against the deck, and he couldn't see anything. Then he happened to glance upward and saw a German on McMurphy's tail. The captain was going into a spiral to try to get away from him, but the German was following him down, the line of tracers coming into contact with McMurphy during at least part of every loop. Trevor calculated an intercept path so he'd come up under the German.

Trevor got him in the crosshairs and opened fire. A couple of shots fired, and then his gun jammed. He quickly pounded on the gun and forced it to eject the bad cartridge. He had perhaps four or five seconds before he lost the chance to take the other pilot by surprise, so he pulled the plane back into position and started firing. Amazingly, the line of tracers found their target on the first volley, and he saw the bullets tear across the cockpit as the German slumped forward in his seat. His aircraft was already in a dive, and with no one to hold it in position, it started into an uncontrolled spin to the earth. McMurphy finally pulled out of his dive and looped up to see what had happened. Trevor eased into a large banking turn to the west and watched as the German crashed onto the runway of the aerodrome at full speed. He felt the inevitable rush of adrenaline and exulted in his kill. Then he felt sick to his stomach.

McMurphy pulled up beside him and motioned for them to go home. Trevor had to use both hands the whole way home to stay on course. Fortunately, there were no other battles to fight, and they landed thirty minutes later.

When they were firmly on the ground, McMurphy shot out of his aircraft and came bounding over to Trevor. "Richards, you got two kills on a single mission. That's Lufbery or Meisener kind of flying."

"I'd like to tell you that it was all planned, sir, but the truth is it all happened so fast, I never could have prepared in advance."

"That's exactly what it takes to succeed. Listen, you saved my life, and I will never forget it. We had an amazing morning."

"Yes, sir, we did." Trevor wanted to be enthusiastic.

McMurphy looked at him steadily. "I saw what Gledhill did for you. I don't know why he couldn't pull the trigger on his guns, but it's obvious he wanted to give you a chance, no matter what it cost him. As far as I'm concerned, he died heroically in battle, courageously engaging a German aircraft. I'd like to write his family without any mention of his failing to fire any shots. Is that something you think I should write?"

Trevor was enormously relieved to hear McMurphy say that. If it was so important to Alan that his father be proud of him, the last thing they needed to report was that he froze in battle yet again. He was so bound and determined to play a role that he was willing to commit suicide. Trevor swallowed hard to hold back the tears. "Sir, that's exactly how I think you should write your letter. And, with your permission, I'd like to write the Gledhills too, not to talk about the battle, but to tell them what a fine person he was."

McMurphy's lip actually trembled. "You do that, Richards. You should do that."

Chapter Fifteen

HAND-TO-HAND COMBAT

By late June, Dan had been in almost constant combat longer than he cared to think about. Yet now he was at the end of a four-day leave, and he was actually hurrying toward the trenches. The paradox of it all was that Dan, like so many other men, left the line beleaguered and emotionally spent, with the sole thought of escaping to the safety and peace of the billet, only to find himself anxious to get back to the line almost as soon as he started his leave. Why was it so hard to relax away from the battlefield? And why go back willingly into the nightmare? The first time to the line could be blamed on naïveté, but what excuse was there for going back time after time? There was a handful of British and French who had somehow survived for nearly four years without being killed, and they just kept going back up to the front, sometimes even after being injured. It just didn't make sense. In time, Dan realized that the reason was the desire to face one's fears rather than live in anticipation. Uncertainty is the enemy of serenity. So it was that once he reached the front, he easily took up the now-familiar post of sniper.

As word of his marksmanship spread down the line of the trenches, he was often in demand to be "loaned" to a neighboring unit to take out some enemy stronghold with sniper fire. That meant he spent most of his days in a parapet focusing on obscure targets more than a hundred yards distant where a machine gun nest or perhaps another sniper emplacement was causing trouble. Sometimes he'd sit all day with nothing to shoot at. Other times he might stare for an hour or more, waiting for some sign of movement in order to fire instantly when a target presented itself, since the enemy would never pop up for more than a few seconds. From what he could tell, he was successful about fifty percent of the time, although he never had any desire to keep track of his kills, as some people did. Somehow it seemed wrong to keep score of human life. Periodically, the Germans would call in an artillery barrage when they thought they'd figured out where he was firing from, but he kept on the move enough that they couldn't really zero in on his position.

In time, the trenches somehow seemed normal, and Dan moved up and down the interconnecting passageways with confidence, not really having to think about where to take a turn or where he could stop to chat with the different units. Snipers were welcome about anywhere, and frankly, he enjoyed the chance to hear some new conversation once in a while. One of the things that amazed Dan the most was how diverse the American deployment was, with soldiers from all over the United States. In just three months, he was sure that he'd heard over a hundred different dialects, and it fascinated him how rich the English language was as soldiers from each region used their colloquialisms to express themselves.

It struck Dan how odd the war was. Here at the front, there were periods of turmoil interspersed with mind-numbing periods of boredom. Most days there was little action, which left the men to clean up their portion of the trench and then play cards or sit around talking. It was probably a lot like being in prison. Then there would be a battle, and everybody would rush around like crazy, firing weapons like a bunch of madmen in a frenetic attempt to protect themselves; and then it would just end, and people would go back to what they were doing before, mostly trying to act like nothing had happened. That was the most bizarre time of all—the wind-down period after a battle. While in the process of cleaning up the trench from someone who had been killed, they'd talk about home, family, or their girlfriends while studiously avoiding the subject of the deceased, as if it would bring bad luck to talk about him.

The other thing that puzzled Dan was how there could be all this mayhem at the front while, just ten miles back, the countryside was lush and green, with farmers tending their crops as if there were no war. He knew of farmhouses that were completely undisturbed, where officers dined with the locals on fresh eggs and meat, eating their marmalade and toast as if nothing out of the ordinary was going on, when, in reality, thousands of men were being killed or wounded daily within earshot of the farmer's house. It was as if it was all too much for a single human mind to comprehend, so everybody put a compartment around his thoughts and just plowed ahead with life.

When he returned to the line after his leave, Dan was pleased to be greeted cheerfully by Jody and Lieutenant Stennis. Somehow the three of them had survived, even though there'd been a lot of close calls. As he reflected on what he was thinking, he had the cold realization that it was bad luck to think about such things, and he reached out and knocked on a wood stake in the revetment.

"I didn't think you were superstitious," Jody said mischievously. "Do Mormons do rituals like avoiding black cats and not walking under ladders?"

Dan laughed. "Mormons aren't superstitious. Superstition is really a bunch of nonsense. But I guess at least one Mormon in France has picked up a bad habit." The truth is that it was hard not to be superstitious, and nearly everyone developed some kind of ritual. It was one way to cope with the stress. Anything to give the illusion of safety. Dan saw that Jody was looking at him expectantly for more explanation. Jody always seemed to turn to him for advice. "I guess we all think we're special," Dan said, "and that if we do things right, somehow we'll be protected."

"Personally, I'm counting on you to say your prayers for me each day. I figure that's the best protection I can get."

"You could say your own prayers, you know. I've told you how often enough."

"I know, and I do try to pray, particularly when the artillery rounds are close. But mine are the desperate kind of prayers. I keep trying to make a deal with God that I'll be good if He protects me, but somehow I don't think He really likes that. But you've got an inside track."

Dan was quiet. He was glad that Jody recognized the importance of spirituality, but he was uncomfortable that Jody put his faith in Dan's prayers rather than his own. It created a sense of responsibility that Dan wasn't sure he could live up to. Still, his friend was a simple person, and if it helped him get through the days, then it was all right. "You can count on one thing, Jody, and that's that I do pray for you every single day. I just don't know how the prayers will be answered."

That night, the bombardment started. Dan had endured bombardments of thousands of rounds of artillery over the course of three months, but he'd never experienced anything like this. The sky itself was one continuous explosion, with the flashes of light so constant and brilliant that at times, he had to shut his eyes to protect them from the glare. Of course, it was the sound that was overwhelming. The concussions struck their bodies almost like a physical blow while shaking the ground like an earthquake that broke down the revetments, no matter how fast and furiously they tried to shore up the walls. Although none of the shells hit them directly, they could see them land at different points up and down the lines, and they listened in horror as the agonized screams of dying men mingled with the interminable sound of the barrage. And, even though they didn't get hit directly, the debris and cordite fumes pouring in on them left them gasping for breath and sometimes in danger of suffocating.

At one point, Jody lost control and started screaming at the Germans to stop. Dan had to grab him by the shoulders and throw him to the ground to keep him from going up and over the top out into no-man's-land. They actually lost men that way who just couldn't stand to be trapped in the trenches anymore while the world went up in flames around them. The urge to run away and get out of the trenches was almost overwhelming. But it would have been even worse to leave what little protection the trenches offered and to try to escape back through the ground that was being churned into rubble behind them. So they had to wait it out, hoping that dawn would see an end to the bombardment.

It did, of course, because the Germans couldn't fire on their own troops while they made their advance into no-man's-land. The ferocity of the bombardment made it abundantly clear that the Germans were preparing for an advance, and the Americans knew full well that the whole purpose of the bombardment was to kill most of the Allied troops in their trenches and drive the rest out in the hope of escaping the bombardment. At the very least, the Germans hoped to destroy the Americans' barbed-wire defenses so they could dash across no-man's-land and into the Americans' trenches for hand-to-hand combat. This was the first time Dan's group would be called on to repulse an attack, and the anticipation was almost as wearing as the bombardment itself.

At 0530 the great guns went silent, just as it was starting to get light. The silence was awesome, and people who spoke did so in a whisper, as if their voices would bring it all back. Their ears were so numb from the noise that it was hard to hear anything, let alone a whisper. Lieutenant Stennis beckoned for everybody to gather around. When they were huddled, he said urgently, "They'll be coming as soon as the sun comes over the horizon. They want the direct morning sun to be in our eyes as they come forward. But we can't wait for them to get into our trenches. You've all got to get ready to fire over the top just as soon as I give the command. Those of you with machine guns, fire a pattern about three feet above the ground. That way the upward trajectory of your bullets will catch the Bosche, no matter how close they are. This is no time to hold back, because they're coming for us. Give it everything you've got." The men simply mumbled some kind of reply, then began checking their weapons. "Be prepared to mount your bayonets, because there's a good chance you'll have to use them."

"So this is it?" Jody said breathlessly. "We're finally going to fight them face to face." Dan didn't say anything. He preferred silence at such times.

But Jody needed to talk. "Do you think there are more of them than us?"

"I imagine that they've brought up as many reinforcements as possible so they can overrun our position, no matter how many fall."

"What do we do if they get in the trench?" Jody said, almost in a whisper. It was obvious that he was terrified.

"We do what we've been trained to do," Dan said firmly. "We stand and fight until the lieutenant calls for a retreat. Then we run like the blazes to get out of here. As fast as you can run, I figure you'll make it to Paris before they get you stopped."

Jody smiled. He knew that Dan didn't like to talk, but somehow Dan always knew what to say to make him feel better. Jody had come to think of Dan as a big brother, even though Jody was actually older. There was something special about Dan. He didn't cuss or tell bad stories, didn't drink liquor or play cards. Of course, all that was strange, but good. Jody felt safe when he was around Dan. He started to say something else, but Lieutenant Stennis raised his arm.

"They're coming! Get ready to start firing." With that, the men moved to the front edge of what was left of their trench. The artillery had pretty well shaken it to pieces, and the sides looked more like a ramp than a wall. But it still provided them the advantage, because they could lie belly-down on the slope and see over the top with very little exposure. Just as the sun tipped above the horizon, they heard shouting. Gazing into the sun made their eyes water, but still they peered ahead anxiously until they saw the silhouettes of men running toward them across no-man's-land.

"Fire!" The trench lit up with the blast of their muzzles, flames shooting out of the barrels some six feet in front of the line. The machine gunners were devastating in their barrage as row upon row of Germans fell to the ground, while those with single-shot rifles did their best to sight in on specific figures to gain maximum advantage. It was really wholesale slaughter—but the Germans refused to turn back. Dan heard a thud next to him and turned to see the fellow he'd been standing next to thrown back, a bullet penetrating his helmet. He put in a new clip and started firing again.

It must have been only a few minutes, but so much activity was crammed into the time that it seemed like hours. The number of German dead out on the field was appalling, but as soon as one German went down, another came up to replace him. It soon became obvious that they were going to force the crossing. At that point, Dan turned to Lieutenant Stennis, who gestured for him to climb into a parapet. As he passed the lieutenant in the trench, Stennis cupped his hands up against Dan's ears and shouted, "Do your best to slow their advance on our position while I get the men out. When they reach that line, no matter what's happening here, you make a break for it." Dan signaled in the affirmative, and Stennis patted him on the back as he mounted the parapet.

It was odd being up there this time. Usually the parapet looked out onto the emptiness of no-man's-land. But today it was the center of fire, and Dan heard the bullets slamming into the sandbags by the dozen. He knew that they would eventually shred the outer skin, then break up the bricks, and finally penetrate through the inner layer. But he had a few minutes and needed to make them count. He leaned into the slit and started picking Germans off one by one. He fired in rapid but deliberate fashion, with virtually every bullet finding a target. He must have killed twenty or more Germans before their advance hesitated. A lot of them started moving to a less hostile area, but some continued toward his position. He reached down for another clip and continued to fire away.

Finally, he heard the rapid fire of a machine gun smashing into his parapet. *They've found me!* The thought filled him with dread and fury. He returned fire at an even more rapid pace. Then he felt the sharp, burning impact of something grazing the side of his head just above his part line. He put his hand up and saw there was a small amount of blood. With a few parting shots, he turned to make his way down into the trench. He was gratified to see that all his buddies were gone, and he hoped to join them as quickly as his legs would carry him.

His foot was on the top rung of the ladder when something flew over the edge of the parapet and caught him with full force, throwing him off the ladder and down into the trenches. A huge German fell on top of him, and as they landed on the boards at the bottom of the trench, the German used the weight of his body to pin Dan to the ground. Dan tried to twist his way out from under him, but the German must have weighed sixty or seventy pounds more than Dan, and no matter what he did, he couldn't gain the leverage he needed to escape.

The German reached behind his back and pulled out a huge knife. Dan put his arm up and caught the German's hand, pushing back with everything he had to deflect the blade away, and was successful on the first swing. Dan continued to wriggle and wrench to try to throw the German off balance, but he was too strong. It took all Dan's strength just to keep the German's arms away from his torso. The German started making jerking motions with his right arm to try to break Dan's lock, and with each motion Dan felt himself losing ground. He tried shouting at the German to startle him, but it had no effect. There was a cold, brutal look in the German's eyes that almost mesmerized Dan. He'd heard the phrase "a murderous look" but had never really understood it until that moment. His opponent's face was flushed with the fever of battle, and Dan knew that he would fight until one of them was dead.

But no matter what he did, Dan couldn't gain any leverage or advantage, and the German kept jerking with what seemed like increasing force. It became apparent that he was not going to be able to hold the German off, so he was concentrating on trying to come up with a strategy as to how he could roll to the side as the blade came down. Just when he expected the fatal blow, the German's face suddenly exploded. Blood sprayed everywhere, and Dan had to blink when some of it went in his eyes. The German tumbled backward, and Dan jerked to an upright position with the weight of the German gone.

Try as he might, he couldn't figure out what had happened. One moment he was about to be killed, and now he was sitting with a dead German lying on his feet. He shoved the body off and rolled around to look in the opposite direction to see who'd shot the German. There was Jody running toward him.

"Are you okay?"

"I am now. Thanks for coming back."

"We gotta get out of here right now." Jody reached down and pulled him up. Dan grabbed his gun, and the two of them started racing down the communications tunnel. At about thirty yards down, they saw Lieutenant Stennis waving them to hurry up. Dan was ten yards from the lieutenant when he heard bullets sing past from behind, and then he saw a look come over the lieutenant's face that gave him a cold chill. Dan turned to see what Stennis was looking at past him and saw Jody lying facedown in the trench, a bullet wound to the back of his neck.

"No," Dan shouted at the top of his lungs, and he turned to race back to his friend.

Stennis shouted at him, "O'Brian, leave him where he is and come on. The Germans aren't fifty yards behind you."

Dan stopped and turned to the lieutenant. "I've got to help him," and he turned to go back.

"He's dead, and we'll be dead too if you don't come right now!" The lieutenant had run back to him by this point and now grabbed him by the shoulders. "I'm giving you a direct order, O'Brian. Run now!" Whether it was training or fear or simply the inability of his brain to process anything else, Dan started running—running as fast as he'd ever run in his life. Once he stumbled over a dead body, but he quickly recovered and kept running. He heard Stennis behind him, but right now, that didn't seem to matter. He just ran until he came to the end of the trench, and then it was up and out, running toward the protection of the nearest trees. As he got closer, his mind registered that he didn't hear Stennis anymore. He turned and saw the lieutenant maybe thirty yards behind him. Stennis motioned for him to keep going, so Dan ran. Finally he found some trees, and he turned to see if he needed to help the lieutenant. Stennis came stumbling forward, though, and finally made it.

Breathlessly, Stennis said, "How in the world did you learn to run like that?" He was bent forward, hands on his knees, gasping great quantities of air. Dan was still breathing hard, but it was nothing in comparison to the lieutenant.

"It comes from not smoking cigarettes. I've tried to tell you they ruin your health and take your wind away." The irony of his remark made him laugh. What a stupid time— and place—to worry about somebody's health.

"Well, I don't know about that, but, my goodness, can you cover the ground when given an order." They laughed. About this time, friendly artillery started landing in the space between the former American trenches and their position. "We've got to keep moving out of here. If any of these shells fall short, we're going to be a statistic, and your award-winning four-hundred-yard dash is going to be in vain." The two of them set off at a jog toward the rear in hopes of finding safety. Before going very far, they encountered American troops moving forward to try to establish a new line, so they turned to join them.

"I'm all out of ammunition," Dan said. A supply sergeant brought him a canister of shells, and Dan moved to a position where he could fire on the advancing German troops. It was here that his skill really played a useful role because he could hit them maybe two hundred yards farther back than any of the others. It was unnerving for the Germans to watch their comrades fall without knowing where the fire was coming from. Eventually, by nightfall, the consolidated American line was filled in with enough strength that the German advance was held in check. Then, with additional artillery support, the Germans finally turned tail and ran. Another one of their attempts at a break-through had fizzled.

When it was over, Dan slumped down in place and fell asleep with his back against a tree.

* * *

Two days later, the unit was finally able to move back to its original position in the trenches. Dan made the trip filled with a sense of dread, hoping that he would find Jody's body so it could be properly buried, yet cognizant of the fact that it would be in pretty rough shape by this point. As they approached the communications trench, Lieutenant Stennis came up and silently put his arm on Dan's shoulder. At the spot where they'd been ambushed, they saw that the body was still where it had fallen. There were flies circling the bloated corpse, which Dan brushed off. He turned the body over and found that Jody's face was discolored but still recognizable.

Stennis said quietly, "He was a good soldier."

"And a good friend." Dan dragged the corpse toward the entrance of the tunnel so that they could get it out of the way of the troops who were returning. Stennis helped him lift it up and over the edge. The stench was almost overpowering, but Dan treated the body with care. When they had it on the lip of the trench, he asked permission to seek out a burial party. Protocol required that the body be taken back to supply, where it would be properly identified and then taken to a military cemetery for interment. Dan had to walk nearly half a mile to find a group, and when they tried to brush him off, he turned insistent. When they figured out it was a friend, they set aside what they were doing and came with him. Apparently Stennis had seen his approach from a distance, because when Dan got there, all the men of the unit were assembled.

"I thought we might have a brief memorial service."

Dan looked up gratefully. "Thank you. He'd like that." It was extremely unusual to show any sort of remorse like this, and Dan knew that Stennis was doing it for him, not Jody. Still, he was glad.

"Maybe you could say a few words about Wilkins, and then I'll finish it off."

"Would you mind if I sang a song first?"

Stennis looked at him in surprise. "I didn't know you sing. By all means."

Prior to this time, Dan had never found occasion to sing on the battlefield. He thought of all the songs he knew, having sung at a number of funerals before the war, and he finally settled on a sectarian hymn that Margaret Richards had taught him when he was in his negro-spiritual phase of training. It was written by a sea captain who had felt remorse for transporting slaves prior to the Civil War and who later turned his life over to God. Dan chose it because it was Jody's favorite hymn—in fact, about the only religious song he knew.

With a voice filled with emotion, Dan started singing the haunting melody of "Amazing Grace." At first he worried he'd be too emotional to sing, but his years of training asserted themselves, and his voice filled with confidence as his rich tenor rang out across the shell-torn battlefield. The men were startled by the strength and clarity of his singing. By the time he reached the third verse, something odd had happened. Dan didn't notice, because he was so involved in the song, but Stennis did. The entire battlefield had grown silent, and men's heads could be seen above the trenches up and down the line. Apparently they were as surprised as Stennis to hear such a wonderful song providing a contrast to the grim work they faced in finding the rest of the dead and preparing them for their final resting places.

When he was finished, the words hung in the air. Then Dan quietly talked about the simplicity of Jody's soul and the kindness of his heart. "In some ways, he was far more experienced than I'll ever be, having grown up on the streets. But in another way, he had the innocence of a child, with a simple faith in friends and life. Those of you who have read the Bible know how much Jesus loved children, and I believe that He will welcome this one home with open arms." Then he went silent.

Stennis stepped forward and thanked him, then read a few verses of scripture, ending with, "I am the resurrection, and the life: he that believeth in me, though he were dead, yet shall he live." Turning to the group, he added, "We all see a lot out here. What I saw the other day was a man who was in the clear turn and run back into the trench to save a friend. He ended up losing his life so that someone else could live. I don't know what finer tribute could be said of a person than that." Then, turning to Dan, he asked if he would sing one more song. "I think it's done us all good."

Dan's face flushed a bit, because it was very hard for him to keep his emotions inside. But he felt it was the least he could do. At the end of the service, Stennis and Dan carefully lifted the body onto the corpse wagon and thanked the men who had taken time to wait for the service. When the wagon moved off, the men descended once again into the trenches to begin reinforcing the revetments and rebuilding the parapet that had nearly cost Dan his life. He was relieved to find that the Germans had recovered the body of the soldier who had attacked him.

Chapter Sixteen

DRACHENS AND
AN ALBATROS

When Trevor first arrived at the front, he was taken aback by the callousness with which pilots treated the death of one of their comrades. Some deaths got past the emotional defenses, as when Raoul Lufbery, the American ace of aces, was shot down within six miles of his own aerodrome. After surviving all kinds of battle for more than two years in the French Escadrille and then seeing almost daily combat in an American unit, he'd seemed invincible. It was easy to believe that he had some special charm that would see him through the war. But it wasn't to be. After his death, the men in both squadrons held an elaborate funeral service with a number of aircraft flying less than fifty feet over his open grave to drop flower petals. Lufbery's death cast a pall on the whole camp.

The pilots in the 95th didn't have the same reaction for Alan Gledhill. Most hardly took notice at all. The few who did were either indifferent or hostile, saying that he should never have been in the Air Service. But Josh and Trevor mourned him. Trevor and Alan had been together for more than nine months, and the ache from his death was so profound that Trevor resolved never to grow that close to another pilot again. It just hurt too much. Josh was more stoic about it, but his relative silence showed that he was shaken as well.

Unfortunately, or perhaps fortunately, the war didn't leave a lot of time to dwell on such things. Josh and Trevor now started flying together on most missions, and Trevor's confidence increased dramatically because he had a good, solid wingman. Returning from a strafing run behind German lines one day, Josh tipped his wings in the direction of one of the huge German "drachens." Located about two miles behind the front lines, these giant observation balloons were tethered to powerful motor trucks on the ground and floated some two thousand feet above the battlefield, giving them an unrestricted view of more than ten miles. Both sides used them to great effect as the observers in them peered through telescopes to spot changes in the enemy's deployment of troops and location of artillery.

The gigantic tube-shaped German balloons appeared to be the easiest of all targets, and they did indeed attract more than their fair share of ground-based artillery fire. But in spite of all the ordnance thrown up against them, most was wasted, because as soon as an artillery piece had found the balloon's range, the trucks on the ground would simply drive down the road a hundred yards or so, and the guns would then be off target once again.

Of course, airplanes could adjust instantly to any changes in location, and the large, stationary balloons created enormous temptation for pilots on both sides of the conflict. However, they made a dangerous target—in fact, the single-most-dangerous targets in the war because of the massive amount of ground-based defense put in place to protect the balloons. Not only was there archy to consider, but at just two thousand feet above the deck, high-powered guns could send up a sheet of bullets that virtually surrounded all approaches to the balloon. It took a very brave—or very naïve—pilot to go after one of the balloons.

When Josh tipped his wing toward the balloon, Trevor tried to signal that he didn't want to participate, but Josh

ignored him and peeled off to the north under full power.
Trevor grimaced but followed. Since Trevor was the senior
officer, it was up to him to come up with a plan of attack.
Catching up to Josh, he indicated a battle plan, using his
hands to show a steep climb followed by a controlled spiral
directly from above the balloon at high speed, firing down
on the balloon from far enough up to avoid the majority of
ground-based bullets. Of course, there would be archy, but
the Germans would have to be careful so that the shrapnel
from their artillery shells didn't fall back on their own
balloon. Josh grinned and signaled back that Trevor should
lead the way. So from a safe distance out, they started
gaining altitude, climbing to nearly fifteen thousand feet.
Once at his chosen altitude, Trevor circled his aircraft into
position directly above their intended target, then shoved
the stick forward to initiate a dive while simultaneously
bringing the stick sharply to the left to start a spiral pattern.
He estimated that he should start firing at approximately five
thousand feet, knowing full well that the chance of hitting
anything from that distance was remote. Still, gravity would
be working to his advantage by pulling the bullets straight
down as opposed to its usual effect on a bullet shot out horizontally.

As he started down, he had to concentrate to keep track
of his speed and direction while spinning in what appeared to
be an uncontrolled spiral. Trevor grinned to himself. *Old
Elmer Peterson would be losing his lunch right about now if he
were doing this!* Elmer was the one who had gotten sick on
the roller coaster at Saltair and who would often wobble after
just a few trips around the merry-go-rounds at the city park.
As the air grew warmer, Trevor felt the airspeed increasing, so
he had to widen the spiral to slow it down. When he reached
five thousand feet, he pulled out of the spiral so that he could
concentrate better on firing the two Vickers machine guns.
At this point their tactic had apparently worked, since he

hadn't been hit. In fact, he was surprised he didn't encounter more ground resistance, so he held firm for another five hundred feet, then pulled the trigger. It was gratifying to see the line of tracers heading straight down, and even from this height he could see them hitting the top of the balloon.

Then the balloon started moving out of the line of fire. Obviously, the crew of the ground truck had figured out what was going on, and they'd started a quick move. Trevor decided he'd done whatever damage he could, so he pulled out of the dive into a sharp ascent to try to get away from the bullets that were now being thrown up with a ferocity he'd never experienced before. With the balloon out of their line of fire, the German ground protectors were giving it everything they had. Fortunately, he managed to climb back to a safe height, where he circled lazily to taunt the archy. He gazed anxiously below to see how Josh was doing and was relieved when he saw him climbing steadily up and out of harm's way. When they both reached the top, Trevor led them off to a safe distance, where they could watch the effect of their fire.

Of course, they hadn't caused an explosion, since they weren't loaded with incendiaries. Trevor circled for a while to see if there was any damage to the balloon. It looked like it might be sagging a bit, but nothing too noticeable. By this time, they were getting low on fuel, so he signaled a return to base, where they landed approximately fifteen minutes later. Aside from the excitement of diving on the balloon, the mission had been a bust, with nothing to show for their time—which is why Trevor was surprised to see John Getty come bounding out at full speed, followed by Captain McMurphy. When he exited the aircraft, McMurphy yelled, "Get anything?"

"Afraid not," Trevor called back while narrowing the distance between them. When he got into conversation range, he said, "We did take some potshots at a balloon, and

I think we wounded it a bit, but nothing that we can confirm." Josh had joined them at this point.

"Balloons, huh? You both decided you have a death wish or something?"

"Actually, it was my idea," Josh said, sensing that they might be in trouble. "But Lieutenant Richards came up with a plan of attack which minimized our risk."

"And what would that attack plan be, Lieutenant Richards?"

Trevor was instantly defensive. They hadn't taken unusual risk, and the balloon was certainly a legitimate target. The worst thing a person could do was return to base with a full ammunition belt.

"With all due respect, sir," John Getty broke in, "why don't you give them the news?"

Trevor and Josh looked at him in surprise. Finally, McMurphy burst into a grin and said, "There were only about ten thousand Allied soldiers watching you two. They hate that balloon, which is why the whole trench line burst into applause after your attack." Trevor waited for what was coming. "Seems that your bullets must have ripped big enough holes in the fabric that the gas floated out. Anyway, the whole big mess eventually collapsed to the ground. Reports are that the pilot parachuted out from around fifteen hundred feet, barely enough for his parachute to open. Congratulations!"

"We got a balloon," Trevor said with an amazed grin. "I can't believe it—a balloon!"

Josh actually started jumping up and down with excitement. "Nobody gets a balloon on their first try . . . nobody!" Coming up and hugging Trevor, he said, "This is my first kill. I actually got a kill." Then he sobered up a bit. "Or did I?"

"What do you mean?" Trevor asked.

"Well, we both attacked, so who gets credit?" Then he caught himself and said, turning to McMurphy, "Trevor's the one who should get credit, because he was the first down, and it was his plan that made it happen. I'd have just flown head-on and probably gotten killed."

"No," Trevor interrupted, "it was his idea. I'd have never dreamed of attacking it, so Josh should get credit."

"If I could get you both to shut up and stop complimenting each other, I'll tell you how it will be reported." They turned and looked at McMurphy. "It's obvious that neither of you know whose bullets did the fatal damage—it probably took both of you. So we'll credit it as a half a kill for each of you. That means you're finally in the game, Lieutenant Brown, and you're at two and a half, Lieutenant Richards, half the distance to becoming an ace. Congratulations." Josh started jumping again as McMurphy turned to walk away in disgust. They heard him mutter, "It's only a big fat balloon, for heaven's sake. My mother could have hit it with a pistol in spite of her cataracts." Josh and Trevor burst out laughing.

Trevor turned to his aircraft, where he saw Getty poking his fingers into some of the holes through the fuselage. "I count twenty," he said, "accounting for entrances and exits." Then he turned to look at Trevor. "You better not think of going after another one of these things. You can bet that the Germans will adjust their firing patterns to protect against this type of attack in the future." Trevor nodded. "Not only that, but you've got my aircraft all shot to pieces, and we'll be working all night to get it patched up."

"Does it help to know that the balloon looks worse?"

Getty looked up and smiled. "Of course it does. And you shouldn't think I'm really worried about the airplane. It's the pilot I care about."

Trevor turned to Josh and said in mock amazement, "Darn it, Josh, this means I'm surely dreaming, and I'll wake up to find there was no balloon. I mean, killing a balloon is plausible, but Getty saying something nice about a pilot?"

Getty growled. "You know I said that wrong. It's not that I care about you. It's that I don't want to have to train anybody else. You pilots are just too much trouble. So take it easy next time and do an old man a favor."

"You got it, chief. Now I'd like to buy my wingman a cup of chocolate."

* * *

The next two mornings were fogged in. Not that anyone minded—they needed the sleep. July had been a particularly intense month as the British and French had completely abandoned this sector to American control. The Germans must have thought the Americans' inexperience would make them vulnerable, because they increased the frequency of incursions behind Allied lines. It also appeared they were planning yet another major offensive, because the number of photo-reconnaissance flights was up dramatically, and the pilots in the squadron were flying virtually every day to try to knock down the two-seater recon planes and to engage in aerial battles with their Fokker escorts.

When they reported to the hangar on Thursday morning, Trevor expected the usual assignment to fly east to meet any early morning photo flights. Instead, he was surprised when McMurphy said, "You may be pleased to know that the Air Service has purchased more than 250 new Spad XIII aircraft for your flying pleasure. We can send pilots off to Paris in groups of two to pick up the new planes and to turn in your beat-up Nieuports."

"I've heard the Spads aren't as responsive as the Nieuports."

McMurphy turned to look at the pilot who'd spoken. "They're not as lightweight because they have a water-cooled engine. But they have significantly more horsepower, and you don't have to fight the gyroscope effect. I'm told that what you lose in maneuverability, you more than pick up in speed. Plus, there haven't been any instances of the fabric tearing off the wing, so you can hold your speed in dives and pursuits. I wouldn't get too worried if I were you. Both the Nieuport and Spad are French built, and the French Escadrilles have always chosen the Spad over the Nieuport. They love the powerful Hispano-Suizo engine because it's so much less temperamental than the Rhone. So who gets to go first?"

McMurphy looked up and down the line, knowing that every one of them would love to get the chance to be the first to fly the new aircraft. A lot of them would probably wish for their old Nieuport back, if for no other reason than that it was familiar, but every one of these guys loved technology and the chance to try something new.

"I thought of having a drawing, but that's not very military. Then I thought of giving the honor to the pilot with the most kills, which would make it Wilkinson. But headquarters suggested that we give it to our new 'Heroes of the Trenches,' as they're being called, none other than Richards and Brown, who managed to let the air out of the German sausage earlier this week. Seems it was great for morale, even though it's expected that the Germans will have a replacement up later today."

Everyone turned to look at Trevor and Josh, whose faces immediately flushed. They knew that all the other pilots hated them. Well, at least they were jealous. But still, the chance to be the first was good enough news that they had to work very hard to suppress the natural grins that were pushing up the corners of their mouths.

"Should I consider that an order, sir?" Trevor said crisply. He knew that would really annoy the others.

"What? Oh, Richards. Yes, it's an order. Why don't you take a couple of extra days in Paris so I don't have to have you underfoot? Besides, it will really make everybody here crazy knowing that you're in Paris with some of the finest wine and women in the world, and you'll probably be off to a museum or something." Everybody laughed, including Trevor. He saluted crisply and started toward his aircraft.

Josh hesitated until McMurphy shouted, "You too, Brown. You're one of the heroes, so get out of here and see if you can't get Richards to at least drink some grape juice or something." Trevor heard him mutter, "A perfect waste of a good R&R." But he knew that McMurphy secretly admired him for keeping his standards.

At any rate, McMurphy did his muttering, and Trevor and Josh went over to the hangar where they told Getty and Josh's mechanic to say good-bye to their old Nieuports. "Good riddance," Getty grumbled. "That engine is a pain in the neck that was ruining me for postwar employment. Whoever heard of an engine where the whole darn motor spins around the shaft instead of the other way around? I can't wait to get a water-cooled, standard configuration."

After all the grief you've given me about how much you love this plane. But Trevor didn't share his thoughts out loud. "McMurphy told us not to come back before Monday, so have a quiet weekend, chief." Then they were off and up in the air. As they flew west, Trevor felt unaccountably light and cheerful. He was almost halfway to Paris before it dawned on him that the reason he felt so good was that there was no risk of enemy archy or fighters. He was able to just fly his airplane in any direction he felt like without concern for somebody shooting at him. It felt great. So great, in fact, that when he finally figured out why, he took the plane into a series of barrel rolls, followed by all the aerial acrobatics he could think of. At one point, he looked out to see Josh laughing at him, but then Josh followed suit and pulled off some amazing moves of his own. The two of them probably played in the air for nearly half an hour doing vrilles, reventments, reverses, and spins to their hearts' content. He'd never felt so free, and it was much like being a kid again. It was one of the happiest moments of his life.

On his last dive, he happened to fly down toward a little village, where he was startled to see nearly the whole town collected on the town square looking up and clapping for him. Apparently the beleaguered French were appreciative of an unscheduled air show. He tipped his wings in acknowledgment and then flew on to their assigned aerodrome northwest of Paris.

When they landed and checked in their Nieuports, they were told to take a taxi into Paris to spend the weekend, since it would be Monday, at least, before their new Spads would be ready. Because Josh had arrived at the front later than Trevor, he hadn't had the chance to spend any time in the city. Having grown up in the Midwest near Milwaukee, he had been as isolated as Trevor had in Idaho from the large, cosmopolitan cities of the East, and the chance to see the capital of France beckoned.

Unfortunately, when they arrived, they found the city in crisis mode. When Trevor had spent time there at Christmas, the people had been frightened of an impending German assault. Now the situation was desperate, with the German lines less than thirty miles from the city. On their first night in town, they could see the flashes of artillery off in the distance and feel the deep rumbling sound of the huge guns firing from both sides. When they got out to walk around the city the next day, they were told that many government agencies were preparing to evacuate to preserve important papers. Trevor had hoped to take Josh on a taxi tour, having found that the best way to see the city was to hire a driver for the day. But there were no taxis available this time since every available motorized vehicle was either transporting troops out to the lines or helping people evacuate to the southwest.

Josh and Trevor had to settle for an experience less than they'd hoped for. In a way, it felt good to be there among the average citizens to share their distress and fear. It gave more meaning to what they were doing on the front lines to see just how desperately the French wanted to maintain their independence.

In spite of the inconvenience, they had a great weekend. From their hotel, they could walk to some of the main sights of the city, and they were able to enjoy the open-air cafés where, in spite of the war, many Parisians continued to congregate to talk, fret, debate, and try to find relief from their anxieties. Trevor knew enough French that he could order food and ask for directions, and there were enough natives who spoke English and could offer their assistance when needed. As American soldiers, they were extremely well received because the French knew that if there was any hope of victory, it would be because of America's intervention. General Pershing had recently made a magnanimous gesture to the French and English, offering to release as many troops as needed to shore up their lines. That was a reversal of his intransigence of the previous year, in which he'd steadfastly maintained the position that he wanted American units to fight only under their own command.

During the warm summer evenings, as they strolled along the River Seine, Trevor and Josh got to know each other as friends. Trevor had promised himself after Alan's death that he'd never grow close to another pilot, but the truth was that it was against his nature to remain detached. He was simply one of those people who had to be connected to those around him, so he relaxed and chatted freely with Josh, enjoying even a few days away from the front.

On Monday, they went out to the aerodrome, where they found their new Spads waiting. Trevor was first to take his aircraft up, and he loved it. It was heavier than the Nieuport, but the engine ran much more smoothly, didn't throw off oil, and had an amazing reserve of power that he decided could come in handy in an emergency. Plus, the in-line cylinder block provided a smooth and steady flight that was much easier to control than the Nieuport. After just a few minutes in the air, he could tell that pilots would come home a lot less fatigued after a patrol.

When Josh joined him in the air, they turned for home. He had hoped to circle high above Paris so Josh could at least see the sights from the air, but the urgency of the inva-sion made it unwise to inadvertently terrorize the local population by making them think hostile aircraft were in the area. So they headed straight for their base, arriving a little after noon. Naturally, the other pilots crowded out to see their compact, little planes, and they were peppered with dozens of questions, most of which could be answered posi-tively and enthusiastically.

* * *

Trevor and Josh got the chance to try out their new Spads the very next morning. Arising before dawn, they crossed no-man's-land and went twenty miles into Germany in search of scouting and photo-reconnaissance planes. Trevor's plan was to circle high in the atmosphere, almost at their ceiling, so that no one on the ground would know they were there. The sound of the Hispano-Suizo engine helped in that regard, since it was quieter than the Rhone-rotary and much less distinctive.

They flew large, interlocking loops for more than half an hour before Trevor spotted movement below. Descending a bit, he decided it was a viable target, so he signaled to Josh to follow him down. They let the Germans get west of them while they descended gently and effortlessly behind them, being careful to keep the sun at their backs. As they got down to around ten thousand feet, they could clearly see two Albatros flying above the trenches, with one supporting Fokker flying close behind. They were undoubtedly helping the German infantry sight in on potential targets.

While Trevor didn't like the odds, he decided that the element of surprise would give him and Josh an advantage that was worth exploiting. Trevor cut his engine and continued to drift down until he was directly above and behind one of the Albatros. To make this work, he'd have to zip down and hit the Albatros, then sheer off and up to get out of the way of the Fokker. He hoped to use a revensement to climb up and over and come in behind the Fokker. He and Josh had talked about this very maneuver in one of their many nighttime discussions, so he was confident that Josh would know what to do. Just as he was ready to restart the engine, he saw two puffs of black archy directly east in front of the Albatros at his specific altitude.

The game was up, and Trevor saw the Albatros pilot start up as the Fokker peeled off to figure out where the two Americans were. Knowing it was now or never, down he dove under full acceleration. It was amazing how much more confident he felt knowing that the Spad could take the speed without having to worry about the fabric. Even though the Albatros made a valiant effort to evade him, it was too late. Trevor came screaming in at top acceleration, pulling on the trigger when the Albatros came into his crosshairs. He watched as the string of tracers came lazily across the observer's seat and the observer fell forward in his seat.

The Albatros banked quickly to the left, but Trevor was able to match him exactly and let go with a second round of firing. This time the tracers cut across the engine cowling, right where the fuel tank was situated, and he watched the aircraft burst into flame. There was nothing the pilot could have done. For his part, Trevor had been coming at such a high rate of speed that he had to pull back with full force on the stick to avoid a collision. As his airplane pulled up into a vrille, he actually felt the heat of the burning airplane as he passed within a few feet overhead. He rose as fast as he could, waiting for the moment when it was time to roll to the side to complete the upper loop. In the intensity of the firefight, he'd lost track of the Fokker, and he had very little doubt that he'd soon be in trouble on that account.

Sure enough, as he started to loop down, he saw the Fokker heading straight for him, machine guns blasting. He swiveled to the left and listened in horror as he heard one of the struts separating the upper and lower wing crack in the wind. Before he could even react, the upper right wing collapsed, and he immediately fell to that side, going into a tailspin. He'd never encountered anything like this in all his previous drills and combat, and all he could do was let his hands and feet respond to the aircraft.

Slowly but surely, he started to stabilize the spin, and as he came down to around a thousand feet, he was able to pull out of the dive and swoop into something of level flight. At that point, he found out that his troubles were just beginning. At this altitude he was just a few hundred feet above the ground, with very low airspeed, which made him an easy target for both the Fokker and the infantry on the ground. He could actually see some of their faces as they fired up at him, and he heard the pinging sound of the bullets. A single glance at his back showed that the Fokker was quickly coming out of its own dive directly behind him. He didn't dare take evasive action because his ability to maintain flight was so shaky that any sudden move could easily tear the wing completely loose.

So there it was. He had no way to defend himself. He was under intense enemy fire, and even though friendly lines were less than four miles away, it was pretty obvious that he'd never live to see them if he kept on this path. The only thing he could hope for was that the Fokker would be content to drive him to the ground, where he could crash-land behind

German lines. All of his bravado about how he'd be okay if he was taken prisoner came back to haunt him. He was almost more frightened of a crash landing and being disabled in some German prison camp than he was of dying, and for the first time in his flying career, he felt his heart pounding in his chest as a wave of panic flooded over him.

Because the aircraft was behaving fairly well, he gave a passing thought to holding his heading, but when he started to climb a bit, the Fokker fired a line of bullets that tore up his left wing. It was obvious that he wasn't going to allow any compromise. Even when Trevor signaled his intention to land, the German opened up a new line of fire that made it clear he was going for a kill rather than a forced landing. Trevor started a prayer, fully expecting to meet the one it was addressed to in the next few seconds.

The next thing he knew, he was nearly knocked out of his seat by the sight of an aircraft swooping down directly in front of him, coming from above and the opposite direction. In the midst of his troubles, he'd forgotten about Josh, who was now flying directly for him but shooting past him at the Fokker. The line of Josh's fire passed precariously close to Trevor's aircraft. As he continued to lose altitude, he suddenly felt a hot blast of air sweep past him from behind and a brilliant light reflected on the backside of his windshield. He turned in amazement to see the Fokker breaking up.

At that point, he twisted to the left to see Josh arch up into the sky, where he fired on the remaining Albatros, which was apparently trying to maneuver into position to take its own shot at Trevor. The Albatros decided that it had seen enough, and it broke off the attack and headed for home.

Trevor was now probably two miles from the lines, and the Germans on the ground were firing on him like crazy. That's when Josh flew past with guns blazing as he strafed the ground. Trevor had been so concerned about the next life that he'd forgotten he still had at least half of his unspent cartridges to fire. So he joined Josh in firing on the German ground troops, who immediately retreated inside their trenches. As his poor, little airplane continued its downward drift, he passed from the German side across no-man's-land into the American sector, no more than two hundred feet above the ground. He saw some of the men in the trenches wave as his aircraft floated toward the deck. His next task was to figure out where to land it, which was problematic, since the fields in this area were rife with holes and debris thrown up by the German artillery barrage. No matter where he looked, there wasn't a good option.

It wasn't really important, though, because no matter what he did, he couldn't keep her airborne. He sighted in on the most likely spot and did his best to come in under a powered landing. As the wheels hit the ground, he cut power and attempted to stop the forward roll, but his landing came to an abrupt and inglorious end as he hit a large crater and went nose-up in the hole. Painfully he unbuckled himself from the restraining belts, which had saved him from being thrown into the instrument panel and crawled out of the wreckage. Josh flew overhead, perhaps a hundred feet above the deck, and waved at him with a signal to stay put. So he did. He just sat down on the edge of the crater and watched his little airplane settle into the muck.

After about twenty minutes, some American doughboys came up and congratulated him on killing the Albatros and then started asking all kinds of questions about what the area looked like from the air. Trevor really hadn't been to the trenches before, and he enjoyed the chance to talk to these guys. In the conversation he mentioned that he had a friend who was in the trenches, and one of the men asked who it was.

"His name is Dan O'Brian. He's a sniper."

"O'Brian—I know him. He served with our unit last month."

Trevor jumped up so fast it startled even him. "You know Danny? Do you know where he is?"

"They always send the snipers to wherever there's a particularly nasty job to be done. I think he's about sixty miles from here. I can give you the name of someone in the Signal Corps who could find out for you."

"That would be great. If he's this close, I can probably get permission to visit him."

The sergeant wrote something on a piece of paper and handed it to Trevor.

"You don't know how much this means to me," Trevor said breathlessly. "This guy's my best friend in the world, and now that I know that he's here, I'll find him." The infantry guys laughed and wished him luck. Just then, they heard the sound of a motorcycle approaching and looked up to see Josh's beaming face racing toward them. When he reached the group, he jumped off and ran up and hugged Trevor.

"I thought you were done for," Josh said. "That Fokker could have let you go down, but he was out to kill you."

"So I found out. If it hadn't been for you, he'd have succeeded. You saved my life."

"Aw, shucks," Josh said with a grin. "I've done worse things in my life." Then he added with a smile, "Do you realize we each got a kill? That puts you at three and a half and me at one and a half. Not a bad morning."

"Actually," Trevor said, "this is about the best morning of the war, for me. These guys just told me how I can find out where Danny O'Brian's serving. I may actually get to see him."

Josh smiled again. He knew how close Trevor and Dan were. "That's great, Trevor. Oh, boy, am I glad you're alive!" Trevor felt a wave of gratitude sweep over him as he realized what a great friend he had in Josh. He gave him another hug. Then Josh asked, "Are you ready to go home?"

Trevor turned to the soldiers and thanked them for coming over to see him. Then he asked if Josh would let him drive the motorcycle back to the aerodrome. "It'll bring back some good memories," he said.

Josh cheerfully climbed on the back of the motorcycle and then did his best to hang on for his life as Trevor raced for the base.

Chapter Seventeen

AN ACT OF ESPIONAGE

Army Headquarters, near St. Mihiel, France
July 1918

Dan didn't realize he could be so nervous at the thought of appearing before an army general. He didn't really think highly of officers and had been content to do his part for the war out in the trenches. For the life of him, he couldn't figure out why he was sitting in a waiting room with special orders in his pocket to report to headquarters. If he ever thought of the senior staff, it was mostly with contempt for their inability to come up with a workable strategy to end the war.

He was brought out of his reverie as the general's aide came back into the room. It was an amazing room. As a kid, he'd thought the Richardses' house was the most elegant that anyone could ever own. But compared to this palace, it was nothing. The general had taken over an estate whose owner had fled to safer ground near the Bay of Biscay, and it was to this humble abode that Dan had been driven in a staff car. The house must have had more than fifty rooms and was situated on perfectly groomed grounds about twenty miles from the front lines. There were reflecting pools, fountains, polo grounds, and forests. Inside the house, he'd walked past a grand ballroom with magnificent paintings on the wall and up the stairs to a highly gilded library, where he'd been instructed to wait for his appointment.

It was all well and good, except that he had no idea why he was here or whom he was to have an appointment with. When he'd asked Lieutenant Stennis about it, all he'd received in reply was a shrug of the shoulders. He still didn't understand why he was nervous, since he hadn't done anything wrong that he knew of. But this place was intimidating, and he felt particularly self-conscious since he'd come straight from the front lines in his field uniform. He was the dirtiest and smelliest thing in the house, and he felt frumpy and disheveled as the stiffly starched young men of the general's staff moved purposefully in and out of the room. Their sideways glances told him that they wondered why he was here as well.

Finally, after what seemed an eternity, another second lieutenant asked him to enter a side room. Dan stood up and walked past him, shifting his Springfield on his shoulder in such a way that it made a sharp cracking noise just as he passed the other lieutenant. He secretly gloated as the lieutenant fell back a bit, startled at the sound.

Inside, he faced two officers—a general and a major. But they weren't the ones to catch his attention. He couldn't help but stare at the other man in the room, who was dressed in a perfectly pressed German officer's uniform. The sight so unnerved him that he almost forgot to salute the general.

"You can stop staring, Lieutenant. He's one of us."

"Yes, sir," Dan stammered. He thought about saying something more but instantly decided against it.

"At ease, soldier. In fact, why don't you have a seat?" The general motioned in the direction of a chair, and Dan moved uncomfortably toward it. The chair was made of highly polished cherry wood, and the thought of sitting on it in his filthy uniform made him wince. A scratch was inevitable. But the general and the others took seats next to him without a glance, so he sat down stiffly.

"You're probably wondering why you're here, so I'll get right to the point. There's a member of the German chief of staff who's going to be visiting the city of Metz twenty-one days from now. We've learned about the visit through some highly confidential sources, and I need to tell you that one of them lost his life after getting us the message. He chose to swallow a cyanide pill rather than run the risk of having the Germans extract from him what information he possessed."

Dan swallowed hard.

"Needless to say . . ." he glanced down at a paper he held in his hand, then looked up. "Needless to say, O'Brian, everything you hear today is confidential. Is that understood?"

"Yes, sir." He said it with as much conviction as he could put into his voice, given that he was completely intimidated by the whole experience.

"You're here because we're hoping you'll volunteer to accompany Major Franklin here on a covert mission behind enemy lines. It's an extremely hazardous assignment, and the truth is that you may be forced to take the same kind of action as our informant, should things go badly." Dan swallowed even harder. "The reason you were selected is that reports from the front tell us you're an excellent marksman with experience as a sniper. Is that true?"

Dan wanted to sound brilliant, but all he could muster was his third, "Yes, sir." He realized he must have sounded like an idiot, but he didn't know what they were talking about, so it was hard to give any more response than that.

"Here's what we've got in mind. This officer is a legitimate military target. He's also one of the men who is responsible for most of the resistance we've encountered in this sector. He has a brilliant mind for strategy and is, I believe, personally responsible for the plans that have cost us thousands of lives." He paused, cleared his throat, and then looked directly at Dan with a cold look in his eye. "We want him dead, O'Brian. We want to send a team into Germany to kill him so he can no longer create the plans that are interfering with our ability to prosecute this war. Do you understand what I'm saying?"

Dan's mind reeled at this, and before he could check himself, he blurted out, "You mean you want me to assassinate him?"

The general sat back in his chair and said, "That's probably not the word I'd have chosen, but yes, that's exactly what we want you to do."

"But why me, sir? I've never had any experience at anything like this. Certainly you must have others who do this sort of work."

This time the major spoke. "There are three reasons you've been asked to volunteer. First, our records show that you took four years of German in high school and two years in college. Is that correct?"

"Yes, sir," Dan replied. "I'm a music major, and it helped to have a German background for some of the work I was doing. Plus, my father wanted me to learn German because of its value as the international language of science." Dan felt defensive, almost like speaking German was unpatriotic or something.

"We're not condemning you, O'Brian. We're glad to have someone with at least a basic working knowledge of the language."

"While I can read and write in German, my speaking would be awkward, I'm sure, since I've never really spent time in a German-speaking environment."

"As you'll see, that isn't crucial. The second reason we selected you is that our records indicate that you're unmarried with only a father back home. Your mother passed away several years ago, and you have no living siblings."

It made Dan uncomfortable to think they'd taken the trouble to learn all this about him. He'd always figured that once he filled out his enlistment papers, they'd been filed away in some filing cabinet back in the States, never to be looked at again. Obviously that wasn't the case.

"No, sir, I have no one but my father. My brother was killed early in the war." He saw a clouded look come over their faces, which probably meant they were concerned about his father having already lost one son in the war. Since Kelly had been killed while serving under foreign command, their records might not indicate anything about him or how he died. "I should add, sir, that my father and I are not close, so that would not present any obstacle to my serving." He felt his face flush, which annoyed him, but it was the truth.

The major nodded his head. It was obviously a statement he didn't want to follow up on. "The third reason is that your field commander has given you the highest rating possible for both your marksmanship and your loyalty. We need both of those in this assignment." Dan blushed again, but for a very different reason. He felt that Stennis respected him, but it was gratifying to think that he'd actually sent up a recommendation in his behalf.

"So the question is, will you accept an assignment to go into Germany? We believe that it has the potential to move the war effort ahead by months, if not years. In fact, there's no amount of men you could take out in the trenches that would equal this one deed."

A hired assassin! Dan shook his head in disbelief, while saying firmly, "Yes, sir. I'll do it." At that moment, when he was feeling nothing but contempt for himself, the words, "It is better that one man should perish than that a nation should dwindle . . . and perish" came into his mind. The enormity of the task staggered his conscience and made him want to throw up. Yet Dan knew the truth of what the general had told him. It was the German leadership that had brought this horror on the world, and it was the German leadership that continued to push its men into battle even though it was becoming obvious that Germany would eventually lose. It was they who had such a callous disregard for human life that they kept feeding men—and even boys— into the trenches with no thought of what it meant to their families and friends back home. They were willing to sacrifice everything to prove the supposed invincibility of the German race. Somehow they had to be stopped, and Dan decided that if he now had the chance to stanch the flow of blood by this act, then he was prepared to do it. He just hoped he could one day look at himself in the mirror again. Looking down, the thought struck him that the filth of his uniform was a fitting symbol. He felt as dirty as his uniform.

"Tell me what I need to do, sir."

"That's the spirit," the general said brightly. "Let me tell you a little bit more about Major Franklin, here." Dan turned to face the major, who smiled wanly at him. "Major Dennis Franklin's father worked for a German company before the war. The major was raised in Hamburg until he was fourteen years old, and then his family moved back to their home in St. Louis. His German is flawless and spoken with a native accent. Plus, he knows the customs and history of the land better than he knows American history. He will be the one to accompany you on this mission, and he will be in command until the event is successfully concluded."

Dan studied Franklin's face carefully. It was important that he know what kind of man he was so he knew how to relate to him. He was relieved to see that in spite of a stern, hard-set jaw, there was compassion in his eyes. Without even speaking a word, he was able to communicate to Dan that he was not a cold-blooded killer either, but, rather, a man of conscience who was doing this in behalf of his country and the men who were fighting out in the trenches.

His thoughts were interrupted by the general. "Now, there will be some papers for you to sign, O'Brian. In essence, you will waive all rights as a United States citizen. If you're taken prisoner, we will do nothing to aid in your release. The Red Cross will not be informed, and the German authorities will be told that you acted on your own. I'm afraid that all the risk is being transferred to you and Major Franklin. Do you understand?"

Dan actually smiled. "I understand enough to request some of those cyanide pills you spoke of earlier." He thought it was clever, but no one else smiled. They simply assured him that he would have an adequate supply.

* * *

The next fourteen days were the most remarkable of Dan's life. Once clear of the general and his adjutant, he and Major Franklin moved into a remote house on the estate, where Franklin started an intense briefing on how they were to carry out their mission. There were no resources that were not placed at their disposal. A group of engineers had created a scale replica of the city of Metz on a huge table in a hunting lodge next to their house. Using that as a guide, Franklin showed Dan the safe house where they would stay. It had been selected to give him a clear shot from an upper window down into the plaza where the general's automobile would pass. Specialists from Springfield created a custom-made gun for him that fit his body perfectly, and they equipped the gun with the most accurate optical sight available. He was given as much time as he desired to practice shooting, until the new weapon became a simple extension of his own body. Finally, he spent the last five days speaking nothing but German. It wasn't expected that he'd ever have to talk, but it was crucial that he understood what others were saying so he could respond appropriately, even if only with a glance or nod of the head. He was surprised at how much of his German language lessons came back to him, and he couldn't help but remember old Professor Braun shouting at the class in his thick Prussian accent back at Idaho State Academy. Now the lessons he'd learned in that faraway place might be the means of saving his life.

While two weeks were hardly enough time to prepare fully, it was all the time they had. The rest of the time was

needed to land behind German lines, make their way into
the city, and discreetly take up residence well in advance of
the general's arrival so that there would be no alarms or
suspicion raised. As he was driving to the airfield, Dan carefully checked the documents that had been forged in his
behalf. Even an untrained eye could see the superb quality of
the workmanship. He also reviewed his personal history.
According to the story written for him, he'd grown up in
Hamburg, very near the spot where Major Franklin actually
grew up. They decided it would be helpful if they got in a
jam for the major to be able to answer questions in Dan's
behalf, since they were supposed to have grown up in the
same area. His German name was Lieutenant Weill, a lieutenant on assignment as an aide to Major Hoffman. With
that level of clearance, he and Franklin could move easily in
any circle.

When they arrived at the aerodrome, Dan's heart skipped
a beat. He was finally going to have the chance to fly in an
aircraft. He was disappointed that the nature of the mission
would prohibit him from writing about it to the Richardses,
who had become his informal conduit to Trevor. For some
reason, any letters he posted directly to Trevor were
completely censored and returned. But if he passed along
nonmilitary information to the Richardses, they'd include it
in their next letter to Trevor, who would respond back to his
parents to pass information back to Dan. It took weeks that
way, but at least they had a general idea of how the other was
doing. At any rate, he'd have to wait until the war was over to
tell Trevor about the flight. But it would be great to have an
idea of what Trevor was experiencing in the air.

At least Dan *thought* it would be great to know what it
was like to fly. When he climbed into the front seat of the
high-altitude fighter, he was optimistic about what a great
experience it was going to be. Ten minutes later, he'd have
volunteered to walk to Germany. On the first swoop up, his

equilibrium was thrown out of kilter, and everything after that simply added to his misery. At one point, he was so sick he had to lean over the side to throw up. As he looked back up, he could see that it amused the pilot to no end, and he knew he'd be the topic of conversation back at the aerodrome that night. Of course, as the nausea continued, he didn't care who talked about him; all he wanted was to get down onto solid ground again. He was able to appreciate, intellectually, how interesting the world looked from this vantage point, but his stomach made a greater impact on his thinking. The only thing that really caught his attention was the passage across no-man's-land. As he followed the line of trenches that extended in both directions, he felt a sense of futility over the tiny piece of that line that he'd been defending. Maybe it made a difference, but from up here, it wasn't obvious how.

The second thing that bothered him was that they just kept climbing. Franklin, who was flying in a second aircraft, had explained they would gain as much altitude as possible in order to pass undetected above the German lines. The problem was that it was cold and getting difficult to breathe. He had as good a set of lungs as anyone, but when the aircraft reached its ceiling at sixteen thousand feet, it was easy to get light-headed.

Just when he was feeling desperate, he heard the engine sputter and stop. It took a few seconds to realize that all this was according to plan, but in those few seconds, he almost panicked.

The aircraft drifted lazily on the air currents, and slowly they descended in a great spiral toward the ground. Dan was struck by the silence, and he actually had the presence of mind to enjoy the feel of the air as it warmed up and blew past his face. Looking at the ground, everything seemed to approach in slow motion until they actually got close to it. At that point, everything sped up, and he found himself

gripping the sides of the cockpit. They came into line with a
large field, and he watched in mild terror as the ground
came up to meet them. There was a huge bump and then
another as they bounced down the field toward a line of
trees. Once they came to a stop, the pilot tapped him on the
back and indicated to him to get out as soon as possible. He
really didn't need the prompt, and he unstrapped himself in
record time. Just as soon as he and Franklin cleared the field,
the two aircraft took off, assuming as steep an angle of
ascent as the aircraft could achieve until they were out of
sight.

"We have a two- to three-hour walk ahead of us to a
shelter where they'll put us up for the night."

"How did you find somebody here in Germany who
would collaborate with us?"

"The Germans aren't the best occupiers. After the last
war, they managed to alienate many of the farmers who have
French relatives. As soon as the war broke out, both sides
began to cultivate a network of potential supporters. There's
always a risk that you're going to be taken in by a double
agent who will betray you, but so far the people we are
staying with have proved completely reliable, even when
we've set them up in situations where they could obviously
sabotage our efforts. So I think we'll be safe."

"Sounds reassuring," Dan said a bit glumly. He was still
in awe of the fact that he was marching deeper into the heart
of enemy territory wearing a German uniform. He assumed
that Franklin would find his way through back roads or even
through the woods and was quite startled when they confidently walked onto the main road leading toward Metz.
Most cars passed them by with an odd look, but when a
military vehicle approached, Franklin held up his arm and
forced it to stop. In flawless German, he informed the occu-
pants that his car had been disabled by a mechanical
problem, and they could either take him and the lieutenant

to the nearest town or surrender their car to them. Since one occupant of the car was also a major, that led to an interesting discussion—one that ended as soon as Franklin showed his top-level security clearance. There was a lot of German grumbling, but the other major made two of his associates get out and wait alongside the road while he turned the car around to take them back into the nearest village, some fifteen kilometers' distance. As they pulled into town, Franklin brusquely told them to drop him at the mayor's office, then gave a crisp salute and a perfunctory, "Danke schön." The other major's car flew off in its original direction without so much as a reply.

Franklin led Dan into a small restaurant, where they ordered dinner. Dan was amazed at how steady the major was, even when he started talking jovially with a group of officers at the table next to theirs. Dan had assumed they would eat in silence. Instead, he became absolutely terrified a few moments later when Franklin invited the officers to join them at their table. He wanted to give his superior some kind of signal with his eyes, but the major simply refused to look at him. What he hadn't understood initially was that none of the other officers, all higher ranking than a lieutenant, would deign to talk to a lowly lieutenant. So as he sat there, he eventually figured out that he was safe from having to say anything more than an occasional "Ja" or "Nein," nodding his head at appropriate intervals. At first, he had a difficult time following the conversation because it moved so fast, but in time, he started to understand more and more of it. That's when he realized that Franklin had purposely set this up so Dan could get acclimated in this small village rather than in Metz.

When the evening ended, Franklin led them out into the now mostly empty streets of the village and walked confidently through two intersections before turning right. "My family used to visit one of my father's business associates

here, so I know this place from when I was a child," he said
in German. At the end of the street, he knocked on the door
of a two-story townhouse, and they were ushered in by an
elderly man and his wife. Introductions were made in
German, and Franklin gave them no reason to think that
Dan was American. Wisely, the couple didn't ask any questions but ushered them to an upstairs room, where they
stayed the night.

The next morning, they enjoyed a large country breakfast, which was probably a sacrifice with the German
rationing, but it was crucial that they have plenty of energy.
Dan didn't know how they were going to get to Metz until
Franklin led him to the local police station, where he requisitioned a driver and car, using forged orders. Once again,
Dan was amazed at both the planning involved in the operation and Franklin's panache in carrying it out. They had
about an hour's drive through some of the best scenery he'd
ever seen in his life—verdant, green fields and heavy forest.
As the car labored its way up the mountain on which the
city was located, he had to suppress the sense of wonder that
overtook him. It was like moving into a fairy tale with the
ancient buildings standing proudly in the late morning sun.
Even the sound of the soldiers passing by was consistent
with his imagination of what this part of the world would
look like. For just a few minutes, he forgot the mission they
were on and was content to just soak in the wonder of being
in a strange, new place.

Finally, they came to a stop in front of a military headquarters, and Franklin had the driver place their bags on the
curb. The driver took off, expecting they would enter the
building. Instead, Franklin hailed a cab, which picked them
up and whisked them off to a hotel about one block from
the main city square. Checking in, the major paid cash and
requested a room overlooking the street. He chatted with the
clerk, paid his compliments to one of the ladies in the lobby,

and then casually ascended the stairs to their second-floor room. Once inside, he put his finger to his lips to indicate that Dan should be quiet. It was a good thing, too, because Dan was about to start into a monologue about how terrific a job the major was doing. It wasn't until Franklin had checked the seals around the door, put his ear against each of the walls, and checked out the window that he finally said, in a very quiet voice, and in German, "Very nicely done, Lieutenant. Your behavior is consistent with your rank, although you should stand more stiffly whenever we come to a stop."

Dan was about to ask why, but Franklin continued, "You will unpack your things and prepare for our assignment." Dan quickly realized that meant he should get out his rifle, which had been disassembled to fit into a regular suitcase, and reassemble it. He carefully unpacked the weapon, oiled each of the parts, and then locked each part into position. He mounted the sight and carefully aligned it until it was perfect. Then he put the gun under the bed, as previously instructed.

For the balance of that week, he and Franklin got up at 0530, went downstairs and ate breakfast, then marched confidently down the street as if they were going to the military headquarters. Instead, they turned into a side street and entered a small business establishment, where they were led to a back room. It was there that they met with a handful of local resistance leaders who briefed them on the upcoming visit, rehearsed with them their escape route, and generally planned for all contingencies. At promptly 1700, they slipped back onto the main street, returned to their hotel for two hours, and then they went out to dinner from 2000 to 2200. At 2230, they always showed up at their hotel, acknowledged the night clerk and any guests, and then went up to bed. "The only thing that makes Germans nervous is lack of precision and consistency," Franklin had told him.

"So long as we're predictable and reliable, they're not likely to give us a second thought. If we showed up even five minutes late for any of our scheduled appearances, they'd start talking." Dan didn't really understand, because he felt so out of place that he thought it must be obvious to the whole world, but he had total confidence in his superior.

On the day of the operation, they left for the "office" at their regular time but circled back quickly around the block and climbed an out-of-the-way fire escape to reenter their hallway from the alley. Franklin checked to make sure that no one was in the hall, and then they slipped ever so quietly into their room. He listened at both walls and determined that one of the neighboring rooms remained unoccupied, while the residents of the next room had gone out for the day. No one was supposed to know that an important person was coming through town that morning, but they'd both sensed tension in the air, which told them that at least some of the city residents knew something was up. At 1100 hours, Franklin told Dan to get his weapon out and sight in on the spot where the general was expected to pass. Dan quickly assembled the weapon, secured the silencer, and loaded live cartridges into the chamber. He had to stand back from the window so that no onlookers would see him, but he practiced until he was confident he could get the shot off, even if the target was only in range for a second. Then Franklin repeated carefully how Dan would distinguish the general from the others in the car. Dan appreciated the review, even though he'd looked at the pictures at least a hundred times before.

At precisely 1200, he took his position at the window, rifle raised and ready. "Remember, lieutenant, this may save thousands of both Allied and German lives. What you're going to do is an appropriate act of war." Dan knew that and had no plans to hesitate, but it was still reassuring to hear it again.

At 1205, there was a disturbance in the street as a small crowd started to move to the spot where the car was expected to come into view. Franklin stepped forward and muttered something in German that Dan couldn't understand. "What it is it?" he asked urgently.

"I don't know for sure. It may be protesters. Our contacts warned us that there's a small insurgency group here that is bound and determined to interfere with the general's arrival to protest the continuation of the war. I hope they don't get in our way."

Dan raised his weapon again, and Franklin told him when the car came into the square. Because of a number of obstacles, there was only one spot where he could take the shot. If he missed, there would be no other opportunity. Franklin started counting down, "Ten, nine, eight, seven, six, five, four . . ." As he reached two, Dan put his finger on the trigger. He saw the front of the large Mercedes come into view and was ready to squeeze the trigger. Just as the general came into his lens, he started to pull the trigger when someone came between him and the general. Somebody in the crowd had rushed the car, and in horror, Dan saw a flash of a gun as the protester was shot by one of the general's bodyguards. He tried to get a second sight on the general, but the guards had shoved the general down into the seat, and the car sped up and out of view before he could do anything. He'd been holding his breath and now found it impossible to exhale. He'd been so tense and ready to fire that it was difficult to get his mind to let him remove his finger from the trigger.

"Stand at ease, Lieutenant," Franklin said quietly. "We lost the opportunity."

Dan put his weapon down to his side. "Can't we find another spot?"

"I'm afraid not. They'll likely divert to a different destination. At the very least, security will be doubled or tripled, and the general will never ride exposed like that again."

"But this can't be happening! We've come so far, and it's so vital!"

Franklin sat down on the bed. "This is what special operations are about, I'm afraid. You work days and weeks for an opportunity, only to have it taken from you. Now, Lieutenant, pack your weapon so we can get out of here."

"Where are we going?"

"Back to the rendezvous, of course. There will be airplanes waiting for us tonight at 1900, and we don't want to miss our ride. Unless you've come to like living behind the German lines."

Dan shook his head. It was all too unbelievable. To mentally prepare for something like that, only to have it evaporate, was just so frustrating. "The most exasperating part of all this is that those protesters could have gained far more than they'd hoped for if only they hadn't interfered."

"But they didn't know that, did they? Such are the fortunes of war."

To make a clean break, they sneaked back down the fire escape, came in through the front door, and announced that they were checking out, explaining that they had been summoned to Berlin. The desk clerk expressed his regret that they had to leave but efficiently cleared their account and sent a bellman to collect their things. There was nothing in the room to raise suspicion, and the major and lieutenant got confidently into a cab that took them to the train station. Once at the train station, they took a different cab to the local military police, where they requisitioned a car, using Franklin's authority. This time they didn't ask for a driver, explaining that they would be back in several days. That obviously annoyed the officer in charge, but there was nothing he could do about it. Two hours later, they were out in the middle of the country, proceeding to the rendezvous point.

It was then that they came upon a guard station situated in an odd location along the road. Franklin looked at the fence that extended in each direction and realized that this must be the equivalent of a provincial line. Undoubtedly, the Germans had set up the checkpoint as something of a forward post to protect the city. As they drew closer, Franklin spoke suddenly in English. "O'Brian, I've got an idea. You need to be prepared to draw your pistol when I give the order. We're going to get out of the car and talk to the guards. I'm going to order them to disrobe. If either one gives me trouble or attempts to draw a weapon, you've got to shoot him. Do you understand?"

"No, sir, but I'll shoot if you give the order."

Franklin laughed. "Of course you don't understand. I'm not sure I do either. But whatever you do, don't put a hole in either of their uniforms. They've got to be in perfect condition. Do you understand that?"

"Yes, sir."

The car pulled up to the small booth, and Franklin got out of the car, throwing the guards off balance.

"Halt," one of them shouted. "You should remain in your car."

"Please," Franklin said in a fatherly voice. "We've been traveling for hours, and we need a break. Do you have some coffee you can share?"

"Who are you?" one of the young men asked. "We need to see your papers."

"You can see that I'm a major, and this is a lieutenant. Of course we'll show you our papers. What about that coffee?"

One of the guards took Franklin's papers, which were, of course, in perfect order.

"We'd be honored to share our coffee with you, sir. We actually brewed a fresh pot in case the general asked for some." At that, the other guard gave him a fierce glance, but Franklin pretended not to have noticed the remark. Meanwhile, Dan stood at the door with his hand ready to go for his pistol. But the two guards had relaxed by now, and both turned their backs on the Americans. At that point, Franklin gave Dan the sign to draw his weapon, and each of them pointed their guns at the two guards who, when they turned around, dropped the scalding coffee to the floor. One started for his gun, but Dan simply raised his pistol to indicate he was prepared to shoot, which prompted the guard to raise his hands above his head instead.

"Very good move, Corporal. I'm afraid that we're going to have to ask you to take off your uniforms. We're going to need them."

"What?" the one started to say, but Franklin waved his gun in his face, and the two men very carefully took off their weapons and put them on the floor of the shack. Franklin indicated that they should kick them over to him. Then they proceeded to disrobe until they were standing in nothing but their underwear. Franklin bound their hands and legs, ordered them into his car, throwing in one of their uniforms, and then told Dan to change into the other uniform. When Dan was dressed, Franklin told him to stand guard until he returned. He then got into the car with the two Germans and drove off into the woods, returning perhaps twenty minutes later dressed as a German guard.

"What did you do with them?"

"Don't worry, Lieutenant. They're alive and well. They're tied up in some trees in a location where they'll be spotted in the morning. We'll be long gone by then, and they'll be able to answer honestly that they have no idea where we went."

"But why are we doing this?"

"Don't you remember what the one guard said?"

Dan tried to recall what he'd heard. It was all so unreal that he'd been concentrating on whether or not he'd have to shoot one of them. But then it came back to him—*coffee for the general.* "Do you think the general's going to come this way?"

"I'm not sure, but we have nearly three hours to waste, so why not do it here? If the general comes, you'll need both your weapons. I'll step out first to interrogate them, and I'll order them out of the car. That will infuriate them, but I'll explain that we've heard of saboteurs in the area, and we've been ordered to increase security. When they get out, you will need to step forward with both your rifle and your pistol. At that range you should be able to point your rifle from the hip, I would think."

Dan acknowledged that he could.

"Good, I want you to point it straight at the general, with one of your pistols pointing to whichever guard is on the general's left side—make that to the left of the general, using your left arm as reference. Do you understand?"

"Yes, sir. I will."

"Lieutenant, if they actually come to this checkpoint, I intend to kidnap the general. I only want to kill him as a last resort. If we could actually get him back to our lines, the intelligence could be invaluable. I don't mind tying up his guards, like we did the others, but we can't risk losing this venture because of them. If they make any move whatsoever, you have to take them out immediately. If they manage to shoot me or it looks like the general can escape, then kill him too. That is vital."

"I understand. I'll do whatever the situation calls for."

"Good. Now, let's have some coffee." Dan declined and tried to relax while explaining why. Talking about the Church helped pass the next hour.

In the course of that hour, only five or six vehicles approached the checkpoint. Franklin quickly processed all the people who approached in a way that caused no suspicion. Just when it was getting close to the time they'd have to break off the plan and head for the rendezvous point, they saw two powerful headlights bobbing down the road from the east.

"This could be it. Move back into the shadows."

Dan pulled out his rifle and inserted the clip. Then he checked his pistol, holding it in his left hand. He listened intently as the car pulled up. Franklin spoke in clipped German. When he heard the order for everyone to get out, he knew that this was the moment. He had to wait, though, because there was an argument from the car. Franklin held his own, speaking in a firm voice, until Dan heard the doors swing open. He listened for the telltale signs that would indicate all three were out. Then he stepped forward from the shadows and out onto the platform, both guns in full view. One of the guards instinctively raised his weapon, and Dan fired, hitting him directly in the chest. The other guard raised his weapon, and Franklin fired, killing him on the spot. The general attempted to jump back into the car, but Franklin yelled at him to halt. Dan opened and closed the bolt on his rifle to give him an audible warning, and the general turned to face them.

"What is the meaning of this?" he demanded.

"We're taking you with us as a prisoner, Herr General."

The general laughed. "You're taking me prisoner, this far behind our lines? There's no way you'll get through to the front lines. Don't be ridiculous."

"Perhaps we are ridiculous, Herr General, but for now, we're in control. Here's what we're going to do." Franklin then ordered the general to step forward, then he quickly tied his hands and gagged him. He then ordered Dan to keep his weapon trained on the general while he disposed of the guards' bodies. He returned quickly. "I checked on our other guards, and they're still doing well, if a bit miserable. I hid the bodies of the general's guards in a spot where it's likely to take some time for anyone to find them." Then, turning to the general, he ordered him into the car with Dan seated next to him, a pistol in the general's rib cage. Franklin proceeded to drive the general's car the short distance to the landing field.

At precisely 1900, they heard an odd swishing sound. Fortunately, there was still enough light to see the two airplanes coast in to land. At that point, the general blanched and attempted to make a break for it, but Dan tackled him to the ground. Franklin dragged him up roughly by the knot holding his hands together and forced him to walk out onto the field.

"What's this?" one of the pilots asked. "We're supposed to pick up two passengers, not three. Where do you think we can put all of you?"

"I don't care if you strap one of us to the fuselage," Franklin said firmly. "We're all going out, and we're going out right now."

The pilot thought about objecting, but the look in Franklin's eye and the three weapons that he and Dan held convinced him otherwise. "Fine, but one of you is going to have to sit with that German in your lap. It won't be comfortable."

"He can sit on my lap," Franklin said.

Dan spoke up. "No, sir. I'm the one who was sent to get him, and I'm smaller than you. Plus, if there's a problem, it's better that I go down than you. You're worth more to the war effort."

Franklin didn't protest. They first strapped Dan in and then forced the general to sit directly on top of his lap. They could have had him kneel in the cockpit if it were not for the duplicate joystick. It would be too easy for the general to throw the plane out of control. When the great bulk of the general settled onto Dan's smaller frame, he groaned a bit but wrapped his arms around the general, with the barrel of the pistol stuck firmly in his rib cage. The general's hands were tied behind him, which made things even more uncomfortable, but it meant he couldn't get to any of the controls. Franklin moved to his escape aircraft, which still had its engine running in idle, mounted the wing, and climbed into the cockpit. Dan used the brief lull to speak directly into the German's ear. "If you so much as move your leg an inch to affect the control of this aircraft, I'll shoot you. Don't think I'll hesitate for even a moment. Do you understand?" The general remained motionless, so Dan jabbed him with the pistol. "Do you understand?" This time the general nodded in the affirmative.

In less than a minute, their engines were racing, and they were accelerating down the field at full throttle. The pilot had to wait far longer than he wanted before letting the aircraft lift off because of the extra weight of a third person. They clipped the branches of a tree as they cleared the end of the field, but they were airborne. Dan expected to get motion sickness again, and he did get a bit queasy, but nothing like the first time. For his part, the general was well behaved, and the flight ended forty minutes later with an uneventful landing at the aerodrome they'd taken off from a week earlier. It was a huge relief to have the general lifted out of the cockpit, and when Dan got out, his legs felt like lead weights until the terrible pins-and-needles tingling started. But he was able to stand on his own. His head felt as if it were in a vise, thanks to a throbbing headache, and he was suddenly overcome by a wave of nausea. Perhaps it was the release of all the tension or simply the motion of the flight finally catching up with him, but he involuntarily threw up again, much to the delight of the air crew that was starting to move the aircraft back to the hangar.

Franklin walked behind the German until they were met by the American general who had first asked Dan to participate on the mission.

"What's this?" he asked breathlessly.

"I'm afraid the plan went awry," Franklin explained evenly. "Protesters interfered with our original mission. But fate presented a new opportunity, and with O'Brian's help, we succeeded in kidnapping the good general."

The American general burst out laughing. "This is just too good to be true! Congratulations to both of you. I can't wait to hear all the details." At that, he took control of the prisoner and ordered the ground crew to offer whatever assistance Dan and Franklin needed. What Dan needed was a cup of hot chocolate to settle his stomach, followed by a good night's sleep. An orderly assisted him in both endeavors.

* * *

Dan didn't see anyone the next day, so he spent his time walking around the general's estate. On the second day, Franklin came over to report on what had happened.

"It seems that our dear general is more self-serving than patriotic. He's convinced that the Allies will win, so he's telling us everything we ask so he can gain favor after the war's conclusion. The result of our mission far exceeds anything we could have hoped for."

"But won't the Germans adjust their plans when they figure out he's been kidnapped?"

"Probably, but that's all right. The disruption of their battle plans will be unnerving to a people so accustomed to order. Plus, they'll never know how much we've learned from him, so they won't know exactly how to react. Uncertainty is a great friend in this instance."

"I'm glad you thought of the idea," Dan said sincerely. "I thought all was lost."

"Don't underestimate your contribution," Franklin replied. "It never would have succeeded if you hadn't been prepared. The crucial moment was when his guard drew his weapon and you reacted exactly as you should. I wish you could tell your friends about the role you played, but, of course, this must never be shared."

"I understand," Dan said. "I'm just glad I could help." Then, in a softer voice he added, "And I'm glad I got to work with you, sir. It's an honor and a privilege. You may be the bravest person I've ever met."

Franklin smiled. "You can join us in Special Forces, if you like. You're brave enough yourself, and I'd love to have your companionship."

"Thank you, sir, but for now I'd like to return to my unit. A trench is a lot less nerve-racking. But if something else comes along, you can call on me again." Franklin extended his hand and gave Dan a firm pat on the back. With that they parted.

As he rode back toward the line, Dan had the feeling that he had finally done something worthwhile that could really make a difference—not just a difference in battle, but a difference in ending the war. It felt good.

Chapter Eighteen

A CHOICE OF
RISK OR DUTY

Trevor was grounded for nearly a week because of trouble getting a replacement aircraft. It was all right with him this time, however, because he used the time trying to set up a trip to visit Dan. It turned out that finding a sniper was more difficult than one might think. At first, he rather naively tried to place some calls himself but was quickly informed that in the military, one has to follow proper protocol. He placed a request with Captain McMurphy, who was sympathetic, who then placed a request with his superior officer, who was sympathetic and placed the request with the staff of General Billy Mitchell, who were mostly indifferent but still willing to try and help. Then the request started traveling down the chain of command of the infantry. In spite of the fact that Trevor had provided Dan's full name, date of birth, location of enlistment, and parents' names, the terse word came back up through the chain that the army could not confirm that such an individual existed.

"What do you mean, they can't confirm that he exists? I know he exists! My mother gets letters from him and passes them on to me!"

"I know, Richards, but you get these guys in Special Operations, and the army's reluctant to give out any information for fear of compromising their safety or their location."

"Captain, I spoke to a guy who saw Dan not five weeks ago. So it's not like he's exactly a secret. There's got to be some way that the army can arrange a meeting, maybe without using our names or something. I just gotta see him." He looked at McMurphy with imploring eyes. "It would be a crime to be this close and not see your best friend."

McMurphy was about to argue, but he knew that Trevor had done a good job and deserved this. It wasn't much to ask. "Let me see what I can do," he said with a sigh. This time, on McMurphy's personal recommendation, General Mitchell took a personal interest in the case, and that started moving things along. The final compromise came in a terse missive.

> Lieutenant Richards may wish to present himself
> at Army Group Headquarters on August 15, 1918, at
> 1300 hours in an active battle sector that will
> be disclosed in a subsequent telegram. We cannot
> confirm that any person of interest will be at
> that location at that specific time, so Lieutenant
> Richards should judge the advisability of a trip
> accordingly. Should he choose to come, he should
> provide up to three code words that would be
> recognizable only to selected individuals and
> that will not compromise the ongoing security of
> operations in the area.

Trevor read the missive and glanced up with a puzzled look on his face. "What exactly does all this mean?"

"It means," McMurphy said, "that they'll get in touch with your friend and tell him he's to meet someone at his group headquarters on August 15. But they won't tell him who it is, and they won't tell you where it is until that morning."

"Oh," Trevor said with furrowed brow. "What does it mean about code words?"

"You really are innocent, aren't you, Richards? It means that you should pick three words that have no military meaning but that would help your friend recognize that he's meeting you."

"Oh," he said again, but this time with a smile. "I'm finally getting it." McMurphy shook his head in exasperation.

"Here are the words: Indian, Stearns, and Steinway."

"I won't even ask. I'll let you know when confirmation is received."

"Thanks, Captain. I hope it's okay if I take my airplane up there, maybe even give Dan a ride?" McMurphy nodded, then dismissed him. He hoped things would work out so Richards could see his friend. It would be even better if the war ended so they could just go home together.

* * *

Trevor sent back the code words ten days before August 15. In the interim, he managed to fly a number of mostly routine missions. He couldn't tell if McMurphy was trying to protect him, but he and Josh were sent out on more than their fair share of reconnaissance missions, which were much less likely to encounter hostile aircraft than a search-and-destroy mission. It was boring, but he was glad to get in some easy flying time in the Spad so he could practice maneuvers with it. Even though the Spad was heavier than the Nieuport, he found that he liked the extra power and stability.

A couple days before he was scheduled to take off to see Dan, he sat down to write a letter to his parents. Overall, it was pretty positive because he didn't want to worry his mother. Still, he thought his father would enjoy hearing about the battle in which he was driven down and nearly murdered just inside enemy lines, so he included just as much detail as he thought he could get away with without pushing his mom over the edge. He also had to be general enough that it would get past the censors. The main thing he wanted to get across was what a great thing Josh had done for him in driving off his attacker and then accompanying him across no-man's-land back to friendly lines where he crash landed. As he read back over what he'd written, he was amazed at how exciting it sounded, thinking maybe he ought to be a writer. Then he looked at his spelling and realized he should never be a writer.

About two-thirds of the way through writing the letter, just after telling them the exciting news about his upcoming visit to Dan, he was scrambled to take off on a rescue mission. A German Fokker had decided to take out an American reconnaissance flight, and the American's escort had been shot down. Trevor and Josh shot out of the barracks at a dead run and jumped into their waiting aircraft for an immediate takeoff. Within five minutes of the call, they were in the air and were at the reported site of the attack within ten minutes. Unfortunately, it was too late. They could see the smoldering remains of the American aircraft just inside friendly lines. Flying down for a closer look they saw some doughboys pulling the bodies of the fliers out of the wreckage.

For some reason, it made Trevor unaccountably angry. The Germans were just doing their job, but it seemed so unfair that these guys would lose their lives so close to base. He indicated to Josh that they should go looking for the German, and Josh nodded his assent. So up they went, passing over no-man's-land in a search pattern that took them farther and farther behind German lines. After about half an hour of searching, Trevor was about to call it quits when he spotted the faintest speck out of the corner of his right eye. He turned and headed in that direction, assuming it was an Allied aircraft on its way home. Suddenly, the other aircraft turned and dived on him, and he knew instantly that this was no ally. He peeled off to the left in a maneuver that usually brought him into the clear, but as he pulled out of the roll, he could see that his attacker was directly behind him. He shot up in a revensement to try to get behind the other aircraft. But when he came out of the loop, he found that the German had simply completed a horizontal circle that left him in a favorable position to fire on Trevor again.

He turned to find Josh, but in vain. Trevor could see only the German, who was proving himself almost impossible to shake off. Trevor listened anxiously as the bullets passed through the space between his wings, one actually hitting one of the wires that laced the upper and lower wing together. Finally, in desperation, he shot straight up into the air, then looped into a steep spiral dive. He made the loops of the spiral just wide enough and erratic enough that it would be almost impossible for someone to draw a consistent bead on him. In spite of his precaution, he felt a bullet slam into his console, shattering the wood panel. As he gained speed, he was grateful that he didn't have the old Nieuport because he was now going straight toward the ground at nearly two hundred miles per hour, spinning wildly as he went.

At one thousand feet above the deck, he knew he had to pull out. What he didn't know was if the German had bought into his ruse or if he was coming behind him to take up where he'd left off. Trevor asserted control, and the Spad responded instantly to his touch. He came swooping out of the last spiral just two hundred feet off the deck and then flew parallel with the ground below tree level. Just as he turned to glance up, he heard another bullet slam into the left upper wing less than a foot away from his face. With little conscious thought, Trevor did something he'd never thought of—or practiced—before. He headed straight for the tree line at full speed, even though he was below the top of the trees. Having accelerated to nearly 190 miles per hour in the dive, he was tearing along just feet above the ground, knowing that in this position it would be difficult for the German to fire on him. Since the best angle of attack was from above, the German would hit the deck if he did anything other than follow. That meant the German had to fly parallel to the ground with only the chance to fire horizontally—a much more difficult shot. Not only that, but at this altitude he'd have to concentrate on the task of flying, not shooting.

Sure enough, the bullets stopped as he approached the line of trees at breakneck speed. For this to work, he'd have to stay calm. If he broke too soon, the German would be on him in a flash. What Trevor wanted was for the German to break early so that he'd be in an upward climb when Trevor pulled up. That would allow Trevor to literally come up and fly upside down in the German's direction, giving him the chance to return some fire. It was risky, but there was nothing else he could think of to do. His heart was pounding as the trees loomed in his face. Calculating the very last point at which he could mount, he pulled back on the stick with everything he had, and the Spad shot up and over in a matter of seconds. He'd timed it close enough that he felt a jolt as his wheels ripped the upper branches off the tree he'd sighted in on. But he made it clear of the trees.

He'd flown upside down plenty of times but had never come into it this quickly, and he found himself disoriented by the g-forces that pulled on his body. He had to concentrate extremely hard to bring the aircraft under control, flying upside down in the opposite direction of his previous heading. He knew the other pilot was probably above him, so he did a quick roll into the upright position, then pulled back on the stick to go into a climb. He knew he'd guessed right when he saw the German shoot down toward Trevor's previous position.

Trevor completed his banking roll and came in nicely behind the German, managing to fire off six or seven hundred rounds at the German. At least some of them hit the aircraft, but the enemy pilot continued unfazed into another round of aerial acrobatics. In the course of the five- or six-minute battle that followed, Trevor managed to hit the German on two or three occasions, and he heard his own airplane get hit at least as many times. Finally, as he rose in one last desperate attempt to gain the advantage, he saw the German suddenly peel off and head back deeper into Germany.

Trevor looked around desperately to see if someone had come to relieve him, but the sky was empty. Slowly he gained altitude and took a couple of sweeps around the area to see if he could find Josh, but he was nowhere to be seen. So Trevor headed for home with a heavy heart. He decided that the only thing that had saved him must have been that the German was running low on fuel and had to break off the fight. One thing was certain—this particular German pilot was the best pilot he'd ever encountered anywhere. If they'd kept up the fight, Trevor was fairly certain he would have lost the encounter.

When he reached his airbase, he was distressed to find that Josh hadn't returned. He walked around the base nervously until he finally had to turn in. He tried to sleep, but concern over Josh made it impossible to get anything more than a few minutes of sleep between the long periods when he lay awake, trying not to think about Josh or what might have happened to him. Even the little bit of sleep time he did get was tortured by disturbing dreams and images.

The next morning, he went to the control tower to see if they'd heard anything, but there was no news. He walked out to his aircraft and went up on a morning reconnaissance which was uneventful. As frightening as the previous day's encounter had been, he almost wished for some action to keep his thoughts occupied. When he landed, he looked for signs of Josh's aircraft, but there weren't any. He taxied up slowly to the hangar, surprised that John Getty wasn't there to greet him. He switched off power and descended from the aircraft, walking heavily toward the hangar. That's when Josh came bounding out, all smiles and yelling for him to hurry up.

"Where have you been?" Trevor asked incredulously.

"Be quiet and take a look." Josh pulled up his shirt and showed Trevor a nasty red gash across his breast where he'd been grazed by an enemy bullet. Amazingly, the skin was hardly torn. It was more like an oozing burn. "While you were down on the deck trying to get yourself killed, I was fighting with your guy's buddy. Man, was he good! I twisted and turned every way I could think. Suddenly, I felt this sharp pain across my chest, and I thought I was surely going to die. Instead, the impact surprised me so much that I pulled to the left and nearly hit the German. I don't know if he thought I was crazy or something, but he circled around, fired a few shots, then took off. I was turning to come down and help you when I saw that he'd somehow hit my propeller, which was spinning unevenly. I knew if I didn't get out of there, I'd crash-land in Germany. So I fired a few shots in the direction of your friend and then headed for our lines. I managed to make it to our lines and set down about thirty miles from here. It wasn't until late this morning that I could find a ride back. Can you believe that I came this close to a bullet?"

Trevor couldn't believe how relieved he felt. So instead of saying anything, he just gave Josh a big hug. Finally he whispered, "I'm glad you made it. I had a pretty bad night last night thinking about it."

Josh looked at him seriously. "Thanks. I was worried about you too. You had your hands full with that guy, and I didn't know if you'd make it back either."

Trevor shook his head and said, "I don't know what this war's coming to when you have to put up with stuff like that." At that, they laughed and turned to go to the mess to get something to eat.

Later, back in the barracks, Trevor finished his letter to his parents. It was pretty somber, really—much heavier than he'd have liked it to be. But the truth was that he'd had some pretty rough flying, and it was hard on his spirit. He actually found himself wondering if Dan would make it to their reunion or if he'd get killed first. He had to shake his head to try to clear his mind.

By the time he finished with the letter, it was getting dark outside. He was restless, so he went to find Josh to see if he wanted to go running. Josh was playing cards with some of the other pilots, but he quickly agreed to a run. For a long time, they didn't say anything, but just ran at a pace that was stiff enough to make Trevor breathe hard. As he bounded along, he remembered the hundreds of miles he'd run with Dan when the world was so much simpler. It felt good to press himself until it hurt, and without thinking about it, he picked up the pace in an attempt to really stress his body.

"How does a person say 'Uncle'?" Josh called out breathlessly. That broke Trevor's concentration, and he slowed down to a jog so Josh could catch up.

"Sorry, guess I was lost in thought. It felt good to push myself hard enough that I could stop thinking about everything that's been going on." They came into a small clearing, and Josh asked if they could sit down for a while. Sitting on the ground with their arms on their knees, Trevor finally caught his breath.

"So you went to MIT," he said casually.

"I did. Great school, if you like science."

"My father and grandfather wanted me to go there, but I didn't want to go that far from home." Trevor laughed. "Now look at me. I'm in the middle of France."

"I don't know if you ever told me what you majored in."

"Mechanical engineering. Stanford doesn't have a program for aeronautics yet, so I worked on a mechanical engineering degree. It helped me understand about stress and design, so it was good. Kind of boring, but stuff I need to know. What did you major in?"

"A new field, actually. I was studying radio and other wireless devices. We were one of the first to transmit the human voice through the air in such a way that it could be picked up by a distant receiver."

"Wow, that's great. I know that radios have started to be used in the war. I bet it's not long before they have them in airplanes so that pilots can talk to each other."

"Probably not too far off, although it's pretty hard to tune them right now, and with everything else we have to worry about, I don't know how a person would find time to babysit a radio."

Trevor nodded his head knowingly.

"So what are you going to do after the war?"

"I met a couple of guys at Stanford who want to go into business. We'll probably do aircraft design or something. I'm not the type to be happy at a desk or design table, so I see myself as a test pilot. I think there's going to be a big future in aviation, maybe carrying the mail and other supplies, or even passenger service someday."

Now it was Josh who nodded.

"Hey," Trevor said, "in peacetime, a pilot would have plenty of time to work with a radio. If we could build an airplane with air-to-ground and air-to-air radio, it would really give us a leg up in marketing. Why don't you come to California and join us?"

"What? You're kidding, right?"

"I'm serious. Radio and airplanes have got to go together. Believe me, the guys I know come from money. If they want to start a business, they can afford to do it. And with our practical experience, we could come up with designs to really make a difference. I know that I'm always finding things on our airplanes that I'd do differently."

"I do too," Josh said. "California, huh? I've never been to California."

"Well, you'd love it. Everybody does. I've been mostly in the Bay Area, although I suspect that the aircraft industry will settle more to Los Angeles, where the weather's even more temperate. Palm trees and beaches are pretty nice. And they've got fantastic roads to ride a motorcycle on."

Josh agreed to think about it. In fact, Trevor could see that he was really considering it. They got up and ran back to their barracks, where they talked for another hour before Trevor finally fell asleep in mid-sentence. Josh woke him up and told him to go to bed. As Josh fell asleep, he started dreaming of palm trees.

Chapter Nineteen

MUSTARD GAS

"O'Brian, you've got to calm down. You're taking risks that you've never taken before. I know you're excited to see your friend, but you're getting sloppy. I've had to call you down from the parapet twice! I've never had to do that before."

Dan dropped his head. "Sorry, sir. I guess I'm not thinking straight. It's just that after the mission I was on, it's hard to get back into the routine."

"Well, anywhere else in the world, I'd tell you it's okay to take some time to adjust. But it's not okay out here. One mistake and you'll leave on a stretcher. So wise up."

"Yes, sir." Then, as the lieutenant turned to leave, Dan added, "Thanks." Stennis just shrugged and moved on.

The very next day brought great news for Stennis and bad news for Dan. The lieutenant had received orders to report to the headquarters of the general staff. In explaining it to the men, he said that he'd been posted as an aide to one of the generals. His father knew someone in Washington, and this was the result. Everybody congratulated him, but the lieutenant felt guilty about leaving. After dismissing the others, he asked Dan to come over where he could talk to him privately.

"I'm going to recommend you to take over the unit, O'Brian."

"What?" Then, catching his lack of proper etiquette, he added, "Begging your pardon, sir, but I'm not fit to take over your command. I can't do what you do. I'm just a marksman."

Stennis frowned. "Of course you can do what I do. There's no one better." Dan was about to protest again, but Stennis interrupted him and continued. "Let me ask you something, Dan. If I were killed in battle today, who would the men turn to for leadership?"

"I guess they'd turn to me, because I'm next highest in rank."

"They'd turn to you because you know what to do. All of them trust you, as they should. You're level-headed—at least, you were until this week—and you're smart." He paused for a moment. "Even more important, you care. I know we're not supposed to, but you do. And that means everything to the men."

Dan sighed. "I'd be honored to have you recommend me, sir, but I'll miss you more than I can say. You've become my family out here."

"I feel the same way. I wish that we could have gotten to know each other better, but I know enough to recognize the quality of your heart. And we are family—we're brothers in arms" Dan winced a bit at the brothers part. It was exactly the words his father would have said when talking about fellow members of his union. Dan had a sudden wave of empathy for Frank.

"By the way," Stennis said, "we just got a new recruit, a private by the name of Geoff Green. Would you take him under your wing and teach him the ropes?"

"Sure," Dan said. "I was new up here a couple hundred years ago. I'll get him in shape."

"I don't know if they'll accept my recommendation about your promotion, but in the meantime, I'm appointing you acting commander. I have to leave today." He stood up and turned to leave. "Do a good job here—hopefully, it won't last too long. Once I figure out the lay of the land at headquarters, I'm going to put in a transfer to bring you to an administrative post behind the lines. I think we've both done our part for the war here in the trenches."

Dan smiled. "That would be great, sir. Without telling you how I know, I can tell you that life's pretty good for the guys who serve the top brass. Nobody deserves it more than you."

"Thanks, O'Brian. Take care of yourself."

* * *

Trevor stood nervously by the telephone, jumping every time it rang. For some reason, it chose to ring more frequently than he'd ever heard before, each time with news that didn't matter to him. Finally, at around 1100 it rang, and McMurphy answered solemnly. He started writing. When he hung up, he handed Trevor a piece of paper. "Here's the landing coordinates. They say your man will be there. Apparently he sent three code words to match your Indian, Stearns, and Steinway."

"What are they?"

"Maniac, Bourgeois, and Salvation."

Trevor shook his head in delight. "They got the right man." He just couldn't suppress a smile. "I can't wait to see that boy."

"Good luck," McMurphy said earnestly. Then, in an unusual gesture, he said, "You're a good man, Richards. It's an honor to serve with you. Go down there and have a great two days with your friend. That's all they'll let him off. Then come back and help us finish this forsaken war once and for all."

Trevor was touched. McMurphy never showed emotion. "Thanks, Captain. I will. You're the best—and I promise."

As he walked out to the runway, Josh came bounding up. "Do you always bounce?" Trevor asked him.

"Only when I'm happy."

"And why are you happy today?"

"Because you get to do something you've wanted for the longest time. Tell that friend of yours hello for me. Someday maybe he'll come to Boston and give a concert at my grand-parents' house. They're awful rich and have this huge house where they love to show off musicians."

"I'll tell him," Trevor said with a grin. "That ought to cheer him up as much as my visit."

Trevor mounted his aircraft and waved. He saw Josh try to yell something at him, but he couldn't hear over the noise of the engine. So he waved even harder, then roared down the field.

"Fly carefully," Josh repeated quietly as he turned and walked from the field.

* * *

The next few days were pretty routine. The Germans were unusually quiet, which made for a nice break. It also gave Dan a chance to help young Green get oriented to the place without the walls falling down from artillery. He liked Green enough, although something about him bothered Dan. He finally figured it out just the night before they were scheduled to leave the front for supply duty. His form and figure reminded him of Jody Wilkins. Their background was entirely different, but he had the same kind of shuffle to his step and a similarly high-pitched voice. Every time Green spoke, a creepy feeling came over Dan. He knew that he'd never fully worked through the emotions of Jody being killed while rescuing him. Still, it wasn't Green's fault, so Dan did his best to help him deal with his anxiety and to be kind to him. Long before this night, he'd given up on the formal military aloofness that was supposed to exist between officer and enlisted men—it just didn't make sense out here.

Finally, morning arrived, and they were to be relieved on the line. He'd packed his meager belongings into his pack the night before and was ready before sunup. He'd done this dozens of time, so it was routine by now, but somehow he was uneasy. Departing soldiers never knew what the Germans were going to do when one group was exiting and another arriving. Sometimes they'd take potshots while the Americans were crossing the open space leading up to the trenches, which meant there was always a chance of getting hit. Other times they simply ignored them and left the morning quiet. The thing that disturbed Dan most that day was that they hadn't heard any noise whatsoever in no-man's-land during the night. It wasn't like the Germans to leave them completely unchallenged. But in an hour, he'd be out of there and on his way to headquarters. He couldn't suppress a smile at the thought.

That's when he heard the artillery fire, and he instinctively ducked up against the wall of the trench. He listened for the concussion and was startled when the explosion was much more subdued than usual. Another dozen shells landed and exploded, but all with the same dull sound. He was trying to figure it out when word was shouted down the line, "Gas! They've fired gas canisters!" Amazingly, in all his time on the line, he'd never come under a gas attack. He reached for his gas mask while running full speed to alert his men.

They were doing exactly what they were supposed to until he came to Green, who sat there paralyzed with fright. Dan hurried and put his mask on, checked for good airflow, then reached down and shook Green. The sight of Dan standing above him with the gas mask over his face must have terrified him, because Green shrank back against the side of the wall with a look of sheer terror in his eyes. Dan pulled the mask off temporarily to show him who it was, then ordered him to put on his gas mask. When he still didn't respond, Dan ripped open Green's backpack, pulled out the mask, and started forcing it over his head. At last Green came to his senses and reached up to take over. Dan gave him hand signals to help him remember how to activate it. When he saw that Green was okay, he stood up and started down the trench.

By now, he could see the vapor of the mustard gas seeping into the trench, and he knew that it was much more powerful than the old phosgene gas the Germans had first used in battle. Mustard gas could actually seep through a person's clothing. He gestured to the men to make their way to the communications trench. He was gratified when they responded and started moving purposefully to the exit. He was bringing up the rear, mentally counting as he went. One short! Then he realized it must be Green. As he was about to turn around, he was knocked against the wall of the trench by a searing blast of heated air as the Germans began firing real artillery.

As he regained his equilibrium, he stood up, only to hear a terrible gurgling sound behind him. He spun around to see what had happened. As he did so, he struck his face against a board protruding from the parapet that must have been damaged by the artillery blast. He put his hand up, because he'd hit the board hard enough to make it sting, but at the same moment he saw Green lying there, bleeding. *Got to get him out,* was all he could think. After all, he was in command. Dan went back and started dragging Green forward. A stranger, a corporal from farther down the line, came up and helped him move Green to the entrance of the communications tunnel. As they were about to turn the corner, he saw the corporal gesturing frantically about his mask, which made little sense, since his mask looked perfect. Then the corporal reached out and touched Dan's mask, and he realized that he was trying to tell him that it was Dan's mask that was damaged. Putting his hand up to his face, he felt the tear in the rubber and saw blood on his hand when he pulled it down.

The corporal pointed in the direction of the exit and gestured for Dan to run. Terror overwhelmed him as he realized he must have been breathing the odorless and tasteless mustard gas. The corporal almost shoved him ahead, gesturing for him to run. A panic unlike anything he'd ever felt made him weak in the legs, but then he started running. He should have stayed with Green, but he felt like he would suffocate if he didn't get to fresh air. So he ran. He tried to hold his mask together against his face, which put him a little off balance. Finally, he made it up and out of the trench and was running as fast as his legs would carry him across the open field when he felt a sharp blow to his rib cage which knocked him to the ground. Looking down, he saw blood.

* * *

The farther north Trevor got, the worse no-man's-land looked. He could never have imagined that it could be worse than in his own sector, but looking down was downright depressing. The Germans had attempted a major advance over this territory, and the effect of hundreds of thousands of artillery shells had left the ground looking like a weird moonscape. On any normal day, he would have broken off his scheduled flight path and flown across the German lines to find some target, but today he was resolved to get to his destination just as quickly and safely as possible. As he got within five miles of the spot where he expected to find group headquarters, however, he saw the Allied lines covered in green fog. Mustard gas! It could stay around for days, hugging the trenches and filling the low spots to make life miserable for the ground troops. Another mile closer, and he saw that the Germans were actually in the midst of an attack across no-man's-land. He couldn't watch the Germans pour in on the Americans without doing something, so he went down to complete a strafing run across no-man's-land. His approach was completely unexpected, and he was able to break up a huge group of Germans running straight for the Allied trenches.

* * *

Dan felt himself being lifted up by another figure in a gas mask. He wanted to help the guy, but he simply didn't have any strength. The uniform was funny, and at first he thought it might be a German. Then he recognized it as British and saw a chaplain's insignia. *I'm being rescued by a priest!* Somehow the thought amused him.

Perhaps because he wasn't involved in running, he became aware of bullets whipping past, and he turned his head to see some Germans racing after them. *Probably killed that corporal in the trench who was helping Green.* Dan never ceased to be amazed at how many thoughts his mind could cram into his consciousness during an emergency. He saw the shadow of an airplane pass overheard, not twenty feet above the ground. He winced and tried to duck, but his rescuer just kept on going. Perhaps a minute later, the same aircraft came flying straight for them, just feet above the deck, and as soon as it passed overhead he heard it open fire on the Germans. It all seemed so surreal. He was being rescued by some stranger, unable to help or to defend himself, while some pilot was providing cover fire for the rescue. It was so incredible. He seemed to watch it as a passive participant, almost like watching a stage play. He was also able to turn to see that the Germans had given up the chase and were racing back to the trenches, probably scared out of their wits by the airplane.

* * *

Trevor had intended to pull up and clear of the Germans, who were now firing their rifles at him, but for some reason, he banked to the left, keeping close to the ground as he crossed back onto the American side. He was trying to read his map to figure out exactly what heading to follow when he saw something that made his blood chill. There on the ground, not two hundred yards in front of him, were two Allied soldiers hobbling toward the tree line as fast as they could. It looked like one was wounded and being helped by the other. Coming behind them was an advance group of German infantry. Trevor pulled up, roared ahead, and did a sharp banking turn, using both rudder and ailerons, and came back straight for the Germans. As soon as he'd cleared the two Americans, he started firing. Of course, the Germans had seen his approach, so they'd dived to both sides of his flight path. Still, he managed to hit a couple, and as he swooped up and over, he was gratified to see the others struggling to regroup. He decided to make sure, so he came back over the heads of the Americans, who were now almost to the trees. He opened fire and chased the Germans back toward no-man's-land. Some of them actually dove into the American trenches they'd just worked so hard to clear.

Coming up and around, he started to get back onto his normal flight path when he saw a German Pfalz flying close to the ground off to his right. Circling behind it, he discovered that the German was firing on a convoy that was exiting the area where the gas was the heaviest. On the open road like that, the Americans were perfect targets, and the German was having a heyday. He gulped and climbed a bit so he could dive down on the German from the side. He didn't want to approach from behind, as he would run the risk of firing into the convoy himself. As he drew within a hundred yards, he could see that the German was unaware of his presence. He shortened the distance and then opened fire. The German really didn't have a chance as the line of tracers tore directly through the cockpit. The force of his bullets must have knocked the German's body to the left because the aircraft banked down steeply and crashed into the ground within a couple of seconds.

Trevor gulped again. He'd never had that easy of a kill, nor one that was so obviously helpful to his own troops. He pulled up to see if any other Germans were lurking about. The twang of a bullet breaking one of his cables gave him his answer. A German was coming in from the six-o'clock position, directly behind him, and he had to take immediate steps to evade him. Going straight up into a climb, he looped himself over and managed to get behind the German on the downswing. Coming up behind him, he fired another round and was able to pull the line of tracers directly into the German aircraft. That's when his guns jammed.

"Dang it," he shouted to no one. Hammering away on the closed breech, he managed to clear the jam just as the German came straight for him. Trevor fired and saw the German's engine spout flames. But the German still had power and passed directly under him at a combined airspeed of about two hundred fifty miles per hour. Trevor looped back around to make certain he'd driven the German down, only to see that the German had also made a turn and was heading toward Trevor from the two-o'clock position. It was obvious that the German was going to go down, because the flames were now going up and over his windshield. Trevor hoped that he'd jump rather than get burned alive. But the German held his course and lifted the nose of his aircraft, as if to ram him as a last gesture of defiance.

Trevor was about to pull up on his stick when he was slammed into the back of his seat with a force that seemed to knock the wind out of him. *I've heard that sound before*, he thought, *but where?* Then it came to him. *That's exactly the same sound I heard when Danny shot the bear that attacked Leonard. That dull thud of a sound.* Glancing down, he saw his flight suit getting wet directly above his right breast. *But I don't feel anything. If I've been shot, I should feel something, shouldn't I?* He wondered where the bullet had come from. *I bet that other pilot got one off in time. Amazing. We shot each other.*

The force of the impact had thrown Trevor back hard enough that his hands had followed his body in pulling back on the joystick. Even now the airplane was in a steep climb, too steep for the power he was giving it. Knowing he needed to level out, he ordered his arms to push forward on the stick but realized he couldn't feel his arms. He tried to push forward again, but his body simply didn't respond. The airplane came to the top of its ascent. Usually Trevor enjoyed the feeling of reaching the uppermost point of a stall. But this time he couldn't feel it. He just knew it was happening because the sound of the motor told him. As the aircraft started to slide back, he noticed that his field of vision was growing dark from the outer edges in.

Slowly, the aircraft tipped forward. As it did, Trevor slumped forward against his restraining seat belts, which forced his hands forward on the stick. Or, at least, that's what he assumed happened, because he felt the airplane start into a dive.

You can do this. You've gotten out of tight spots before. You've just got to concentrate. His head hurt, though, and he realized that it was the only pain he could feel. With just the slightest sense of panic, he talked to himself once more. *You can do this.* The airplane began to pick up airspeed.

* * *

As they reached the line of trees, Dan felt the fellow who had been carrying him buckle beneath him. He tried to catch himself, but as soon as he put weight on his feet, the wound in his side stabbed at him with such intensity that a wave of pain flooded over him. The last thing he remembered was collapsing to the ground as his field of vision went dark.

Part Three

THE SHATTERED
DREAMS OF AUGUST

Chapter Twenty

TRANSFERRED
TO ENGLAND

A field hospital in the American sector near St. Mihiel, France
August 1918

"Hey, Yank! Are you awake?"

Dan stirred uneasily in the hospital bed and tried to open his eyes, but to no avail. The wild and disoriented dream reasserted itself, and he tossed uneasily in the bed.

The voice returned. "Lieutenant, you need to wake up. You've been asleep for two days."

Forcing his eyes open, Dan attempted to focus his thoughts and figure out where he was. The disorienting pressure in his head made it feel like his brain was being crushed in a vise. He tried to groan but was surprised to find that his voice refused to respond. Finally, he forced himself to roll to his side. A searing pain in the right side of his face told him that particular action was a huge mistake, and he cried out as he rolled to his back. While trying to bring the ceiling into focus, he reached down to feel the thick bandages that wrapped the right side of his body. There were also bandages on his face, and they were growing wet from the tears that seemed to stream from his eyes.

The voice from the left side spoke to him again, in a strong English accent.

"I don't think the burned area on your face is as bad as it probably feels. I heard the doctors talking, and they say it will heal without much disfigurement."

Very carefully, Dan rolled to his left side and did his best to focus on the voice. He could make out the shape of a bed and distinguish the difference in color between the white sheets, the green blanket, and the flesh-colored face that looked back at him. But he couldn't see the face clearly.

"Where am I?" That's what he wanted to say, but all he heard was a growling sound that in no way resembled his own voice. He was surprised when the stranger seemed to understand what he'd said.

"You're in a field hospital in France. I'm afraid you've had a rough go of it."

In spite of the covers and the fact that it was August, he shivered in the bed.

"Do you want to know the extent of your injuries now or wait until you feel better?"

It was an odd voice, very deep and resonant, yet somehow upbeat and cheerful. Each sentence seemed to end on an up tick. *What a forsaken place to be cheerful!* Still, the stranger seemed to have some kind of skill at calming the panic that Dan felt rising in his throat, and he desperately wanted the man to keep talking. "Tell me the worst of it," he growled. "That's the best way for me to deal with whatever's happened."

"Ah, very good, then. That's the approach I'd take myself. First, let me introduce myself. My name is Philip Carlyle, a Church of England chaplain in the British Expeditionary Force and presently on the disabled list myself." He managed a chuckle. "I had a small disagreement with a German bullet, and it retaliated by taking out a piece of my right leg."

Locating the sound of Carlyle's voice, he was able to focus his eyes enough to make out some features. It appeared that he was tall and maybe a little bulky. He had dark hair and very large eyes, although Dan couldn't distinguish the color.

"As to your condition, I'm afraid you came under mustard gas attack. Something must have happened to your gas mask, because there are burns on your face. The medical staff can advise you better than I, but as I've listened in on their conversations the past few days, it seems that you inhaled quite a bit of gas, which may have damaged your lungs. Your eyes are very puffy, but apparently full sight should return with the passage of time."

Dan closed his eyes. *So it wasn't a bad dream. I really was under attack.* In his mind, he could picture the trench where he'd spent the previous seven days, not counting the days he'd been here at the hospital. He remembered pulling the mask on, feeling the anxiety while waiting for the air to flow through the charcoal filter, and starting to move out to the escape trench. At that point, his mind started replaying the scene like a movie reel. Once started, he couldn't stop it, even though he knew that he should if he wanted to keep the panic down. He could sense that he was breathing rapidly and shallowly, and the pain in his chest warned him he had better calm down.

He was suddenly aware of Philip Carlyle talking to him again, and he realized that he really hadn't missed any of the conversation. "After helping your comrade to the escape trench, you came above ground and started running. That's when a bullet grazed your rib cage and knocked you to the ground. I suppose that's where I came in. I was running with the best of them when I saw you fall. I could see that you were in no shape to get up, so I half-pulled you up on my shoulder and started dragging both of us forward. We almost made it, too. It was just as we reached the trees that a stray bullet caught me in the leg, and we went down in a great heap. Fortunately, there were others to get us into cover. It took another thirty minutes before they could get a stretcher in to bring you out to an ambulance. And now, here we are—roommates in a Red Cross hospital tent while they're trying to figure out what to do with us."

"What happened to Geoff Green?"

Carlyle was silent for a few moments. "I'm afraid it was too late for him. From what I understand, he was already dead when you reached the escape trench. You really should have left him, but from the way you've hung on to life here, I guess that's not really in your nature."

Dan settled back into his bed and let the tears flow freely.

Suddenly, he sat up with a start. *Trevor—what happened to Trevor?* Turning to Carlyle, he said, as clearly as his throat would let him, "A friend of mine that I grew up with was supposed to meet me the day I got gassed—an airman by the name of Richards. Have you heard anything about him?"

"So that's who you've been talking about the past two days. I wondered, because you seemed so anxious to see him."

"So have you heard anything about him? He's the kind of guy who would come looking for me if I didn't show up where I was supposed to."

A nurse, who had come to the foot of Carlyle's bed a few moments earlier, joined the conversation. "An airman, you say? There hasn't been anyone looking for you, but I did hear some of the men talking about some kind of amazing aerial combat a few days ago. Perhaps it was your friend."

"What did they say?" Dan asked urgently.

"Just that a unit on the ground had come under bombardment from two German aircraft when an Allied plane came blazing out from the sun and attacked both of them. From what I gather, it was an unusually bold maneuver that succeeded in downing both German aircraft. The men said that the pilot had saved at least fifty Allied lives by his daring."

"But what happened to the pilot—is he all right?"

The nurse looked back with compassion. "I'm afraid I don't know that part of the story. I had to move to another patient."

"Can you go ask them what happened?" Dan pleaded.

"I'm afraid I can't—those men have been moved out of the hospital. But I'll try to ask questions up the line and see if I can find something out for you. What did you say your friend's name is?"

"Richards. Trevor Richards. An American pilot who was supposed to come visit me."

"I'll try," she said gently. Then, even more softly, "I'll try. In the meantime, you've been talking way too much. Captain Carlyle here needs to let you get some rest." She glowered at Carlyle, who shrank back into his pillow. "The doctor told me to give you another shot for the pain." With a speed and dexterity that prevented him from raising any protest, she slipped a needle into his left arm. "Close your eyes now and see if you can't sleep some before it's time for breakfast. You'll start to feel sleepy in a few minutes." With that, she moved out of the room.

Carlyle spoke up in a stage whisper. "I'd try to sleep through breakfast, if you can. Being wounded is bad enough, but eating their food . . . Now I'll be quiet. But I'm glad you've finally joined us."

Dan rolled to his side and said, "I should thank you for saving me. I am grateful for the risk you took. But right now, I don't know if I'm grateful to be alive or not." He settled back into his pillow.

"I wouldn't be too sad—your wounds will heal, and while your voice may not be good enough to sing in the church choir, you should heal to the point that you can get on with your life. One thing's for sure—you don't need to worry about going back to the trenches, not with those wounds."

Settling into the sheets, he closed his eyes and felt a warm numbness start to course through his veins as he thought bitterly of the happy dreams he had once nurtured. As his thoughts started to drift, he pictured the warm days

of August when he had first met Trevor. Dan choked back a
sob. *How could this happen? Why would God let this happen?*
"Why did You let this happen?" Dan said savagely into the
pillow. It didn't answer. Neither did God, for that matter.
Dan struggled to maintain consciousness, but the drug was
too powerful, and he started dreaming again.

* * *

"Lieutenant O'Brian, there's someone here to see you."
Dan's heart leaped inside him, and he rolled over to his back
as fast as the pain would let him. With all his heart he hoped
to look up and see Trevor standing there. In the time since
his conversation with the British chaplain who had rescued
him and the nurse who had promised to see what she could
find out about the pilot the other patients had been talking
about, all he could think about was Trevor's promised visit.

But when he looked up, it wasn't Trevor. Worse, it was
another aviator. "Hello, I'm Dan O'Brian."

The airman reached out his hand. "I'm pleased to meet
you, Dan. Trevor told us a lot about you. My name is Josh
Brown. I was his roommate. We used to fly together a lot."

Dan swallowed hard. "I doubt you've come here to tell
me good news."

Josh reached for a chair and pulled it up to Dan's
bedside. "I'm afraid not. I'm very sorry to have to tell you
that Trevor's aircraft was shot down not ten miles from here.
He carried out an amazing air duel in which he downed two
German fighters before getting hit. The Germans were in
the process of attacking an unmarked convoy that was evac-
uating wounded infantry, and Trevor's action saved at least
fifty lives. He's been put in for a medal." Josh paused for a
moment. "Plus, his two victories gave him five and a half
kills, which makes him an ace. That's something he'd hoped
to achieve."

Dan didn't care about how many kills Trevor had. "Is there any chance he survived the crash? Could he be in a German prison?"

Josh shifted uneasily. "He crashed on our side of the line, and they recovered his body within just a few minutes."

Dan felt himself go cold inside. He expected to cry or to blurt something out, but he just went cold, as if he had no feeling whatsoever. That wasn't true of Lieutenant Brown, he saw, whose eyes had filled with water.

"The people who recovered him told us something that may be a comfort to you. It was to me. Apparently, Trevor was hit by a bullet through his chest. It missed his vital organs but struck his spinal column. Hopefully, it severed all the nerves so that he felt no pain. It's likely he was killed instantly. If not, it's certain that death came quickly, before he hit the ground. Among pilots that's always the best way to go and something we hope for if we ever get hit. It's a lot better than having to think about things on the way down or getting burned alive."

Dan rested his head on the pillow. He wanted to say something to thank this man for coming to tell him personally. He wanted to reminisce with him about Trevor. But he couldn't get any words out. He could hardly get his breath.

"I know how much you meant to Trevor. He talked about you all the time. I guess you guys used to go running together. He said he taught you how to beat him, which we all thought was kind of crazy."

That actually got through, and Dan felt himself smile. He choked out the words, "It's true—Trevor liked to win, but only when you gave it the best effort you were capable of. If he could give you a tip, he was always willing to help."

Lieutenant Brown sat there, a bit uncomfortably. Finally, Dan found some words. "I really appreciate you coming down to tell me. I've been all tied up inside wondering about him. I figured something bad had happened when he didn't find me. But I guess I just hoped . . ." His voice trailed off.

"It's because we all thought so much of Trevor that my C.O., Captain McMurphy, said I should fly down to talk with you. He had to pull a lot of strings just to find you. I guess you do some secret stuff. Anyway, McMurphy told me that I had to find you, no matter how long it took. He liked Trevor a lot." Both Josh and Dan sat quietly for a few moments. "Most times we don't let ourselves get close to the other pilots because the odds are so high that something like this will happen. But with Richards, it was impossible not to get to like him—he was so easygoing and friendly. Trevor talked a lot about your Church. I never knew any Mormons before him, but there must be something really special about your beliefs to turn out a guy like that. My folks didn't really believe in church, so I liked listening to his stories." Josh shuffled a bit. "At any rate, he gave us a lot of hope—me in particular."

Dan knew he should say something, but the lump in his throat hurt so much that all he could force out was, "Nobody lived his religion better than Trevor." Then his voice froze.

Finally, Josh paid Trevor the highest compliment one pilot could pay another. "All that aside, he was as good a pilot as any who ever went into the sky. You always felt safe when he was on your wing."

Dan raised himself up as best he could and forced out an agonized question. "Did he have fun flying? From the day I met him at age fifteen, he wanted to fly an airplane. Did the war ruin that for him?"

Josh looked down at his feet, then back up to Dan. "He was almost poetic about flying. He loved it. I don't think he liked hurting other pilots—no one does. But that's the job here. When it came to flying, though, there was never a time Trevor griped about it. He seemed to be one with the airplane, as graceful as a trapeze artist. The last thing I'll remember about him, assuming I make it out alive, is the grin on his face when he said he was flying down to meet you. He literally bounced out to the field. I think his last day was a good one right up to the end." He paused again.

Dan took a moment to compose himself. "Thanks for telling me that. I want to remember him the way I always knew him—happy and cheerful."

"By the way, Trevor always spoke about what a terrific singer you are. I hope whatever happened to you doesn't interfere with that."

Dan sighed. "Mustard gas. Only time will tell, but right now my voice sure doesn't sound like it will ever come back. Even if it does, they tell me my lungs will never be very strong. It's been a rough couple of days."

Josh's face fell. "I'm sorry to hear that. I'll hope the best for you, though. I'm awfully glad I got to meet you. Now I know why Trevor liked you so much. Good luck in your recovery." Lieutenant Brown got up and left the hospital with just one glance back.

Dan laid his head back on the pillow. The cold, empty feeling inside made it feel like his stomach would collapse on itself. He didn't want to be here. He didn't want to be alive.

"Lieutenant, I'm sorry for the news." Dan turned his head to look at Philip Carlyle.

"Me too. It's kind of consistent, though, with what's been happening in my life lately."

"I couldn't help but overhear the part about your singing voice. I didn't know that you were so good. I would have never said what I did the other day about how lucky you were, even if you can't sing in the church choir, if I knew about your musical skills."

"Well, life is hard. They say I'm lucky to be alive."

"Perhaps there is hope for your voice. I can't help but believe that your life will take a turn for the better."

Dan reacted instantly, striking out in a sudden fury. "You think my life's going to get better? Do you want me to tell you about my life? I'll tell you about my life. I grew up with a father who couldn't stand to be around me and a brother who liked to beat me whenever he got the chance. Getting shot in the ribs? That's no big deal. I got kicked there more times than I can count. I spent the better part of my life trying to find excuses not to be home. Then the Richardses moved to town, and I actually had a friend and a place to go where they have a real family, the kind you hear about in church. Then Trevor's mother taught me music—I mean *really* taught me music—so I had that in my life. Finally, when things were starting to get really good, one of our best friends got attacked by a bear, and I had to shoot the bear while Trevor tried to pull it over backward . . ." He choked on his own breath momentarily. "I'm the one guy in the world who never wanted to kill anything, and now I've killed bears and men by the dozen." He swallowed back a sob. "More men than I can count, and every single one of them probably had someone back home who loved them."

He choked back his tears, and then the anger reasserted itself. "After that, Trevor got to go off to a world-class university, and I had to stay home at a nondescript academy. But I stayed with it and got a degree. Not much of a degree, but a degree. And then, because of Trevor, I finally got a chance to go to Stanford to study for a master's or maybe even a doctorate degree in music. Stanford, the finest university in the western United States. But, of course, America joins the war, my father calls me a coward, and I enlist out of spite—some spite against him, isn't it? So here I am. My best friend is dead, my voice is ruined, my father still hates me, and I've got nothing. Nothing! So you think my life's going to take a turn for the better? I hope not, because every time it has before, things have just ended up worse." The effort exhausted him, and he went into a coughing fit so severe it frightened him. Finally it subsided, and he lay back on the bed, exhausted. The handkerchief in his hand was covered with blood.

"I know it's hard right now—"

"Would you just be quiet and leave me alone! I know you're a priest and all that, but I simply don't care right now. It's pretty hard to think about God when He lets someone like Trevor get shot down . . ." Then he could say no more. The lump in his throat simply hurt too much, and he flailed to his side, actually enjoying the pain it caused. He wanted to hurt. He needed to hurt.

Dan was so furious that he wanted to stand up and tear out his stitches; but his system shut down, and against his will, he started to fall asleep. As he dozed off, he thought, *Maybe God will take pity and make it so I don't have to wake up again. Maybe the nightmare will end. Oh, please, God, make it end!*

* * *

But he did wake up. It took a few moments to clear his head and to realize where he was. Then he remembered the visit from Lieutenant Brown. He could feel Philip Carlyle watching him, but Dan didn't have it in him to talk to anybody. When the nurses came around, he rejected the food they offered. When it was time for a shot, he received it without comment. When the doctor came by to check on his dressings, he just mumbled that everything was fine. His fury was spent, the anger gone. Whenever he started to feel pain or sorrow, he just went numb again.

By the end of the third day after Josh Brown's visit, the doctor instructed an orderly to help him force food into Dan's mouth. He tried to resist, but they plugged his nose so that he had to swallow. It was like that for another two days until he finally relented. But he still didn't talk. His medical condition was getting worse—he could feel that. The pain in his side was constant, and he suspected that he had an infection. He started going to great lengths to keep the nurses or doctors from examining the wound. He wanted it to get bad enough that they couldn't do anything about it when they did find it. But the next morning he woke to find new dressings. They'd changed it in his sleep.

* * *

On the sixth day after Josh Brown's visit, Dan found himself in a conversation with the doctors. He was listening to them and talking to them, but something was different. It was as if he was observing the conversation as if he was watching another person talk for him.

"Lieutenant, we've done all we can do for you here. Your bullet wound should clear up, although it's worse than we originally thought. You're likely to have trouble raising your arm on that side. The skin on your face will certainly heal, although there will be scarring. It shouldn't look too bad, though. We've certainly had a lot worse in here. Do you understand what I'm telling you?"

"Yes, sir, I do," Dan heard himself reply.

"As to your voice, Captain Carlyle has told us about your singing. I wish I could hold out hope that full function will return, but the truth is that it's not likely. Your lungs have lost significant capacity, and the long-term effects of mustard gas are unknown. But we suspect that you'll have trouble the rest of your life. Although you're not fully recovered, we need the space, and so we have to transfer you to England where you can get the kind of support you need. More than anything, you need cold, moist air for your lungs to heal."

They're going to transfer me to a sanitarium. They think that the real problem is in my mind. He thought about it for a moment. *They're probably right.*

Then he heard a different voice.

"Doctor, if young O'Brian is to go to England to recuperate, do you suppose you could arrange for him to come and live at my house? We have a large estate near London, and it would provide the kind of serenity that I believe he needs. Since I have to go there myself while my wounds heal, it would be no problem for me to take him with me."

Dan tried to say something, but oddly, his voice wouldn't work.

"Oh, yes," he heard Philip Carlyle reply. "We can certainly provide nursing support, as much as is needed."

"You're a very lucky man, Lieutenant."

"I don't want to go to England. Why don't you send me back to America? Or just let me go back to the front lines. Maybe I can do some good there."

"I'm afraid not, Lieutenant. This war has strange rules. Men who want to go back to the front often aren't allowed to. It's only the ones who don't want to be there whom we can trust." The doctor smiled and added, "You may not appreciate it at this moment, but Captain Carlyle here is giving you a rare gift. I hope you work through your troubles. God bless." The doctor went over to a table and started filling out some papers, most likely Dan's and Philip's transfers.

Dan lay still for a few moments. "I suppose you expect me to be grateful?" Dan said, with a distinct edge in his voice.

"I don't really expect anything. Frankly, you're not much of a neighbor. But I feel compelled to try to help you. Perhaps it's the Spirit of the Lord that you talk about in your dreams. At any rate, I've always wanted to play the role of the Good Samaritan, and you're the best candidate I've ever had."

That took Dan by surprise, and he actually laughed. "You've got your work cut out for you, my Good Samaritan friend." He breathed in a few times. His lungs hurt on every inhale. "It's much more than my body that needs healing. I think I've lost myself, and I don't know how to get me back. I don't know if I even want to come back." He felt a lump rising in his throat, which he hated. It hurt so badly to think about Trevor that he didn't think he could bear it.

"It's not likely that even the two of us working together can accomplish what you need. But perhaps with the Lord's help, we can."

"If there is a Lord. I certainly haven't seen His hand at work lately." Hot tears dribbled slowly down Dan's cheeks. Philip started to say something, but once again Dan rolled to his side and closed his eyes.

Chapter Twenty-One

A FLICKER OF HOPE?

Thirty miles from London
September 1918

Carlyle Manor was amazing. The house—or, rather, the mansion—was made of stone, with turrets in three corners, steeply gabled roofs covered in grey slate tiles, and windows with glass rippled from age. Because he was in an ambulance when he arrived, Dan didn't immediately get to see the grounds and gardens, but in the days after his arrival, he was able to go out for walks in a wheelchair. His legs weren't damaged, but his side was still tender, and the doctors had given strict orders that his lungs should not be taxed for at least two or three months. So he and Philip Carlyle, both in wheelchairs, were pushed around the grounds by servants.

The grounds were magnificent. Having grown up in the high desert of southern Idaho, where water was always in short supply and sagebrush was the native ground cover, Dan was astonished to see acres of well-manicured grass, tall green hedges lining the walkways, and flowering hydrangeas at every intersection. He loved the vine-covered walls of the servants' houses as well as the magnificent trees in the groomed sections of the grounds. The formal gardens were surrounded by a thick forest, and on his first day strolling the grounds, he saw a deer peek its head out from behind a bush. A stream ran through the property and into a small lake directly behind the house. The dining room looked out on the lake. A rustic stone bridge crossed the stream, allowing access to the forest that surrounded the entire property.

"You really meant what you said when you told the doctors your property would provide serenity, didn't you?"

"I've always loved this place. We have a townhouse in London where my parents are, but somehow I've never been one for the hustle and bustle of the city. Out here a man can be alone with his thoughts."

Dan turned and looked at Philip. "Why are you so kind to me? I'm just another American who got gassed. There must be tens of thousands like me. Why are you doing this?"

Philip smiled. "There are certain native tribes in which tradition holds that if you save a man's life, you remain in his debt forever. Since I saved yours, I suppose you became my responsibility."

"Isn't that just backward? I should be the one who is in your debt."

"That's the usual way, all right. I think what these tribes have figured out is that when you intervene in another person's life in such a direct and forceful way, you change his destiny. Who's to say you have the right, or that they want your help? Consequently, when you take that choice on yourself in behalf of the other person, you are bound to them."

Dan didn't say anything for a few moments. Finally, he started to open up a bit. "I wanted to die back in the hospital. There was a time when I was very angry with you for saving me."

"I know. You suffered greatly in the days after the attack—mentally more than physically, I think."

"There are still times when I get panicky and wonder how I'll possibly survive, and then I pray for a release. But God didn't listen when I asked for protection, so why should He when I ask for the opposite?"

"Has it occurred to you that He did offer protection in the guise of me?"

"I've thought it. But then I wonder why He didn't protect Trevor. It seems so arbitrary."

"About this Trevor . . ."

"Please," Dan said in alarm. "If I hope to have any chance of keeping the panic feelings down, I just can't talk about Trevor. That wound is still too new."

"Sorry. I understand."

They continued on for some time until it was obvious that Dan was starting to droop, so Philip instructed the servants to take them back to the house. Every time he entered the manor, Dan was shocked again by its opulence. There was a great entry hall with twenty- or thirty-foot-high ceilings. The ceilings were supported by massive carved beams that were supported by ribbed vaulting. To the right was a drawing room at least four times the size of the Richardses' drawing room, and next to that an extensive library. In the back, with windows looking out on a tiled patio next to the lake, was a large ballroom. The kitchen and servants' quarters must have been to the left, because he observed the servants coming and going through a swinging door beneath the stairwell. The bedrooms were upstairs, which presented a problem for the two invalids. Because all the young men on the staff had been called off to war, it would have fallen to the older men to carry them up and down the stairs. For convenience, two hospital beds had been set up in the parlor so they could spend their days there.

After a few days at the manor, Philip started putting weight on his legs for a few minutes each day, and it would be only a matter of weeks before he could walk with crutches. Dan was also able to support himself but quickly ran out of breath even at the effort of crossing the room. Probably the best thing to happen since arriving was the opportunity to take a hot bath each afternoon. The warm water felt wonderful on the wound in his side. Plus, the moist, humid air was obviously good for his lungs. The first time Carlyle's personal doctor took the bandage off Dan's face, Dan was shocked at what he saw but took comfort from the doctor's explanation that the tender, pink skin was actually a good sign that his face was healing. The doctor felt that there would be very little disfigurement to the tissue but that it was likely there would be permanent discoloration. Dan had never really thought a great deal about his looks, and he was genuinely surprised when the doctor said, quite sincerely, "You're a very handsome man. I don't think this will interfere with your ability to attract the interest of young ladies." He'd never considered himself handsome. Trevor was a different story, with his wavy, blond hair and blue eyes. He'd always been attractive to the opposite sex. Thinking about Trevor again, he started breathing quickly, as if he were suffocating; but he'd started to learn how to calm that response. He tried not to think of the memories of home, because each time he did he got melancholic and frightened. It was so strange to deal with these new emotions. He'd felt anxious before, but never panic-stricken as sometimes happened now. It was a terrifying feeling until it passed.

One afternoon, after he'd been at Carlyle Manor a few weeks, he spoke quietly with Philip about something that was bothering him. "I appreciate your hospitality," he said hesitantly. "But, even though I know I'm not in very good shape, I feel like I should get back to my unit. There are men dying out there while I'm living in the lap of luxury. Somehow I feel guilty."

"A lot of soldiers feel that way. It's why some very good men have been going back to the trenches for almost four years now—even after being wounded and withdrawn from the line. I've talked to a lot of them, and I think there's a couple of reasons for their feelings of discontent."

Dan gave him a look that asked him to continue.

"First is a feeling of loyalty and guilt—just as you expressed it. But beyond that is a sense that the person involved is missing out on something important and exciting. There's simply nothing in civilian life to equal the adrenaline one feels in combat. I think it becomes almost addictive. So men go back, even when reason says they shouldn't."

"Reason would say they should never go in the first place!"

"True, but most of us feel a loyalty to our country, so we go, and we become completely involved in it. Then along comes a wound, and we're out of it. One day, action; the next day, inactivity. It's quite a different pace. I think it overwhelms the mind to go from a dangerous, action-packed scene to total quiet and calm. It's disorienting, to say the least."

Dan had to agree, even though it made no sense that he'd miss the activity of battle. He'd hated it, but the enforced inactivity of his condition, coupled with the natural quiet of Carlyle Manor, was almost as bad. His wound made him an invalid incapable of caring for himself, and that was hard to deal with. Plus, all his plans for the future were gone. It felt so lonely and hopeless. He wondered if he'd ever feel content again.

* * *

As the days passed, Dan began to regain some sense of self. He hated it when the dark days came, when he felt overwhelmed by hopelessness. But then Philip would challenge him to a table game, such as chess or checkers, and his mind would be lifted out of despair for a time. As he began to regain strength, he was left to wonder what he could do with his life. Singing was obviously out, and that was what he had wanted most.

One day, as he was exercising by walking from one piece of furniture to another, he was so exhausted that he needed to sit down and rest. When he reached the grand piano, he slumped down on the padded piano seat. Without really thinking about it, he started moving his fingers on the keys. Before he knew it, he was playing one of the songs that Margaret Richards had taught him—nothing too sentimental, but one of the light classics. About that time, Philip and his father came into the room.

"I didn't realize you played the piano," Philip said enthusiastically.

"He doesn't just play, he plays it very well," Lord Carlyle interjected. "I pride myself on recognizing talent, and this boy knows something about music."

Dan was startled enough that he stopped playing. "I'm sorry," he said. "I sat down for a rest, and I suppose habit took over. To be honest, I didn't realize I was playing. I should have asked permission."

"Rubbish. People who have developed a skill have a natural right to play. I simply own a piano, but what use is that? Nothing more than an expensive piece of furniture. You can play it, though, so rightfully, it's yours to use," Lord Carlyle said.

"Dan," Philip said, "you've fairly well convinced yourself that you've lost your future in music because of your voice. Yet you have all kinds of talent with the piano. Why can't you take that up again?"

"Tell me the last time that you listened to someone playing the piano on a gramophone or in the musical theatre or the opera. Sorry, but the world is full of great pianists. My talent was singing."

"Perhaps." Philip was thoughtful. Even after just a few weeks together, Dan had come to know that such thoughtfulness usually meant Philip was up to something. He also knew better than to ask what it was, since it never brought a reply until Philip was ready.

* * *

In the course of the next four or five weeks, Philip and his father found numerous occasions to invite Dan to play for them. It irritated him at some level, because he knew they were trying to draw him out of his doldrums and convince him he had something left to offer the world. But they were his hosts, and generous at that, so he felt it would be churlish of him to refuse their requests. In time, he started practicing without their invitation. The piano did give him a chance to express his emotions. On some days, his playing was placid and serene; on others, it was furious and angry; on still others, it was hesitant and confused. But with little else to pass the time and not wishing to impose himself on Philip all the time, the piano provided Dan a much-needed diversion, and he was grateful that the family let him play.

Then, one day, Philip surprised him with a question. "Have you ever played the pipe organ?"

"The pipe organ?"

"Yes, you know, like the ones found in churches."

Dan thought back to the little foot-pump organ that he'd played hymns on for Junior Sunday School at the First Ward building. "Not really. Just occasionally for church. The balance of the keys is so different from the piano that it's hard to get excited about. Plus, I have no idea how to use the pedals."

"I'm going over to my church this afternoon. You know what day this is, don't you?"

Dan sighed. "It's November 11, and at 11:00 tonight, the armistice takes effect—the eleventh hour of the eleventh day of the eleventh month. At last, the madness of the war is over."

"There will be celebrations all over England, and probably everywhere else in the world. But I don't feel up to attending them. Not even the midnight mass. But I do feel I should go to church on a day as important as this. And my leg is getting well enough that I feel I should offer my services, at least on a limited basis. Would you care to ride with me?"

The chance to get out was exciting. Dan sometimes felt like a prisoner, even while residing on this beautiful estate. "I'd like that. I hope I won't get in the way."

"Oh, I don't think you'll get in the way."

* * *

Dan had never been inside a cathedral, and he was amazed at the grandeur and scale. Philip explained to him that all cathedrals are designed with a building footprint in the form of a cross. They entered with other worshippers at the base of the cross and walked up to the intersection of the crosspiece, where the ceremonies and sacraments were performed. Candles lined the walls, and magnificent gilded statuary adorned the breastworks. Dan was taken aback by the gold statue of Christ hanging on the cross, since such a representation was not part of his religious upbringing. Still, he felt a marked spirit of reverence in the place that felt good. But it was the stained glass windows that made him catch his breath. They were stunning, with the sun sparkling through the thousands of colored panels that told the story of Christ's life in pictures. He could only imagine the thousands of painstaking hours that skilled artisans had spent creating them. As he gazed upward, he felt his spirit rise, something that had eluded him for many months.

He looked around while Philip talked quietly with a well-dressed man standing to the side of the altar. In a few minutes, Philip came over and said, "I have something to show you, if you think you can make it up some stairs." Dan agreed to give it a try, and they moved off to a door near the entrance to the church. They begin climbing a long, circular staircase built of heavy, carved wood. Dan had to stop every four or five steps or his lungs started to hurt. Just when he thought he'd have to turn back, they came out on a platform high above the back of chapel. The balcony looked out on the cathedral, and he marveled at how different things looked from this vantage point. The grey columns naturally led one's eye heavenward, where giant ribbed vaults were supported by ornately carved columns, much like those at Carlyle Manor, except on a much grander scale. Philip put his hand on Dan's shoulder and turned him to face the wall. There he saw the pipes of the organ—not as large as the Tabernacle organ, but certainly impressive. In front of the pipes were choir seats, and up above the seats a stained glass window that sparkled in the sun.

"Care to play it?" Philip said casually.

Dan laughed. Then, before Philip could inquire further, he said, "I'll play it, but it won't sound like much, since I only know how to play on one register."

Philip smiled. He'd previously talked with the professional organist, who now appeared in the doorway. This rather diminutive man came over and turned on the electric air pumps, pushed a series of levers, and invited Dan to sit down.

"Control the volume with your right foot by pushing on that pedal. Each of these controls modifies the stops that add or subtract pipes. You can set different stops for each keyboard register so that you can mix sounds as needed."

"Thanks," Dan said, "but I think I'll start out with something simple." He ran his fingers idly up and down the keys and was startled at the volume. He quickly extended his right leg to turn down the volume—perhaps something of a mistake, since a sharp pain stabbed at the site of his wound. Once he got the volume settled, he started playing an old familiar tune that he'd always wanted to hear on an organ, "Deep River." It was impressive but lacked any real depth.

"Why not try playing your bass clef on this register and the treble on this one?" the organist said. He pulled a few levers to set the stops. Dan played the same notes, but this time the organ thundered on the deep cross-melody he played on the bass clef.

"Very good. Now, do you see that pedal right there? I'm sure you already know that the foot pedals are arranged like the keyboard. You can use them to provide a sustained tone while your hands play out the melody. Pick one or two that you think would give the music substance and give it a try."

Dan was intrigued, so he picked out two and started the song. When he depressed the foot pedal the first time, he was so startled that he lifted his hands off the keys. The rumbling of the pipes was more than he'd bargained for. "That sounds wonderful," he said.

"Give it another try." He did. One of the things Dan had always been known for was his ability to improvise an arrangement. As he gained confidence, he changed the harmony on each verse to create a changing mood that enriched the simple melody. When he finished, Philip applauded.

Dan looked at Philip and returned his smile ruefully. "All right, so you have me intrigued. This was a good experience." He turned to the church organist. "Thank you."

"By the way, my name is Max Hellenberg."

"I'm Dan O'Brian. Thank you for letting me play."

Philip was embarrassed that he hadn't introduced them properly, but he'd been so anxious to get Dan engaged in the process without his becoming suspicious that he hadn't taken time.

Dan stood up to leave. "I'm kind of tired—all this stretching has made me sore."

"Yes, we should be going."

"Before you leave," Max said, "could I ask if you'd be willing to return? Philip told me a bit about your skill at the piano, which doesn't always translate into ability at the organ. In fact, sometimes it works against it. But you adapted to this instrument very quickly today. It's remarkable, in fact, considering you've never really played before. I'd like the chance to teach you more."

"So that's what this visit is about, Philip? Another attempt to make me productive?"

"Believe me, I wouldn't offer my time if I didn't see potential," Hellenberg interjected.

Dan looked at the two of them and, in spite of the conspiracy, decided that he had really enjoyed the experience, so he agreed to return.

On the way home, he asked Philip about Max Hellenberg.

"Max? He's actually quite accomplished. He teaches music at Cambridge University." He heard Dan's intake of air. "He's actually considered England's finest organist."

Dan turned to him with an expression of pure astonishment. "What have you done to me? I can't play with somebody like that. I thought it would be enjoyable to learn a few fundamentals of playing the organ. Why would you want to waste the time of someone like Max Hellenberg on me?"

Philip smiled. "It seems to me that Max Hellenberg can decide for himself whom he wants to teach. Besides, you may only get one more session with him, so try to make the best of it."

Dan shook his head. "I just can't believe you—you never let up! By the way," he added, "there's been something nagging at me lately. Just how is it that a British chaplain happened to be in the American lines the day I got shot and gassed? That doesn't make a lot of sense."

"It does if you believe God is interested in you."

Dan paused. "Even if I accept that He is, the military still had to give its permission."

"Just down the line from you was a large group of Americans who were members of the Episcopal Church.

There were enough of them to warrant their own minister. Unfortunately, there were no American Episcopalian chaplains available, and since the Episcopal Church is part of the worldwide Anglican communion, it made sense to send in a British chaplain—me. But on the way, I got involved in helping you. So you see, God really does work in mysterious ways."

"At least when it involves you, He does," Dan said dryly. Philip smiled.

* * *

Dan had more talent than he gave himself credit for, since the offer for a lesson some time turned into six months of weekly lessons, with daily practices mandated in between. The church organ wasn't always available, so Philip made arrangements with a neighbor who had a pipe organ in his home.

With the passage of time, Dan's health improved considerably, and the stretching he did helped his wounded ribs to the point that he could use his right leg with very little pain. He also regained enough capacity in his lungs to walk a mile or more on the grounds of the estate before coming in for a rest.

One day he finally raised enough courage to ask a question he'd been dreading. "When are they going to release me from rehabilitation?"

"What?" Philip said.

"When are they going to send me home? I'm getting well enough to travel."

"The doctors haven't released you yet."

"But that's because you keep intervening in my behalf. I think you've bought off your family doctor."

Philip stopped what he was doing and looked at Dan directly. "Do you want to go home?"

Dan was subdued. "I should want to go home. But whenever I think about it, I start to panic. I know I can't go on living off your hospitality forever, but I truly have come to love it here."

"Two things you should know. First, our local doctors have recommended that the American army discharge you here in England. It's against standard protocol, but we have some influence, and indications are positive that it can be accomplished if you consent. Second, my parents have talked to me about it, and we're very happy to have you live with us as long as you like. My father enjoys hearing you play, and my mother enjoys playing the role of benefactor for your studies. Have you noticed that your rehearsals are starting to draw crowds?"

"No, I haven't noticed that."

"They have. In fact, the bishop approached me the other day to ask if you'd like to try playing in church one of these Sundays. I know that you're not Episcopalian, but it's not at all unusual for someone who's not a member of the congregation to play."

It took only a moment for Dan to make up his mind. "I would like to play—something simple, of course. But it would feel good to make some kind of contribution. Besides, I think I'd like to attend church with you."

Dan's first performance was received extremely well, which encouraged him to perform again. Within the month, he started attending weekly and was invited to play on a regular basis, even accompanying the choir. Soon his days were filled with music and new friendships with the professional choir directors and members of the choir. Eventually, they asked him to become one of the paid organists.

"I don't know if I can do that," he said to Philip. "In my church we don't have a paid clergy, and somehow it seems wrong to be paid for assisting in a worship service."

Philip laughed. "You've wanted to start being productive again, and this is a way for you to earn your own way. I want you to continue to live with us, but at least you'll have some spending money so that we can go into London once in a while. I believe that God would allow you this opportunity."

Finally, Dan agreed.

* * *

As the anniversary of his transfer to England passed, Dan was finally settled in. He had a job and a home with a family that cared about him. He even enjoyed going into London for recreation once in a while. Max Hellenberg was extremely complimentary and had put him through an accelerated course of study. Dan suspected that the Carlyles paid him for his time, but no one ever said anything about it, and he felt uneasy bringing the subject up.

One night, Philip asked if he'd like to attend a musical production being put on in the West End, the theatre district of London. Dan was nervous at the thought of dating but soon found that he enjoyed being in female company. The girl was pleasant and attractive, and she made no mention of the discoloration on his face. When he looked around the restaurant, he could see why. There were a good many veterans, some without certain limbs and others with burns far worse than his.

Although it seemed unreal, he had, with the help of Philip, started to build a life for himself. The frequency of his anxiety episodes had diminished and seldom occurred during waking hours now. The price of all this was an almost complete severing of any connection to his past. He felt guilty that he hadn't corresponded with his father, or even with the Richardses. He had a stack of unopened letters from Sister Richards that he wanted to open, but each time he thought about it, the dark cloud of anxiety threatened, and he had to get up and move around to shake it off. He concluded that his isolation in England was a small price to pay. Perhaps someday he'd contact the people at home, but for now he was content.

Chapter Twenty-Two

ROYAL PERFORMANCE

London, England
January 1920

One morning, a little after breakfast, Dan was trying to read a book to fend off boredom when Philip said, a bit tentatively, "I hope you don't mind that I looked at one of your books during our passage across the Channel." Dan could hardly remember the passage or anything about the journey through England.

"I don't mind. But I don't have many books."

"One was called the Book of Mormon. It's written in the style of the Bible, but it certainly is different from the Bible in most regards." Philip saw Dan go quiet. "I haven't talked to you about it before because of your reticence when it comes to discussing religion."

Dan didn't say anything immediately. Whenever soldiers in his unit found out he was a Mormon, they'd ask some stupid question about gold bibles or polygamy. After that, he was marked as being odd. It was discouraging enough that he had done his best to conceal his membership. It was not that he was ashamed, but a trench wasn't necessarily the best place to talk about it. Now, apparently, Philip was going to start in on him. Dan had heard stories about ministers and how they liked to tear the LDS Church apart. Even the thought of talking about the Church made him vaguely uneasy. Still, he was accepting Philip's hospitality, so he couldn't avoid talking to him.

"I grew up in The Church of Jesus Christ of Latter-day Saints. Our members believe that the true gospel of Christ was lost to the earth through apostasy but that it was restored by revelation through the Prophet Joseph Smith. One of the evidences of his calling is that he was inspired to translate a set of ancient gold plates written by descendents of Joseph, Israel's son, who had traveled to the American continent anciently. My church accepts this additional record as scripture. It talks a great deal about Christ." He braced for Philip's reaction, expecting a challenge at best and charges of blasphemy at worst.

"Curious. You told me that the members of your church believe this record is scripture—what do you believe?"

That caught Dan off guard. "I used to believe it was true. I love its teachings. We had this wonderful priesthood quorum instructor who could tell the best stories from the Book of Mormon and make them relevant to what was happening in our lives at the time. But now, after the trenches, I don't know what I believe. I'm not sure I even believe in God." His anxiety escalated alarmingly, and he felt himself starting to perspire.

Philip nodded. "Many soldiers have that reaction. Some turn to God because of the stresses of the battlefield, while others recoil from the teachings of their youth when they see the viciousness and inhumanity of war. I personally saw so many instances when I thought God's hand was involved in a soldier's life that my faith is actually stronger than it's ever been."

Dan was reassured by Philip's calm reaction, containing none of the usual hysteria that went along with an announcement of the name of the Church. Dan wondered why. "Have you ever heard of the Mormons before?"

"Oh, my, yes. They have classes about them in our divinity school. About fifty or sixty years ago, the Mormons made quite a splash in this area, converting thousands and taking them off to Utah. We're taught to shun them like the plague and to preach of the perfidy of their doctrines. They're labeled as a cult, you know."

"So why aren't you shunning me?"

"Because I don't believe in all that. God speaks in many languages and ways, and who am I to say that He couldn't talk to Joseph Smith or through this book?" Then he looked at Dan earnestly. "Dan, I've read your book, and I get some strange feelings when I read it. Would you mind if I ask you some more questions about your church?"

Dan started to say, "Of course not," but a different kind of dread swept over him like a thunderstorm, and he felt his heart pounding in his chest. Once again, it was difficult to catch his breath, and he started gasping for quick, shallow breaths.

Philip was instantly alarmed. "Are you all right?"

"I don't know what's happening to me. I feel like the room is closing in. Maybe it's better if I don't think about the Church right now. I don't know why my emotions are so volatile, but they are." He went silent, and Philip could see that he was struggling to control his breathing, his eyes darting from side to side. It was the same kind of look he'd seen in men under fire.

"I understand," Philip said evenly. "Perhaps this is a good time for a stroll in the garden. I believe the air would do your lungs some good."

"Thanks," Dan said. "Thanks for understanding."

I wish I did understand, Philip thought to himself.

* * *

"Are you ready for the concert tonight?"

"I'm as nervous as a kid about to give his first piano recital."

"My father's invited all his friends. I'm afraid he's been playing you up a great deal. But we're all confident that you'll do well. Best of luck."

The event was set to correspond with Palm Sunday, perhaps the most glorious day in Jesus' life, when the citizens of Jerusalem hailed him as the Messiah. Dan had always hoped it had given Jesus some consolation for the dreadful week to follow. When they arrived at the cathedral, Dan was delighted to see it filled with hundreds, perhaps thousands, of pungent Easter lilies. Their beauty and fragrance filled him with joy.

The church planned to celebrate with a special service of choir music apart from mass, and Dan was invited to play an organ medley of his favorite Easter hymns.

When the moment arrived, he set the stops for each of the registers. In the course of his original arrangement, he planned to use all three registers. The massive chapel was filled with worshippers. Dan's heart raced, and he actually felt himself saying a mental prayer. The prayer seemed to calm him, and the trembling in his hands subsided. As Dan's solo started, a hush fell on the room as he quietly played the opening strains of "He Is Risen," growing to a great crescendo at the end, followed by the haunting melody of "He Died! The Great Redeemer Died," and concluding with "Christ the Lord Is Risen Today." The organ responded enthusiastically to his touch, and he was able to create sounds that he felt may never have been heard before. More than anything, he wanted to create a tribute that would resonate in the hearts of the listeners. But as he lost himself in the music, he forgot all about the people and simply played what his heart was trying to express. When the last grand crescendo came to an end, he looked up to see the entire crowd standing on its feet. Since it was a concert, everyone felt free to applaud.

He took a modest bow and was about to leave when Philip came out. "Do you see who is down there?"

"No, who?"

"It's Edward, Prince of Wales, for heaven's sake. He's applauding you as loudly as the rest."

"The Prince of Wales?"

"Yes. My father didn't know if he could actually make it, so he didn't say anything. Besides, if people had known that the prince was coming, they very likely would have clogged the roads so that he'd have had trouble getting through."

Dan took a second bow.

"Pay attention to the prince. If he stands up, that means you'll be required to perform an encore."

"What?" Dan said in horror. "I don't have an encore prepared." He looked down in misery as the prince, acknowledging the crowd, rose to his feet and gently tipped his head.

"Oh, my, you've got to do something right now," Philip said breathlessly.

"What? What should I do? I don't even have music here!"

"Play something from memory. Anything. I've heard you play hundreds of songs before." With that, Philip exited behind the organ console, and Dan tentatively made his way back. Sitting on the bench, his heart was pounding wildly. He was actually thrilled. But what to play? Without knowing what would emerge, he reset the stops and started playing.

The significance of the melody that emerged escaped him at first. He was concentrating so deeply that his fingers worked automatically to play the keys while his mind tried to work with the arrangement. The music started out as a single trumpet playing a lonely, forsaken sound. Halfway through the first verse, he added a second finger, also trumpet, to provide a haunting countermelody. By the end of the first verse, he'd added some simple chords, but still the music conveyed a feeling of endless longing and sorrow—

and hope. As he started the second verse, the tempo picked up in intensity as he added additional stops to increase both the richness of the score and the feeling of encouragement. By now, the organ was singing beautifully, as if it had been built especially for this song.

It was in the fourth verse that Dan finally realized what he was playing, and when he did, he felt himself start to weep gently as the words came into his mind. *And should we die before our journey's through, Happy day! All is well!* He brought in the stout reinforcements of the lower pedals. *We then are free from toil and sorrow, too; With the just we shall dwell!* Suddenly, the images of Trevor and Brother Richards and Elmer and Sam and Leonard came vividly into his mind, and he faltered briefly. But the music simply had to get out, and so he moved to full crescendo as he finished the song. *But if our lives are spared again to see the Saints their rest obtain, Oh, how we'll make this chorus swell—All is well! All is well!* Then, to end the song, he repeated at maximum volume and force, *All is well!* The chapel trembled as the organ resonated throughout the great expanse of the hall, the last note fading in an echo that never fully seemed to disappear.

The song ended, but Dan didn't hear the applause. He didn't even stand up until Philip came out and put an arm around his shoulders. He was unaware of the Prince of Wales standing with head bowed. Instead, he was sobbing, sobbing as if he could never stop crying. The audience assumed it was because he'd been carried away in this beautiful but vaguely familiar tune. But Philip knew it was more. As quickly as it was honorable to do so, he pulled Dan from the organ console and into a private side room.

Max Hellenburg had the presence of mind to step up to the organ to accompany the choir on their last song, aware that something awesome, and perhaps awful, had happened to his pupil. When the concert was over, he positioned himself in front of the door where Philip and Dan were cloistered so that he could fend off the many well-wishers.

* * *

In the vestibule, Philip sat with his arm around Dan's shoulders while he sobbed. It seemed as if he could never get control of himself as his shoulders heaved up and down. Philip let him cry.

Finally, he said, "Can I do anything, Dan?"

"I don't know how to stop crying," he said miserably.

"Tell me about that song, will you? It was the most stirring thing I've ever heard."

Dan looked up helplessly. "It's called 'Come, Come, Ye Saints.' The words were written to comfort the Mormon pioneers who had been driven from their homes and who were working their way across the central plains of America to Utah in covered wagons."

Hoping to calm him, Philip continued, "Can you tell me why it has such great significance to you?"

Dan didn't know. "Maybe it's because I sang this once in the Tabernacle in Salt Lake City. The president of our church, the prophet, told me that I should always share my music with other people. Maybe I'm sad because I can no longer sing, as he told me to."

Philip considered for a moment. "At first you said your prophet told you to share your music. Then you said your singing. Can you tell me which it is?"

Dan caught his breath and looked up. He thought back to 1912, and he was in the Tabernacle. "He said, 'Share your music.'" Then he added thoughtfully, "He never said anything about singing." He wiped his face a bit. "I always thought I'd gone against God's wishes by losing my voice, but maybe He knew what would happen."

"I believe that God knows everything, even the future of a boy from Pocatello, Idaho."

Dan had regained enough control that he could talk now, at least in spurts that were only occasionally interrupted by a wayward sob.

"But there's something more to the song." His throat grew tight. "In the fourth verse, the words talk about what happens to the Saints who died on the journey. It calls it a happy day for them." He let out a wail as the significance of the words hit him. "Oh, Trevor, how could it be a happy day for you? How could Trevor's dying be a happy day?" He started sobbing again as tears streaked his cheeks and fell to the floor.

After a few moments, Philip said quietly, "Perhaps that's why the song affected you so strongly. It made you think of your friend."

Dan felt himself panicking now. There was nothing he could do to stop it. He stood up and paced the room, moving restlessly from corner to corner.

"What is it?" Philip asked anxiously.

"I don't know. Whenever I think about Trevor or about my church back home, I get panic-stricken. I don't know what to do, Philip. I feel like I'm going to die."

Philip moved over and grabbed him firmly around the shoulders. "Dan, it's time for you to work through this. You've been avoiding it for more than a year. You've got to figure out why you react this way."

Dan looked at him incredulously. "Why do I react this way? Because my best friend died!"

"I think it has to be more than that, particularly since you have the same reaction when you try to talk about your church. Please tell me what comes to mind when you think about your church."

"I can't, Philip. I just can't!"

"Is it your doctrine?"

"No, I love the doctrine." Then he added quietly, "I miss the doctrine. I miss it desperately."

"Then what comes into your mind when you think about your church?"

Dan closed his eyes, and he was in the classroom with Jonathon Richards and the other boys. He could smell the chalk on the slate blackboard, he could feel the smooth, polished surface of the chair under him, and he could see, as vividly as if he were there, the pale green walls opposite him. Then he saw Jonathon Richards, and he let out a cry.

"What is it?"

"It's Brother Richards. I can't face him. I can't face this thought."

"Why can't you face him? I thought you liked him."

Dan turned with a wild look to his face. "Like him? I love him. He was . . . he was like my father."

"Then why can't you face him?"

"Because I killed Trevor," Dan said savagely.

Philip stumbled back. "You what?"

"I killed Trevor, don't you see? He was coming to see me! He would never have been where those Germans were if he hadn't been coming to see me! It's because of me that he's dead, and now I have to tell his father." He crumpled to the floor, sobbing again.

Philip sat down next to him. "So that's it. That's what you've feared to face all this time."

Dan didn't look up. He wanted to cease to exist, to simply disappear.

Philip let him sit for a while. "Dan, I need to talk to you. Can you listen to me for a minute?"

Dan turned angrily. "You're going to tell me it's not my fault. Don't you think I know that? But I feel like it's my fault, and it will never go away."

"Actually, I have something far more important to tell you. But first I need to ask a few questions."

Dan sat sullenly.

"This friend of yours, Trevor—from the few occasions when you've talked about him, I got the impression that he volunteered for air service. Is that correct?"

"Yes."

"Do you think he knew the risks when he went in?"

Dan turned with a glare. "Yes, he knew the risks. But still—"

"My next question. If, on the morning your friend woke up to come see you, someone had told him that if he embarked on the journey, it was absolutely certain that he would be killed, but that if he went he would be in the position to save the lives of more than fifty wounded Americans, what choice do you think he would make?"

Dan tried to talk. He wanted to argue with Philip. But it was hard to let go of the guilt. It had wrapped itself around Dan's soul, building up layers of fear and dread, much as an oyster tries to protect itself from a grain of sand. He wanted to hold on to the agony. It had become part of him.

Philip pressed him. "I'm afraid I'd like you to answer this one. If he knew that he had the choice of staying and protecting his own life or flying that mission to save the others, what would he do?"

"He'd go on the mission, and you know it."

"Dan, the only person who is served by your accepting guilt for Trevor's death is the adversary. Through the war, he destroyed your friend's body. Through guilt and regret, he's trying to kill your soul. Can you see that by trying to take responsibility for what happened to Trevor, you're actually diminishing the meaning of his sacrifice?"

That caught Dan off guard. "What do you mean?"

"Trevor must have been a kind and generous person. The scriptures say, 'Greater love hath no man than this, that a man lay down his life for his friends.' When Trevor moved against the odds to protect those people, he was completing the most selfless act of love that a human being can offer. It was a magnificent thing, something that should be treasured. I can't tell you why it was required of him, but when he was faced with a choice, he made the one that offered life to other people. If he hadn't come to see you that day, fifty black letters would have been sent to parents, wives, and children back in the States. Trevor gave those men life by offering his own. You should not take that away from him."

"I need a priesthood blessing," Dan said plaintively. "I need my church. I miss my church. I need to find peace. I know you're right in what you're telling me, but my heart still hurts. The reason I've had all this anxiety when I think of home is that I haven't wanted to face Brother Richards." The face of Jonathon Richards intruded into his thoughts, and he ducked to avert his gaze. "I wish God would speak to me and help me feel better."

Philip steadied his own breathing. This was the moment when he could finally help his friend take back his life. "Dan, in a city the size of London, there has to be a congregation of Mormons, and I will find it for you."

After a moment, Dan quieted down. "Thank you. Maybe, if I can talk to a bishop or someone, it will help. Maybe . . ."

Finally, after Dan sat quietly for perhaps two or three more minutes, the anxiety attack started to fade. Eventually, Dan looked up and smiled at Philip. His breathing was almost normal, and he felt as though he could finally stand up to leave. "I guess I let people down by disappearing after the encore."

"Don't be foolish. They loved you. You're an American, so you probably don't understand what a great honor it is to perform for the prince. And to receive an ovation! This was truly a remarkable evening." Taking Dan's arm, he opened the door. "I think it's going to be all right, Dan. I believe maybe now you can heal."

Chapter Twenty-Three

A FATEFUL TELEGRAM

London, England
August 1920

Philip found a small LDS congregation and drove Dan there the very next Sunday. When Dan and Philip walked into the small restaurant that was rented for use by the Church on Sundays, the local members first thought they were American missionaries. When Dan explained he was an expatriate, they adopted him into their branch. Philip asked if he could stay through sacrament meeting. Then priesthood meeting. Then Dan invited him to stay while he received a blessing from the branch president. For the first time in their relationship, it was Philip who wept, explaining that all his life he had wondered why the charge to call for the elders of the church, as explained in James, was no longer active.

In the course of the next few months, Dan continued to play the organ for the Church of England, then made a mad dash to his own services. He and Philip had lengthy talks about the LDS Church, its doctrines, its scripture, and the Spirit that enlivened it. When Philip announced his intention of resigning his position at his church, his father reacted angrily, saying that he didn't care a thing about whether Philip was a priest or not but that he had better not get any ideas of leaving the Church of England. "It's all about propriety with my father," Philip explained. "He doesn't care if one believes in the church, just that one attend it—or, at the very least, that one not leave it. It would be socially unacceptable for a government minister to have a son who converted to some obscure American sect." So Philip stopped attending services with Dan.

Even though no one said anything, Dan felt a different spirit in the Carlyles' home after that, so he found a small apartment closer to the branch. He liked his life in England, and his performance for the prince had created opportunities for him to perform on both the organ and piano. Professor Hellenberg even arranged a recital at Cambridge. The American embassy said it would do what it could to help him secure a permanent visa. He hoped he could find someone to share his life with while strengthening his little branch of the LDS Church in England. He tried to convince himself that he was no longer afraid to go back to America, but the anxiety he'd felt was so powerful that even though he knew he'd made progress in working through it, he was reluctant to face the fear again. He still became emotional when he thought of Trevor, but in a different way. There was poignancy about it now—not so bitter, mostly just sad. He felt the same about Jody Wilkins and Geoff Green and all the others he had known.

Then, one day, while Philip was visiting, there was an unexpected knock on the door. A military courier presented himself. "Are you Lieutenant Daniel O'Brian?"

"Yes, I am."

"I have a telegram for you that has been forwarded through military channels. Please sign here." Dan's hands trembled as he signed the manifest. He opened the telegram carefully. It was from Sam Carter.

Pocatello, Idaho, USA
Your father is very ill cancer STOP Suggest you
return immediately STOP Please telegram your
intentions STOP Sam

Dan handed the telegram to Philip, who, knowing of Dan's struggle with his father, asked, "What are you going to do?"

"I don't know." Dan shrugged. "The last words my father spoke to me were, 'Get out.' I've done my best to honor his command."

"It sounds like he may be dying."

"Maybe he's already dead," Dan said dejectedly. "Why should I leave England if he's not even alive? I don't want to go back."

"What does your heart tell you?"

"My heart is about the least reliable organ in my body. I can't trust what it tells me." But he was surprised to find that he wasn't anxious. It was more of a cold, empty feeling. He'd spent so many years getting past the anger he felt toward his father that he just couldn't face the thought of feeling that way again.

"I could go with you, if that would help."

Dan turned sharply. "You, go to America? But your life is here."

"Dan, you had to come to England to find your life. I have resisted my heart by not learning more of Mormonism. Yet whenever I read your scriptures or study the writings of your leaders, my heart tells me I need to find out for certain if your church is true. Do you realize how significant it is that your doctrine says that 'men are, that they might have joy'? Most religions teach that happiness is to come in the next life, that we should suffer here. But Joseph Smith taught that this life should be joyful. What a remarkable, dynamic approach to life." He looked wistful for a moment, as if there were something missing in his life that he wanted desperately. "At any rate, perhaps I have to go to America to discover what God has in mind for me. I want to see Salt Lake City and feel for myself if there is a prophet on the earth again. If it's true, it will be the most momentous discovery of my life."

"But the Spirit of the Lord can speak to you here—not that I wouldn't be grateful to have you come with me."

"I'm concerned that the Spirit has already spoken to me. But there is a problem. As much as my father inhibits and dominates me, I still love him. To join your church here would imperil his career. Perhaps if I go to America, I can find a place for myself."

"You'd be willing to leave your beautiful home and the security of your inheritance?"

"Do you remember the scripture that your Pearl of Great Price is based on? 'Again, the kingdom of heaven is like unto a merchant man, seeking goodly pearls: Who, when he had found one pearl of great price, went and sold all that he had, and bought it.' If this is what God has in mind for me—my own pearl of great price—then I must give up everything, if need be, to acquire it. At the very least, I need to go to Salt Lake City and find out for myself what is true."

Dan smiled. "God must love both of us to bring us together. I'm sure that you saved my life by intervening in my behalf, because the despair was simply too profound for me to endure on my own. No matter how difficult I acted, you never gave up. Now, perhaps I can help you find something of value in return." He sighed. "Even if it means facing my father."

* * *

The train pulled into Pocatello at 3:00 A.M. Philip yawned when wakened, but Dan had been awake for hours. He had to face Frank, and he didn't know what to say. As they walked onto the platform, it struck him that he didn't have a car, and it was highly unlikely that there would be any cabs at that time of night.

But as they stepped into the terminal, he saw Sam standing there, who, when he spied Dan, opened up his arms and strode across the station to hug him. "We missed you, buddy. We missed you every Sunday."

Only then did Dan realize how much he had missed Sam. "I can't believe you came at this hour of the night."

"I'd have stayed here 'round the clock, if necessary. The world just hasn't been right without you guys." He dropped his gaze. "We were sorry to hear about Trevor. There was a big article in the newspaper about the medal he earned and all. But we didn't know anything about you except that you'd been wounded." Then he clapped his hands on both Dan's shoulders. "You look good. Thanks for coming home."

Dan fought down the panic in his stomach. Hearing Trevor's name reminded him that he'd soon have to face the Richardses. But after a deep breath, he was able to respond. Turning to his right, Dan said, "Sam, this is Philip Carlyle. He's a friend who let me recuperate at his home in England. I had some trouble with a gas attack and had to stay in a humid environment."

After shaking Philip's outstretched hand, Sam presented a young woman and said, "I don't know if you remember Sarah Long. She was two years younger than us at church."

Dan turned and smiled. "I remember Sarah. May I ask why you are here? And where's Mary?"

"She's home with our son. Sarah's here because she's one of the nurses who takes care of your father. She's the one who got in touch with me."

Dan looked at her. She was really lovely. He took her hand and actually felt himself blush when she smiled. Clearing his throat, he said, "Thank you for helping my father. But you should know that he and I parted on very bad terms. I'm not sure he's going to want to see me."

Sarah replied quietly, "He told me about your argument. He doesn't talk a lot about you, but he did mention some of the medals you've earned. Even though he's never said it, I believe he wants to see you. In fact, I believe he would have died days ago except that I told him you were coming."

Dan swallowed hard. "Well, then, should we go directly to the hospital?"

"He's sedated right now. Cancer is an awful way to die. Maybe you can stay at his house tonight, and we could pick you up first thing in the morning."

Dan's stomach flipped, and the panic came on stronger than it had in months. He gripped the bench he was standing next to in order to steady himself. Almost in a whisper, he said, "I'm not sure it's a good idea to stay at his house. I may have a problem with that. I know it's late, but maybe we could go to the Richardses'."

"They don't live here anymore," Sam said flatly. "After Trevor was killed, Brother Richards accepted a transfer back to Salt Lake City so Sister Richards could be close to her family. They've been gone for nearly a year."

"Oh. I see." Dan just stood there.

"You can stay at our house—although it's a little crowded."

Dan didn't know what to do. He didn't want to impose on Sam, but he knew he wasn't up to going to his childhood home.

"I've got an idea," Philip said. "I see that there's a rather stately hotel just half a block from here. Don't you suppose they would have a room?"

Dan looked out at the Yellowstone Hotel. "It would be great if they did."

Sam helped them with their luggage, and they checked into a room. Sam promised to pick them up the next morning at nine o'clock.

* * *

Dan had always been frightened of his father. He was one of those men whose barrel chest gave him an ominous appearance. At least it appeared that way to a little boy. So he was completely unprepared for the frail figure that lay in front of him. The body was completely different, wasted away to skin and bones. But his face was the same. Dan recognized the face. He pressed his hand against his stomach to try to calm himself.

"Father, it's me, Dan. I've come to see you." He immediately stepped back from the bed. Frank stirred and slowly opened his eyes. After focusing on Dan for a moment, he rolled to the other side without comment, leaving Dan and Philip standing there awkwardly. Finally, to break the silence, Dan said as forcefully as he could, "I'd like you to meet a friend of mine who's taken care of me since I was wounded in France. This is Philip Carlyle."

Philip angled around the foot of the bed so that Frank would see him. Finally, Frank looked up and said, "I guess I should thank you for taking care of my boy. Since no one here in America knew what was happening to him, I guess it's lucky he made friends with the English to watch out for him." Then he fell silent. Philip immediately picked up on the tone in Frank's voice, remembering that Dan had told him how much his father resented the English.

After a few more moments of being ignored, Dan felt his face flushing as the old anger started to swell up inside. Memories swirled in his brain, and he found himself wanting to reach out and shake Frank, in spite of his current condition.

"Dan was wounded in action, sir, while trying to save another man. In doing so, he was gassed, severely injuring his lungs. That's why he had to spend time in England." Philip's voice was remarkably even.

Frank rolled to his back and looked at Philip with narrowed eyes. "He always did like the English . . . it only makes sense that he'd want to live there. He probably should have stayed there—for his health." With that, Frank rolled back to his side and pretended to go to sleep. Philip looked up at Dan and gave him a resigned smile.

For his part, Dan wanted to scream. He wanted to turn
Frank to face him and tell him that he had no right to insult
Philip or Jonathon Richards or anyone else, whether they
were English or not. At least they'd taken an interest in him.
At least they treated other people with decency and good
manners. As the anger escalated, he was startled to find that
he actually wanted to hit this shriveled wreck of a human
being. Philip caught his eye. He could tell that Philip
wanted him to keep trying, which just made him angry at
Philip. Dan simply turned and walked out of the room.
Philip shrugged his shoulders at Sarah and followed Dan out
into the hall.

"Dan, you shouldn't take it personally. He's in a lot of
pain . . ."

Dan grimaced. The last thing he needed was a lecture.
"Philip, I can't talk about this right now. I know about his
pain. I know about his condition. But there's nothing I can
do about that. I shouldn't have come home. I knew it was a
mistake. But I did, and right now I need time to think. I've
got to figure out what to do, if anything . . ."

As Dan rocked slightly from side to side, Philip could
see the effort it was taking for him to calm down his anger
and hurt. Feeling Dan's need for some space, Philip said, "I
think I'm going to take a walk around Pocatello for a bit and
see if I can find that candy palace you told me about. Maybe
I can bring you something?"

Dan looked at him, distracted. "What? Oh, candy. That
would be good." Philip slipped quietly around a corner and
down the stairs.

Dan sat down on the high-backed wooden chair just
outside Frank's door, rested his elbows on his knees, and held
his head in his hands. Sarah Long came out of Frank's room.

"I'm sorry," she said hesitatingly. "He's never been like
that. Sometimes he doesn't talk a lot, but he's never been so . . ."
She struggled for words. "So abrupt."

"Never to anyone but managers and his second son." Dan didn't even look up. "Oh, and Englishmen. It's not enough to hate just his local antagonists—he's got to hate an entire race as well."

"He's been given drugs—" Sarah started to say but was interrupted when Dan sat up quickly in order to stop her from going on.

"I know he has. I'm sure that's why he said what he did. I'm all right. I would just like to be by myself for a while." Sarah started to protest, but Dan put his head down again to stave off any further conversation. She moved off down the hall.

The emotions swirling inside Dan were contradictory and confusing. On the one hand, he felt an almost burning hatred for the way his father had treated him. On the other, he wanted desperately to go into his room and try to comfort him. He wanted the chance to say something nice to Frank and even dreamed about hearing something nice in return. He wanted, just once, to have his father simply accept him. It was so frustrating. And that it happened in front of Sarah and Philip was embarrassing.

At the deepest moment of his reverie, he was startled when a voice spoke to him from the chair to his left, almost jolting him from his chair. He hadn't even noticed that anyone had come up, let alone sat down next to him.

"I'm sorry," the person said. "I didn't mean to startle you." Dan looked up and saw an older man sitting next to him. He had a leathery face and wore the coveralls of a railroad man. His face seemed familiar, but Dan couldn't place him.

"You're Frank O'Brian's boy, aren't you?" The old fellow was eyeing him up and down.

"Yes, sir. I'm Dan, his second son."

"I thought I recognized you. I haven't seen you since you were a boy going on the train to Salt Lake City with a bunch of your friends and Mr. Richards."

Dan looked at him quizzically and then realized it was the engineer who had let the teachers quorum tour the cab of his locomotive. In spite of his dark mood, he smiled at the memory. Just recalling that wonderful day lifted his spirit. "I'm sorry. I know you were the engineer the day we went to Salt Lake, but I can't remember your name."

"Newsome. Tom Newsome."

Dan smiled. "You guys gave us the ride of our life." They both laughed.

"I thought Richards was surely going to write us up. But he never said a word about it." They sat quietly for a moment, recalling the experience. "Your father was so proud that day. He told me over and over that you were the boys' leader who helped get the trip organized. He's told me a lot about you through the years. Whenever the military sent a telegram, he'd read it to whoever was nearby in the union room."

That brought Dan up short. "My father talked about me?"

Tom Newsome looked up, surprised. "Of course he did. He talked about you a lot through the years." The look of astonishment on Dan's face caused Tom to pause for a moment. Then recognition seemed to dawn, and he said quietly, "You had an argument with him before you left for Europe, didn't you? He started to talk about it briefly one day but caught himself and stopped. I guess you haven't talked with him much."

"No, sir. I'm afraid we haven't talked at all."

"I'd forgotten that, because he used to share things from your letters."

"But I didn't write him any letters." Dan's confusion was obvious. "We left on bad terms, so I didn't ever write to him."

"Maybe that explains something I've wondered about," Newsome responded. Dan looked at him quizzically. "I saw the return address on one of the envelopes he got and was surprised it was from Salt Lake City. That seemed kind of strange, but I just figured the army transferred it from there."

Dan caught his breath. "It must have been Margaret Richards. She probably sent him the letters I sent to her and Brother Richards. She probably thought he was lonesome. That would be like her." Dan grew quiet. His anger had been derailed, leaving him to try to figure out this new information that had come along.

"He's a very good man, you know." Dan turned and looked into Tom Newsome's eyes. "I don't know what happened between the two of you, but I do know that he's a good man. His word is his bond, and he's made a real difference for the working men in this town. There'll be a lot of people at his funeral."

Dan didn't know what to say. What was there to say? Obviously, Frank could talk to Tom Newsome and a hundred other men—people Dan didn't know. But he never talked with any of the people who had mattered in Dan's life. He cleared his throat. "I'm glad that he talked with you. For some reason, my father and I could never seem to connect. He wasn't very interested in things that mattered to me."

Newsome didn't raise his voice or argue. He just asked a question. "So the fact that you and your father couldn't talk was his fault?"

"What?"

"Your father didn't want to talk to you, so the two of you didn't get along."

"With all due respect, Mr. Newsome, things may have been different inside our house than they were in the union hall."

Tom Newsome sighed. "I'm not trying to make you feel bad, son. It's just that I've got a boy that's hard for me to talk with, too. We both want to, but somehow the words always get tied up. From my side, it's like he's ready to get angry at me before I even say something. I try to see it from his side but just can't seem to make it out. Maybe it's like that with your father."

"Maybe. All I know is that everybody seems to know about Frank O'Brian but me. It's like we lived in two different worlds while sleeping in the same house."

Tom Newsome stood up. "I'm sorry things were hard for you two. I don't know if it will help, but I can tell you this—your father is proud of you. He told me so himself on more than one occasion. Maybe that counts for something."

Dan stood up and shook Tom's hand. "Thank you, Mr. Newsome. Someday maybe I could sit down and talk with you to find out more about my father. I'd like to get to know more about him, and I probably won't learn it from him. Are you going to go in now?"

"For just a minute, to let him know all the boys are out there pulling for him. I won't take long."

It was perhaps ten minutes later when Tom Newsome came out of Frank's room. "He's awake now. I told him you were here."

"What did he say?"

"He just said he knew that. Good luck, Dan." Tom patted him on the shoulder and walked slowly down the hall.

It took Dan a good five minutes alone in the hall to get up his courage again. He put his hand on the doorknob and went into the darkened room. Frank looked at him but didn't say anything. He didn't roll over, either. Dan pulled up the chair next to his bed and just sat there. It was hard not to say anything, but he was determined to leave the first words to his father. As the wall clock ticked away the seconds, the noise sounded almost as loud in his ears as the concussion of artillery. Still, he was determined to remain silent.

Finally, Frank said quietly, "So how are your lungs doing, now that you're in this dry air?"

"They hurt, actually. It's like a burning in the middle of my chest. It's hard to get my breath sometimes." Frank grunted as if he understood.

"You got shot, besides that?"

"Yes, sir, a bullet grazed my rib cage. It's healed up pretty well, although I'm a little stiff sometimes. But it's all right."

"That's good."

"Yes, sir." Dan waited a bit before saying, "I'm sorry about your cancer. I didn't know until I got a telegram from Sam. Then I came straight home."

"I'm managing all right. It shouldn't be too long before you don't have to worry about me anymore."

Dan stood up and looked directly at Frank. At first he wanted to respond to Frank's sarcasm. But he hesitated and looked directly into his eyes and was startled by what he saw. They were hollow and dark, and he saw something in them he'd never seen there before—fear. And pain. In an instant, all of Dan's anger seemed to evaporate. Instead of the all-powerful Frank O'Brian, he saw a lonely, dying man, and his heart ached for the tortured soul lying in the bed. His voice caught as he said, "Father, can we call a truce? Can we just talk to each other for a few minutes?"

"A truce? So you want me to just forget all the times you passed on my invitations to go hunting so you could go over to the Richardses' house? You want me to forget that you preferred that Richards kid's company to your own brother's? Just put all that away. Is that what you want?"

Dan reeled. It was the same old story—somehow Frank was trying to make it his fault again. "No, sir, that's not what I'm proposing. If I've hurt you, like you say, then you can hang onto that as long as you like, just like I'll probably hold on to all the times you didn't come to my concerts or field trips with me."

"Like you wanted me there. How could I have found room with all the others you really wanted to attend?"

"Father," his voice broke. "Father, a truce simply means you agree to leave things where they are. The past is what it is. Can't we just accept the fact that things weren't the way we wanted them and at least have some time now? Can't we just talk with whatever time is left?"

Frank looked into Dan's eyes this time. Dan could feel them searching him, testing to see if his offer was sincere. Dan was surprised to find that it was. He no longer wanted to recite all Frank's crimes. He just wanted to hug his father. It's all he'd ever wanted, really.

So he did. He reached down into the bed and gathered his frail father into his arms and hugged him. At first Frank resisted, trying to pull away. But Dan held tight. Regardless of what Frank wanted, this was what Dan needed. Then, hesitantly at first, Frank hugged back. He hugged back with all the strength he could find in his weakened condition. Dan felt tears on his father's face mixing with his own. "Dan, I'm sorry we didn't get along. I always wanted to. I just didn't know how. You made it hard."

Dan started to pull back, but Frank pulled him close. "I'm not accusing—I'm just telling you how it was. I'm sorry it was like that."

"I'm sorry too, Father. I'm so sorry." They separated.

Frank cleared his throat. "I accept your offer of a truce. I'd like to talk, if we can. I'd like to find out what's happened to you." Then, quietly, "I'd like to know what to expect when I die." And then Frank O'Brian started sobbing. The invincible tower started to crumble, and Dan and his father wept together. All that was left of the O'Brian family finally found a bridge—a tentative bridge, to be sure. At last the wall between them was breached.

* * *

In the course of the next few days, Dan spent most of his waking hours at Frank's bedside. It was difficult to talk at first, but when Dan started asking questions about Frank's childhood, about how he'd met Dan's mother and how he'd felt when Kelly died, the words started to come in a torrent, as if everything that they'd wanted to talk about had to come out now that time was short. Dan was able to talk about the military and some of the horror he'd endured. It was then he began to see why the union men loved his father. Frank was able to counsel him about how to deal with injustice, how to yield when necessary, and how to fight when possible. It was remarkable to see his father through the eyes of an adult. They were two men who had been battered by life, yet were still alive and facing it.

Finally, the bridge was strong enough to stand the greatest test of all. This time it was Frank who took the initiative. "Dan, when you came to see me the day we learned that Kelly had died, I didn't intend to call you a coward. I don't know what I expected out of seeing you that day." He caught his breath at the memory. "I was so angry about what happened to Kelly—the futility of it all. There he was, fighting a war for governments—big, capitalist governments that couldn't care less about their workers— and he lost his life the first day. I was angry at him for going, and I was so devastated that he died. He loved me, you know." He realized what he'd just said and how it might be interpreted, so he looked away. "At any rate, I just wanted to hurt someone . . . hurt them like I was hurt. And who better to hurt than you? It was a well-rehearsed game." Then he looked up, with something of fire in his eyes. "But why did you have to choose that moment to finally react against me? I'd said mean things before, and you just took it. The last thing I wanted to happen was for you to lose your head and go and enlist. That's the last thing I wanted . . ." His voice trailed off.

Dan staggered a bit to realize that the attack that day was intentionally designed to hurt him, as if that was his role to play. His face flushed. But this time he would not lose his temper, so he replied evenly, "I guess it was the proverbial straw that broke the camel's back. After a lifetime of failing to measure up, I just couldn't stand it any longer and had to do something."

Frank hesitated. "Well, I provoked you, and now you've lost your voice. All you'll have to remember about me is bitterness."

Dan wasn't prepared for this moment when he would finally get to say something. Even though he'd dreamed of it on so many occasions, he hadn't really expected ever to have the chance. But it was here. Finally, collecting himself, he said, "Father, I'm the one who made the decision. I did it in anger, and I've learned from that. But the truth is that I helped some people out there and, may Heaven forgive me, I hurt some people. At least give me the dignity of owning up to my own decision."

Frank looked up, surprised. "Well, I never expected that. If you'd hit me, that would be more justice." Then, collecting himself, he continued. "I guess you've become a man, son. I guess that you have some steel after all."

Dan didn't know what to say, so he just sat there. Finally he heard Frank whisper, "I'm sorry." Then Frank started coughing again, and Dan lifted his back to ease the spasms. At last the words had been spoken.

Very quietly, Dan said, "I honestly don't know what to say. The proper thing would be to accept your apology, but I have a lot of unresolved emotions. I will pray so that I can accept it. I'd like to—it would be good for both of us. At any rate, thank you for saying it."

Frank lay back on his pillow, exhausted from the effort. "That's better than I could have hoped for." He placed his withered hand on top of Dan's and closed his eyes.

Emotions Dan was unprepared to feel washed over him. His goal in coming to Pocatello was to find some honorable way to make an appearance of patching things up with his father so he could die with the illusion of peace. What he didn't expect was a genuine reconciliation—and certainly not to hear his father apologize. He should have felt wonderful, since this is what he'd always wanted. Having spent a lifetime building resentment, it was harder to forgive and seek forgiveness now than it should have been. It would take time—and there'd be plenty of time after Frank was gone. He said a mental prayer and then whispered quietly, "I love you too, Father."

* * *

Frank lingered for a few more days. As the end drew near, he grew increasingly apprehensive. Finally, Dan asked if he'd like a blessing. Frank's eyes grew wide, but he said that he would. Dan asked Bishop Peterson and Sam to join him in giving his father a blessing. It was the first time he'd performed a priesthood ordinance in many years. In the course of the blessing, Dan spoke words that were unexpected, giving Frank permission to leave this life in peace. When it was over, Frank said, "Thanks," then closed his eyes. It was his last conscious moment. "Remember me to Mom and Kelly," Dan whispered quietly, then kissed his father's face.

The combination of morphine and pain overwhelmed Frank, and he slipped into the coma that finally provided relief. In the end, death came quickly, and Dan was at his side.

Chapter Twenty-Four

A TIME TO MOURN, A TIME TO HEAL

Even though Frank's death was expected, the actual moment of passing was still a shock. Fortunately, Bishop Peterson was there to help Dan make the funeral arrangements and plan and conduct the program. Dan asked one of his father's old friends to read a life sketch, with Sam giving a short talk on the plan of salvation. Philip suggested that Dan play an organ solo, which seemed like a good idea. "For once, he'll have to attend one of my performances," Dan said dryly. Then Bishop Peterson would conclude with some brief remarks.

His conversation with Tom Newsome had given him a hint that a fair number of people would turn out from the railroad, but when Friday arrived, he was unprepared for the crowd that showed up. There were more than a hundred men and their wives, each expressing their sympathy and the loyalty they felt to Frank.

Approximately fifteen minutes before the funeral was scheduled to start, they closed the doors where Dan had been receiving mourners. Since he was the only one in the family, he asked Philip to offer the family prayer. The prayer was both beautiful and comforting. Philip's lifetime of devotion seemed to open the heavens, and Dan felt a warm spirit come over him that eased his anxiety and helped him feel equal to the ordeal before him.

Just minutes before the meeting was to start, Dan was moving toward the stand when he felt a powerful arm grab his shoulders. He turned to see Leonard Whitman smiling at him. "How are you holding up, Dan? Are you all right?"

Dan almost fainted. "Leonard! How did you get here? This is so . . ." Dan had made it through two days with no tears, and now, suddenly, they came flooding out on his cheeks as he grasped Leonard in a lingering hug, grateful to be in the arms of his oldest friend. "I've missed you terribly, Leonard," he whispered in his ear. "Particularly since Trevor . . ."

"I know, Dan. I know. I still can't think about it myself. I just wish I could have been there to help you. Now you have this to deal with as well."

Dan straightened up. "It will be a lot easier with you here. Believe me, it will be a lot easier. How did you know to come?"

"Sam called me. He's the one who has kept in touch with everybody since our group broke apart."

Dan turned and looked at Sam, who was smiling at him from the stand. "He's been terrific to me," Dan said. "I wouldn't even be here for Father's funeral if it wasn't for him."

"Well, you better get up on the stand. It's time to start. I'll be here when it's done, and we can talk."

"I'd like that a lot—just like the old days." Dan watched as Leonard limped off to a seat near the front row, where he sat down next to his wife, who was holding a beautiful, little girl in her lap.

The service was shorter than most funerals of the day, which was all right, considering that Frank wasn't much for church anyway. The tributes were sincere, and Dan's organ solo filled the chapel in a way that no one in Pocatello had ever experienced before. He'd chosen a selection from Antonin Dvorak's *New World Symphony*. The haunting melody of "Goin' Home" stirred the imagination and gave expression to the sense of longing a person feels to return one day to a heavenly home. The people who remembered Dan as a boy, mostly for his singing, were moved deeply by the power of his playing. At the conclusion of the service, Dan followed the pallbearers, all members of Frank's union, as they lifted the casket into the hearse for the drive out to Mountain View Cemetery. Just as he was about to get into the car, he looked up and saw Jonathon and Margaret Richards walk out the side door of the chapel. Losing complete sense of place, he turned and ran over to them, throwing his arms around Jonathon Richards, who embraced him warmly. "I missed you," Dan said quietly.

"We missed you too—more than you can imagine. I'm sorry we have to meet in these circumstances."

When Dan stepped back, he saw that Jonathon had aged. His hair had turned gray, and his face was wrinkled. The years had been hard.

Margaret stepped over and hugged him. "You look wonderful, Daniel. And your musical tribute was magnificent."

Dan was suddenly self-conscious. "You're kind not to mention my face," he said as he lifted his hand to his cheek.

"Don't be full of nonsense. Your face looks fine. You should consider it a badge of honor that shows you were willing to sacrifice for our country." Then she added, "It's just so wonderful to hear your voice and know that you're well."

Jonathon asked, "I know you have to go right now. Do you suppose we could get together to talk for a few moments sometime in the next few days?"

"Of course. Of course we'll get together." Then Dan looked around quickly from side to side. "Brother Richards, can I ask a favor? I'd planned to dedicate the grave, since I have no other family. And," he swallowed hard, "and even though I haven't written or anything for the past year, I'd like you to ride out to the cemetery with me, since you're as close to family as I'll ever have. Maybe you could even dedicate Father's grave. That would help me a lot."

Jonathon's face turned an ashen gray. "Oh, Dan, don't apologize. I'm sorry I didn't do more to find you. It's been a hard time, and I haven't really been myself. You've got so much more to worry about than not sending us letters. Of course we'll come with you to the cemetery. It would be an honor to dedicate your father's grave." Then he added, "Although I'm not so sure your father thought very highly of me."

"You're not doing it for him. It's for me."

Jonathon smiled, and they walked arm in arm to the car.

And so Dan found himself surrounded and supported by friends. From the forlorn day in France when he'd awaken to find his life forever changed, he'd felt totally alone in the world. Now he suddenly realized that he'd really never been alone. Seated between Margaret and Jonathon, with Philip in the facing seat, he felt secure for the first time in years.

* * *

The only natural way for the group to get together again was to share a breakfast. The day after the funeral was tied up with details, so they met the day after that. This time it was as the invited guests of the Richardses at the Bannock Hotel, where they were staying. Dan, Philip, and Sam, Leonard, and their wives were invited guests. Jonathon asked Dan if he could arrive a few minutes early for a private conversation with him and Margaret.

"I hate to bring this up so close to your father's funeral, but Trevor asked us to share something with you before he died. Do you think it would be okay right now?"

Dan clouded up. "We might as well. I've been thinking about him every day since coming home anyway."

Jonathon took a moment to compose himself. It was obvious that he'd practiced this so he could get through it. "Shortly before he died, Trevor sent us the following letter. Rather than try to sum up what he said, perhaps I should just have you read it." Jonathon handed him a well-worn piece of paper.

France, August 15, 1918
Dear Mom and Father,

I've got just a few moments, but I wanted to write. You'd be amazed at how beautiful France is right now, in spite of everything men are doing to tear it up. The war is filled with such ironies. There are farmers getting ready to harvest crops just a few miles from the front lines. Yet in no-man's-land, nothing can grow because of the continuous bombardment. From the air everything is beautiful—even the battle scenes, in an eerie sort of way. But the death is real, and so it quiets down your enthusiasm.

I'm flying nearly every day now, and I still love it. There is such freedom in the air, and the aircraft have improved to where they're just swell to handle. I like the reconnaissance missions best, since you don't have to shoot at anyone and you hope it gives the Allies information they can use to save some of our soldiers. The dogfights are exciting, and you can't help but get excited when you get a kill. My only problem is that whenever that happens, I think of Sam and Danny and how they feel about killing. Then I get subdued. The only way I've been able to make peace with myself is that it's the only way to bring this carnage to an end—we need to win the war as soon as possible. So I do my best, trusting that the Lord will work it all out.

Dan read silently about the mission where Josh Brown had saved Trevor and helped him get back to friendly lines, where he crash-landed. He felt a twinge of guilt that he hadn't given Josh more time when they'd met in the hospital. It was obvious Trevor had liked him a great deal. When he finished that story, he saw the almost scribbled sentence at the bottom. *Been called up on alert. I've got to go.*

The text that followed was written on a different type of paper. It was obviously written later, and the tone of the letter changed substantially.

> *It's hard to be happy here sometimes, though I try to keep my spirits up. So many of my friends have been killed. You almost don't want to get to know people. I had a close call today—there was this German pilot who was really good. Fortunately, he ran out of fuel and had to turn back. The good news is that I get to go see Danny. Whenever I feel sorry for myself, I remember that he's down in the trenches, and that's so much closer to purgatory than what I put up with. At least I get to go up into the clouds and have the silence of the air around me. He has to put up with artillery shells falling at random intervals. It must be maddening. I plan to take him up for a ride, whether he wants to go or not. I'm so excited to see him, I can hardly stand it.*

Dan had to put the letter down for a moment. He didn't dare raise his eyes to look at Jonathon. Finally, he wiped his eyes with a handkerchief and continued.

> *Well, I'm about out of time. I hate to write this next paragraph because it will worry you. But since the odds are stacked against me, there's always a chance that I won't make it home. If that's the case, will you please give my things to Dan? He'll be able to get more use out of them than you will. While I've had a lot of great friends, he's still the best. Tell him I love him like the brother he is. Thanks for being such wonderful parents. I love you.*

P.S. This is exactly where I'm supposed to be—I feel it in my heart. So please don't worry about me.

Dan put the letter down and tried to say something. He opened his mouth, tried to talk, and closed it again. Finally he squeaked out, "I just hope the day comes when I can think about him without crying."

"We do too," Jonathon said bleakly.

"Brother and Sister Richards . . ." Dan's voice caught as they looked up. He struggled with himself, as if he were trying to make a difficult decision. He was obviously in some kind of pain, but they refrained from interrupting him. Finally, he said, his voice tight with emotion, "I need to apologize to you for not coming home sooner. I should have been here to help . . ." Margaret reached over and took his hands in hers. He took strength from that and continued, "I wanted to see you, but I went through something of a black period where I just didn't feel I could face anyone. I actually wished that I could have died out there. I was all torn up inside about Trevor and about my voice . . . I guess I tried to avoid feeling the pain by avoiding the people I love. I didn't even open your letters, let alone reply to them. But I did save them. At any rate, I'm sorry I left you alone."

Margaret smiled, but before she could say anything, Jonathon spoke up. "I actually understand much better than you might think, Dan. I went through my own period of darkness. When I heard about Trevor, I got angry—really angry. That was something new for me. I'd never felt anything like that before. Life has been so good to me, and now everything was wrong. Trevor was gone, you were hurt, and I was furious—furious with the political leaders who'd started this mindless war, furious with Trevor for wanting to go. And . . ." Hesitating, he dropped his eyes. "I was angry with you for not getting in touch." Then he looked up. "I was even angry with God for letting this happen. Can you imagine that? Mostly, though, I was angry with myself for not stopping the two of you. I was just heartbroken to lose my boy." Tears filled his eyes, and he couldn't talk. Now Margaret took her hands from Dan and put her arm around her husband's shoulders. "In the end, I came to realize that this wasn't about me and how I felt. It was about Trevor and all the others like him who volunteered to do something noble. My anger did nothing for them—in fact, it somehow diminished them. So I've been trying to let go of the grudge I've felt. With God's help, I've made some progress."

"It's interesting that you'd say that," Dan said. He glanced over at Philip, who was talking with Leonard and his wife as they entered the room. "I eventually came to the same conclusion, but I needed the help of a friend to do it. I'm sorry I gave you reason to be angry at me."

Jonathon reached out and hugged him. "I'm not angry. I should have come to England and found you. We could've come. I couldn't make myself deal with it. I guess we were all wounded, in a way. Just know that we love you, and we're glad you're safe and sound." Dan melted into his shoulder and felt sustained by the old bond that had existed between them.

"What about you, Sister Richards? Are you all right?"

She looked wistful. "I never got angry, or even sad, really. Somehow I knew the day he left on the train that I wouldn't see him again. I've just felt incredibly lonely, particularly when Jonathon immersed himself in his work." She sighed. "Fortunately, I've had my family to help out, and I've done a lot of volunteer work. Plus, I was blessed with a good memory, so I get to visit him whenever I like." She smiled as if she saw him in memory. "So I'm getting by."

"You also found the time to send copies of my letters to my father," Dan said quietly.

Margaret glanced up with a guilty look and started to explain, but Dan interrupted. "Please don't feel bad. I'm actually grateful you did. Apparently, it meant something to him, because he talked about it to other people. There's still a lot about our relationship that is tough to understand, things I'll probably never understand or feel right about, but at least we parted on decent terms. The letters you sent on were part of that." He smiled. "At the end, I had a chance to lose my temper again, but maybe I'm learning something about life, because I bit my tongue, and things worked out much better than I could have hoped." Margaret relaxed and took his hand again.

Gathering his strength, Jonathon said, "I guess the thing I admire most about Trevor is that he relished life and lived each day—or, at least, most days—very well. In the end, we're all going to die, and the only thing that matters is how well we lived. When I feel bad about Trevor, I always take comfort knowing that he lived well. That's what I admire about Trevor . . ."

Dan managed a smile. "And the thing I've always admired most about you, Brother Richards, is that you always found things to admire about Trevor—and about the rest of us. You and Sister Richards have been our biggest supporters."

Jonathon cleared his throat. "Thank you. At any rate, we've sorted through his things and hope you'll come to Salt Lake when it's convenient. For example, you are now the owner of an Indian motorcycle, which may be more of a curse than a blessing." He tried to smile.

"Wow," Dan said. "I think I'll actually enjoy riding it from the front seat instead of behind the teenage madman that used to give me rides." Even Margaret laughed at that.

Then he added, "I'll never be able to thank you for everything you've done for me. You both mean the world to me."

Margaret took his hands and said, "All right, then—that was an important conversation, and one we needed to have. But this is a day to reflect on our blessings and to comfort you in the loss of your father. So we'll keep Trevor in the back of our mind as a happy memory."

Just then, there was a stirring in the room, and they looked up to see a handsome young man in military uniform enter the room with Bishop Peterson and his wife.

"Oh, my good heavens," Dan said. "It's Elmer Peterson. I can't believe it!" He rushed across the room, and the two friends embraced. After all the years apart, the four boys from the quorum joined each other in a big group hug.

"How did you get here?" Dan finally asked Elmer.

"Sam sent a telegram. I caught the next train out of Washington and pulled in just a few minutes ago. Father had told the Richardses I might make it, so he invited them to join us for breakfast. We wanted to surprise you."

"Well, it worked," Dan said happily. "We're all here." Then he added softly, "Well, almost all of us." That left everyone with nothing to say.

Elmer finally broke the silence. "Maybe, for just this one day, all five of us will be together again—at least, for a few hours."

Everyone nodded, and Dan said quietly, "I hope so." Then he smiled at the thought that Trevor might be able to join them in spirit. Turning to Elmer, he said, "You're a full captain! What have you done to earn that?"

Elmer grinned. In some ways, it was hard to recognize him. His face had hardened and matured. With jet black hair, he was actually quite handsome and carried himself with a new sense of self-assurance. "It turns out that I did well building military codes. It wasn't just a fluke in the testing. They've offered me a full-time commission, which I've decided to accept. Hopefully, we can keep America strong enough that we don't have to go through another war like that ever again."

Dan smiled. "I'm glad that the war was actually good for you, Elmer. I'm glad something positive came out of it."

"Hear, hear," the others responded.

Dan looked up and saw Philip standing over by the Richardses. He motioned for him to come forward, and he introduced him to the group. "This is Philip Carlyle, the man who saved my life." Then, a bit more quietly, he went on. "Even when I didn't think I wanted it to be saved. He's also interested in the Church. I know you'll all like him a great deal."

They shook hands, and Leonard said, in his modest fashion, "In view of what Philip did for Dan, I propose we make him an honorary member of the First Ward teachers quorum." Philip laughed and conceded that he would consider that a signal honor. And so he became one of them.

With that, Jonathon Richards called everyone to breakfast, and they sat down to a hearty meal that was almost as sumptuous as those in the old days. Even though the event that brought them together was somber, the joy of being together soon had them laughing and chatting much like in the old days. When the Richardses left town later that afternoon, they invited Philip to come and stay with them while he looked around Salt Lake City, which he promised to do as soon as he had helped Dan straighten out his affairs.

* * *

That evening, as Dan and Philip sat at dinner at the Yellowstone Hotel, Dan looked up from his food and said quietly, "I think I'll go stay at my house tonight."

"Do you want me to come with you?"

"No, I don't believe so. I think it's time I make peace with the past. It's time to let go of the ghosts." He smiled weakly, as if gathering his courage. "I need to start thinking about the future. I need to talk to the Lord about it." He smiled at Philip. "I think maybe now I'm ready to do that."

HISTORICAL NOTES
ON WORLD WAR I

Pulitzer Prize–winning historian Barbara Tuchman wrote three outstanding books relative to the First World War, including *The Guns of August* and *The Zimmerman Telegram.* But to understand the political and social conditions that led up to this great conflict, one needs to turn to *The Proud Tower,* which talks about the social order as it existed in the twenty-five years prior to the outbreak of war in August 1914.

Europe in the late-nineteenth century was dominated by a number of hereditary monarchies that were related to one another by marriage and alliances. For example, Queen Victoria of England was mother or grandmother to the future king of England, the kaiser of Germany, and to the wife of the czar of Russia—three of the major combatants in the war. There were indirect family relationships with the other European monarchies as well. As long as Queen Victoria was alive, Britain was able to prevent the outbreak of war that always simmered beneath the surface of European politics. Austria-Hungary, which had been the foremost European power for nearly a thousand years, was in decline, with the most obvious sign of the breakup of the empire being the formation of an independent German state in 1870 under Chancellor Otto von Bismarck and the King of Prussia, Wilhelm I, who declared himself kaiser (king) of the new German state. In the Franco-Prussian War (1870–71), Germany had beaten France on the field of battle, forcing Napoleon III into a brief and humiliating exile, before withdrawing back to traditional lines, with the significant exception of retaining the fertile

Alsace-Lorraine region on the border. This humiliation left France perpetually unhappy with their aggressive neighbor and anxious to regain their lost territory.

Germany, meanwhile, wished to exercise dominance over European affairs, and by the time Kaiser Wilhelm II ascended to the monarchy, it became almost an obsession. He hated the urbane influence his British uncle King Edward, who succeeded Victoria, had in international affairs but was wise enough not to cross him. When King George ascended to the throne, however, Wilhelm started aching for a chance to strike out against France on the assumption that George was weak and would keep England at bay. To keep England out of any conflict, the kaiser built an incredible fleet of powerful dreadnaught battleships in a direct challenge to England's traditional dominance of the oceans. England viewed Germany's fleet with alarm since the small, island country was completely dependent on imports to feed its people. Rather than confront Germany directly, the British played their traditional foreign policy based on keeping balance between the various powers so that no one nation could dominate.

It was into this politically charged atmosphere that the various nations formed alliances to protect one another should another nation challenge them.

But there was far more at work in the world than international politics. The Socialist movement was gaining strength in each of the nations of Europe, with workers forming international alliances through their unions. As business prospered with advances in technology, workers were often left out of the abundance while owners amassed huge wealth. Strong social currents sought to break up these concentrations of wealth. Ancient grievances against royalty and aristocracy added to the fire.

Generally, there were two approaches by the civil agitators. First, there were those who called for political reform within the existing social structure to provide social benefits from both employers and the government. This group met with some hard-earned of success, with a number of employers providing modest health care benefits to industrial workers, while improved sanitation was made a priority by communities. Even old age insurance was considered. The reformists looked for practical solutions rather than revolution.

In contrast, there were powerful forces within the unions that called for the total overthrow of regimes to be replaced by benevolent, worker-oriented governments that would share the wealth of the nation equally. It was felt that with proper provocation, the workers would spontaneously rise and throw off the shackles of business and government in a glorious revolution that would usher in a utopia of worker equality and comfort. This idealistic approach rejected improvements in everyday working conditions since it was felt this would reduce pressure on the workers to rise up in revolution. There was a small group within these movements, called Anarchists, who thought that the use of terrorism and assassination could light the fuse. In a series of well-publicized acts of terrorism, the Anarchists set out on a course of assassination (eventually killing six heads of state, including President McKinley in the United States) and acts of violence (most prominent of which was the bombing of the Paris Opera House and the Hay-Market rebellion in Chicago). Governments clapped down on civil liberties in an effort to contain the discontent.

When war actually loomed, the reformers were disappointed that patriotism and nationalism proved a greater hold on the workers' loyalty than their common international goals. Thus, the German workers eagerly took up arms to aid Germany's war effort with little thought of their "brothers" in France and England, and vice versa.

While many theories have been advanced as to why the world came to such a violent war in the first decades of the 1900s, the German-Prussian ambition seems to be a primary cause. When Archduke Franz Ferdinand, heir to the throne of Austria, was assassinated, it was Germany who goaded Austria into making unreasonable demands on Serbia, knowing full well that Serbia would refuse to comply. On its own, Austria would never have had the military wherewithal to bully Serbia, but they were backed by an iron-clad treaty with Germany.

Germany was also aware that Russia would see an advance by Germany into Serbia as an act of aggression against their borders and would thus be forced to mobilize. That is why Germany warned against mobilization, essentially demanding that Russia leave itself completely vulnerable to a fully mobilized German army. Again, the likely outcome was that Russia would declare war, with France obligated to follow. All this would provoke a war that would allow the Germans to launch a lightning strike through Belgium into France and quickly dominate Western Europe. Once that was accomplished, they could challenge the economically impoverished Russians at their leisure. It was felt that England's navy would have little effect on the ground war, and their almost nonexistent army would be meaningless to the ultimate outcome of the conflict.

What is clear in retrospect was not nearly so obvious at the time, at least to the nations who eventually became the Allied powers. Although most of the nations of Europe had the uneasy sense that war between Germany and France was a real possibility, few could have guessed that the assassination of Archduke Ferdinand by a lone anarchist in Sarajevo on June 28, 1914, would be the event that would bring the world to flames and eventually crumple most of the European monarchies. After all, previous acts of terror by the Anarchists had failed to ignite war. Unfortunately, this time Germany used the assassination as an excuse to invoke the complex set of alliances that quickly drew all of Europe into the Great War with dominolike speed.

Austria-Hungary declared war on Serbia July 28 for failing to comply with a long list of demands that would have effectively ended its independence, as well as for harboring a criminal Anarchist. Russia started mobilizing for war at this time. This was a tremendous threat to all its neighbors, because whichever country mobilized first had an automatic advantage if hostilities broke out. Accordingly, Germany warned Russia to stand down.

When Russia failed to comply, Germany declared war on Russia August 1 and immediately started mobilizing troops for the Eastern Front. Russia declared war on Germany and Austria.

Germany invaded Luxembourg the next day.

Because of France's alliance with Russia, Germany declared war on France August 3. France responded by declaring war on Germany. Austria-Hungary declared war on Russia.

Germany invaded Belgium August 4, despite Beligum's neutrality, as part of a sweeping and well-organized attack against France. England declared war on Germany in honor of its treaty with Belgium.

Austria-Hungary declared war on Britain and France August 12.

Thus, in a matter of weeks after the assassination, all of Europe was swept up in a great war that everyone assumed would be over in just six weeks. Germany counted on crushing all resistance between the German border and Paris so that their conquest of France would be a *fait accompli* before Russia could effectively bring its millions of troops to bear on the Eastern Front. At the time, Germany did not take England as a serious threat, with Kaiser Wilhelm II boasting that if the English actually landed any troops on the continent, he'd have to call the local police force to deal with them.

France, on the other hand, counted on launching a devastating counterattack against Germany to the south of the German offensive and directly across the rugged border between France and Germany which would send French troops deep into the heart of Germany. This strategy would isolate the invading German troops far behind enemy lines, where they would falter because their supply lines were cut. At least that was the plan at the beginning of August 1914 when marching troops called back to loved ones, "We'll be home before Christmas!" Little could they imagine that it would require 37,000,000 casualties and four dreadful years before the war finally came to an unhappy end.

Eventually, the First World War played out in numerous theaters across the world.

Eastern Front. Germany invaded Russia on Germany's eastern border, originally hoping to hold the massive but ill-equipped Russian army at bay while it successfully dominated Belgium and France. Russia struck back against Germany with surprising strength, however, which frustrated Germany. Even though Russia was eventually defeated at the battle of Tannenberg in East Prussia, its counterattack in Galicia forced Germany to withdraw troops from the Western Front in the war against France at a key moment, which may have doomed Germany's ability to execute its six-week plan for overwhelming France. Thus, even though Russia was defeated in each of its major battles early in the war, it played a key role in sapping German strength in the west. Eventually, Russia was unable to keep Germany from invading deep within its territory, but the sheer size of the country made it impossible for Germany to hold onto the conquered territory. Before the war was over, the Bolshevik Revolution in 1917 ended the life of the czar of Russia, as well as all his heirs, and the Russians and Germans concluded the treaty of Brest-Litovsk that left Russia independent and no longer a threat to Germany's war in the west.

Western Front—Belgium. This was the scene of the most ferocious fighting and which brought Britain into the war. Belgium had maintained a strict policy of neutrality in the hope that it could stay out of any wars between Germany and France. But the temptation to sweep north through the low countries and flank the French army was too great for Germany to resist, and it issued an ultimatum to Belgium to surrender its neutrality so that the German army could pass through its territory. Belgium refused and put up a spirited resistance, fighting against the overwhelming force of the German army at each step of Germany's sweep through the country. Although Belgium's effort was doomed from the beginning, it infuriated Germany to have its plans interfered with, and Germany spent a great deal more time subduing Belgium than it wanted. The Germans were unusually cruel to any Belgian city that resisted, often taking the most prominent citizens into the village square and executing them in front of their wives and children. This aggressive policy brought the enmity of all the Allied powers against Germany and formed the basis of a very successful underground resistance effort against Germany for the balance of the war. When combined with Russia's initial success in the east, Germany fell behind schedule in its advance toward Paris, which eventually allowed the Allies to consolidate their strength enough to push back against the German advance.

Western Front—France. Most of the fighting of the First World War took place on French soil. Only toward the end of the war were France and the Allied Powers able to push the Germany back onto its own territory. It was along the eastern borders of France that the trench system developed and where the combatants fought back and forth for nearly four years. At times, the German lines came within sixty miles of Paris, only to be repulsed and pushed back for a period. The problem for the German army, of course, is that as it advanced, its front became progressively larger, while the French resistance was able to consolidate its lines.

Italy—Austria. While the war between the Allies and Germany raged in the north, Italy and Austria fought each other on their mountainous border. The goal of Italy was to capture additional territory. The goal of Austria was to maintain its border—an easier proposition. While the fighting was often fierce, Italy was never able to force its way across the border, and it actually yielded land during the course of the war.

Gallipoli. Turkey's entry into the war on the side of Germany in October 1914 opened a new theater of war. Ironically, the clash soon became primarily that of Britain versus Turkey. Britain first decided to force passage through the Dardanelles, the narrow passageway between the Mediterranean Sea and the Black Sea, so that it could strengthen its military alliance with Russia. With heavy guns sited high above the water on both sides, Turkey was able to pound the British warships and stop their advance. Under the goading of First Sea Lord Winston Churchill, marines were dispatched to fight, which led to a crushing military defeat for Britain. A second landing on the western side of the Gallipoli Peninsula was also repulsed by desert-smart Turkey. Heroic action on the part of the navy succeeded in rescuing many survivors, but the battle itself needlessly consumed a great deal of resources without contributing to the ultimate success of the war. It also led to the forced resignation of Churchill and created a stain on his public credentials.

Pacific Theater. At the outbreak of war, Britain requested that its South Pacific colonies of Australia and New Zealand attack German colonies in the area. They were joined in this effort by Japan, who soon declared war on Germany. While successful in stopping the flow of exports to Germany, Japan used the war as a pretext to make military advances against German colonies in China in order to establish its own foothold in that vast region.

Africa. Britain's war in South Africa to subdue the German colonies there ended up as a long, protracted campaign against internal dissent and a wily German adversary under the leadership of General Paul von Lettrow-Vorbeck. After initially inflicting actual military defeats on the British, he eventually led a guerilla war that lasted the duration of the war and was the last German commander to surrender.

Mesopotamia and Palestine. Much of the fighting between Turkey and Britain took place in Mesopotamia (modern-day Iraq) and Palestine. The war in Mesopotamia was initially very successful, with Britain making great advances up the Tigris and Euphrates Rivers. History shows that Britain should have retreated a bit to consolidate its gains and hold the territory, but instead, it fought to maintain control of Damascus at a huge loss of life and, in so doing, gained the enmity of the Muslim world. The battles in Palestine were also notoriously costly with little military significance. After the war, Britain tried to hold on to Mesopotamia, but eventually found it too much trouble.

In the end, nearly 250,000 Allied lives were lost in these sideshows with little effect on the ultimate outcome of the war.

President Woodrow Wilson won reelection in 1915 on the campaign slogan, "He'll keep us out of the war." A year and a half later, he stood before Congress to solemnly request a Declaration of War against Germany and its allies. America's traditional antipathy to European wars was overwhelmed by the public's reaction to Germany's declaration of unrestricted war on the high seas, which put American civilians and commercial fleets in jeopardy of sinking without warning. After the attack on the Lusitania in 1915 that killed numerous American civilians, the country was in no mood to endure further humiliation. When the contents of the Zimmerman telegram, mentioned earlier in the book, were made public, the outcry for war was overwhelming. And so America entered the war in 1917.

In the end, the outcome of the war was a matter of mathematics—How many young men could each side send into the trenches before they ran out of bodies? With America's entry into the war, the math inevitably favored the Allies. But Germany still had a chance if it could defeat its European foes before America could effectively mobilize for combat. There were no rapid deployment forces in 1917, and it would take time to mobilize a massive war effort. Germany felt that it could conquer France and defeat England before America could land troops in any significant numbers. Once again, as at the beginning of the war, Germany nearly succeeded on a number of occasions. Its new commander, General Ludendorff launched three massive strikes deep into France. But each time he came tantalizing close to Paris, the Allied lines constricted to the point that they could defend themselves and hold the line while the German forces were spread thin by their elongated lines. Each time, Germany was repulsed.

America's mobilization became decisive approximately one year after officially entering the war when more than 100,000 troops per month arrived in Europe and the American Expeditionary Force under General John Pershing was able to assume responsibility for an ever-increasing portion of the front lines. Even though America was actively engaged in the war for a little over six months, it was the decisive six months that finally brought Germany to heel. America suffered 237,135 casualties, of which 48,909 resulted in death.

Interestingly, it wasn't the leaders who sounded retreat. Eventually, the frontline German soldiers, routed from their well-established trenches, began to abandon the front line in an increasing panic. The kaiser was shocked when he ordered everyone back to the line to find that the troops no longer obeyed him. On November 9, 1918, the kaiser abdicated, and two days later at 11:00 P.M. on November 11, an armistice went into effect ending what was, up to the time, the bloodiest conflict in history. The world was stunned as the guns went silent, then broke out in tumultuous joy at the thought that the Great War (as it was known by then) was finally over.

The Allied powers met at Versailles Palace in France to work out the terms of the armistice. America argued for leniency in the war reparations imposed on Germany, and the damages imposed were relatively light compared to previous conflicts. It was the fashion of the time to have the conquered nations repay the cost of a war incurred by the victors. So great was the cost of the Great War, however, that the German people seethed with resentment as they were kept in poverty while sending payments to England and France. Adding to their sense of outrage was the feeling that they had not been beaten on the field of battle but had agreed to an armistice—negotiated peace—to finally end the senseless killing. Yet, in their minds, the Allies treated them as if they had uncondi-tionally surrendered. Plus, the Allies simply declared Germany to be a democracy while giving them very little assistance and guid-ance as to how to live and operate in a democratic system. For a people who were accustomed to living under the leadership of strong, military leaders for more than a thousand years, the project was almost doomed to failure in the absence of a patient and continuing presence on the part of the Allies. But the great democracies retreated into their own borders to lick their wounds and to attempt to recover from the horrors of the war. Such were the conditions that gave rise to Adolf Hitler and the Nazi party.

For his part, Woodrow Wilson, a religious and pious man, sacrificed his health and personal credibility to establish his Fourteen Points program to nurture the defeated nations and bring them once again into the fellowship of nations. Unfortunately for Wilson, he was not one to compromise, and in his stern refusal to allow any changes to his plan he was unable to sell his own country on the need to remain a part of European affairs. On November 19, 1919, the United States Senate refused to ratify the Treaty of Versailles or to join the League of Nations. The seeds for an even greater and more devastating conflict were thus planted and simply needed the poverty and frustration of the Great Depression to grow. The promise of the "war to end all wars" was an illusion, and it would fall to World War II—the grudge match that would finally settle Europe's old scores.

* * *

Many historians feel that Germany came within about one week of reaching its goal of conquering Paris before the end of its six-week timetable. Had it succeeded, the war likely would have ended with Germanic hegemony established over Western Europe. But it wasn't to be. Once Germany fell short, France and Britain were able to force Germany back toward its historic borders where the battlefield settled into something of a permanent fixture on the French and Belgian landscape. It also provided the context for the most devastating form of war yet conceived by man—trench warfare.

The Great War of 1914 was one of the first to rely almost exclusively on conscription for its supply of soldiers by all combatants. Previously, Britain had always relied on highly skilled professional soldiers, while other countries often hired mercenaries who sold their fighting abilities to the highest bidder without regard for national loyalties or ideology. The cost of training professional soldiers was enormous. Because the available supply was limited, the generals and officers who relied on these men were very cautious in exposing them to danger and seldom deployed them when the expected casualty rate was expected to be too high. But with the implementation of the draft, the military leaders of World War I had a seemingly endless supply of bodies to send to the front. They came to accept appallingly high casualty rates with a callous disregard that was perhaps best stated by Joseph Stalin, a young agitator in Russia, "The death of one man is a tragedy. The death of a million is a statistic."

The military and political leaders of the era seemed to lose all sense of proportion as they used up successive waves of conscripts in the bloodbath of the continental war. For example, the first group drafted in Britain was completely spent by the end of 1915. This was hardly a problem, for just as soon as another wave of young men reached the age of the draft, they were sent to the front lines with little training. In time, the British soldiers came to be identified as the Class of 1914, Class of 1915, etc.

The most obvious adjustment to this new reality was a tolerance of trench warfare, perhaps the most deadly form of combat ever encountered in the long and bloody history of the world. After the huge initial assault by Germany in the first six weeks of the war, they were forced back to a static battle line by the combined weight of the French and British armies on the Western Front. Once the German lines had constricted to the point that the Allies could no longer prevail, both sides settled into fixed positions along the entire line leading from Belgium in the north to Switzerland in the south.

Because of the risk of machine gun fire raking the troops who stayed at ground level, the German army started digging trenches to provide protection. The British and French armies quickly adopted the same technique, and within a matter of weeks, semi-permanent trenches slightly deeper than a man's height snaked along the entire front. The trenches became the killing field where millions lost their lives as the opposing generals vainly sought to gain the advantage with huge, mostly futile attacks that were easily repulsed by the other side. For nearly three years, the relative positions of the two great opposing armies hardly changed as the body count climbed into the millions.

Two features served to make trench warfare so appalling. First was the use of artillery against fixed positions. One British soldier wrote that in his first week in battle, they endured a daily barrage of more than 200 to 300 heavy artillery shells within a 300-yard radius of their trench. Over the course of the war, this led to the death or disability of millions of frontline troops.

The second reason trench warfare produced inordinate casualties was that men advancing up and over the trench were exposed to the full force of machine gun fire spraying bullets by the hundreds every minute the trigger was pulled. The machine gunners had the luxury of sitting inside a reinforced parapet, while the advancing troops moved across the open expanse of no-man's-land, working their way through barbed wire that was used liberally in front of each side's trenches to slow an advance and to keep the enemy troops exposed to defensive fire for as long as possible. When any major advance was planned, the offensive side would first rain thousands of artillery shells on the enemy's trenches and wire with the ever-optimistic assurance that it would completely break down their defenses. Then sounded the cry for the infantry to advance. Unfortunately, artillery fire was largely ineffective in tearing up the barbed wire and instead created huge shell holes that made the advance even more difficult.

Colour-Quartermaster-Sergeant Robert Scott Macfie tells of watching 130 men of his unit of the Liverpool Scottish go forward into battle. While they were gone, he carefully set out one tin of cookies for every five men in their tents in the billets behind the lines to give them some comfort when they returned. He was anxious to feast with them when they returned. Several hours later, they heard the distant sound of bagpipes, and after a while, a handful of men crossed through the gates in tattered clothing. He called out for the men of Y Company, and only one came forward. In the next few hours, another 25 straggled in, many wounded. By 0530 the next morning, only 40 had returned out of 130 deployed. The rest were killed, wounded, or taken prisoner. Such was the casualty rate of soldiers on the Western Front.

Life in the trenches was unlike anything ever experienced in battle, before or since. In these trenches, men ate, slept, went to the latrine when one was available, and sheltered themselves from the hail of artillery that periodically, and unrelentingly, hazed them during the interminable days and nights they spent at the front. As the months and years dragged on, they lived through rain, fog, and the bitter cold of snow, sleet, and ice with nothing more than their winter clothing, and the occasional small cooking fire that allowed them to warm their coffee and tea. Sometimes they'd fire off rounds of ammunition into the ground to warm their hands on the barrel of their gun. The spring was often the worst, when the snow of the winter started to melt and the rains of April and May filled the trenches with water, sometimes up to their waist. The good clay soil of France turned to a muck so thick, it would suck in a soldier's feet to the point he couldn't extract himself without assistance. The single leading cause of disability was trench foot, a condition in which a man's feet and toes began to rot inside his water-soaked boots because there was no way to keep his feet dry. Many a veteran spent the rest of his life a semi-invalid because his feet were so injured by the days he spent in the trenches.

Because the risk of the sides of a trench caving in from artillery or water was so high, the men were kept busy reinforcing the sides with revetments and improving the drainage in the bottom of the trenches. The revetments were built using sandbags the entire length of the trench with stakes driven into the bottom of the trench and connected by wire to stakes on the upper lip of the trench. Planks ran the distance of the trench across the bottom to give something firm to walk on, otherwise no progress could be made when water filled the bottom. Periodically, great sump-holes were dug to collect the water with small wooden bridges built across the sump.

At night, the men lived in small dugouts at the backside of the trench where they hollowed out a small room that they reinforced with two walls of sandbags and covered with a sheet of corrugated iron layered with an oil-sheet under it in an attempt to make a waterproof roof. When possible, a latrine dugout was built along the line so the men could relieve themselves without filling the bottom of the trench where they had to stand all day. This attracted rats and other rodents and had to be cleaned out regularly by a soldier who was assigned as a "sanitary man," usually older men who did their work without complaint, even though the stench was overwhelming.

Supporting trenches were dug perpendicular to the front line trench to facilitate communication and to provide ingress and egress for the soldiers as they moved into position, and as food and supplies were brought forward to meet their needs. The effect created a massive labyrinth hundreds of miles long that was surrounded on both sides by a landscape forlorn of vegetation or life. Giant shell holes pocked the earth and mocked the grand designs of the generals as artillery failed to outstrip the ever-fresh supply of replacement troops that came forward to serve their respective countries.

It was a constant challenge to maintain morale in these abysmal circumstances, so each of the major armies came up with their own approach. The British tried, where possible, to follow a routine of three days in the trenches, three days doing support work moving back and forth across the ten miles that separated the trenches from their supporting operations where food, ammunition, and other supplies were brought forward, followed by three more days in the trenches, and finally three days rest in billets, back out of range of artillery where they could dry off, get hot meals, and rest up.

The demands of battle sometimes interfered with the schedule, and individual groups ended up spending ten days or more in the trenches on the front line. It was generally these men who were the ones to suffer from one of the first recognized psychological disorders called shell shock, the result of living under the mental cloud of constant artillery bombardment that assaulted the ears, filled the air with the thick smell of cordite smoke, and killed or wounded one's friends in a seemingly random and totally unpredictable pattern. A shell-shocked soldier became unresponsive and detached from reality and was a danger to both himself and his unit because of his propensity to take bizarre risks that exposed the unit's position.

Among the many technological advances in the art of warfare that manifested itself in the First World War, aerial combat was by far the most romanticized part of the battlefield. While it was difficult for the civilian population to cope with the pure carnage of the trenches, the propagandists on both sides of the conflict were able to capture the public's imagination with tales of chivalrous conflicts in the air between warriors who followed the ancient traditions of combat. Thus was born the cult of the "Bloody Red Baron," Manfred von Richthoven, of Germany as well as the aces of the Allies.

The truth is that air warfare was cold and calculating with an extremely high casualty rate. America's Eddie Rickenbacker, the top ace with the most kills, called aerial combat "scientific murder." Yet the young pilots of the time loved the thrill of testing their machines in combat and eagerly looked forward to each new advance in technology. From a handful of aircraft at the beginning of the war to tens of thousands by the end, World War I provided the fledgling aeronautics industry the chance to build an entirely new form of transportation from the ground up, and the war effort clearly compressed the pace of advances in aviation science by decades. From the first flimsy aircraft at the beginning of the war to the deadly fighters and bombers that were in use by November 1918, aircraft provided a new context for fighting that would become preeminent in the Second World War.

REFERENCES

Brown, Malcolm. *The Imperial War Museum Book of the First World War: A Great Conflict Recalled in Previously Unpublished Letters, Diaries, Documents, and Memoirs.* Norman, OK: University of Oklahoma Press, 1993.

Dowswell, Paul. *Weapons and Technology of WWI.* Chicago: Heinemann Library, 2002.

Eisenhower, John S. D. *Yanks: The Epic Story of the American Army in World War I.* New York: Free Press, 2001.

Gittins, H. Leigh. *Pocatello Portrait, The Early Years, 1878 to 1928.* Moscow, ID: University Press of Idaho, 1983.

Graves, Robert. *Good-bye to All That.* New York: Doubleday, 1998.

Nordhoff, Charles, and James Norman Hall. *Falcons of France.* New York: Arno, 1980.

Prior, Robin, and Trevor Wilson. *The First World War.* Washington, D.C.: Smithsonian Books, 2004.

Rickenbacker, Eddie. *Fighting the Flying Circus.* Alexandria, VA: Time-Life Books, 1990.

Schuster, George N. *The Longest Auto Race.* New York: J. Day, 1966.

Treadwell, Terry C., and Alan C. Wood. *The First Air War: A Pictorial History, 1914–1919.* London: Brassey's, 1996.

Tuchman, Barbara W. *The Guns of August.* New York: Ballantine, 1994.

———. *The Proud Tower: A Portrait of the World Before the War, 1890–1914.* New York: Ballantine, 1994.